Clay Park
Growing up Gay

Cameron De Cessna

Forward

We often hear of the 1950's as a time of blissful innocence in America. During the first two or three years of the 1950's, the Second World War was over, the bloodiest portion of the Korean Conflict was about to end and the Cold War was still pretty much unknown to most Americans. It's funny how Americans often define and divide our historical periods by whatever war happened to be starting, raging or ending.

It was the decade of Truman and Eisenhower, chrome embellished cars, classic early television and the rise of suburbia in many parts of the country. If you ask most people today over sixty-five to what era, they would most like to return, many would say the fifties. It was the time before the proliferation of the atomic bomb, the race for the moon and Viet Nam even though during the mid to late fifties, President Eisenhower was sending troops to Southeast Asia to "train" the locals in ways to defend against communism. It's funny how that worked out.

If the popular television shows of that era like *Ozzie and Harriet* and *Father Knows Best* were to be believed, it was a time of happy and stable families living in beautiful, friendly, crime-free neighborhoods. *Television Dad* wore a suit and ties *all the time*, as he faithfully worked and provided for his family. *Television Mom* was a selfless, stay-at-home, loyal housewife who cleaned and cared for the home and kids while having absolutely no ambitions of her own. The typical *Television Household* averaged two or three beautiful, *white, Television Kids* who went to school, studied hard, respected their teachers and *never* entertained thoughts of civil disobedience. Television was just as reliable defining true Americana then as it is today, it would seem; entertaining, yes --- realistic, no.

In some ways, the fifties *were* a kinder, gentler time for some Americans, but certainly not all. Ask any *"colored person"* who was a

1

child during those times. They'll probably remember asking their mother or father why they had to go to a separate, poorly funded and run-down school, use a *Colored Only* restroom or drink from a *Colored Only* water fountain. Ask any child who was foreign-born and perhaps spoke another language or whose parents held unpopular political views such as socialism or god-forbid, communism. Ask the children of Kentucky and West Virginia coal miners who grew up in the ramshackle company towns and villages of Appalachia during the fifties watching their fathers slowly dying from black lung and cancer as they barely eked out a living, deep in the bowels of dark, damp and dangerous coal mines. Life wasn't kind and gentle to them. It was damned hard.

Every era has had its difficulties and struggles. Life is not ideal. It never has been, nor will it ever be, a perfect world. Today we live in an age of miracles with spacecraft taking breathtaking, high-resolution photos as they zoom past distant Pluto, computers that have nearly reached the level of human intelligence, medical breakthroughs that have extended our life spans at least two decades longer than someone born in 1900. Even with these and other modern wonders we still have religious fanatics and mentally unbalanced individuals who willingly blow themselves up in a crowded marketplace, open fire with automatic weapons in a crowded nightclub, church or school, or fly jet planes into skyscrapers. As I write this, we've recently elected a poorly educated, inexperienced and socially crude president who turns his head from the reality of a warming earth, the possible extinction of half the world's species and perhaps our own species as well.

I say all of this to establish that life is never perfect. Life has always been a struggle and will continue to be. The fifties were no exception.

This is a story set in 1953. It's not a true story, but it could have been. It's not a story of a black child, a poor child or an immigrant child, all of whom would have lived a difficult life in those so-called *kinder and gentler* times. This is the story of a *gay child*. A boy who in 1953, comes of age at fourteen, sadly realizing he is so utterly different from his peers and is beginning to fathom how very hard his future might well be. During that period, even the word gay had not come into common use with the public in general. Harsh and demeaning terms like *queer* and *homo* were most often used.

Being gay is nothing new, of course. Gay men and women have been --- and will continue to be --- born that way. Their interests are governed by whatever genes they end up with. Few, if any persons

2

choose to be gay; it's simply another aspect of the diversity of life, one that thankfully, is finally being understood. At least intelligent people not fettered by archaic religious dogma and superstition-fed hatred are coming to recognize the realities of being born gay.

As I mentioned already, Clay Parker is not a true story, but it could have been. It's the story of a boy who has already suffered much in his life before the onset of adolescence hands him another surprise as he begins to show a sexual interest in other boys. Put yourself in Clay Parker's place throughout this tale and try to imagine the confusion, the fear and the sorrow of facing such a thing alone in a world that shuns or openly hates anyone who is different --- especially one who is sexually different. To whom could Clay turn to explain the alien thoughts, emotions and desires beginning to plague him? How could he begin to adjust to, and prepare for, what was ahead in his life?

In 1953, it would have been a terrible burden for a fourteen-year-old boy, especially one like Clay who had already lost his entire family to fire and had suffered disfiguring burns. Imagine what it would be like for a boy like Clay, forced to live with a hateful and abusive aunt and uncle who were compelled to take the boy in as a family obligation. Imagine a home without love, without forgiveness, without any understanding of anything or anyone who was so completely different.

As you read of Clay's struggle and ultimate triumph, put yourself in his place. If you're gay, you'll understand better what a boy in that era might have felt and experienced. This author did to some extent, although I came of age in the nineteen sixties, a confusing time for other reasons. If you are not gay, try to see things from Clay's perspective and understand there have been many boys and girls who have had to go through similar struggles all alone, filled with confusion, fear, loneliness and sorrow. As you read, ask yourself; *how would I have coped with such a burden at fourteen?*

Do not judge another until you have walked a mile in his moccasins.
Native American Proverb

Judge not, that ye be not judged.
The Bible, King James Version - The Gospel of Saint Matthew, Chapter 7, Verse 1

Empathy is the first step to understanding.
Cameron De Cessna

This novel is dedicated to the victims, survivors and families of the June 9th, 2016 terrorist attack on Club Pulse in Orlando, Florida and all similar crimes of prejudice and hatred.

Clay Parker
Growing Up Gay in 1953

Chapter 1

It sometimes seemed to Clay as though he spent half his waking hours running: Running to school, running to town, running through the woods of Southwestern Pennsylvania and running from his family --- if they could be called that. Since he was ten and a half, he'd learned many ways to avoid being around them and home --- their home. Nothing about it seemed home like to him. It was a place to eat, sleep and avoid as much as possible once his household chores were completed. He mostly ran to avoid his uncle, Warren Waters, a contemptible tyrant who Clay had learned to dread with all his heart.

Clayton Alan Parker was fourteen and even though he was forced to live with his maternal aunt, Martha Waters, her husband Warren and their two miserable sons, he could in no way consider their house near Sand Patch, Pennsylvania, to be *his* home. Peter and

4

Paul, eighteen and sixteen respectively, were every bit as mean and hateful as their father. His Aunt Martha, even though she was a blood relative, was nearly as cruel in her own way by allowing his cousins get away with making his life as miserable as possible.

Clay was running toward the house today from the small, eight-room school in Sand Patch, knowing full well that he dare not be late arriving, as chores were waiting. The house was a two-story, brick and clapboard structure located roughly a mile and a half north of town. He'd owner an old bicycle he could use to travel to and from school for a few months in the fall of 1952 and the first two months of 1953. It was so rusted and broken down, however; that it literally fell apart in late February due to the daily pounding it took on Highway 160, a rutted and pot-holed road winding through town and northward to where his uncle's place was. He remembered the sound beating he'd taken after he'd carried the parts of the bike home one afternoon in blowing snow. His uncle had bought it second hand for five dollars the previous summer and Clay often wondered what the beating would have been like if it had cost ten.

After the bike gave up the ghost, Clay decided it was easier to depend on his legs, at least until he could buy a bicycle with his own money, if he ever found a way to earn some. He was given no weekly allowance --- even though his two cousins were --- and figured he'd have to depend on his legs for transportation for some time to come. There wasn't much around Sand Patch anyway that couldn't be reached on foot. Now, all he had to worry about was wearing out another pair of shoes and hear his aunt and uncle rail about the cost of a new pair.

His best friend was Albert Stiles, also fourteen. Albert's dad was a full-time carpenter and --- as far as Clay went --- part-time shoe-repairman who did what he could to keep the boy's shoes in repair, as he knew how unreasonable Warren Waters could be. Clay helped Albert with his chores from time to time to keep on Mr. Stile's good side. Clay often wished he was Albert's brother and could live with the Stiles family and share in the love always present in their home.

Clay was small for fourteen and somewhat skinny. He had dark brown hair, brown eyes and stood four feet eleven inches tall. It bothered him to be shorter than most of his friends in school, but recently he was encouraged because he had finally started growing and growing fast. In just two months, he'd grown a full inch. He kept a record of his height by making faint pencil marks, every two weeks, on the backside of his closet door where his fastidious aunt wasn't likely to spot them. His rapid growth in height wasn't the only changes he'd noticed. Other, less obvious changes were taking place that excited him and confirmed he was finally growing up.

Often he wished he still lived in Bedford, a nearby Pennsylvania town, with his mother, father and younger brother, Timmy. The little village of Sand Patch was quite a change from Bedford and wouldn't be so bad if it wasn't for his aunt, uncle and cousins. At least he had a good friend in Albert.

Sand Patch was a small country village perched on the summit of Big Savage Mountain, one of the densely forested spines of the Allegheny chain that ran from West Virginia, through Maryland and into Pennsylvania. The pass at Sand Patch was at an elevation of 2,800 feet and the Baltimore and Ohio Railroad, years before, had taken advantage of the saddle-shaped passage across the Alleghenies while constructing the mainline between Cumberland, Maryland to the south and Pittsburgh to the northwest. Even still, the mainline ran through a tunnel that passed beneath part of the town.

As he ran toward home, Clay heard the lonely wail of a locomotive struggling northward up the fifteen mile long, two percent grade out of Hyndman, Pennsylvania, just north of Cumberland. It was probably hauling either coal out of West Virginia, or a string of boxcars loaded with any number of products from the factories and farms of Central and Western Maryland or the docks of Baltimore.

Clay loved the railroad and the giant steam engines that pounded across the mountains. He especially favored the mighty Mallets, for they were the grand masters of steam power with double pairs of pistons working  in tandem to conquer the relentless pull of the valleys below as the long trains struggled to reach the pass at Sand Patch. Mallets, built in the nineteen twenties and thirties by ALCO, the American Locomotive Company, were like two locomotives combined in one massive body and were the longest and most complex steam locomotives ever made in America, if not the world. Nothing sounded like them, and no locomotive pulled or worked as hard. Clay would give anything to ride in one of their cabs as they toiled across the Alleghenies.

He would probably be late if he took a slight detour to catch sight of the train as it passed through a rock cut to the right or east of the road along which he was running. He'd have to cut through the woods to reach a point where he could look down along the cut and see the mighty engines pass. More than likely, there were two Mallets working in tandem; at least it sounded like two.

Once in a great while, the load was so heavy that a third Mallet or even a fourth was attached to the rear end of the train to help push the cars up and over the crest of the Alleghenies. He lived to see such a train. He'd seen three Mallets in a train once, but never four. He doubted the train today was such a rare spectacle, but he still wanted to see those mighty engines thunder along the rails. It might even be worth a beating if he ran a few minutes late. As he once again heard the Mallet's plaintive whistle calling, he decided it was and took a path through the woods to the right. The railroad cut was less than five-hundred feet away and he was pretty sure he could make it in time.

Clay wasn't sure how much longer he'd be able to see and hear the great engines, for, little by little they were being replaced by diesel-electric locomotives. The diesels were exciting to watch in their own right, but nothing --- absolutely nothing --- compared to the iron dragons of the rails that had powered the B&O --- America's first chartered railroad --- during the last hundred years. More and more he heard the garish sound of air horns instead of the lonely, ghostly wail of a steam whistle. America's railroads were growing and evolving just as Clay was growing and changing. His boyhood was nearly behind him as he faced the challenges and confusions of adolescence and manhood.

The train today might very well beat him to the cut. His sides were aching with the strain of running uphill through the woods, dodging old trees and thickets of thorny brambles, struggling to reach the end of the crude trail. He

7

felt like a locomotive himself puffing and striving to make the grade and reach the cut. The locomotives had already passed through Sand Patch tunnel just south of town --- he'd heard the whistle signal for the switch tower just beyond the tunnel's exit --- but still they struggled, for most of their load was far below the town, striving to drag the train back to Hyndman.

Soon, as the last of the cars, including the inevitable blue B&O caboose, passed the signal tower at Sand Patch, the engines would have to start throttling back and applying their air brakes to check the train's decent along the  western side of Big Savage Mountain. It was nearly all downgrade from Sand Patch into Meyersdale, Pennsylvania, thirteen miles to the west.

If the train used a helper engine, its brakeman would have to run along the side of the locomotive to its very front and pull the coupler release to enable the helper to unfasten itself from the caboose and the rest of the train. Sometimes the caboose crew would do the job if a spare brakeman happened to be available aboard the caboose. The helper engine or engines would then slow to a stop and then run in reverse all the way back to Hyndman or Cumberland to prepare for the next assist job with another train.

Un-coupling was done on the fly as it wasn't practical to stop a moving train to make the separation. It was also extremely dangerous for the brakemen who had to perform the maneuver. One had fallen to his death beneath the wheels in the few years Clay had been living in the area. The new diesels had electrically controlled couplers that allowed the engineer to do the job with the touch of a switch in the locomotive's cab, but the older steam engines had no such device and union policies and directives kept it that way to protect the jobs of brakemen. Clay's uncle Warren was a brakeman for the B&O and often was the one to perform the dangerous duty as he worked the trains running between Cumberland and Pittsburgh.

Clay reached the cut just in time. Two massive Mallet

8

locomotives, numbers 812 and 315 were pounding along the rails within five hundred feet of where he was standing. He hadn't missed them. Clay was on the wrong side to spot the engineer but did catch sight of the fireman in the lead engine. The man looked up along the ridge of the cut, spotted the boy and waved. He turned to the engineer and said something. The engineer gave two short toots of  812's whistle as the fireman waved once again just before the cab of the lead engine moved out of sight. The fireman of 315 waved too as the second locomotive struggled through the cut.

Clay recognized him as Lester Mills, a quiet, gentle man who lived a little north of Clay's house on State Road 160. He always had a kind word for the boy whenever they met or passed in town.

It took another four minutes for the train to pass through the cut. Clay counted ninety-three hopper cars loaded with coal before the B&O caboose rattled past. The train's conductor, always the crewman officially in charge of a train, saw Clay from his elevated perch in the caboose's cupola and waved as well. The helper engine --- if there'd been one --- had already un-coupled back in town.

Not all cabooses on American railroads were red. The B&O used light blue for its rolling crew quarters and freight conductor's office. Painted on their side was the royal blue, circular B&O herald sporting the U.S. capital dome. The caboose's designation number, 188, was painted in royal blue both along the rear of the left side and on the end of the caboose. The train's flagman stood on the rear porch of the caboose and he too waved to Clay as the train trundled on toward Meyersdale.

Clay broke his reverie as he lost sight of the caboose when it disappeared around the curve of the cut. "Oh darn! I'm really gonna be late," he said aloud as he turned and ran back along the path through the woods. Just before he reached the road, however, he caught one toe on an exposed tree root and went sprawling. Throwing both hands forward to ease his fall, one encountered a sharp piece of shale and Clay felt it slice into his palm just behind

9

his right thumb. He sucked his teeth from the pain and ventured a look at his hand. The shale had gouged an inch-long slice along his skin and blood was dripping from the wound. It wasn't terribly deep and wouldn't need stitches, but it sure was bleeding.

The boy gathered himself and stood up. Taking a blue bandanna handkerchief from his left pocket, Clay did the best he could to brush dirt from the cut, wrap the wound and staunch the flow of blood. He noticed that his blue jeans had been torn as well when he fell. One knee was ripped open along an inch long tear. He hadn't noticed any pain there, but his mind had been more focused on the pain in his hand. His pant legs were too tight to pull up, so he unbuckled his belt, unfastened his top button, unzipped his pants and dropped them past his knees. This was hard to accomplish since his right hand was wrapped with the makeshift bandage, but he eventually was able to get a look at his knee. It was a bit scratched up but was by no means as serious as his hand.

Just as he was about to pull up his pants, he heard a laugh from just ahead of him and looked up to see a blond-haired boy about his same age grinning at him as Clay stood there with his pants down. It was Albert Stiles, his best friend, so he wasn't as embarrassed as he might have been if it had been a strange boy or, god-forbid, a girl.

"What the heck happened to you, Clay?"

"Hey, Albert, I fell and cut my hand."

"I was riding by and heard something make a noise in the woods, so I stopped and walked back here. The last thing I expected to see was you with your pants down." Albert chuckled and added, "Thought at first you were taking a crap in the woods."

"No, I tore my pants and was looking to see how bad I'd skint up my knee. I'm gonna get a lick'n at home for sure. I'm late coming home from school and now I've torn my good school pants. Uncle Warren is gonna wear out my rear end for sure."

"Why's he so darned mean, Clay? I came by to talk with you two days ago and he ran me off saying I wasn't to bother you when you had chores to do. He even threatened to give *me* a lick'n."

"Gees, I don't think he'd do it 'cause he knows your pop would come after him if he did. I'm sorry he was mean to you too. He might have been drinking. He's back at it here lately."

"I'm sure sorry you lost your folks and had to come live with that old buzzard, but at least you coming here was good for me. You're my best friend."

"You're mine too, Albert." Clay was trying his best to pull up his pants, zip them and fasten his top button with his aching hand still wrapped with cloth.

Albert asked, "You need a hand?"

"Naw, I just about have it. The dang buttonhole is too darned small for the button."

Clay finally managed to finish. He'd felt a little self-conscious as he noticed Albert looking at the dark, wrinkled, burn scars along his legs as he pulled up his trousers. Considering all, he was fortunate to be alive. He had barely made it out of the house the night it caught fire and burned to the ground, due to faulty wiring. His parents and little brother hadn't been as lucky and all had perished in the inferno. He'd been burned over a third of his body when his pajamas caught on fire and had spent nearly seven months in Bedford Memorial Hospital recovering from the third-degree burns that had left scars on his legs, chest, belly and left arm. The pain he'd suffered then was beyond belief and left him with an ever-present fear of fire.

Thankfully, Clay's face and neck had been spared and most people never knew he was so marked by the flames. He wore long sleeve shirts and long pants even in the summer months so fewer people would notice. Albert was okay though and as Clay's best friend, had seen him completely naked when they frequently went swimming during summer months in a millpond west of town.

Clay dusted himself off and started toward the road which was less than thirty feet away. Albert gathered his bicycle from the weeds near the highway where he'd dropped it before going to investigate the noise of Clay falling.

"Get on the handlebars; I'll give you a lift. That way you won't be so late."

"Thanks. Just don't wreck us 'cause I've lost enough blood for one day," Clay said with a chuckle. "Sure wish I still had a bike. I get tired of running and walking everywhere."

"I bet, especially since your uncle is always bully-ragging you about being on time. What's his problem anyhow? I bet he ain't that way with *his* boys."

"Oh no, Saints Peter and Saint Paul can do no wrong. I think the only way he'd punish them is if they did something nice for me. He eggs them on sometimes when I'm around just hoping they'll make me more miserable."

"Wish you could move in with us. Mom and Dad often talk

11

about your uncle and how cussed mean he is."

They chatted as Albert peddled them along the road toward Clay's house. It was about five minutes later when they saw the picket fence marking the Water's yard. Albert turned in at the open driveway.

Clay whispered, "Oh, crap. He's out and he's mad. You better drop me here and make tracks, Albert, or he'll give you heck too."

"Yeah, he don't look too happy."

"See you sometime this weekend unless I'm grounded. I'll try and come by your house. Wish they'd let me use the telephone, but you know what they're like."

Albert hit the coaster brakes and skidded to a stop in the gravel drive. "Good luck, Clay. I'll see you when I see you." Clay jumped off the handlebars and started walking toward his uncle's porch where the man stood with crossed arms, wearing a scowl.

"What the hell happened to you, boy?" he hissed as Clay reached the bottom concrete step, five steps below where his uncle stood. "Your school pants are torn up. What you got to say for yerself? Did you fall off'n Albert's bike?"

"No, sir, he gave me a ride after I fell along the road running home. I cut my hand up pretty bad and tore the knee of my jeans. I'll sew 'em up tonight, myself. Aunt Martha won't have to do it. I'm sorry. It was an accident."

"Get in the god damn house, you worthless piece of shit. I waste my money buying you nice clothes and you tear 'em up like they was nothin'." Clay had mounted the steps and was passing by his uncle when the man suddenly fist-slapped him square in the center of his back, knocking him nearly off his feet.

"Ow! Please, Uncle Warren, don't hit me. It was an accident!"

"So was that. I was aiming for the back of your damned head, you impudent son of a bitch!" Warren started slapping and hitting Clay as the boy tried his best to escape the worst of the blows and get inside. By the time he'd reached the front door, Warren had managed to land half a dozen blows. Clay ran for the stairs and clattered upward toward the relative safety of his room. His uncle, thank god, remained at the foot of the stairs cussing at him. The cussing he didn't mind. He was used to that. He never could get used to the beatings though, for every blow reminded him how much he hated the man. He'd smelled liquor on Warren's breath as he passed and that always signaled trouble.

12

Clay wanted so much to cuss back at his uncle, but he'd learned long ago that only brought on worse abuse. He fled to his room, closed and locked the door and stood panting at the foot of his bed. Tears were beginning to flow, not from pain but from shame and anger. He whispered to himself, "Mom and Dad, why did you have to die and leave me with that old devil." He continued thinking silently; *I wish I could have died with you. At least you're at peace and so's little Timmy. I'm glad Timmy never had to live here with these creeps.*

The thoughts of his parents and little brother overwhelmed him and he flung himself on the bed and cried silently into his pillow, cursing his uncle, aunt and cousins, for he could hear Paul and Peter laughing downstairs as Warren bragged about the lick'n he'd just given Clay.

His hand was aching and Clay realized he still needed to tend to the cut; it should be washed and disinfected. He sat up on the side of the bed after wiping his eyes with a corner of the pillowcase. Clay un-wrapped his right hand and saw the cut was red and swollen, but at least the bleeding had stopped. He went to the door and listened. His uncle and cousins were still talking in the parlor downstairs, so he unlocked the door and turned left toward the bathroom only to nearly run into his aunt who glowered at him and looked at his hand.

"What in the name of heaven did you do now? I swear, I never saw such a boy as you. Where are you going in such a hurry?"

"To the bathroom to clean up this cut; I don't want it to get infected. I fell and cut it on a sharp rock; it's full of dirt."

"Tore your pants too, I see. Well, don't expect me to drop everything and mend them. You can just wear them that way to school on Monday."

"I'll sew them up myself, Aunt Martha, if I can use your sewing box."

"Humph. I suppose you'll make a right mess of that. I'll give you needle and thread after bit. Your uncle said you're to miss supper, so you can sit and sew like a girl while the rest of us eat."

"Yes, ma'am, that'll be fine. Let me get washed up and put a bandage on my hand."

"Let me see it." She grabbed his wrist and wrenched it over so she could see his palm. He opened his hand to let her see.

"It ain't too bad. Unlike your britches, you won't need stitching. Get in the bathroom. There's a bottle of iodine in the medicine cabinet. You can use it; just keep over the sink and don't spill any of it, 'cause it stains something fierce. There's gauze and tape there too. Don't waste any more than you have to. That first aid stuff costs like the dickens."

Clay made his way down the hall to the bathroom, entered and locked the door behind him. Starting the hot water and adding just enough cold to keep it from scalding him, he washed the wound carefully, doing the best he could to remove any dirt that had been driven into the cut. It stung from the water, but pain didn't bother him. Pain was an old companion to the boy who had suffered such hideous burns at ten. After cleaning the wound, he dried it as best he could and opened the medicine cabinet. He gave one glance at the iodine bottle but opted instead for a similar bottle of mercurochrome. It too was a good germicide but did its work without the biting pain of iodine. He applied the red liquid liberally with a medicine dropper and cotton swab, dabbed it semi-dry and wrapped the wound from a roll of gauze. Using a length of first aid tape, he completed his repairs. The hand would be sore for a while, but the wound would soon heal.

He had to pee, so he opened the commode, unzipped his pants and proceeded to relieve himself. While doing so, he thought about some of the changes his body seemed to be going through lately. Over the past four months, he had started growing hair above his privates and it was now fairly thick, black and curly. His penis too had grown nearly an inch in length over the same period and often became hard in the morning. It sometimes did the same when he thought about certain things. Friends of his same age had talked about growing hair down there nearly two years ago, but for some reason, his hadn't started appearing until he was fourteen. He'd had his fourteenth birthday on January third and almost as if that was the magic trigger, within a few weeks, his body started changing. It was now Friday, April 10, 1953, and he was pleased to be finally catching up to his classmates, at least in height and hair.

Unusual thoughts and fantasies had begun to invade his mind. Some fantasies that appeared to come from nowhere bothered him a great deal, as they seemed unnatural and somewhat disturbing. As he finished peeing while thinking about these same topics, he felt himself beginning to harden below. He drove the strange thoughts from his mind, stuffed himself back in his pants and zipped up. The hardness persisted for a little while, showing through his clothing

14

and he had to wait a few minutes before leaving the bathroom, all the while feeling ashamed of what he'd been thinking about that had caused the reaction.

Clay had a number of questions he wished he could ask of someone, but again, he was too ashamed to seek out help. His uncle would be the very last person he would depend upon for help on such a topic.

In 1953, sex education was undreamed of in the Pennsylvania schools, especially in the small rural school he attended. Most of the teachers there were older women; he'd never be able to ask them about what he was feeling.

Clay returned to his bedroom and sat once more on his bed. As the weekend was beginning, he had no homework to do; that was the reason he hadn't needed to carry home any books or supplies. There were chores that must be attended to, however, and since he would have no supper this evening, he figured he'd best get started. He changed into a set of work clothing and as he did so, felt an odd wetness on the front of his boxer shorts. He thought perhaps he hadn't been careful and had leaked a bit after peeing, so he made sure his door was locked and pulled down his underclothes. He was surprised to find that the tip of his penis was wet and shiny with some slippery liquid. It wasn't pee. He pulled back his foreskin, squeezed along the shaft of his penis and was surprised to see a large drop of clear, gooey material ooze from his opening.

He was growing hard again as he felt the substance. It was very slippery and the tip of his penis felt unusual as he rubbed the wet stuff over it. As he hardened, more of the liquid dribbled out. He removed it and smelled. All he could smell was the normal odor of his foreskin. No matter how many times he bathed or cleaned himself, his foreskin would develop that odd scent within a few hours. Strange as it seemed, he kind of liked the odor and just the smell of it lately was enough to make him grow hard.

There were so many new things happening to him down there that both confused and intrigued him. Rubbing that stuff on his penis felt nice, but he had to get to his chores, so he stopped and once more pulled on his clothing. Soon he was ready to leave the room and get to work. Once in the garden, his mind turned to his duties and, as he weeded the bean and turnip rows, he thought no more about bodily changes and all the strange daydreams that seemed to haunt his thoughts.

After finishing, he returned to the house just as the family sat down to eat. His uncle looked at him with a smirk as if to say, 'How's it feel to go to bed hungry?' Clay gave him no satisfaction and smiled as he walked past the family and climbed the stairs to his room. He remembered he had a small box of soda crackers and a half jar of peanut butter stashed in the rear of his top dresser drawer. He often stashed a few non-perishable food items he'd spirit out of the pantry when his aunt wasn't around, especially for emergencies like this. The peanut butter crackers would suffice for supper. Clay was skinny anyway and missing a meal at this house was common. It was often his aunt and uncle's punishment of choice. He wasn't sure if it was to punish him or save on food costs. His aunt was terribly stingy with everything else, so he was sure the food savings made her happy.

He turned the brass key locking the door behind him after entering his small bedroom, even though his uncle always gave him hell for locking the door. Lately, he wanted privacy more often from the rest of his relatives. He seldom thought of them as *family*. Clay associated that word with love and there was no love between him and the people downstairs.

Sometimes he wished he could pack up and leave Sand Patch, take off on his own somewhere and maybe find another family like Albert's who would care about him and maybe even love him a little. As he stretched out on his bed, tears appeared at the corners of his brown eyes as often happened when he thought of how different and good his life had been before the fire.

Chapter 2

 **W**hile munching on a stack of peanut butter crackers, Clay spent the rest of the evening deep within the pages of a good book. An avid reader, books were his escape. He was halfway through Jules Verne's classic, *20,000 Leagues Under the Sea*, exploring the coral kingdoms with Professor Aronax, Ned Land and Captain Nemo. He'd recently learned that Walt Disney was planning to release a movie of that name in early summer starring James Mason, Peter Lorie and Kirk Douglas; he wanted more than anything else to see that picture. His chances were slim, however, as his relatives would never take him. For a big-name motion picture like *20,000 Leagues*, it would mean a trip to the Strand or Liberty Theatre in Cumberland, Maryland --- the largest city in the area --- located across the Mason Dixon state line, south of Sand Patch. It was a fifty mile round trip over twisting mountain roads and his aunt and uncle would never consider such a trip for a mere movie.

Maybe he could go along with Albert when his parents took him to see the film. He'd seen several other movies that way before. The last time, however, he got a thorough beating as he'd failed to tell his aunt and uncle where he was going that Saturday afternoon. If he'd asked, they would have said no, so he accepted the beating as a fair trade for the pleasure of seeing another Disney film, *Peter Pan*. He often felt like one of those Lost Boys in Neverland and thought how grand it would be to live on a magical island with a group of boys with no grown-ups or girls. Wendy was okay, but one girl was enough.

He'd read for nearly two hours and had finally gotten so sleepy that the heavy book fell backward from his fingers striking him painfully on the chin. He had nearly bitten his tongue as he jumped awake grabbing at the heavy tome before it could fall to the wooden floor and maybe wake his uncle or aunt. He found and marked his place before laying the book aside. He pulled off all his clothes and got into his pajamas before crawling beneath the sheet and turning off the light. It was only then he remembered he hadn't taken a bath, but it was too late now to worry about it. He'd take one tomorrow. He snuggled down and soon drifted off to sleep.

He had been thinking about movies and his dreams that night carried him into the plot of one of his favorites. Older movies were often shown at a small theatre in Meyersdale. Albert's folks tried to take him along every so often, once they realized his relatives did nothing for the boy. A few weeks before, he'd seen a classic film from the early forties, *How Green Was My Valley*, starring Walter Pidgeon, Maureen O'Hara and thirteen-year-old, Roddy McDowall portraying a young Welsh boy. A more involved adult drama was

being played out in the film, but Clay, for some reason, was fascinated by the young actor whom he found to be strangely appealing and nice-looking. At one point in the story, the young boy had fallen into a half-frozen stream, become ill and nearly died. Clay was surprised as he started crying uncontrollably as he saw the boy lying crippled and helpless in bed. He wanted to hug that boy, tell him he would be all right and that he loved him. The Welsh boy eventually got well and Clay was able to feel better.

Now, in his dream, he was running through the fields of Wales with the boy from the film. Clay hadn't noticed the young actor's name in the credits, but he could easily picture his handsome face in his mind. As dreams often will do, his memories of the movie became mixed with his own memories. He imagined himself and the young star swimming in the millpond as he had done many times with Albert. And, like it was with Albert, Clay was wearing nothing and neither was Roddy. They splashed and played, dived and swam until his movie idol turned and smiled at him as they stood near one another in the water. Clay leaned forward and kissed the handsome boy's lips.

Clay woke with a start, surprised at what he'd just dreamed. He dreamed he'd kissed another boy and liked it. He was painfully hard down below as well and felt terribly confused and ashamed. What was wrong with him? This was not the first time he'd had similar dreams, but never had he imagined *kissing* another boy or even wanting to. But now, for some reason, he *was* thinking about it. The dream seemed so real and exciting. Maybe he was just missing his younger brother whom he'd often hugged and kissed because they were close. But he'd never kissed Timmy on the mouth like he just dreamed he'd done with the Welsh boy from the movie. He loved Timmy as a brother. With the movie star, it was different. He could close his eyes and imagine the moment all over again; he felt himself stir below. He reached down and found himself wet again.

Clay felt sick. Something was horribly wrong with him. He'd heard a boy at school talking about boys who liked to kiss other boys. They were called sissies or queers and no one liked them. They were boys who liked to dress up in girl's clothing and walk around in high heels, put on makeup and play with dolls. He didn't want to do any of those things, but the thought of kissing a boy like the boy in the movie made his thing get hard.

"I'm going insane, like my aunt Louise," he whispered as he sat up in bed, turned on the light and started crying. She had been committed to an asylum after trying to take her own life years before when Clay was about nine. The family didn't talk much about Louise after that. Other than his Aunt Martha, she was his only living relative; obviously, Louise couldn't take him in. He was relatively sure Aunt Martha qualified as being insane in a few ways too.

But thinking of Aunt Louise didn't help. It only made him question his own sanity. *Any boy who dreams about kissing another boy he saw in a movie has to be a little crazy*, he thought as he felt below once again. He was soft by now but still that damned slippery stuff was pouring out of his opening. *Maybe I have an infection and it's affecting my mind. Maybe I need to see a doctor, but how in the world will I ever explain what's happening without dying of embarrassment. If only I had someone, I could talk to about this.*

Clay looked at his alarm clock and found it was four-twenty in the morning. He felt sleepy but was half-scarred to go back to sleep and maybe dream again about the Welsh boy. Part of him wanted to, and that was more disturbing than the dream itself. He turned off the light and lay down. Within a few minutes, he drifted off and at least dreamed no more about running and swimming with young Roddy.

The next morning, Clay awakened a little before eight. Breakfast on the weekends was normally later, so he knew he hadn't missed it. Uncle Warren hadn't said anything about 'no breakfast' at least; he'd done just that several times in the past. Clay was hungry and his stomach growled as he threw aside the sheet and sat up on the side of the bed. As usual, he was hard and had to pee in the worst way. He felt and was pleased to find that there was none of that weird clear pus, or whatever it was, leaking from him this morning. He put on a blue, terrycloth robe to help cover his erection, as he knew it wouldn't go down until he emptied himself. He didn't want anyone seeing him in his pajamas looking like this. The robe was loose and floppy and covered him well enough to get by. He opened his bedroom door, peeked out and saw no one else in the hallway. He padded down the hall to the bathroom and closed the door.

After peeing and finally losing his hardness, he changed the bandage on his hand. Most of the soreness and redness was gone. He returned to his room and put on clean boxers and a pair of old gray dungarees. He still had to make repairs to his school pants sometime this morning. He really hated that he'd ruined his pants, but it *was* an accident and couldn't be helped. He was growing out of them and the school year was almost over anyway. He left his room and went downstairs to see about eating.

Upon reaching the kitchen, he saw his aunt at the stove and said, "Good morning, Aunt Martha; can I help you with anything?" He thought maybe an offer of help might ease the tension of the previous night.

"Set out some bowls, milk and sugar. We're having cinnamon oatmeal. Does that suit you?"

"Oh, yes ma'am. I like oatmeal, especially with cinnamon." Clay did as she asked and prepared the table for the rest of the family. As he did so, his two cousins clumped into the room and took their seats along one side of the table.

"Where's Pop?" asked Peter, the elder of the two.

Martha answered, "He got called out early this morning to fill in on a train crew making a run from Hyndman to Pittsburgh and on into Ohio somewhere; Cincinnati I think. He won't be back until Monday, more than likely, or until another eastbound train heads this way and he can either work on the crew or deadhead his way back. At least he'll be getting overtime and we can use the money, especially since some of us are careless and tear up their good school clothes."

"Sorry, Aunt Martha, it was an accident. I fell. I wouldn't do something like that on purpose." Clay was trying his best to get on her good side. He was exceptionally happy his uncle was out of the house for the rest of the weekend. He took one place setting from where Warren normally sat and put the plates and silverware away.

"Albert called for you about a half hour ago, Clay," his aunt said with an air of irritation. "I want you to tell that boy not to waste my time having to answer the phone all the time for your playmates." Paul snickered at the word playmate, a word usually reserved for small children.

"I'll tell him, ma'am. Uh, may I use the phone and call him back?"

"You may not!" she said as she spooned oatmeal into his cousins' bowls. She filled her own next and then set the pot back on the nearby counter, completely forgetting to give Clay any. Clay got up and filled the bowl himself, secretly glad because he got to spoon out a much larger portion than his aunt would have given him. As he took his place at the table, she continued: "If you want to talk to Albert, you can walk to his house once your Saturday chores are finished."

He made the mistake of saying, "But Peter and Paul use the phone to call their friends."

His aunt's spoon stopped a few inches from her mouth dribbling oatmeal as she simply stared at him as though he was some exotic insect that had just landed on the table and might bite or make a stink.

"Peter and Paul both work and contribute to the family income. When you find a job someday and pay your share, you can use the phone too. Eat now and be glad we feed you."

"Yes, ma'am." He finished his breakfast in silence.

Clay's Saturday chores included washing the clothes, running them through the wringer on their Sears and Roebuck washing machine and hanging them out to dry in the backyard. Usually, that took the better part of the morning as Saturday's wash had accumulated for several days and included his uncle's work clothes.

After eating, he got right to the task and separated the clothes into four loads according to color and type of fabric. His aunt's dresses and under-things were always done separately and required great care as they were more delicate and he cringed to think of what might happen if he were to ruin or tear them. He lived in fear that someday one of his aunt's satin nightgowns would get tangled in the wringer and be shredded; he was sure his butt would soon suffer similar damage. Thankfully, she did her delicate nylon stockings by hand.

All went well and by noon, he'd taken down the last dried load from the line in the backyard. Luckily, a warm breeze had been blowing all morning and the clothes dried quickly. He was glad his aunt wouldn't let him use the iron and insisted she do that herself. He folded the last few sets of clothing and set them in stacks near the ironing board.

After lunch, he asked, "I'm all finished the laundry, Aunt Martha. Can I go to Albert's house now?"

"I suppose. Behave yourself and try not to tear any more of your clothes. Remember, before the weekend's over, you need to sew those school pants."

Her reminder gave him an idea. He'd washed the damaged pants and now removed them from the stacks as though to take them to his room. Instead, he planned to take them to the Stiles house to ask if maybe Albert's mother would mend them with her sewing machine. She was such a kind lady and treated Clay as though he was a member of their family. She reminded him of his own mom; another reason why he often wished he could move in with Albert and his folks. She even gave him a hug occasionally.

He gathered up a few things including the torn pants and stuffed them into a canvas backpack he often used. While his aunt was busy with the ironing, he managed to swipe a few apples and oranges he and Albert could eat while playing or exploring near Albert's home. He wished it was a little later in the season and they could go swimming at the old mill where they often swam during the summer months. For just a minute, he thought about seeing Albert naked like his dream of the young actor.

Whoa! I shouldn't be thinking of things like that. Albert's my best friend and I shouldn't want to see him naked. That's kinda sick. But, deep down, Clay knew his thoughts wouldn't go away. For some reason, lately, he often thought about seeing Albert without clothing; it was one of the troubling things he daydreamed about in school and at home in the evenings as he lay in bed before drifting off to sleep. Albert didn't look much like the movie boy who had dark hair but had golden blond hair, bright blue eyes and the most beautiful smile. He again thought about Albert naked and how he looked at the millpond all wet and dripping and...

Clay felt himself stirring down below as he left the house toting the backpack and thinking about Albert's bare body. *I gotta think of something else. This is sick. I'm no sissy or a damned queer. It's just a daydream. I should be thinking about girls.* He tried to imagine swimming with Linda Wilcox, a pretty, red-haired girl who sat near him in school. She too was in eighth-grade and seemed to like him. As he walked north along the road toward Albert's place, he envisioned Linda taking off her clothes and walking toward him near the pond.

Having never seen a girl naked before, he was having a rough time imagining what she might look like. He'd once caught a brief glimpse of one of Peter's dirty magazines and it had some naked women in it. Peter caught him however before he could get a good look, boxed his ears and kicked him out of his room with a threat to do something called cat-straightening to him if he caught him messing with his magazines again.

His vision of Linda was forming as he strolled along the road, but try as he might; she looked like a boy without clothes. He knew she didn't have a penis, but somehow he saw Linda with a really long and thick one. It was bare, pink and smooth like Albert's was, without foreskin like his own. She had a boy's chest too with small, dark breasts like Albert's. In his mind's eye, Linda face slowly became Albert's. *Maybe I am queer,* he thought with an element of sadness and self-disgust.

He started as a car passed by him, tooted its horn and a short distance down the road pulled to a stop. It was Lester Mills; the fireman on the Mallet he'd waved to the day before. Clay ran ahead to the car, an old '39 Buick, as Mr. Mills slid over, unlocked and opened the passenger door and asked, "Hi, Clay. Can I give you a lift?"

"Thanks, Mr. Mills. I'm only going to Albert Stiles's place, but I sure wouldn't mind a ride."

"Well hop in." Clay climbed aboard and closed the door. Les slipped the car in gear and continued down the highway.

"That was you up on the side of the cut yesterday, wasn't it?"

"Yes, sir; I sure love to watch those Mallets. I'd give anything to take a ride on one someday."

"I wish I could help you, Clay, but it's strictly forbidden by the railroad. That, and the fact the Mallets are about to be retired within the next year or two."

"Really? That's a shame."

"As they break down, or need expensive parts, they'll be replaced with diesels. I plan to train for another job with the railroad soon. Not much need for a fireman when there isn't a fire. I'm tired of breathing coal smoke and dust anyway. It's starting to make me cough all the time and I'm only thirty-three, so I figure I better get a safer and healthier job."

"What kind of job?"

"My foreman said he'll recommend me for conductor training since I have an education and can handle the paperwork."

"Well, that's good, Mr. Mills. At least you won't be put out of work."

"There will still be men on the trains called firemen, but they'll really be diesel trouble-shooters and repairmen. I'm simply tired of the noise and smoke and think it'll be nice for a change to work as a conductor and be the man in charge of the train. I'd prefer to get a job on the passenger trains as a conductor. They pay best and once I'm trained, I'll qualify."

"Nifty."

"Yeah, passenger trains are mostly all pulled by diesels now too, so no more coal smoke and filth. Tell you what, since you like watching trains, I'll talk to my bosses and ask if someday I can take you to the roundhouse down in Cumberland and let you look a Mallet over up close. It won't be a ride, but at least it's safe to look one of the engines over while it's parked in a roundhouse stall."

"That would be something!"

"Think your folks would let you do that? Your uncle's a brakeman. I'm surprised he hasn't shown you around the yards himself."

"Uh, my uncle isn't very nice, Mr. Mills. I doubt he'd let me go to Cumberland with you either. He's got some funny ways about him."

"Yeah, I suppose you're right; I've worked with him before and know how he is. Sorry. Well, here's Albert's house; hope the ride helped you out."

"Thanks heaps, Mr. Mills. I liked talking with you. Anything to do with trains is fun to talk about. Maybe someday I'll get a job with the B&O too."

Mr. Mills pulled to a stop as he said, "Take my advice, son. Look into some other line of work. Railroad work is not as attractive as it seems. You have a good head on your shoulders; use it for a better job and career."

Clay thanked him again and hopped out saying, "Maybe I can chat with you again someday. You're a swell guy, Mr. Mills. See you later."

"Anytime, Clay, anytime." He smiled at the boy as he put the car in gear and drove off toward his home, another third of a mile along 160.

Clay ran from the road to Albert's front porch and just as he reached it, Albert and another boy, Toby Anderson, who also lived along 160, opened the front door and stepped out. Albert said, "Hey Clay, I was hoping you'd call."

"Hi, Albert, you know my aunt and uncle won't let me use the phone. They gave me heck 'cause *you* called me on it. I had to do half a week's laundry too before I was free to come over. Hey, Toby."

Toby nodded and said, "Hey."

"Did I hear a car? Did your uncle give you a ride?" Albert said incredulously.

"No, that was Mr. Mills from down the road. He's a fireman on the B&O. He stopped and asked me if I could use a lift."

Toby frowned a little as he looked back toward the highway and said, "Uh, Clay, I'd be careful taking rides from Mills. Some people say he's kind of odd and might even be dangerous. My dad told me once he's probably queer and to stay away from him."

"Queer? What's queer about him?" asked Clay. "He seems like a nice guy."

"Yeah," added Albert. "He's spoken to me too and he's pretty nice. My folks like him."

Toby went on with lowered voice, "You know, queer --- like he likes other men and maybe even boys. Dad said he used to live with another man and they both loved each other 'till the other guy tried to kill himself and had to be put away."

"Loved each other, like they kissed and stuff?" asked Albert.

"Yeah, can you imagine two guys wanting to do something like that? Jesus!" Toby said with an air of disgust.

"I've heard a little about people like that, but not much," said

Clay, as he thought back to his recent dreams and inwardly cringed to hear how Toby felt about the subject. "What else do men like that do?"

"Uh, before I tell you, let's go to Albert's clubhouse in the backyard. I don't want to talk about it out here. Albert's mom might hear us through the window and that wouldn't be good at all."

They took a shortcut through the house so Albert could tell his mom where they'd be playing. She said hello to Clay and gave each of the boys four, fresh-baked cookies, wrapped in paper napkins, to take along to the clubhouse. Clay asked about the sewing and she told him she'd be glad to help and took the pants from him before the boys went out the back door.

Once in the home-built shack, located in one far corner of Albert's backyard, they sat down on some wooden benches and munched on their cookies. Clay opened his backpack, passed around the apples he'd brought and reminded Toby to tell them more about the queer guys who liked to kiss.

"Well, the real name for them is homos or homosexuals. Dad told me to be careful if I'm ever out playing and some guy comes up, gets too friendly, and wants me to go home with him or off in the woods or something. Some homos like to do stuff with boys as well as men."

Albert asked, "What kind of stuff?"

"Well, play with their privates and kiss them and that sort of thing. They're real sick and sometimes get sent off to prison for doing stuff like that."

"And you think Mr. Mills is like that?" asked Clay.

"Dad's not completely sure, but he's heard rumors about the guy's boyfriend and told me to avoid being around him. If I was you, I'd be real careful, Clay, taking a ride from him."

"Yeah, okay. I'll be careful. He seemed nice and didn't say anything about going to his house."

"What did he talk about?" asked Toby.

"Well, you know how much I like trains and steam engines. He said he might be able to take me into Cumberland to see the big locomotives in the roundhouse there someday. Trouble is my uncle would never let me go."

"See there. Already he's asking you to go someplace with him and you hardly know the guy. He's gotta be around forty years old. You need to stay clear of him, Clay."

26

"Yeah, okay. He said he was thirty-three. I really haven't heard that much about homos before. Are there a lot of guys like that?"

Toby shook his head and said, "I don't know. He's the only one around here I've heard about. I bet they stay real secret. I sure wouldn't want anyone to know if I was like that. I think I'd jump off a bridge or something if I found out I wanted to kiss another boy or a man, instead of a girl or woman."

The rest of the afternoon, the three young teens played in and around Albert's yard and the woods behind his house. They walked to a nearby beaver pond and felt the water in hopes it was warm enough for a swim, but it was still too cold. They'd have to wait at least until late May to brave the water. Somehow, now, Clay wasn't as anxious to skinny dip with Toby around for he feared he might get hard when he saw the other boys and they'd think he was queer. Now that he knew how Toby felt, he found himself somewhat disappointed in his friend although he couldn't figure out why.

The next few days and nights Clay found himself thinking about some of the new ideas Toby had planted in his head. He wondered about Mr. Mills and if he really was a man who liked other men. He thought about the movie star boy and nearly always got hard as he closed his eyes and pictured the handsome young actor. He thought about how Albert looked when naked as they swam last summer. That always made him hard, too. He'd only gone skinny-dipping with Toby once; it was when they were about eleven and now, Clay could hardly remember what Toby looked like without his clothes. More and more, Clay was thinking he might be queer and more and more he began to panic as he realized that someday people might hate and distrust him the same way Toby and his dad distrusted Mr. Mills.

He was still puzzled why, whenever he got hard, he leaked that slippery, snot-like stuff and how odd and good it felt when he rubbed it around with his fingertips. More and more Clay had found himself looking at other boys at school as they studied or moved about the classroom. He especially noticed that a few of the boys in his eighth-grade class, who wore tighter pants, showed an interesting bulge in their trousers. Seeing that always made him hard and occasionally wet down below as repeatedly he asked himself, *What is wrong with me?*

The state school system operated a truck that visited each rural school every month or so exchanging about five hundred library books at a time so students could read different books without having to go to a large city library. On Wednesday of the same week he'd played at Albert's house, Clay browsed through some of the new books the library truck had recently dropped off. One was a large book about classic motion pictures and he was excited to  find that one of the movies featured in the book was *How Green Was My Valley*. It had a glossy page with four pictures from the film and one was a studio shot of the young actor that so fascinated him. The caption gave his name: Roddy McDowall.

Then, Clay did something he had never done before. He first looked around to make sure no one was looking and then carefully tore the page from the library book and hid it in his notebook. To Clay, one of the greatest sins was to tear or deface a book and now he'd done it to a *library book* --- a book that belonged to *everyone*. But for some reason, he had to have that picture.

That evening, behind the locked door of his room, he used scissors to separate the photo of Roddy from the other three. He hid it behind a framed photo of his mom, dad, little brother and himself taken just prior to their death in the fire. He kept that photo on his nightstand; now, hidden behind his family, was the photo of young Roddy. The other three pictures from the movie, he burned with the trash as they were of other actors and actresses from the same film and of no interest to Clay.

Every so often, just before turning out the lights at bedtime, Clay would slip that photo out from behind his family picture and gaze at it until he became hard and often wet. Sometimes before putting it away, he'd kiss it too, even though he felt guilty afterward. He'd hide it and try to go to sleep quickly in the hopes he would have another dream about his movie idol.

Chapter 3

Clay continued to worry about his strange daydreams and occasional night dreams as they kept featuring other boys his age or young men. More and more he was realizing he might be queer. Try as he might, he could not get excited by thoughts of girls or women.

On one occasion, while using the bathroom, Clay noticed his aunt or cousins had left the Sears Roebuck catalog on the counter beside the commode. He browsed through it while doing his business and happened upon the section featuring women's underclothing. He'd heard Toby saying how he'd often used the catalog to get a *boner,* as he put it, so Clay thought he'd give it a try. Nothing happened. Much to his chagrin, he found he did get an erection when he looked at the photos and drawings of boys and young men in underwear; especially tight-fitting briefs like those Albert usually wore.

What makes me this way? How can I change? Will I always be this way? These were constant questions on the boy's mind. He considered tearing up the movie photo, but for some reason, couldn't bring himself to do it.

In late May, Mr. and Mrs. Stiles took Albert and him to see the movie, *Lassie Come Home* in Meyersdale. Imagine Clay's surprise and joy when the film stared a fifteen-year-old Roddy McDowall and Clay's desires and dreams were again inflamed by the handsome young actor. Like Clay, Roddy had grown up too and in one short scene, the now teenaged actor was dressed only in somewhat revealing long underwear. Clay became aroused and within a few minutes, felt himself growing wet.

Unfortunately, not long after seeing the movie, Clay was devastated to learn, after browsing through an almanac at school, that McDowall was born in *1928* and was now *twenty-five years old,* practically middle-aged in Clay's mind. Only on the silver screen would Roddy be forever young.

It was on the last day of May, just before turning out the light to sleep, that something new and extraordinary happened. While Clay was again looking at his photo of Roddy, his penis, by now nearly five inches long when hard, felt especially sensitive and ticklish. The door was locked, so he continued touching himself, moving his foreskin up and down and squeezing the head of his penis while sliding his slippery fingers rhythmically over and around the exposed tip. He had recently read in a health book at school that men produced sperm cells in their testicles necessary to fertilize an egg cell and create a baby. He had concluded that the mucus was not from an infection, but was in reality, his sperm.

He was harder than he could ever remember being and was especially wet and sensitive. Tonight, something deep inside of him was tensing and feeling better than ever before. Slippery stuff was pouring from his opening as he looked at the photo and imagined Roddy was there beside him in his long underwear and he was kissing the handsome teen and touching him the same way.

All of the sudden he felt new sensations deep within his lower body as he squeezed and stroked. His penis grew harder still and something inside was drawing back and drawing back and... Suddenly his lower body was filled with the most wonderful feeling as silver streams of warm, liquid began spurting from his penis and falling on his neck, his chest, his belly. Repeatedly it surged until his chest and neck were spotted by seven or eight clots of the white, warm and odd-smelling liquid. He'd never felt anything like it, but now, after many indescribable spasms, his penis started feeling irritated; his body was jerking and he was forced to stop.

What is this stuff? He thought as he felt the warm, white liquid and gathered enough on his fingertips to smell. It had an alien odor, somewhat like musky, wet leaves after a spring rain or some exotic, rare mushroom. "This is my sperm," he whispered aloud. In his mind he reasoned, *the clear stuff is only to make me slippery. This is wonderful. If this is my sperm, I'm old enough to be a father.* He used a bandanna handkerchief to wipe away the slippery, sticky white liquid that was here and there on his neck and chest. He was able to solve a few other mysteries about procreation that had escaped him up until now. *A man must stick his penis inside a woman's opening and squirt his sperm up inside her. That's how it reaches her egg cell and makes her get pregnant. The clear stuff is just to make a boy or man slippery and feel real good as he moves in and out of her opening.*

The whole process seemed odd to Clay. He'd never had any interest in girls, or their openings down below and the thought of putting his penis inside one was not at all appealing. *I must be queer because I'd rather let a boy rub me while I rub him and make us both feel good like what just happened.*

Clay's penis had gotten soft as he cleaned himself. Now, as he imagined another boy, maybe one who was as handsome as Roddy or Albert, stroking his penis, he began to grow hard once more. He squeezed along his shaft and some leftover white stuff --- sperm --- flowed out of his opening. He used it to rub himself and at first, it was a tiny bit irritating, but that soon faded as his body became tense once more and he knew if he kept it up, his body would probably squirt out more.

After two or three minutes of pleasurable rubbing and further fantasies, he felt the muscles below gathering and tensing until he shivered and watched as four more clots of sperm spattered on his belly. It didn't feel quite as good and not as much came out, but it was still wonderful. This time, after the last pulse, Clay smelled and then tasted some of the semen from where a glob of the slippery stuff was running slowly down and over his fingers. It tasted salty and sweet at the same time and smelled so pleasantly unusual. *I wonder how long I've been able to do this? I could have been doing this a long time ago; I just didn't know. No one told me about this. I wonder if Albert knows about this and does it too? Should I ask him? Probably not.*

He was feeling very sleepy for some reason even though he was still excited. After squeezing out the last few drops and wiping off his belly with the handkerchief, Clay turned out the light and fell asleep. He hadn't even bothered to unlock the door, or get dressed once again in his pajama bottoms.

He awoke to someone pounding on his door. His alarm hadn't gone off because he'd forgotten to wind the clock. *Criminy! I'm late for breakfast and school!* He tossed aside the sheet and realized he was naked. His photo of Roddy was wrinkled and lying on the bed where he'd rolled over on it as he slept.

His uncle was yelling, "What the hell have I told you about locking this goddamn door? Open it right now, boy!"

Clay tucked the photo inside his pillowcase and pulled on his pajama bottoms as he said, "Okay. I'm trying to get dressed, just a minute." He went to the door and turned the brass key in the keyhole. His uncle pushed the door open so forcefully that he nearly knocked Clay down. His uncle looked around the room as though expecting to see something he could yell at the boy about.

"Thought you said you was getting' dressed. You're still wearing your nightclothes. Looks to me like you just got up. Did you wind and set your damned clock? "

"I must'a forgot. Sorry. I over-slept. When you knocked, I was about to dress. I locked the door so no one would come in when I was bare. I'm fourteen now, Uncle Warren, and need some privacy when I'm dressing." He said this last part in an accusing way and realized his mistake immediately.

His uncle backhanded him and Clay went down hard on his backside. Before he could crab along backward, his uncle grabbed him by one arm, jerked him to his feet and started raining blows across his sides and chest.

"Don't you ever back-talk me, boy! I'll fuckin' kill you next time you do that. You ain't my son and I don't like you, but I'm stuck with you. As long as you're under this roof, eat'n my groceries, you'll talk to me with respect! You hear?"

"Yes, sir, I'm sorry. I was half-asleep. I didn't mean to get smart-mouthed with you. Please don't hit me again."

Instead, the vile man shook him and shook him hard. "If I want to hit you, by damn, I will. What you want doesn't mean crap! You hear?"

"Uh huh, yes, sir, I know."

His uncle finally turned loose of him and he lost no time in backing away from the wild-eyed man.

"Now get dressed and leave the door unlocked. Matter of fact, give me the goddamned key." Warren snatched it from the keyhole on the inside of the door as he went past. "You can't lock it, if'n you got no key. What you been doing anyway, playing with yourself? I better not catch you doing that. I'll cut it off, if'n I do." He slammed the door as he left.

Clay was panting from anger and fear, a common emotional mixture around his uncle. He changed clothing quickly and hid the Roddy photo in the picture frame before he forgot about it. Thank God, his uncle didn't know about that. He probably *would* kill him.

He thought as he headed to the bathroom, *what am I gonna do? I can't live much longer in this place with these people.* He started crying as he stood before the commode and relieved himself. The scarred skin on his chest and legs was stinging terribly this morning, especially in places where his uncle had slapped him. As he grew, the scar tissue had to stretch and often got sore and prickly. His chest and belly had been especially bad lately and felt like ants were crawling all over, itching and stinging him.

At least I haven't had so many dreams about the fire lately. His preoccupation with his awakening sexuality had replaced the nightmares he'd struggled with since he was ten, right after the fire. He used to wake up screaming and if that woke his aunt and uncle, he often got a paddling and a warning to 'get over it', or 'be a man'. Never once had either of them hugged him or tried to console him. *If I stay in this place much longer, I'm gonna get to be as mean as they are. I'd rather die than be like them.*

He used a small amount of petroleum jelly to rub on his thighs to help ease the stretching pain in the scar tissue. A doctor, last year, had prescribed a special medicated lotion for his skin, but it cost two dollars a tube and after his aunt bought it once, she never bought any more. As he looked at his legs, he thought, *I'm so damned ugly now. Even if I am queer and ever find another queer boy to do things with, he'll probably not want to touch these damned ugly scars. God, I wish I could have died with Mom and Dad and Tim.*

By the time he made it downstairs to the kitchen, breakfast was over as he'd slept too long. It was a little past his usual time to leave for school and he'd have to run faster than usual to make it on time. He remembered to grab his lunch box from the refrigerator --- he'd made a couple of cheese and ham sandwiches and packed it the night before --- and in the process nabbed two apples that would serve for breakfast along the way. His aunt saw the apples and glared at him, but chose not to say anything. He went through the living room and snatched up his book bag, stuffed the lunch box in it and headed out the front door. One apple he stuffed in his left pocket, the other he gripped in his hand.

He'd sewn two shoulder straps on his book bag so he could carry it on his back. Clay shrugged into the straps and started running as soon as he stepped off the porch. The golden delicious apple in his hand was cold, sweet and ripe; he bit deep and chewed while running. He was halfway through the second apple and a quarter of the way to school when he heard a car approaching from behind.

Looking back, he saw it was Mr. Mills in his old Buick. As the car passed, Mr. Mills slowed down, leaned out and said, "Need a ride to school, Clay?"

Thinking about what Toby had said for only a moment before dismissing it, Clay said, "Yes, sir. Thanks. I'm running late." The Buick ground to a halt and Clay ran around to the passenger side and climbed in. What could the guy do to him between here and school anyway?

"How is it you don't have a bicycle, Clay? I know you live too close to school to ride the bus, but you still should have a bike." Clay looked at the man and thought, *why can't I have an uncle like him? He's a stranger and cares about me.* Clay felt a hint of tears in the corners of his eyes and blinked to fight against them as the man slipped the car in gear and started along the road.

"I had one, sir, but it was old and rusty and fell apart last February. My uncle wouldn't get me another. If I had an allowance or could find me a job, I'd buy one. They're pretty expensive though. School will soon be out for the summer, so maybe I can earn one."

Clay saw that Mr. Mills was dressed up today, so he couldn't be going to work on the B&O. "You off today, sir?"

"I'm off for several days, Clay. I just finished a series of long hauls back and forth between Cumberland and Baltimore. I've been on the job for seven days and that's all the union allows. They require a four-day layoff before I can go back after a week like that. I don't mind the long hauls, though; it means a lot of well-paid overtime. I make nearly twice what I'd usually make on short runs. Two more runs of work like that and I'll be able to pay off some debts I recently took on."

"That's good. Uncle Warren is always cussing about his mortgage payments. I think he blames me for taking away family money that he could use toward paying off the loan."

They rode along in silence for a few minutes until finally, Mills said, "Listen, Clay, I work with your uncle sometimes and forgive me if I criticize him. Maybe it's none of my business. If you think so, tell me and I'll shut right up, but your uncle makes good money. There's no way that you're a burden to him and your aunt. I believe both of your cousins work too. He's such a nasty son ... Well, he's just plain mean sometimes. Even the men at work don't care much for him."

Mr. Mills reached over, gave Clay's arm a quick squeeze, and said, "I know about what happened to your folks and I'm very sorry you have to live with Warren, Martha and their boys. You're completely different from them and deserve better. Sorry if I've insulted them, but I'm just telling it the way I see it."

"No, it's okay, Mr. Mills. You're right. They're just plain mean and sometimes I hate living with them so much I want to run away and never come back."

"Well, son, do the best you can and please, don't run away. Believe me, the world's a lot more cruel than your aunt and uncle."

"I guess it is. I'll do the best I can."

"Good. The school's just ahead. You have a good day and study hard. It's the best way to get away from this place. Get a good education and in a few years you can go wherever you want and be anything you want to be."

"Thanks, Mr. Mills. Thanks a lot. I'll do the best I can."

"Call me Les. We're friends now, Clay. Be good in school, son."

Clay jumped out and after closing the car door he smiled and waved at Les thinking to himself, *There's no way that man would ever hurt me.* He watched until Les's car was out of sight. His final thought before turning and walking toward the school building was, *He called me son. I wish to God, I* was *his son.*

A few days later, on the fifth of June, school let out for the summer. Clay was pleased to see that he'd passed eighth-grade with very high marks. Four years before, even though he'd spent nearly a half year in hospital after the fire, he'd been helped by a young male nurse who worked with him not only on coping with his burns and learning to walk again but spent extra time tutoring him so he could keep up with his studies. As a result, when he returned to school, he was actually ahead in most subjects and able to fit back in without having to repeat a grade.

Clay would be starting high school in the fall as a ninth grader. This meant he would be able to take the school bus to Wellersburg, a small Pennsylvania town located eleven miles south of Sand Patch, along route 160, a mile from the Maryland state line. The bus would even stop right in front of his house. Nevertheless, he still wished he had a bicycle for the long summer that stretched ahead. For one thing, he was toying with the idea of visiting Mr. Mills occasionally and a bike would make that much easier as his house was nearly a mile north of Clay's home. No matter what Toby said, he wasn't afraid of the man who was the first adult, other than a few teachers and Albert's folks, to show him any kindness above and beyond the ordinary since his family had died.

Clay was completely flabbergasted that evening when his older cousin, Peter --- who had just barely graduated high school --- offered Clay his old bicycle for free! Peter was preparing to move to Eckhart, Maryland to start work in a coal mine and had recently bought an old but serviceable car. Clay stammered his thanks and was so surprised at the kindness that he moved toward his cousin to give him a hug.

He never made it though, because his cousin pushed him away saying, "Hey! What are you doing? You queer or something? Guys don't hug. You ain't no little boy anymore. Shake hands, but for shit's sake, don't ever try and hug me. Real men don't ever hug each other."

"Sorry. Thanks though. I'll take good care of it, I promise." He shook hands with Peter.

Uncle Warren had to make a nasty comment, however, "I'd a made him work for it, or pay you, Peter. You'll spoil him."

The bike was a nice one made by the Murray Company and was metallic blue with hand-operated friction brakes, twenty-six-inch tires that looked almost new, twin side baskets and a large front basket. Peter had used the bike to deliver newspapers for a while a year before. Clay thought that maybe he could get a job doing the same thing now that he had a way to get around. He'd look into that as soon as he could. Peter also gave him a can of car wax, some Three-in-One Oil and a tire pump to go with the bike. Other than a few token presents of clothing at Christmas, it was the first gift Clay had ever gotten from the Waters family.

He could hardly wait until morning to take it for a ride to Albert's place and maybe even farther to Les Mill's home. He wouldn't tell Albert, however, about his plans to visit Les in case it got back to Toby. After what Toby had said, he didn't want to hear any further rumors from Toby about Les. It didn't matter to him if Les was queer anyway. It looked like he was too and maybe Les was someone he could carefully ask a few questions of, once he got to know him better.

Chapter 4

Saturday morning dawned bright and clear. After doing his usual four loads of family laundry and eating lunch, Clay headed for the county road with his new bicycle. He was amazed at how well it handled and how quiet it was compared to his old bike that rattled and squeaked no matter how much oil or grease he applied to its rusty axles and bearings. He'd have to get used to hand brakes as his old bike had only coaster brakes activated by reversing the pedals.

It took him no time at all to reach Albert's place, but he was disappointed to find his friend wasn't home. His grandmother was visiting, however, and told Clay the family had gone shopping in Cumberland at the Sears and Roebuck store. They wouldn't be back until around six. Clay thanked the lady and took off north along 160, headed this time for Les Mill's house. A few minutes later found him turning into the man's driveway. Les owned a comfortably large, two-story, brick and frame home centered on several acres of neatly kept land. The front of the property was outlined by a whitewash-painted, rail fence. The right side and rear of Les's property were bordered by dense woods. To the left were a neighbor's fields planted in timothy and oats. In the distance over the rolling landscape, Clay could see the peaks of the neighboring farmhouse, silo and barn. The gate to Les's driveway was open, so Clay peddled along the gravel drive to the front of the house where he parked in front of a neat brick garage attached to the right side of Les's house.

So far, he'd seen no sign anyone was home. There was a chance that Les was working a train. If so, he might be gone for several days. His Buick wasn't visible, but it could be in the garage. Clay walked his bike close and peeked in one of two windows set in the large garage door. Les's Buick was there, so he must be at home. Clay parked his bike on Les's front walk and climbed the steps to the porch. He knocked on the varnished oak door that had three rectangular windows stair-stepping along its upper panel. To the left and right of the door were two windows both curtained with sheer, white material having a lacey design. The windows were open for ventilation but screened. So far, there was no answer, so he knocked again, a bit louder this time. Still, there was no answer.

Clay figured Les might be in his backyard, so he left the porch and walked around the left side of the house. Two other curtained windows were along that side, but a third window had no curtains. He felt a little wrong for doing it, but he peeked inside anyway as he called Les's name. It was a kitchen window. There was no one there but a cat.

The black and white cat was lying on a small table across from the window. It looked up from its sleep and mewed as it spotted Clay in the window. Because the window was open and screened, Clay could hear the cat as it mewed twice. It got up from the table, arched its back in a stretch, jumped to the floor and crossed the kitchen. From there, it jumped to the windowsill and started rubbing itself back and forth against the screen as though wanting to be petted. The sill was just wide enough to allow the cat to make the turn and sidle back and forth. Clay placed his hand against the screen and said, "Hey, kitty. How are you doing? Is Les home? Did he go off and leave you all alone? You're a nice kitty." The cat started purring at the sound of Clay's voice and rubbed its jaws against the pressure of his hand on the screen.

Clay left the cat and the window and went around to the back porch and a door that obviously opened into the kitchen. He knocked there again, but still, no one answered or came into the room. He could now hear the cat mewing on the other side of the door. Clay pulled open a screen door and took hold of the solid door's knob to see if it was unlocked or not. It was unlocked, but Clay didn't open it. He'd look around some more.

It was then that he noticed another small building, nearly hidden by a grove of blue spruce trees about a hundred feet behind the main house. It had a peaked roof, was painted white and trimmed in green, like the upper floor of the main house. A flagstone path wound through several well-tended flowerbeds toward the smaller building. Clay followed the path and as he drew nearer the building, he could hear piano music. The building was built slightly above ground level and he used the two steps to mount its small, flower-trimmed porch. To the left of the door was a two-person porch swing and to the right was an old leather Davenport sofa.

Shelves bearing terra-cotta pots of flowers were mounted beneath each of the windows. Clay peeked in the right-hand window where most of the music was coming from; inside he saw Les sitting at an upright piano with his back turned toward Clay. He was expertly playing some very difficult-sounding classical music. Clay was mesmerized by the sound. He'd heard piano music before, but

38

never anything like this. Les was deep into the music as it built to a finale. With a complicated run of chords and notes, the piece ended with a flourish and Les raised his hands from the keyboard.

Clay was about to go to the door and knock but hesitated when he saw Les raise his hands to his face and rub his forehead. At least it looked that way from behind. He'd wait a minute before knocking to be polite. It was then, however, that he saw Les bow his head and from what Clay could see, the man was sobbing, his whole body wracked with emotion. Clay felt embarrassed to see Les this way and wasn't sure what to do next.

Something was wrong. Maybe Les needed to talk to someone. Then again, maybe he would be embarrassed to learn that Clay had seen him crying. Clay couldn't remember ever seeing a grown man cry. Some part of him wanted to hug the man and make him feel better, but he hardly knew him.

He felt like an intruder peeking in the window and watching the man who was plainly having a difficult time. He backed away from the window intending to leave quietly, except his sleeve caught on a cracked section of one of the flowerpots resting on the sill and knocked it over. It hit the porch with a crash. Clay nearly wet himself in fright. Inside he heard Les say, "What the heck?"

Les came to the window and looked out, seeing Clay standing there gritting his teeth and looking sorry. He smiled at the boy and came to the door. It opened and Les said, "Clay! What are you doing here? Are you okay?"

"I'm so sorry I broke your pot of flowers. I heard you playing music and peeked in and... My sleeve..."

"It's okay. Please, come on in. I uh, was just finished playing. I have plenty of other pots. That one was cracked and about to break apart anyway. I'll re-plant the petunias later. I'm so glad to see you, really."

Les stepped aside to allow the boy to enter. Clay was still mumbling an apology as he entered the parlor. "Sorry, I'm so clumsy. My shirtsleeve caught on the pot and... Wow! It's like a little house in here too. I knocked at the big house, but no one was there except your cat. She's nice and tried to get me to pet her through the window screen."

"That's Debussy. She's actually a he, but is missing a few parts."

"Huh? He looked like he was all there to me."

Les laughed and said, "I had him neutered when he was little and now Debussy's like me; a confirmed bachelor."

"Debussy? That's a strange name. What does it mean?"

 "Well, I named him after one of my favorite music composers, Claude Debussy. In fact, I was playing some of his music when you arrived; a piece called *Arabesque*. It's one of Debussy's best-known pieces --- the composer, not the cat." Clay chuckled and Les ruffled his hair.

"You look like you could stand a cold glass of lemonade. I made some a little while ago and now I have someone to share it with."

"Thanks. That sounds good. I am kinda hot and thirsty."

"Great. I don't get much company and it's such a pleasure to see you. I guess school's out for the summer, right?"

"Yes, sir, and I'm glad. I needed a break. Next year I'll be going to the high school in Wellersburg."

"Wow! That's great. You're getting all grown up, son." Clay felt good as he heard Les call him son again. If only he was. Clay followed Les into a small room with a sink and a small refrigerator. There was no stove, just a two-burner, electric hot plate, so it wasn't a real kitchen. There was another door leading off from the one with the sink, but Les closed the door on that side before opening the fridge and taking out a glass pitcher of lemonade. He took two glasses from a shelf and poured them each a drink.

"Your music was wonderful. I've never heard anyone play like that in person, only on records, or on the radio. There's a man at our church who plays, but he's pretty awful and misses notes all the time. I hope you aren't angry for me listening and peeking in the window. I didn't want to disturb you."

"Oh, no, I'm glad to have your company."

"Mr. Mills? Sorry. Les, are you all right? I hope I'm not being too nosy, but after you played it looked like you were feeling kind of bad. Is everything okay?"

Les looked at the boy and opened his mouth as though to say something, but couldn't. He looked away for a moment and Clay saw he was having trouble.

"Sorry. I didn't mean to..."

40

"No, Clay. It's all right. I *was* having a rough time. I get to feeling kind of bad sometimes, living alone out here. I lost a real close friend a few years ago and sometimes I get lonely. The piece of music I played was one of his favorites and it made me think about him. I miss him very much."

"I know what that's like. My whole family died when I was ten and I still get lonely. I cry sometimes too. I'm sorry you feel bad. Did he die, Les?"

"Yes, he eventually died. He had some mental problems because he had been hurt badly during the war. I still miss him terribly, but it was probably for the best; he was very unhappy. I'll eventually get over it. See, even grown-ups have problems that make them sad sometimes."

"If I can do anything, please let me know."

Les sniffed and said, "Well, just having you visit today has made me feel a hundred percent better. Let's go up to the main house. You can finish your lemonade there and meet Debussy. He gets lonely too. I've been thinking about getting him another cat for company for those times when I'm off on a long train ride."

"What will you name him?"

"Humm --- maybe another composer, how does Rachmaninoff sound?"

"Huh? Rockamanakoff?"

Les laughed and pronounced slowly, "Rock-man-a-noff. Hmm, no, I wouldn't do that to a cat. He's another of my favorite composers though. Sergi Rachmaninoff was a Russian composer who lived in America until his death in 1943. Sometime I'll play you some of his music. It's very complicated. He had these impossibly large hands and could reach keys most other pianists can't. I'm lucky I have long fingers and can manage his music pretty well. Maybe Sergi, his first name, would serve as a good name for a cat, but not Rachmaninoff."

"How'd you learn to play piano like that? I'd never think a locomotive fireman would play stuff like Rockman... that guy."

Les chuckled, "Well, I wasn't always a fireman. Once I was a music teacher in Baltimore. I went to a college there and received a degree in music."

"Why did you quit and start working for the railroad?"

"It's a long story, Clay and one I won't be able to tell you today. Things simply didn't work out and I had to leave the school. Now I just play for myself and occasionally do some painting and drawing. I like art as much as I do music. Of course, now I can play for my good friend, Clay. Next time you come over, maybe I'll tell you more and I'll certainly play for you if you'd like. But today, I'm all played out. Come on up to the house. Did you walk all the way here?"

"No, that's one reason I came by. I've got a nice bicycle now. I couldn't believe it, but Peter, my oldest cousin, gave me his blue Murray. He got a car and is leaving home to work in the coalmines, south of here. The bike's like new and boy is it fast and easy to pedal."

"That's great. Now you can visit me occasionally. Always call first though in case I'm out on the railroad. I'll have to give you my number; I paid a little extra so it wouldn't be listed in the phone book. I don't want a bunch of salesmen calling me all the time."

"I'm not allowed to use the phone, Les. My aunt and uncle say since I don't help pay the bill, I can't use it."

Les frowned and shook his head. "What's wrong with your folks? It's the same cost no matter how much you use the phone unless you're calling long distance. That simply doesn't make sense. You're what, thirteen?"

"Fourteen and a half, I know it doesn't seem right, but that's the way they are. Maybe I can call you from a neighbor's house. There's a pay phone at the Esso station too, just down the road toward town. I could use it."

As they reached the house, Les opened the back door and invited Clay inside. He ruffled Clay's hair as he passed and warned, "Be prepared for the love cat. He'll want to make friends."

He was right, for no sooner had they entered, Debussy pushed his head into Clay's shin and then started rubbing around Clay's ankles.

"Is it okay to pick him up?"

"Oh sure, he loves it." Clay raised the friendly cat, cradled him upside down in his arms, and nuzzled the cat's soft, warm belly. Les wrote his phone number on a slip of paper, folded it and tucked it into Clay's shirt pocket while the boy held the loving cat. The cat purred and started moving his paws in the air, one after the other, as if he was pushing at something.

Clay giggled and asked, "What's he doing with his paws?" The cat's eyes were now closed in blissful satisfaction.

"I've never been quite sure myself. Most cats do it though. I think maybe it's something left over from when they were kittens. Kittens push at their momma's belly for milk. They only do it when they're very happy. You've made a friend."

"He's a nice cat. I like him."

"I've had him almost three years now. I picked him out from a litter of all white cats but one. He's the color of piano keys so I named him Debussy after my favorite composer."

"He's a really pretty cat and so friendly too."

"Do you have a pet at home?"

"Noooo. Aunt Martha won't let me. She says cats and dogs are dirty and that a cat will get on your bed at night and suck away your breath, but I don't believe that."

"You're right. It's just an old wife's tale."

"Well, that's Aunt Martha --- an old wife."

Both shared a laugh at Clay's joke.

Les said, "Uh, Clay, does anyone know you're visiting me today?"

"No. I went to Albert Stiles's house --- he's my best friend --- and he wasn't home, so I rode on to your house. It's okay though. My aunt and uncle never ask where I'm going, where I've been, or when I'll be back home as long as I get my chores done. I gotta do my chores first or else."

"Or else what?"

"I either get no supper, lunch, or breakfast, whatever's next, or I get a lick'n."

"By lick'n, you mean a spanking, right?"

"A spanking would be on my rear end, but with Uncle Warren, it's wherever he can reach. When I first came to live with them they couldn't spank me or hit me cause I was still healing up. Now that I'm better, they do whatever they want."

Les was frowning with concern. "Does your uncle ever hit you with his fists?"

"He has a couple of times, but it's usually the back or palm of his hand."

"You said you were still healing when you first arrived at their house. What did you mean?"

"I was burnt in the fire that killed my folks and my little brother. My legs, arms, chest and belly were burnt pretty bad. I still have loads of scars."

"I'm sorry, son. I had no idea you've been through so much. I'd heard your family was lost in a fire but didn't know you were hurt too. Did you have to spend a lot of time in a hospital after the fire?"

"Uh huh. It was up in Bedford where we used to live. I was in there for a little more than half a year. I had to get skin grafts on a few of the burns. I had a super nice nurse who helped me to learn how to walk again. He helped me do exercises to stretch the new skin and scars, and helped me keep up with my school work too."

"I noticed that even on a hot summer day like today you wear long sleeve shirts and long pants. Is it because of the scars?"

"Uh huh. I don't like strangers staring at me. Some of the scars are pretty bad looking, but they don't hurt as much now. The ones on my legs sting and itch, but it's mainly because I'm growing taller and they have to stretch as I grow. Uh, I don't mind showing you the scars if you want to see them. I only show them to close friends I trust."

"It's up to you, Clay. If you want me to see them, I'll look."

"The ones on my left arm aren't so bad, but the ones on my chest and stomach look the worst. I'll show you my arms and belly. He put Debussy down, unbuttoned his shirt and took it off. He then pulled off his tee shirt. Les looked at the boy's chest and stomach where there were several wide patches of dark-colored, wrinkled skin. The boy's arms were thin and one, the left, was marked by a patchwork of scar tissue running several inches from his wrist and upward. His navel was nearly invisible as some of the scar tissue was more apparent there. Clay had a bit of hair beneath his right arm, but not the other. His left armpit was marked by scarred flesh.

"My back is okay. The fire didn't get me there." He turned around and showed Les his back. It was smooth and unblemished.

Les looked but was so affected by what the poor kid had gone through that he became emotional, sobbed once or twice and had to wipe away a few tears.

"Oh, Clay, I'm so sorry you had to suffer so much and lose your family too. You are one brave young man. Thanks for showing me."

44

After Clay put his tee shirt and outer shirt back on and tucked them in his pants, Les stepped close and opened his arms to the boy. The gesture was so unusual and unexpected, that Clay just stood for a moment not knowing what to do, but then he started crying and moved into Les's arms for a warm hug that felt so nice. It had been so long since anyone had hugged him like that and he wanted to stay in Les's embrace the rest of the afternoon. He was crying with abandon now and was surprised to hear Les doing the same thing.

Soon the hug ended and Les turned loose. "Clay, I hope it didn't bother you to be hugged like that, but I felt like we both needed a hug. I have a feeling you don't have anyone at home who cares enough to do that. Even though you're fourteen, you still need someone to care once in a while; everyone does. Uh, it would probably be best if you didn't tell your folks that I hugged you. They might not understand and take it the wrong way. I only did it because I'm your friend and I wanted you to know that I care about you."

"That's okay. It was nice; I won't tell anyone. You're right, they'd take it all wrong. I tried to give my cousin a hug last night when he gave me the bike and he pushed me away and said I was acting like a queer. He said real men don't hug, but I think he's full of shit. Oops, sorry. That just popped out."

"That's okay. I think he's full of shit too." Les laughed a bit and ran his fingers through Clay's hair once more. "I'll never tell. Listen, Clay, since no one knows you're here it's probably best that you don't stay too long. I have to drive into Somerset anyway this afternoon so you'd better head back home. I have a train to catch tomorrow morning and I won't be back for --- let's see --- uh, four days. I'll be back on Thursday. If you want, you can pay me a visit then."

"Sure, I'd like that."

"A lot of people around here don't like me much. I think they believe I'm a hermit or something and I don't want to give them any reason to gossip about me having you visit. Sometimes people say things that aren't true and it can cause other people a lot of grief. For a while, we'll keep the visits short and secret. Okay?"

"Sure. I don't mind doing that. I'll be sure and drop by on Thursday."

"Good. The train I'm working will be going all the way to Saint Louis and then I'll work another coming back. If I can, I'll get you a

45

little something in Saint Louis. Humm, I know just the thing for a surprise."

"Really? What is it?"

"A surprise. If I tell you, it won't be. Be patient, you'll love it. Right now, you need to head on down the road. Where's your bike?"

"By your front porch. Thanks, Les. This has been one of the best days since I moved to Sand Patch. I really like you and I'll miss you this week until Thursday."

"I'll miss you too. Be good and be careful." Les led the boy through the house from the kitchen into the dining room and out the front door. There he ruffled the boy's dark brown hair and was surprised when Clay turned and flung his arms around him once more and hugged him tightly.

"I love you Les and wish *you* were my uncle."

Before Les could respond, Clay turned loose, ran across the porch, pounded down the steps and grabbed his bicycle. He turned once and waved before straddling the bike and heading for the road. As he turned toward home, he waved once more. Les waved back with tears still sparkling in his eyes.

"I wish I was your uncle too, son. I really do."

Chapter 5

Clay could hardly wait for Thursday to arrive. On Sunday morning --- Clay's least favorite time of the week --- he accompanied his aunt and cousins to church. His uncle would normally attend as well; but he had been called to work a two-day shift on a westbound freight. They required Clay to attend each week because they insisted he should be raised in a *Christian Home*, even though the rest of the week none of them prayed, said grace, or treated each other --- especially him --- in any way that would please Jesus.

They attended the Calvary Baptist Church of the Blessed Savior, in Wellersburg where their pastor, Rufus Tarn, re-introduced his flock each week to the horrors of hell-fire and eternal damnation. Clay knew all about fire and felt sometimes as though he was living now in his own private corner of hell with his aunt and uncle.

This morning's sermon was centered on the story of Sodom and Gomorrah, two ancient cities somewhere in the Holy Land where everyone was so bad God decided to wipe them out with some fire and brimstone of his own. Clay had heard a carefully edited version of the story before in Sunday school, but now that he was older, some aspects of the story seemed to take on new meaning. As Pastor Tarn talked of the sins of Sodom, he mentioned the sinfulness of, 'men lying down with other men'. When younger, Clay had always pictured a kind of large dormitory room where a lot of men slept on cots or padding on the floor. Now, however, he was discovering that the story was all about men doing more than simply sleeping in the same room. The story was all about queer guys.

The story went on to tell how God finally let a fellow named Lot and his family leave the city because they were the only good people there. They were told to leave and not look back when the city was destroyed but Lot's wife, simply had to see what she was missing and disobeyed God. She peeked. God turned her into a chunk of rock salt. There were a lot of things going on in that story. More than Clay had realized before.

First, he couldn't believe that everyone in those two towns was evil. What about the little kids and babies? God burnt 'em up. What about married folks where husbands were sleeping with their wives, going to work and having kids? God burnt 'em up. What about the old people, the grandpas and grandmas? God burnt 'em up.

Then there was Lot himself. When some angels came to visit him and see the wickedness of the city, some of the queer men in town came to his house and asked Lot to send out the angels so they could 'know them'. Clay was old enough now to realize what was meant by 'know'. It meant those men wanted to have sex with the angels who happened to be men. What really bothered Clay, was that Lot, instead of telling them to get lost said, 'Let me send my daughters out to you. Make love to them instead of my guests.' Now what kind of a daddy would do that and tell strangers to have sex with his own daughters? God *didn't* burn Lot up for saying such a thing, but should have, in Clay's opinion.

Then there was Lot's wife; she didn't do anything wrong except get curious. When she heard and maybe felt the heat from the heavenly fire raining down on the town she took a quick peek. Heck, anyone would do the same thing. God didn't burn her up, probably  because Lot was standing next to her and might have been roasted himself in the process. Instead, God turned her into a pile of salt that would dissolve as soon as it rained.

Clay concluded God was kinda mean in those days. Maybe He was still learning how to be a good god; maybe He made a few mistakes too. It seemed that over the years, by the time He helped Mary have Jesus, God had gotten a little nicer. Not too nice though; he let Jesus, his own boy, get crucified by the damned Romans.

Finally, the story part of the sermon was over and Pastor Tarn got going on Sodomites. He talked about them in such a way that small children in the church might not be able to figure out what he was really talking about, but now that Clay was older and wiser about men who might want to lay with men, he saw things in a whole new light.

The preacher said, "There are Sodomites among us," meaning there were some right here in Southwestern Pennsylvania. The sermon was taking a whole new direction; a direction Clay didn't especially like. The church was hot inside, to begin with, but Clay felt himself growing warmer and beginning to sweat. He listened more carefully than he'd ever listened to the preacher's ravings before.

"My friends, we are all in terrible danger. Living among us there are those who would bring unspeakable harm to the gentlest and most precious of our loved ones; our children. There are men who would corrupt and befoul the innocence of our babies. They would teach them the ways of the flesh before their rightful coming of age and lead them into the sinful ways of Sodom and Gomorrah. We must be ever vigilant and protect our beloved young from these beasts who would seek out, befriend, influence and corrupt young men and boys with their foul ways." Pastor Tarn paused and scanned the congregation before continuing.

"Think carefully, my friends, before you send your children out each day to school, to the scout camp, to the very neighborhoods in which they live and play. The foul Sodomites are out there waiting for your young children, like jackals stalking a herd of innocent, young antelope, carefully selecting the weakest and most vulnerable to prey upon."

After the sermon, the service droned on through several long-winded prayers, seemingly countless other Bible readings and five or so never-ending hymns accompanied on the piano by Mr. Weathers, a balding, middle-aged man who managed; it seemed, to miss one or two notes out of every ten. The horrible musical delivery reminded Clay of Les and his flawless skill at the keyboard. In light of the sermon and the piano music, Clay was reminded of what Toby had said about Les and the rumor that he might be one of the men Pastor Tarn had been talking about. Clay knew full well that Les was too kind and too gentle to do anything harmful to him or any other child.

Clay tried to visit Albert on Sunday afternoon, but no one was home. Again, if he was permitted to use the phone, he could have saved a trip. Just for the heck of it though, he rode farther along the road to Les's house even though he knew Les would be gone until Thursday. Knowing that, Clay walked his bike around to the back of the house before parking it and mounting the back porch. He was surprised to find an envelope tucked in the back door with his name on it. He tore it open anxiously and read the short message inside:

Dear Clay,

*If, by chance you drop by, find this note and want
to say hello to Debussy and keep him company for a
little while, you are welcome to do so. First, however, you
have to solve a little puzzle that I've left for you. I know
you are bright enough to do it. Here's your first clue:*

First, look in the space, where I've had to replace,
The thing that was broken; I've left you a token.

Your Friend, Les

Clay was amazed. Les trusted him enough to go in his house and
pet Debussy. He could hear the cat meowing from behind the locked
kitchen door and talked to him from outside. He went to the window
and tapped. Debussy jumped to the windowsill and began moving
back and forth as before. This time, though, the window was closed.
He'd have to have a key to unlock the back door. Maybe the clue
was a way to find a key. He looked at the note once again.

First, look in the space, where I've had to replace,
The thing that was broken; I've left you a token.

What had Les replaced? He walked around the house looking for
anything that looked new such as a windowpane that may have been
broken. It would look clean and new, but Clay soon found that Les
kept all of his windows clean and none looked recently replaced.
The grout around them was faded from age; new grout would be
bright white. "I'll check the little house in back," he said to himself
in a half-whisper.

Before he even reached the small building's porch, he grinned as
he solved the first riddle. He'd spotted the petunias; they'd been re-
planted in a new flowerpot. Smiling, Clay ran to the replaced pot
and lifted it up expecting to find a door key. Instead, he spotted
another slip of paper. It was a second clue that read:

Find a door small, I won't open 'till fall.
It will open for you, to find the next clue.

This was fun and Clay was amazed that Les had gone to the
trouble of making a treasure hunt game and make up rhyming verses
just for him. *Now, what kind of a small door would be outside the
house where I could find it?* he thought as he walked around the

little bungalow. He found no small door. He ran to the big house and circled around it twice. It was on his second trip past the front left corner of the house when he spotted the small, metal, coal door set in the cement wall of the foundation. It was where a coal company would deliver coal in the fall to prepare for the winter. Most coal chutes were kept locked to keep small children from climbing in and becoming trapped, but Les had purposely left the little door unlocked. Clay opened it and found another note. This one read:

> Its arms hang so sadly, so sorry it seems.
> A nice place to sit, and enjoy your daydreams.
> In winter, its green coat is lost to the cold.
> In spring and in summer, its tears you behold.

The riddles were getting harder, but Clay was having a ball. No one ever since his parents were alive had done something especially for him. "I love you, Les!" he shouted loudly this time. "I wish you were my uncle or even my dad. I love you!"

What could look sorry and lose a green coat? Maybe it was a tree whose summer and spring coat was green. But what kind of tree was sad? He stood near the coal chute and looked around the front and side yard. There were a number of trees but none looked sad. What would make a tree be sad? Clay ran around to the back of the house and scanned the yard. In the very back corner was a tree that instantly registered. "A weeping willow; it's sad because it's crying."

> Its tears you behold.

"Oh, Les, that's so clever."

He tore across the yard and found a small wooden bench was built in a circle around the base of the old tree.

> A nice place to sit and daydream.

He saw no note at first, but when he bent down and looked under the bench, he saw a note thumbtacked beneath one of the seat boards. He pulled it out and read:

> This is the last of my riddles for you.
> This is the final and hardest clue.
> Go fifty paces from where you stand.
> Aim for the farthest corner of land.
> A special stone lies there below in the grass.
> Beneath it, for you, is a tool made of brass.
> Keep what you find as my gift just for you.
> You're always welcome, my friend, oh so true.
> Les

Clay stood by the circular bench and looked around. The willow was at one corner of Les's land. The farthest corner of his land was beyond the big house, but due to the upward slope of the land, he could see it from here. He started pacing and counting as he walked in that direction. At fifty paces, he spotted a flat rock that had obviously been placed there recently; the grass had been removed to make a place for it. Excited, Clay reached beneath the rock and lifted. It came free and under it, wrapped in waxed paper, Clay found an ornate brass key. It was the key to Les's house. Les trusted him that much.

Clay found himself kneeling in the grass and crying. His aunt and uncle hadn't even given him a key to their house, telling him he wouldn't be allowed to have that kind of responsibility until he turned sixteen. This man, after knowing him only a few hours, was giving him a house key. He dried his tears and replaced the stone.

In his pocket, he had a key ring he used for his school locker key and bicycle lock now that he had a bike once more. He pulled it out and added Les's key. Clay approached the porch and back door. Taking the key in hand, he inserted it in the lock after pulling aside the outer screen door. He heard the door unlock and pushed it open. Debussy was there and ready. As soon as he stepped inside, the cat reached up along Clay's left leg begging to be held. He lifted the loving animal and pulled him close to his face and nose, nuzzling in his soft fur while feeling the lively buzz of his purring. "I love Les so much and I love you too, Debussy. Let's go in the living room and I'll spend some time with you."

First, Clay checked to see if Debussy had plenty of water. Les had a special water container for pets that stayed full for several days. He emptied its reservoir and filled it with fresh water from the sink. Next, he made sure the cat had a good supply of kibble. Another dispenser assured that. A note above the device, however, said:

If you want to give Debussy some canned food, go ahead. There's plenty in the cupboard just above this note. Wait until you're ready to leave and then feed him one whole can. His sandbox should be okay so you won't have to bother with it. He's used to me being gone for several days at a time. There's a dollar bill in the cupboard too, for spending some time with Debussy and feeding him.

See you soon,

Love, Les

52

Clay felt elated that Les was putting this much trust in him and even signed the note "Love, Les" For the first time, he was feeling like a person who counted. He carefully folded the note and added it to the clues from the treasure hunt. He could hardly wait to see Les and thank him for his trust. Clay especially looked forward to getting another hug. He looked in the cupboard and sure enough, there was a crisp dollar bill under a can of cat food.

Up until now, he had only seen Les's kitchen, dining room and front entry room as he walked through the house with Les on Saturday. He picked up Debussy once more and walked into the dining area and front room. It was tastefully decorated with nice furniture and was very clean and neat. Two doors led off to the left and a set of stairs led upward to the second floor. The first door he looked through was standing open and led to a neat, clean bathroom. He was in need of just that sort of room and after setting Debussy on the sink's countertop, he un-zipped and peed.

Leaving the bathroom after flushing and washing up, Clay walked over to a pair of closed French doors. Looking through the glass, he saw a large parlor and library. He opened the doors and went in. Debussy padded along beside him over the rich, oriental-style carpet, occasionally rubbing against his ankles. Two entire walls were lined with shelves loaded down with several thousand books. The room was well lit through several large, French-style windows along the front of the house. A door in the far wall was centered in one of the walls of shelves. He walked over and opened it; beyond were three steps leading down into the garage. There was no car there at present, of course.

The most striking thing in the parlor, however, was a beautiful grand piano. Clay walked around it, running his hand across the satin-finished, black instrument. Gold letters spelling *Steinway and Sons, 1935* were printed on its front. He raised the wooden keyboard cover and taped a few keys. The instrument's tone was beautiful. He re-covered the keys and walked to the bookshelves where he found many titles that sounded interesting. Maybe Les would let him borrow some to read once he got back.

After closing the parlor doors, he and Debussy next took the stairs to the second floor. There he found three bedrooms and another bath. The bedrooms were large and nicely furnished. Clay wondered why a single man would need such a large house, but reasoned it was once his parents' home in the past. The largest bedroom was obviously Les's as its dresser-top displayed a number of photos in frames standing beside personal care items, whereas the other rooms looked more like guest rooms. Some of the furniture in those rooms was protected by dust covers.

Clay felt a little strange as he peeked in a few of Les's dresser drawers. He saw nothing out of the ordinary. The several photos on the dresser featured an older couple, who must have been his parents and a photo of the same two people, looking much younger standing with a smiling teenaged boy who Clay realized was Les at perhaps his own age of fourteen or fifteen. Les had been a handsome young man and apparently was an only child, as there were no other children in the photo.

Only one other photo drew Clay's attention. It was an eight by ten framed picture of Les looking much younger than now and another man of similar age. They were standing side by side with a waterfall in the background; their arms were around each other's shoulders and both were smiling not at the camera, but at one another. Clay picked up the photo and looked on the back of its frame. A notation had been penned on the cardboard backing. Clay recognized Les's neat printing from the clues he still had in his pocket. The writing said:

Todd Garrett and Les Mills
Muddy Creek Falls, Maryland
July 1940

Clay placed the photo back where he found it. *I wonder who Todd was. Maybe he's the friend Les said had been hurt in the war and later died.* Clay saw a sweater draped over a chair back nearby, went to it and ran his hands over its soft weave. He picked it up, knowing it was Les's and brought it to his nose and lips. He could smell the spicy scent of the cologne Les used. He buried his face in the material and breathed in the man's scent. *I wish Les was here now. I can't wait to see him on Thursday. God, I wish he* was *my dad.* He replaced the sweater and left the bedroom. Debussy followed him back downstairs and was quite happy when Clay used a can opener and served him a bowl full of fishy-smelling cat food.

Clay was ready to leave, so while Debussy ate, he petted him saying, "Now you be a good kitty and I'll see you again on Thursday. I love you." He took one last look around the kitchen and headed out the back door, making sure to lock it securely. He retrieved his bicycle, walked it around to the front drive and rode home.

Chapter 6

On Monday morning, after chores, Clay hoped to spend some time with Albert, but after biking north along 160, he found that Albert was spending a week or two with his grandparents in Salisbury, Pennsylvania and wouldn't be back until Sunday a week. His mom smiled and said that Albert had asked her to call him and let him know he'd be gone, but she hadn't had a chance to do it yet and she was sorry he'd made the trip for nothing.

"That's okay. If you talk to him, tell him I'll see him when he gets back. Thanks." He turned around and headed for home. He almost rode on to Les's house but decided not to. Debussy was fine and he didn't want to cause Les any trouble in case some nosy neighbors happened by or saw him going in the house. He wanted to talk with Les about a few things before he again used the key the man had given him.

Clay thought about riding to Toby's place, but somehow, after hearing Toby's comments about queer men, he wasn't as comfortable being around him. It seemed that the only thing Toby wanted to talk about was girls, baseball, girls, basketball and sometimes, girls. Clay wasn't a sports fan and certainly wasn't a girl fan. He felt so out of place whenever Toby discussed them that he preferred not talking with him at all. He returned home and read a book until lunchtime. At two, his uncle returned from his two-day sojourn on the rails looking dirty, disagreeable and decidedly drunk.

Lately, he'd noticed his uncle was starting to drink heavily again. His aunt and uncle had recently had an argument and during the shouting match, Clay heard her accuse Warren of drinking again. Clay remembered that two years before, his uncle had come home drunk several times and Clay soon learned to stay clear of him whenever that happened because Warren got even more mean and abusive than usual when drinking. For a while, he went to meetings somewhere and the drinking stopped. Now, apparently, he was back at it again. Clay cringed to think of what it might soon be like around the house if his uncle got angry with him while drunk.

On Tuesday afternoon, just after one o'clock, his uncle gave Clay an especially nasty look as he passed Clay's open bedroom door on his way to the bathroom. Clay, who had been lying in bed reading, wearing only a pair of gym shorts and a tee shirt, figured it was time to go outdoors, or perhaps take another bike ride even if he had nowhere in particular to go. He closed his door and was in the middle of changing into other clothes when the door was thrown open and his uncle stormed in. Clay was dressed only in boxer underwear, about to pull on a pair of long pants. The door flew back and hit his dresser with a bang and Clay was so surprised that he fumbled the pants and dropped them before he could step into them.

"What the hell have I told you about locking this god-damned door?"

"It wasn't locked. You have the key. You just opened it."

Warren, obviously drunk and maddened by the alcohol, wasn't in any shape to think logically. He growled something and made for Clay with his fists balled up and before Clay could get away, Warren hit the boy's mouth with his right fist and his stomach with the left. Clay collapsed to the floor gasping for air he couldn't seem to find. Blood was pouring from his upper lip and he thought one of his front teeth might have been knocked loose it ached so much. His uncle kicked him twice, once on his left upper leg and once in the butt before he was able to rally enough to roll farther away from the madman. He was able to suck in one small breath of air as his body started recovering from the blow to his diaphragm.

Warren made a drunken rush toward him and thankfully, a small throw rug saved Clay from another kick for as Warren placed his foot on it, it slid on the polished hardwood floor and his uncle went down hard on his rear end with a grunt and a curse. His head also struck the corner of an old wooden cedar chest Clay once used for toys as a child. Warren rolled on his side, rubbed the back of his head and looked around confused. He shook his head just as he spotted Clay.

"You little son-of-a-bitch; I'll kill you for that. Get over here and help me up. I'll teach you not to trip me. Get over here, I said!"

Clay, able to get a few breaths by now, managed to get up, but instead of going to his uncle, he grabbed his clothing and a pair of shoes, ran around Warren --- who made a futile grab for his ankle --- and ran through the open door. His aunt was just coming up the stairs looking perplexed and said, "What happened? What's going on? You're bleeding!"

"Uncle Warren hit me in the face and stomach and kicked me twice! I'm fed up with this place. He's drunk and said he was gonna kill me. I'm getting out of here for a while and if he ever touches me again, I'll call the sheriff and have him arrested. I'm not his damned punching bag!"

"What? He tried to..."

Clay paid no attention and yelled. "He's hit you before too. I've seen him do it and you're too yellow to do anything about it. I wish you and him both were the ones to burn up in the fire instead of my real family. Damn him and damn you and damn this house!"

Aunt Martha was speechless, standing at the top of the stairs with her mouth open, staring at Clay as though she'd never seen him before. Clay pushed his way past her and ran down the steps.

Clay could hardly believe he'd said what he'd said. *But it's the truth,* he thought. *I've got to get away for a while. If Aunt Martha tells him what I said, he probably will kill me.* Clay went through the kitchen and stopped only long enough to grab a few items from the refrigerator and cupboards and stuff them in the backpack he'd retrieved from a hook by the door. In his effort to grab some canned goods, he accidentally turned over a five-pound canister of flour and its contents puffed across the countertop. Instead of leaving it there, Clay grabbed the container and twirled it around spewing the remainder of the flour all over the normally spotless kitchen. He did the same with a similar canister of sugar. *What the heck,* he thought. *I'm in deep trouble anyway, why not do it right.* His uncle's expensive, brass, B&O lunch-box was setting on one counter, so he opened it and emptied a bottle of pancake syrup into it along with a can of ground coffee. He set it on the floor and partially mashed the metal lunch-box carefully with his bare foot. He took a moment to wash his mouth out in the sink and spit the bloody contents on his aunt's once shiny floor.

Clay was still dressed only in boxers, so he pulled on his pants and shirt as quickly as he could, stuffed his socks into one pocket and slipped his bare feet into his tennis shoes. He didn't bother with the laces but grabbed his pack and fled through the back door. He heard his aunt and uncle coming down the stairs. His uncle was cursing loudly, so it was time to vacate.

Clay ran around to the side yard, jumped on his Murray and took off toward the highway, stopping only long enough beside his uncle's shiny, blue, '51 Pontiac to scratch along it with Les's house key. Luckily, he'd remembered to grab the key ring from his dresser on the way out of his room. He wanted to scratch, **DAMN YOU** on the car's trunk lid but didn't have the time. He had to leave!

When he reached the end of the driveway, Clay was unsure which way to go. Where *could* he go? Left and south toward town --- or right and north toward Albert's, or Les's house. More than anything else, he wanted to go to Les's house. No one was home and no one so far knew of his friendship with the man. *But,* he thought, *I don't want to get Les in trouble with the rumors about him. I care too much about him to put him in danger that way.* Clay was crying and just now realized it, with all else that was happening.

What have I done? I've really gotten myself in trouble this time. I just need to find a place where I can think for a while and not be bothered by anybody. He looked up and down 160 as if some flashing sign might magically appear saying:

<<< *GO THIS WAY* or *GO THAT WAY* >>>

Then he thought of a place where he *could* go; at least for a good think. Clay turned left, toward town and pedaled hard. He glanced back to see if his uncle or aunt were out where they could see which way he went. No one was outside, but they still might be watching from a window. It didn't matter, he'd soon be turning off 160 and he doubted his folks would ever think of looking for him where he was headed. Once he was out of sight of the house, he stopped only long enough to pull on his socks and tie his tennis shoes, as he was afraid the flopping laces might become tangled in the bicycle chain and throw him off.

It wasn't long before he reached his turnoff. It was a tar and gravel secondary road turning right or west. There was a gas station and small country store there; Hickory Esso, named for the two giant trees that overshadowed it. All too late, he remembered the dollar bill Les had left him. It, and some extra change he'd left behind in one of his dresser drawers might have come in handy at the small store. It couldn't be helped now. He had to make tracks.

The road he turned along provided access to several played-out coal mines, an abandoned stone quarry and at the road's end, a ruined grist mill that hadn't seen a grain of buckwheat or corn in thirty or forty years. A couple of small, run-down cottages along the road were still home to a few poor families, but other than that, the old road was seldom used. Clay's destination was at the very end of the road.

As he considered what had just happened with his uncle and aunt, he thought the term 'end of the road' was just about right. He wasn't sure he could ever go back to his uncle's place. Of course, if

59

the sheriff ever found him, he'd make him go back, or else he'd have to go to the state orphanage in Bedford. He'd heard tales about that place and he'd rather live in alleys and basements than go there.

He had to be careful on this road as it was notorious for ruts and potholes that opened up after any sizable rainstorm --- potholes that could easily bust a bike tire. He at least had a fine bicycle and had to take especially good care of it now. He figured if he could hide out for a few days until Thursday, when Les returned, he could go to him for help and advice. As he thought of the kind man, his loving cat and beautiful home, he started bawling uncontrollably and had to pull off the road until he got over the emotional response.

I am in so much trouble was all he could think. He was both frightened and relieved an unusual emotional stew for a fourteen-year-old to digest. After a few minutes, he regained control and set off down the road. It wasn't long before he saw the end and turn-around ahead. The ruins of the old mill showed above the foliage to the right of the road's end and that was where he was bound. He dismounted as he reached the end of the hardtop and walked his bike along a rough path that led behind what was left of the mill to the flat flagstone ledge along the millpond. It was a ten-foot wide shelf between the crumbling stone side of the mill building and the drop-off into the millrace and pond. The massive oak waterwheel had long ago rotted away, but its rusty shaft still protruded from the side of the mill like a reddish-black spear.

The millpond was still in good shape, for the small stream that fed it was held back by a stone weir that had been built by stonemasons who knew how to construct things that would last. The pond was about fifty feet across and seventy feet long. Nowhere was it more than eight feet deep. Part of the creek's water entered the pond by way of an elevated stone millrace just beyond and above the ledge where Clay was now standing. Rushing water poured from its end where once the old --- and now absent --- water-wheel turned.

It was a favorite place now for local children and teens that would ride the flume and shoot from the end into the deeper part of the pond below. Last summer he and Albert had come here many times to swim, play and ride the flume. They loved climbing into the millrace farther upstream and allowing the two-foot-deep, fast-moving water to sweep them along a ninety-foot ride before the rushing water cascaded into the millpond.

He wished Albert were here with him now. It seemed strange; he wanted to be alone, but he was lonely. Clay was sweating from his strenuous bike ride in the June heat, so he pulled off his outer clothing until he was wearing only his under shorts and tee shirt. They were sweaty and needed cleaning, so he walked upstream along a stone-paved trail where he could slip into the millrace and ride the rushing water.

It was an exciting ride and Clay whooped with delight as he raced along the slippery channel and shot past its end into the pond, ten feet below. After swimming about for a few minutes, he took off the tee shirt and boxers and hand scrubbed them. Before doing anything else, he returned to the ledge, just below the race and climbed out. He spread out his underwear on the warm flagstones to dry next to his other clothing. He ran naked along the stone path to the top of the millrace once more for another trip down the flume.

After reaching the pond this time, Clay swam across to the other side and back a few times; he finally swam to the weir and sat in the rushing water that poured over the stone ledge into the lower stream below. He noticed a new, wide crack in the weir's wall where much of the water was escaping at high speed through a V-shaped opening. He moved over and sat in the gap. He loved the way the water felt, rushing over his lap and beneath his bare bottom as he wedged himself in the V-shaped opening and held himself there with his knees facing the millpond.

If he spread his legs apart, the rushing water poured up and over the sides of his lap and as it did so, it caused his privates to flutter back and forth in the swift current; it tickled in an odd way and caused him to become hard. Within a few minutes of letting the water wiggle his hard organ, he felt the familiar drawing back for release. *This is pretty nifty,* he thought as he raised himself out of the flow. He let himself rest another minute before again lowering himself into the flow. The feeling was intense and he thought, *Why not? It feels great.*

He laughed as he watched his hard penis fluttering back and forth in the flow like a flag in a fast wind. Clay was rising fast and after stopping a few times and returning to the flow, he decided to let nature take its course. It felt very different than by hand and he was amazed at how much more he seemed to be drawing back doing it this way before the release took place.

Suddenly his body had reached a point where it could draw back no more and his pleasure began. Streams of white fluid burst from his opening under the water and were instantly carried over his lap and away by the rushing water. His body was shaking like never before as he felt a completely new and different release. *This is great. I only wish I could do this with another boy touching me down below or maybe sitting on my lap and facing me as it happens. It would be so great if Albert was here and wanted to be with me as I do this; or a handsome boy like Roddy. I bet he'd love to do this too.*

Clay ceased his fantasies as the pleasure ended. He raised himself out of the rushing flow of water and sat on an unbroken section of the weir just beside the V. It was time to return to reality and his uncertain future.

Looking upward at the sun which was just touching the tops of the higher trees around the western end of the pond, he thought, *It must be about three o'clock. I wish I had a watch. Should I stay here tonight, or try to find a better spot?* He glanced at the ruins of the old mill. *I bet it's pretty spooky around here at night.*

In the past, he'd explored the building several times with Albert and once with Toby. There was little shelter to be found there as the mill's roof had long ago rotted away even though most of the stonework walls remained. They'd seen rat droppings in the mill's partially exposed basement and he certainly didn't want to share his bed with a bunch of varmints.

He felt hungry and a bit sleepy after his swim and sexual release. He walked carefully across the weir's slippery, algae-covered rocks until he reached the stone ledge. He climbed up and walked naked along it until he reached his pile of clothing. He rooted in his backpack and pulled out a can of sliced peaches, an apple and a half pound wedge of longhorn cheddar cheese. Somewhere in the pack was a half box of saltines to go with the cheese. He looked until he found it. The cheese and crackers hit the spot, as did the apple. The peaches posed a problem, however, as he'd forgotten to swipe a can opener from his aunt's kitchen drawer.

He got up and looked around for a sharp rock to use on the can and was pleased to find instead, a six-inch-long, half-inch wide, flat bar of rusty iron. By scraping it on the flagstones for a few minutes, he brought it to a reasonably sharp point and edge. Now with a rock and the sharp bar of metal, he was able to punch through the top of the can, wiggle the metal around a bit and pry up the lid enough to get to the peaches inside. He felt pleased with himself for his inventiveness. *I might have to do a lot more for myself now that I've run away,* he thought as he drank the sweet juice from the can before trying to hook out the peach halves themselves.

He found that by using the sharpened metal bar as a knife, he could slice the peach halves while still inside the can and then more easily hook them out to eat. After eating all of the fruit, he was about to toss the can off in the weeds but stopped himself. The can might come in handy, as he'd neglected to bring along a cup or a glass. He leaned over the edge of the stonework and swished out the can in the millpond, removing all the leftover stickiness and peeling off the paper label. He bent the lid back and forth enough to fatigue the metal and remove it so he could use the can as a cup. In fact, he filled it with water from the clean mountain stream and drank deeply before putting the empty can in his backpack.

His underclothing was dry; he was about to put them back on, but hesitated. One part of him thought about jumping back in the water for another swim and maybe another trip to the V-shaped break in the weir, but he reasoned, *No, it's getting late and I have to find somewhere to spend the night. I can come back tomorrow and have another swim. I'm sure not going back home.*

The swim that afternoon had served to cool and clean him off, but he noticed now that a rather large and colorful bruise had formed along the side of his left leg where his uncle had kicked him. It ached as he pressed on it. He'd already checked his teeth and while one was sore, it wasn't loose, as he'd first feared. His lip had been cut inside where it smashed against his teeth and was raw and sore, but that would heal.

Clay had developed a fair degree of tolerance to pain because of what he'd experienced in the fire. His lip was blue and sore looking as he gazed into a puddle of still water to see what damage his uncle might have done. Leaning around as best he could he saw his left buttock was extremely black and blue from the other kick he'd suffered. *What a stinking, drunk bastard my uncle is. I bet they don't even call the sheriff to report me missing. They're probably glad to get rid of me anyway.*

Clay didn't consider the fact that his uncle and aunt might have to answer embarrassing questions about his injuries if they called the authorities. As it played out, they chose not to say anything to anyone and figured he'd come home in his own good time after a night in the woods suffering hunger pains. They greatly underestimated the youth.

Chapter 7

Tuesday afternoon, about the same time Clay was swimming at the pond, Les Mills was browsing through a store in Saint Louis. His train back to Cumberland and home was due to leave the next afternoon and would arrive in Cumberland around six, Thursday morning, so he had the whole afternoon to spend in the downtown area of the city. The store, Steamboat Hobbies, specialized in beautiful model steamboats like those that once plied the mighty Mississippi, but also carried all manner of other hobby materials and supplies. He'd selected several items for his own hobby needs and was searching now for something special for Clay. As he examined the various items, his thoughts turned to the boy and several concerns Les had about his relationship with the lad.

Les had to be very careful. Several years ago, he had been accused of leading an inappropriate lifestyle when he was a teacher in Baltimore's Academy of Fine Arts. He had been very careful to protect his privacy, but word had reached the school administration that he was living with another man in a one-bedroom apartment. In 1944, that was all it took to bring suspicion upon anyone who worked directly with children and in his case young adolescent prodigies who attended the exclusive school. No wrongdoing was ever reported and nothing was ever proven about Les's lifestyle, but he was dismissed with little notice, paid for two additional weeks and asked to leave the school immediately.

He'd also been providing private music lessons to several other young people in Baltimore as a source of extra income. Somehow, the parents of those children were informed about the school's suspicions and once again, he found himself without work and little cash to see him and his companion through more than three weeks. His roommate, Todd Garrett, was a disabled veteran of World War Two and was unable to work, so in effect, Les was supporting two people.

Todd and he had grown up together in Sand Patch Pennsylvania and as they came of age --- long before the war and college --- they'd discovered they were of a different nature than their friends. They were homosexual. It was during their first few years in high school when they fully realized their nature and discovered they loved one another in this special way. After high school, both were able to start college, as their parents were sufficiently well off to send them to a small college in Bedford, Pennsylvania. Todd was not cut out for higher education, however, and soon was forced to drop out, while Les excelled and began his studies in fine arts with a major in music and composition. He had been playing piano since he was seven on his family's old upright. Todd began working for the Pennsylvania Railroad as a ticket agent in the Bedford Station. They lived together in a small apartment and did pretty well for themselves.

Les was a natural pianist with exceptional talent and soon earned a music scholarship to attend Baltimore City College. He and Todd were about to move there when the Japanese bombed Pearl Harbor and World War Two broke out. Both volunteered for service. Todd was accepted into the Navy but Les was rejected, due to a slight curvature of the spine. He continued his education in Baltimore while Todd went off to war.

In late 1943, Todd's ship, a minesweeper, was torpedoed by a Japanese submarine off the coast of Hawaii and eventually sank. Todd's left arm was crushed, but with the help of fellow sailors, he survived in a life raft, made it to shore and was taken to the naval hospital in Pearl Harbor. The arm was beyond repair and had to be amputated from just below the shoulder, but at least he was alive. By mid-1944, he returned to Baltimore and joined Les, who was about to graduate from the college.

After graduation, Les landed a job with the Maryland Academy of Fine Arts, in Baltimore, as a piano professor and things went well for the two fellows for a while. After the accusations were made, however, and Les lost his job, they were forced to move back to Pennsylvania. Les's father had died a year before and his mother was not well, so he and Todd moved into the family home. Todd's father and mother had also died and his older brother inherited the farm, so Todd made his home with Les.

As in any small town, the gossip mill was in full operation. Soon, people were making comments about Todd's living with Les, even though he was disabled. He and Les had been using that to explain why he stayed with Les and his mother. People still remembered, however, how inseparable the two had been in high school. Les found a job teaching art and music at a Meyersdale grammar school; a true waste of his talents, but it was all he could hope for in the rural area where he was forced to live.

Another problem began to surface, however. Todd had frequently suffered from nightmares and episodes of severe depression right after the war, as he re-lived his traumatic experience on the burning and sinking ship. He'd seen friends and comrades blown apart and severely burned; he'd heard their screams and watched them die before his very eyes. His arm had been pinned and crushed while flaming oil was slowly drawing nearer and nearer to where he was trapped. He fully expected to die from the fire, but two other sailors found him in time, managed to free him from the crushing weight of a smashed bulkhead and pulled him from the spreading path of the flaming oil. He never would forget, however, seeing his comrades roasting and dying nearby and his dreams were often filled with their screams and the horrors of his war experience.

To some extent, while in Baltimore, and even more so in Les's home in Sand Patch, the dreams began to dominate his life. Todd was becoming more and more depressed no matter what Les did to comfort him and keep his mind on positive things. Todd would sometimes become irrationally angry at Les for no reason and the love between them was strained and tested constantly.

In 1948, Todd tried to take his own life with a pistol and botched the attempt. He lost his left ear, sight in his left eye and a portion of his temple sustained some degree of brain damage. He had to be institutionalized. Within a year, Todd had withered away and Les was forced to let go and move on with his life. Todd barely recognized Les and every visit became slow torture for the sensitive young man who never stopped loving his long-time friend. In 1949, Todd died and it was with mixed feelings that Les attended his funeral. On one hand, he mourned his loss, but on the other, he was relieved that Todd was finally at peace.

For a year after Todd's death, Les continued to work at the elementary school, but he was less and less satisfied with his job. He started tutoring students all around the area, in small towns and hamlets as well as Bedford and Cumberland. It meant more travel, but he felt like he was putting his knowledge to better use and hoped to discover some boy or girl who had the potential to become a great player.

It was in Finzil, a tiny mining town just over the state line in Maryland where he found a thirteen-year-old boy whose talent was nothing short of amazing. Both of the boy's parents were uneducated and almost backward due to years of poverty. His father was a coal miner and his mother could barely read or write. Nevertheless, Charles, or Charlie as he preferred to be called, was a musical savant. His ability at the keyboard was phenomenal and once Les discovered him through a tip from a teacher at Charlie's small, one-room school, Les offered to teach the boy at no cost, for this lad had the potential to be an international star of the keyboard.

Because the family had little money and no piano, Les offered to pick the boy up twice per week and tutor him in his own home. Les's mother was still living and he felt comfortable having the boy there where he could learn on a Steinway piano Les had gone into debt to own a few years before. Within a year and a half, the boy was playing at a level approaching Les's and he talked to Charlie's family about allowing the boy to audition at Julliard or some other fine school. Les even offered to travel with him to New York City, if necessary, for the audition. By then the boy was fifteen and growing like a weed. He had it all, talent, good looks, and a kind and winning personality. Charlie was no spoiled, savant brat with his nose a mile in the air, but a humble, somewhat shy genius who would please audiences someday in the great concert halls of the world.

The parents were proud of the boy's talent and agreed for Les to do whatever he could for Charlie. The sessions at Les's home were increased to four evenings a week as they prepared for a trip to New York and Julliard. The boy worshipped the ground Les walked on and was not ashamed to show his affection for his mentor with a warm hug occasionally. Les felt a kinship for the boy almost like a father for a son. Never did Les have any inappropriate thoughts about the lad, or any other youth for that matter. It was true that Les was homosexual, but his attraction was strictly for adults and after Todd's death, he hadn't actively sought out another companion. Les's work became his passion, especially after discovering young Charlie.

Charlie, however, was growing up and, unbeknownst to Les, was discovering his own homosexuality. But at fifteen, he wasn't able to understand fully his needs and wants; he was falling in love with his teacher. It was during the trip to New York, just after the audition, while staying at a low-cost hotel when Charlie tried to show his love for his teacher by climbing into bed with him, revealing and exploring his feelings.

Les awoke that night, surprised and confused as he felt Charlie, now nearly sixteen, naked beside him in the bed, embracing, and kissing him while fondling him beneath the covers. When he saw that Les had awakened, Charlie confessed his love and became even more amorous, but Les had to stop what was happening and do it quickly as he was having wild temptations he never thought he would ever feel. A part of him was excited by the boy's fervent attentions for his body was reacting according to his nature. Thankfully, the other part of him had the strength to end Charlie's advances immediately and do it in a way that would not hurt the poor boy emotionally, causing him to become angry and turn against Les.

He gently told Charlie to stop and for the rest of the night Les talked with the sobbing teenager explaining why this could not be. Both were emotionally drained by morning and Les felt, at least, that he had handled the situation well. Fortunately, their appointment for the results of the audition was not until late afternoon, so both were able to get some sleep.

As expected, Charlie was accepted. Les was overjoyed for a number of reasons. This meant that the world would gain a great pianist; it meant that Les had satisfied his ambition to discover a prodigy and best of all; it meant Charlie would be living far away from Sand Patch, Pennsylvania in just a few short weeks. After their talk, Charlie was disappointed and sad, but understood Les's position and realized he had to find the companionship of young men his own age.

Once back home, Les made sure that for Charlie's last lessons, someone else was always present. He also resolved to completely stop teaching piano and change careers. He applied to the railroad, and since his father had worked for the B&O, he was hired, through the union, as a legacy and sent for training. The pay surprisingly was three times what he'd been earning by teaching at the elementary school. Because of Charlie's attempt to make love to him and his urge to reciprocate, Les no longer felt it was to his best advantage to put himself in a similar position around young people, at least for some time. Les's mother died that year of heart problems and Les, being an only child, inherited the debt-free homeplace.

Now, after several years, Les was re-thinking his stance. He wasn't a bad person for almost succumbing that night. He was only human and had exercised the proper control and done the right thing.

His thoughts now turned to Clay. Having lived in the area for many years, Les had heard of Clay's loss of his family. Les's neighbors --- Albert's parents --- had mentioned several times how they thought the boy was being badly treated and most likely physically abused by his uncle and aunt.

When Les saw Clay on several occasions, he felt sorry for the boy who seemed well behaved, polite and a good person. Something was telling him the boy needed a friend and someone to turn to. That was one reason Les stopped to give Clay a lift the day he spotted him running along the road. Later, when he saw the lad's burns and heard him talk about frequently being denied meals and 'getting a lick'n' for minor infractions at home, Les's heart melted and he decided to be there if the young man needed him for advice or friendship.

Today, in Steamboat Hobby Shop, Les spent fifty-five dollars --- a small fortune in those days --- for a beautifully crafted, HO scale, model locomotive. It was a handcrafted, brass model of a Mallet, the very type of locomotive he often worked on and the type of locomotive doomed to extinction. The locomotive was highly detailed and painted in B&O colors. It featured a device in its smokestack to release puffs of smoke from small pellets one could drop into the stack. Clay would love it.

He hadn't revealed what was in the room beyond his guesthouse kitchen that first day when Clay visited. He would wait until he returned home to do so. Les looked forward to seeing Clay's face as he saw his new model locomotive come puffing out of a tunnel on the elaborate model railroad Les had been building in that room over the last several years. The poor boy needed something to do and be proud of. He needed to learn, most of all, that not all adults were mean and abusive. He needed someone he could trust to be there for him as he grew up; someone to whom he could go with his questions and problems; someone he could trust and love.

Les needed him too. He was tired of the loneliness, the sorrow, the emptiness. The day Clay saw him crying, he wasn't crying about a lost friend as he'd implied, he was crying as a teacher and mentor who could no longer do the thing he was best at --- guiding and inspiring young minds. He was thinking of Charlie, who had recently performed at Carnegie Hall. Already at eighteen, the lad was being hailed as the next, world-class pianist. Les had received an invitation to attend too late to make arrangements and felt that he had let Charlie down. He wouldn't fail to be there next time. He'd written Charlie a letter, before leaving for Saint Louis, to say how very sorry he was to have missed his former student's premier performance and begged Charlie to let him know well in advance next time.

Les gathered his purchases, left the hobby shop and headed back to the railroad hotel, where train crews on layover could sleep for a night or two before their trains departed. On this trip, he'd be working a passenger train, the *Shenandoah #7*, as fireman in a 4-8-4 Baldwin locomotive housed within a bright, B&O blue, streamlined body. Several railroads had built similar streamliners, as they were called, to give a more modern look to steam engines, but the coming of the diesel-electric locos had doomed them as well.

The B&O's passenger trains running between Baltimore and Saint Louis had two different numbers, depending on whether they were running eastward or westward. The westbound train was called the *Shenandoah # 6*, while its eastbound counterpart was dubbed the *Shenandoah #7*.

Les would work the train in shifts with another fireman until he reached Cumberland early Thursday morning, where he would get off and allow the other fireman to finish the run into Baltimore. In a few weeks, he would attend school in Hagerstown to become a conductor and finally leave behind the hot, smelly cabs with their hateful coal smoke and cinders.

Chapter 8

As Les was settling into the railroad hotel in Saint Louis, a little after three, Clay, in Sand Patch, was pedaling hard, heading north along route 160. It was after four o'clock due to the different time zone and the sky  was growing dark as a summer storm swept across the Alleghenies from the west. He'd already passed his uncle's driveway hoping they didn't catch sight of him as he sped by.

He was thinking about spending the night at Albert's place; the little shack where Albert and he often played would be a perfect place to do so. It was substantially waterproof and by the look of the sky, that might be a necessity. Also, Albert wasn't home and his folks would have no reason to come down to the hut and find him sleeping there. His only regret was that he'd not had time to pack a blanket or sleeping bag. He didn't own one, but his cousin Paul did and if he'd had more time before he'd fled the house, he would have grabbed it. He'd make do as best he could. Being June, it shouldn't get too cold, unless the storm hung over the area and brought with it cold air. That sometimes happened in the Allegheny Mountains, due to the elevation, even in June.

Clay would have to be careful as he approached Albert's home as his folks might spot him coming in the driveway. Perhaps he'd have to wait somewhere nearby until dark or dusk. That shouldn't be a problem unless the storm broke. If that happened, he'd have to risk discovery. If the family did spot him he could use that to his advantage and ask to stay there until the storm passed, or if it raged into the late evening, he could ask to stay the rest of the night. *No, he realized, that won't work; they'll call my aunt and uncle to let them know where I am.* "Damn!" His last word was spoken aloud.

He was almost to Albert's place and would have to make a decision soon. A few raindrops spattered on the road and he could smell the exotic, electric odor of the coming storm. It was going to be a doozy! Black clouds were rolling above like Atlantic waves and a bolt of lightning flashed somewhere ahead of him. It was only a few seconds before he heard the thunder. The next burst of thunder followed more quickly after another blinding flash. It wouldn't be long before...

With a crash, a bolt of sky fire hit a tree not twenty yards away along the west side of the road and scarred Clay so badly he felt himself pee, just a bit. He had to laugh, but at the same time knew he had to find shelter somewhere. *That tree could have been me.*

Of all days for a damned storm, he thought. He raised himself off the bike seat, pounded the pedals and flew along the road as the sky opened and the rain came down, drenching him and nearly blinding him to the road ahead. The rain was like ice, stinging as it pelted his face and neck due partly to the speed at which he was pedaling. He could hardly see now and had to slow down in spite of his desire to reach shelter.

Maybe I should just go back home and take my punishment. I could get struck by lightning out here. I wish now I was closer to Les's place. I might need more than Albert's shack in this mess. He looked ahead and finally spotted the driveway to Albert's home just ahead. It was either turn in there and hope for the best, or pedal another third of a mile to Les's house. The rain was getting even colder and now he felt the occasional sting of hail. Pea-sized and then marble-sized pellets of ice spattered against the road, as well as Clay's face and arms.

"What next, God, you gonna make it snow?" He yelled, but the wind and storm swallowed his complaint. His decision about where to spend the night was made moot as another bolt of lightning struck a tree a hundred feet down the road. He turned into Albert's place, careened along the driveway, pedaled around the house and slid to a halt next to the hut. He jumped off and rolled the bicycle into the shed along with him. Thankfully, the ramshackle door had no lock on it. It was still cold inside, but at least it was mostly dry and the incessant wind was thwarted by the walls.

A little rain was blowing in one window with a single missing pane out of six. All four of the windows had been glazed by Albert's dad, but one had been broken by an errant baseball just a few days before. It plagued Clay to recall how he was the one who had hit the foul ball that doomed the window.

He located himself as far from the broken window as possible and hugged his chest in an effort to get his breathing under control. His sides were still aching from the strain of peddling so fast to reach shelter. Clay had never been so wet and cold. His limbs were shaking and his teeth chattering as he looked around for something to wrap himself in. The only thing was a grubby piece of carpet on the packed, dirt floor; one end of it was already soaked by water that was trickling down the wall from the broken window. Within minutes, the rest would be just as sodden. There was an old toy chest where Albert kept a few things, from time to time. He opened it and was overjoyed to see an old pullover sweater and a large, ratty-looking, white towel. They would have to do.

Clay started stripping off his wet clothing. It was fairly dark in the hut due to the storm and would soon be totally dark once the sun set. Now naked, he used the towel to dry himself a little. He wanted to keep the towel somewhat dry, as he might need it to wrap himself up for warmth, so he only used it on his head and face. He would let the rest of his body air dry as best he could. The musty old sweater smelled like a wet animal, but was looking darned good at this point; he could hardly wait to put it on.

As strange as it seemed for him of all people to say, he wished he had a fire to warm himself. Clay suffered from a strong phobia concerning fire and seldom went near one. His uncle made him tend the fireplace and furnace in the winter, knowing it bothered him to get so close to the flames. Warren said, 'You have to get over that, boy. Someday you have to be more of a man and quit being so afraid of fire'. He realized in some ways, his uncle was right about that, but still held a fear for what fire could do. Any person burned like he'd been would feel the same way. But tonight, he almost wished he was standing in front of that thrice-damned fireplace at home, even if he had to put up with his uncle's abusive sarcasm.

Clay still had enough food in his backpack for another day, if necessary. He was feeling hungry, but getting dressed and warm was his first priority. Even though it smelled foul, the sweater was large enough to fit him and then some. It must have belonged to Albert's dad who was slightly over six feet tall and weighed somewhere in the range of two hundred thirty pounds. Clay held his breath as he pulled it on and could hardly wait until his body heat --- at least what was left of it --- could start warming him. The towel he wrapped around his lower parts like a loincloth and tied it the best he could in an effort to defend his modesty somewhat in case someone did come to the hut. It looked to Clay like a baby's diaper, but cold, wet beggars could not be choosers.

Clay next pulled three hard-boiled eggs from his pack and set them aside. Half the crackers were left and half the wedge of cheese. A can of sweet fruit cocktail would provide energy and satisfy his thirst, although all he had to do for that was hold his empty peach can outside under a dripper and he'd have plenty of water within seconds. It was pouring outside as hard as before and hail was drumming a constant clatter on the hut's tin roof. The yard outside was peppered with marble-sized balls of ice. Using his makeshift knife, Clay opened the can of fruit and worked the lid back and forth until he could drink the juice and slowly savor the fruit chunks. Nothing ever tasted as good. He peeled the eggs and after eating them, with the cheese and crackers, soon was satisfied.

By now the light was fading fast as the sun, already obscured by storm clouds, set behind the surrounding ridges. Clay figured it was about seven o'clock by the time he was finished his meal. He was ready to settle in and rather than try to lay down flat to sleep, he moved two of the wooden benches together into one corner of the building to form a platform where he could sit with his legs folded in front of him and lean back against the corner of the shack. Once that was ready, he sat on the platform and drew his knees up. He then pulled the sweater down over his knees and tucked it in around him as best he could. The arrangement worked pretty well and soon he was actually beginning to feel warmer. Surprisingly, Clay drifted off to sleep quickly; he'd had a very busy and nerve-wracking day.

Morning found Clay laying on his side in a fetal position on his small platform. He blinked a few times in puzzlement, trying to clear his mind and figure out exactly where he was. It all came back; he'd made it through the long, wet and chilly night. He remembered getting up once during the night to pee out the door and must have gone back and curled up on the bench before once more falling asleep. Thankfully, it had stopped raining; bright morning sunlight was streaming in through the broken window. He stood up, stretched and suddenly was painfully in need of relieving himself both ways. He wrinkled his nose as he realized one other item it would have been nice to bring along --- toilet paper. Oh well, nature would provide.

He peeked outside to make sure no one was out on the lawn at Albert's place. He couldn't see anyone. The shack was about two hundred feet from the house, so he could probably exit the hut and run into the woods without being spotted. He'd wrung out his wet clothes the night before and spread them out on the old toy chest, but they were still somewhat damp. He at least replaced the loincloth with his nearly dry boxers before pulling on his damp and clingy pants. The smelly sweater had to come off too. It had served its purpose, but until he could give it a washing, maybe at Les's house, he'd had enough of the wet animal stink.

After putting on the rest of his clothes, he felt a little better. At least they were clean from the soaking rain last night and a half hour in the sun would dry them completely. He folded up the towel and smelly sweater and stuffed them in his backpack. He couldn't wait any longer and left the hut, aiming for a nearby path he was familiar with. The air was a bit chilly, but nowhere near as cold as it was the night before. A little way into the woods, he searched about until he found a patch of mullein. Some people called it deer's tongue. It was

a common broadleaf woodland plant that had wide, fuzzy leaves that his dad --- years before when Clay was nine --- told him was a great natural substitute for toilet paper. Feeling the wide, soft, fleshy leaves which were fuzzy like velvet, he quite agreed. These might even be better than toilet paper when it came to softness.

Near the patch of mullein, he peed, then squatted and soon was able to try out the leaves. His dad was right; they were every bit as soft as velvet and did the job quite well.

Clay returned to the hut and gathered his things. Just before leaving, he remembered something he wished he'd thought of before. Albert had a secret cache in the floor of the hut. Clay flipped back the damp carpet and revealed a one-foot square of plywood set at ground level near the center of the hut. Lifting it up revealed a small wooden box Albert had built and buried to hold items. The contents of the box varied from time to time, but Albert kept a few items there on a regular basis. One was a genuine, Swiss Army

Knife wrapped in an oil-soaked cloth to prevent rust. It was bright red with a white cross and shield symbol set in its handle. One thing it had, in addition to two sharp blades, was a can opener, a small file and a screwdriver/bottle opener combination.

Looking further, Clay found a small metal Sucrets box containing two dollars and thirty-five cents in change. He'd have to owe it back to Albert. He needed the money. There were odds and ends of marbles, an official Boy Scout slingshot, bottle caps, paper clips (they might come in handy), a compass, several crayons, a small pocket flashlight that actually worked (that would really come in handy), a coach's whistle, a small circular mirror from a lady's powder compact, three small candles and a box of waterproof camping matches. *Boy, if I'd remembered the trapdoor last night, I could have had light. Oh well, maybe I'll need this stuff even more tonight. I don't know where I'll be then.* He gathered the items he might need and dropped the borrowed treasures in his pack. On the back of the plywood lid to the cache, he used a red crayon and wrote:

Albert   I had to borrow some things for an emergancy.
I will return them soon. IOU $2.35.
Your best friend, Clay

He shrugged into the slightly damp, canvas backpack and walked his bike outside after peeking to see if anyone might be out around the house. He stuck close to the wooded perimeter of the grounds and was able to make it out of the driveway, as far as he knew, without being noticed. It wouldn't matter as much now since it was morning and Albert's folks wouldn't question him being there like they would have before the storm last night. There were still many puddles here and there along the road from last night's storm as he pedaled north on 160 toward Les's house. It was Wednesday and Les was due back on Thursday. Clay figured he'd risk staying tonight either in or around Les's place and see him the next morning. Within fifteen minutes, he'd arrived and walked his bike around to the back porch where he parked it out of sight of the highway.

The key might also fit the front door, but he didn't want anyone on the road, driving or walking by, to see him enter the front door unless Les was home. He unlocked and opened the back door and was immediately greeted by Debussy. He sat down at Les's kitchen table and petted the loving animal on his lap for five or ten minutes. He was purring and pushing with his paws at Clay's knees while soaking up the attention. From time to time, Clay would bend forward to feel the cat's soft fur against his lips and face as he whispered his troubles to the cat and kissed the top of his head.

Clay wanted, first, to change clothes and clean up a bit. He'd have to borrow some of Les's clothing until his clothes were washed and dried, so he went upstairs to Les's bedroom. Debussy padded along behind, rubbing against his ankles each time he stopped long enough for the cat to do so. Clay again felt a little odd going through Les's stuff but figured Les would understand once he explained what had happened. He found a drawer with underclothes and took out a pair of socks and a pair of white briefs. He'd never worn briefs before and wondered how they would feel as he was used to the freedom of boxers.

In another drawer, he found some tee shirts and took one out. It wouldn't be too big on him as Les was rather thin and boy-like in build anyway. Clay found a pair of soft corduroy pants and a long sleeve shirt that would do until his clothes were finished being washed. Looking about, Clay noticed a clothes hamper in Les's closet. He thought, *I'll wash any dirty clothes in the hamper and help Les out.* He saw a wicker clothesbasket nearby, dumped the contents of the hamper into the basket and set it near the bedroom door. Clay then slipped out of his clothing and added them to the basket as well.

Clay went to the bed where he'd laid out Les's clothes and slipped into the briefs. They were a little large for him but would do for the time being. His imagination kicked in about that time as he realized Les had worn the underwear to cover *his* privates and that set off a natural reaction. His penis hardened and Les's briefs were on the rise. Clay giggled, as he looked at himself in a long mirror mounted on the inside of the closet door. He remembered the photos in the Sears and Roebuck catalog and liked the way he looked in the briefs. *Maybe I'll start wearing them someday soon too,* he thought.

He pulled on the pants and used his own belt to keep them up, as they were a few sizes too large in the waist. He had to roll the cuffs several times to adjust the length. The tee shirt and long sleeve shirt fit well enough for now. He pulled on the socks and slipped his feet into a pair of loafers he saw in Les's closet. They were a size too large but would have to do. His sneakers were wet and would have to dry out on the clothesline before he could wear them. He toted the basket downstairs and searched around until he located the door leading to Les's cellar. It was off the kitchen; he'd not noticed the door before. He switched on the lights, went down the wooden stairs, and soon located Les's washing machine. It was a standard machine with a large tub and a wringer. He searched around until he found a box of Rinso Blue laundry soap, separated the clothing into two loads of light and dark colors, and then decided to do the lights first.

He soon had the washer going and went back upstairs to wait for it to wash the clothes for a while. He used the time to fry a couple of eggs and make some toast. After he finished eating --- with some help from Debussy --- he went downstairs and eventually finished the wash. If Clay was an expert at anything, it was doing laundry, as he was the one most often tasked with washing his family's clothing twice a week.

He was about to carry the damp clothing outside to the clothesline but wasn't sure if he should let Debussy outside or not. The cat decided on his own, for as soon as Clay opened the door the cat slipped out, ran across the porch, onto the lawn where he played in the grass, chased a few butterflies, caught and ate a grasshopper, and looked completely happy. After a few minutes and as Clay was hanging up the clothes, Debussy found a flowerbed, dug a small hole and squatted to relieve himself. Clay had never been around cats and was surprised by the cat's actions. He was positively dumbfounded when, after finishing his business, Debussy carefully covered the hole and patted it down. *And Aunt Martha says cats are dirty. Crazy old woman.*

By noon, the laundry was dried, ironed and folded. Clay was back in his own set of clothes and he and Debussy were finishing their lunch. Clay had found the cat's sandbox and tended to it as well. When Les made it home tomorrow, he wouldn't have any chores to bother with and could relax after his long workweek.

Clay wondered if by now his aunt and uncle had called the authorities about him being missing. He'd taken a bath after doing the laundry and looked himself over in a mirror in Les's bathroom. His bruises were even more colorful than they had been yesterday, especially the one on his backside. One whole cheek was purple and blue surrounded with tinges of sickening yellow. His upper lip and part of his cheek were still black and blue, but the cut inside his mouth was healing pretty well; the tooth wasn't hurting any longer. Clay used the upstairs bathroom which had a larger tub and added some nice-smelling bath oil to the water. He'd decided to stay the night here rather than sleep outside somewhere like he did the previous night. He wasn't anxious to repeat a night like that.

He tried picking out a few tunes on the grand piano in the parlor and discovered he was able to do pretty well. He managed to pick out *Silent Night* and *Happy Days are Here Again* and planned to play them for Les when he got home. Maybe Les could start teaching him piano if he had the time. Les had a Motorola radio and record player in his living room and Clay played a few Glenn Miller and Harry James records and listened to the radio.

In one corner of the room was a square-shaped wooden box with a rounded-off square of glass mounted behind two folding doors. It was labeled, Westinghouse Spectrevision and had an on/off and volume knob, like a radio and a round dial with the numbers 2 through 13 on it. Clay wondered why there was no 1.

He knew it was a television. He'd heard about them, of course, and seen them in the Sears store in Cumberland, but had never seen one in anyone's home. Albert's folks were talking about buying one soon and told him he'd be welcome to come over and watch with Albert. His aunt and uncle were vehemently opposed to television, claiming it to be an ungodly invention. It was only recently that two television stations --- one in Altoona and one in Pittsburgh began to broadcast in Southwest Pennsylvania. People were slow to buy the expensive sets and begin watching, as the reception was weak and required a high antenna.

There were several knobs labeled Brightness, Contrast, Horizontal Hold, and Vertical Hold, but Clay had no idea what some of them did. He turned the TV on and after a few seconds to warm up, he heard scratchy sound coming from its speaker.

The window lit up with a grainy picture with fuzzy-looking people moving around and talking. As he watched spellbound, a man was yelling at a lady. Sometimes he seemed frustrated and spoke fast in some foreign language and then the lady opened her mouth wide and cried loudly saying, 'I'm sorry, Ricky. I only wanted

 to surprise you. Fred and Ethel said I shouldn't try to drive our new car, but I wouldn't listen. Awwww.' She was bawling again.

The man let her cry for a minute and then finally said, 'Loocy, is not so bad, just a little scratch. I'll have it fixed and next Saturday, I'll teach you how to drive the car. I was wrong to say that women drivers are a menace. Stop crying, Sweetheart. I still love you.'

They kissed, music played and then a picture of a heart came on the screen and other music started playing as words flashed past, like in the movies, telling who was in the show and who directed it. After that, the picture changed and a man appeared on the screen telling about a furniture store in Altoona.

Clay watched the television for a while amazed at what he was seeing. Another show featured three crazy men, who were always hitting each other and doing silly things; they were kinda funny. Clay saw how a television could be a nice thing to have, but after a while, he got tired of  just sitting there watching it. Debussy had curled up beside him in the easy chair and gone to sleep; he looked a little put out when Clay got up and switched off the television.

Clay took a book from the shelves in the parlor. It was an illustrated version of Jules Verne's *Journey to the Centre of the Earth*. He carried it upstairs and stretched out on the single bed in one of Les's guest rooms where he planned to sleep tonight. He read several chapters, but got sleepy and drifted off. It was after five when he woke up and felt hungry. Debussy had once again curled up beside him. They went downstairs where Clay found some hot dogs in the refrigerator and boiled several in a pan. He also opened a can of baked beans and the last can of peaches from his own backpack. He gave Debussy a can of cat food to eat while Clay scarfed down three hot dogs with mustard, ketchup and chopped onions on buns.

Clay decided to avoid turning on too many lights in case someone, who knew Les's schedule, might spot them and wonder who was in the house. The bedroom he'd chosen was on the rear of the house; he'd picked it for just that reason, figuring a light there wouldn't show from the front as easily.

He watched a little more television, read some more from the Verne book and by nine, was ready for bed. He took a quick bath before changing into a pair of Les's pajamas and he and Debussy crawled in bed. He snuggled with the cat for a little while. He thought about his mom, dad and brother and wished that he'd brought along the picture of them in his room, but there hadn't been time. He also thought of the photo of Roddy hidden behind it and that started him thinking about Roddy and then Albert and then...

He felt a little strange playing with himself as Debussy watched him with obvious curiosity. The cat came close and batted at his moving hand causing him to giggle and push him away saying, "Come on, Debussy, leave me be. This is private." He let Debussy sniff at his hand. He must have smelled the mucus, or else the odor of his foreskin, because the cat licked his fingers a couple of times and once more Clay was surprised. He expected the cat's tongue to be soft like a dog's, but it was rough, like sandpaper. Again, he'd never been around cats before.

Debussy left him alone long enough to finish what he was doing; Clay enjoyed it as usual and used some bathroom tissue he'd brought into the bedroom to clean himself. Debussy watched the whole process, mewed a couple of times as if to say, 'That was interesting' and then curled up beside him. As Clay pulled Les's roomy pajamas up and over his privates he thought, *Les will be home tomorrow and boy, do I ever have a lot to talk about. I sure hope he's not mad at me for coming here, but I had nowhere else to go.* He petted Debussy, as his eyes grew heavy. That usually happened right after he gave himself pleasure. Within a few minutes, Clay fell asleep.

Chapter 9

The eastbound *Shenandoah* pulled into Cumberland's Queen City Hotel and Station at five-ten on Thursday morning. Les, tired from an eight-hour shift in the lead locomotive, swung down from the cab of the Baldwin 4-8-4 Streamliner as a replacement fireman  took over for the remainder of the run to Baltimore. He collected his duffle bag and items he'd purchased in St. Louis from the baggage car and headed for the entrance to the employee section of the hotel. As in Saint Louis, there was a small section of the railroad-owned station and hotel for train crews to use. He went to a communal shower room, stripped out of his coal-smudged and sweat-stained coveralls, grabbed a bar of Octagon Soap and washcloth from his travel bag and stepped under the stinging hot spray of a showerhead.

The water felt great as he scrubbed thoroughly with the Octagon soap. Afterward, he stood beneath it for several minutes, allowing it to wash away not only the soap but the stress of his labor. It wasn't so bad for firemen nowadays as most locomotive fireboxes were fed automatically by machinery. In years gone by, the fireman shoveled coal almost constantly to stoke the ever-hungry fire. The Streamliner used a semi-liquid slurry of ground coal and fuel oil to create the tremendous heat needed to boil thousands of gallons of water into steam that drove the giant engines and their trains. His job was to watch pressure and temperature gauges, adjust the flow of oil and coal mixture and make sure all was operating safely and efficiently. The cab wasn't quite as dirty as in the older locos, but still, he and the engineer were subject to fierce heat, smoke and coal cinders that filtered back from the locomotive's stack. Steam locomotives were dirty and there was no way around it.

After enjoying the shower for nearly twenty minutes, he dressed in normal clothing and as he stepped out of the employees' door again at six forty; he could have been any other Cumberland citizen going about his business. Unlike most railroad workers, he always changed into the type of clothing most any other man of thirty-three might wear in and around a city. Often Les even wore a tie with a lightweight sweater or jacket in the spring or fall. He wore his work coveralls only when on the job. On this particular day, he wore a light green, short-sleeve dress shirt, tie and slacks as he had a stop to make on the way home.

He walked to the employee parking lot of the Queen City Station, unlocked his old Buick and after stowing his belongings in the back seat, got behind the wheel. The car started on the third attempt and soon he was leaving Cumberland and heading north through the Narrows, an ancient river valley where Will's Creek had cut through the mountains over numerous millennia to join the Potomac River.

Les was driving west along U.S. Route 40, the Cumberland or National Road. It was America's very first government-funded highway, had served wagons, and later motorized traffic from Cumberland, Maryland westward into Southwest Pennsylvania and Central Ohio for nearly a hundred-fifty years. In its early years, it was a toll road with tollhouses scattered along the way. From Cumberland eastward, Route 40 was known as the Baltimore Pike, another vital thoroughfare that crossed the mountains and valleys of Central Maryland.

In the small town of La Vale, Maryland, Les passed one of the remaining, octagon-shaped tollhouses. It was a historical building now, housing a small museum honoring the venerable highway. Les was taking U.S. 40 today, rather than his usual route through Corriganville and Barrellville, Maryland so he could pass through the little town of Finzil, just north of Frostburg. He wanted to stop by Charlie's home and congratulate his parents on the young man's recent concert debut.

He hoped to catch Charlie's father early before he went to work and made it to Finzil well before seven. Charlie's folks saw him pull in and met him at the front door, pride evident in their eyes. He gave Charlie's mother a warm hug and shook hands with his father.

"We sure do owe you a lot, Les," said Charlie's dad. "I was so proud of that boy up there in front of all those fancy-dressed folks. I tell you though; I couldn't live in that awful town. My god, the noise and the traffic and... Les, the people in New York are the rudest folk I've ever seen. They'll walk up one side of you and down the other if'n you stop to look around on the street." Les smiled and nodded as he remembered his visit to the city with their son, a few years before.

Charlie's dad continued: "Them subways, now, they's a marvel. Charlie took us all around town the next day. We saw some museums; one had a big round room where they show the stars on the ceiling just like it's night and a park damn near as big as this county. Charlie took us on a boat out to the Liberty statue too. We climbed all the way up into her crown and looked out. He even took us up to the top of the Empire State Building, the tallest building in the whole world! I wish you could have been with us. We owe it all to you and if'n there's anything we can ever do for you, just name it."

Charlie's mom spoke next and said, "Our boy said to give you a hug," and that's just what she did. "He said to tell you he loves you like a member of the family and to us, you always will be. Please plan on coming back sometime soon for dinner. We'd love to have you. Charlie said he's coming home sometime in late August and he wants to see you then, so plan on dinner one night while he's here."

"I will. I miss him and look forward to seeing him. If I'd known about his concert in time, I would have been there. I wrote to him explaining why I couldn't make it. I won't miss the next one."

Charlie's dad glanced at his wife, grinned and said, "Well, Les, we might all have to miss the next one."

"Why's that?"

"It's gonna be over in England. Our boy's going to London, England in July to play for them people over there. He said young Queen 'Lizabeth herself might even be there. A whole bunch of young folk from his school have been invited to play and Charlie's one of them. They'll be going over on an aero plane."

"My gosh, Charles, that's wonderful. You're right; I might have to miss that one. I get free train fare anywhere in the United States, but unless the B&O builds a very long bridge in the next month or so, I won't be able to make it. I'm amazed."

"We're gonna try to go to another concert in Chicago. That one's in September," said Charlie's mother.

"That one I can attend. I'll see what I can do about getting you both rail passes for that and help save a little money. I'll probably be a passenger conductor by then."

"That would be a kindness, Les. Thanks, son," said Charlie

Senior.

"Well, I'm glad I stopped by and caught you both in, but I have to get home. I just worked the *Shenandoah* passenger train from Saint Louis and I'm worn out. I'm going to go home and sleep away the morning and probably most of the afternoon. Please drop in whenever you can and visit. I do feel like we're all family now. Thanks."

Les drove the last leg of his journey, a mere eight miles and was happy to pull in to his home a little before eight. He opened the garage, idled the Buick inside, closed the door and entered the house through the parlor door. He was halfway across the room when he noticed the keyboard cover to the Steinway was open. Frowning, he closed it and was about to go through the French doors and into the living room, but stopped again. The television doors were open. He smiled and thought, *Oh good! It looks like Clay found the clues and paid a visit. What a great kid. Hope he comes by later today.*

He got a drink of water in the kitchen and noticed a used can of baked beans had been rinsed out and left in the sink. He smiled and thought *Clay must have been a little hungry too. What teenager isn't? I wonder where Debussy's hiding? Probably asleep in my bed.* He often found the cat there after one of his long trips. He probably felt closer to him sleeping there.

Les had to go, so he headed up the stairs to the bathroom, unzipped and peed. Still no cat. That was odd. He'd left the bathroom door open as usual and by now expected the cat to come running. Leaving the bath, Les went into his bedroom and was surprised to see no sign of Debussy there either. Instead, he saw two stacks of clean clothing on his dresser. "I'll be darned, Clay must have done my laundry," he said half out loud while wondering, W*here the heck is that goofy cat?*

Les was determined now to find Debussy and started searching the other upstairs rooms. He checked in the front guest room. Nothing. He then walked down the hallway to the back bedroom. The door was closed and he heard faint mewing coming from behind the door. He opened it and was about to reach down for Debussy, but stopped cold. Clay was sprawled on his back, asleep in the bed. He had tossed off the covers and was wearing a pair of Les's pajamas. Les was both alarmed and amused. He was concerned as to why the boy was sleeping here and amused because, like most teenage boys and young men, part of his anatomy was already wide awake and peeking through the pajama fly.

Les walked over to the bed and threw the sheet over the boy in such a way so its folds covered his exposure. He sat down on a bedside chair and looked at the handsome young man wondering what had driven him here last night. Then Les noticed the bruised lip. *Oh, dear God. I bet his uncle did that. What the hell am I going to do?*

He reached out and lightly brushed his fingers through the boy's dark brown mop of hair. It was so soft and Les's heart melted a little more for the lad who had experienced such a terrible time in life so far, yet still hadn't turned mean despite all the pain and suffering from the fire, the loss of his family and the negative influences he'd had to put up with at home. Les couldn't help himself as a few tears filled the corners of his eyes. He bent and kissed the boy's warm forehead.

Les sat back down, took Clay's hand in his, and gently squeezed. The boy sniffed, wet his lips and his eyes fluttered open as he yawned and looked over at Les.

"Hi," said Les as he gave the hand another squeeze, then reached out, and caressed Clay's hair once more.

"Oh, Les! I'm so glad to see you." The boy tossed the sheets aside before realizing what was happening beneath them. He looked down and said, "Oh, crap! Sorry." He covered himself quickly and grinned at Les.

"That's okay. It happens to half the people on earth, son."

"Huh?"

"Half the people on earth are men or boys --- happens to us all in the morning. Don't be concerned. What's going on? Why are you here instead of at home?"

Clay started talking at full speed as he sat up on the bed keeping his lower half covered by the gathered sheet. "Oh Les, I can't go back there. I've had it with Uncle Warren. He was drunk and beat the heck out of me. I've got big bruises on my leg and butt where he kicked me. He almost knocked my tooth loose with his fist. See?" He turned back his lip showing Les the ragged cut. "I want to live here with you and Debussy. I love you Les, and never want to leave. I love Debussy too. He's the best cat in the world and he's smart too. Did you know he covers up his poop? Did you teach him to do that?"

Les had to laugh in spite of the seriousness of the moment. "No,

Clay. All cats do that. It's instinct. Let's stick to more important things than cat poop, okay?"

"Okay. I sure hope you're not mad at me. I owe you some for a few groceries I ate, but I did all your laundry and cleaned up after myself. Please don't be mad and please don't make me go back there." The boy was trembling. He began to cry as though he was wounded. Clay was positively howling. Even Debussy, who had jumped on the bed, backed away and blinked.

"Come here, Clay." Les pulled the boy to him and held him close, rocking his upper body and whispering in his ear. "It's going to be okay, son. Just relax. I'll do everything I can to help you. You go ahead and cry though. Let it out. I know you probably feel like you're about to explode sometimes. When that happens it feels so much better to have a good cry and let it out. I've got you, son, and I love you."

"Oh, Les, I love you too. I wish you were my dad. I miss my real dad and mom so much and my little brother too. He was so nice and so cute. I was so proud to be his big brother." Clay separated from Les's embrace and stared at him wild-eyed. "Oh God, Les, I saw him catch on fire in our bedroom and he was screaming and I tried to get him, but it was too hot and the fire caught on my pajamas and I had to run. I rolled on the floor and put out the fire, but it was all my fault he died. I tried to get him, but the fire pushed me back and swallowed him up. It was all my fault --- Oooooo!"

"Oh God, son, I'm so sorry. I'm so damned sorry. But, Clay, it wasn't your fault. You did the best you could by trying to grab him and pull him out. You were only ten and did the very best you could. I've got you, son and I'll do whatever I can to keep you safe. Maybe we can find a way so you won't be hurt again by your uncle. I'll talk to some people I know who might be able to help."

Clay looked panicked. "Not the sheriff! He'll make me go back there, or send me to the orphanage in Bedford. They beat kids there, Les. I've heard awful things about that place. I want to live here with you and Debussy. Please say you'll adopt me, or even hide me here and not tell anyone. I can't go back! I won't go back! I'll run off again. I don't want to be beaten no more."

"When did it happen, Clay?"

"Two days ago. On Tuesday," he said between sobs.

Alarmed, Les said, "You've been staying here two days?"

"No, just yesterday afternoon and last night."

"Where did you stay Tuesday night?"

"In the hut in Albert's backyard."

"What did Albert's family say about your being hurt?"

"They still don't know. Albert's at his grandma's house. I snuck in there to get out of the thunderstorm and hail."

"Thunderstorm? Hail?"

"Night before last. It was really bad. I was never so cold and wet as I was that night. I almost got hit by lightning, too. I would have come here, but the storm was so bad I had to get off the road at Albert's place."

"Okay, kiddo. Start from the beginning and tell me everything that happened. Uh, fix the sheet first. Your horse is out of the barn again."

"Huh?" Clay looked where Les was pointing. The sheet had fallen to the side and he was once more exposed. "Sorry."

"It's okay. Matter of fact, get dressed. I want to see those bruises anyway unless you're too shy. I have to make a few decisions about what to do and if you've been hurt, we have to get it on record. I may have to take you to a doctor, Clay."

"I'm not shy. Sorry my thing was hard when I first woke up. I have to pee and it does that when I have to go. I'll be right back." Clay ran off to the john and must have left the door open; because Les heard the sounds of falling water followed by a flush. Debussy had followed Clay from the room as well. *Looks like I've lost my cat,* thought Les with a laugh. *Fickle feline! Every cat needs a boy to take care of.*

Clay returned and laid out his clothing. He pulled off the pajama top and Les saw no bruises on his back or chest. With no sign of shyness, Clay pulled off the pajama bottoms then turned to show Les his left buttock and left upper leg. The bruises were extremely severe, especially the one on the boy's backside. Les felt himself growing warm with anger.

"He hit you awful hard, son."

"The bruises are from where he kicked me with his shoe. He hit me in the mouth with his fist. That's what cut the inside of my lip where it hit my teeth. He hit me in the stomach too, but I can't see any bruise there. I couldn't get my breath for a little while after he did that."

The boy turned and Les looked at his scarred tummy but could see no bruising. He saw the boy was not burned around his privates and that was good at least. Part of a man's pride in himself centers on that part of his body. Clay had enough baggage to carry as it was.

"Okay, Clay; get dressed and tell me the whole story from start to finish."

For the next half hour, as Les fixed breakfast for them, Clay told everything that had happened from the time his uncle got home drunk until the present.

"Well," said Les after the tale was told and breakfast was nearly over. "You've had one heck of an adventure this week." He yawned, rubbed his eyes and stared out one of the kitchen windows into the trees beyond the house. Clay could tell he was thinking, so he remained silent.

Finally, Les turned back and spoke. "Clay, I have two friends in Somerset who I want to take you to see. One is in a position of authority; the other is a minister. Both belong to an organization that I also belong to. That organization is dedicated to helping people who find themselves in serious trouble and you certainly qualify. If it were your parents, there would be little these men could do to help, but since your parents are dead and because your aunt and uncle never really wanted you to live with them anyway, these men might be able to make things better."

"Who are they, Les?"

"One's a county judge named Lucius Brand. Judge Brand is a good man and he can work wonders within the law since he's chief judge of Somerset County. The other man is an Episcopal minister, Reverend Abner Brooks. Judge Brand is highly respected and knows me very well. Father Brooks knew my mother and father for years and was a big help when I was trying to get into college."

"What organization do you all belong to?"

"See this ring I wear? Look close. You'll see a design made up of several symbols. What do you see?"

"Well, there's a compass, sorta like the kind you use to draw circles with in school."

"Good. That's exactly right. What else?"

"The other part looks like a carpenter's square."

"Very good, son; you're one smart boy --- heck you're almost a man and I'm very proud of you." Clay beamed at the praise. Les could tell the boy didn't get a lot of that at home. He was positively glowing.

"What's the G stand for, Les?"

"For God, mostly. It also stands for geometry, a very useful kind of mathematics, which my society has always had a lot of respect for. This ring shows I'm a member of the Order of Freemasons or sometimes just the Masons. Ever hear of them?"

"No, sir, are they a secret club?"

"No. Some people criticize the Masons and call them a secret society, but instead, we're a society of secrets." Clay wrinkled his nose and tried to work that out. Les added, "It means we operate in plain sight in most American towns and cities, but we keep certain secrets that our members learn over a period of years as they study our history and learn knowledge that has been passed down for centuries. Some evidence exists that the Freemasons started in the time of the pharaohs in ancient Egypt."

"Wow!"

"Some say their special knowledge of geometry helped to build the pyramids, but that may not be exactly true. No one really knows for sure. It is true that early Masons were builders who guarded the secrets of how to construct great buildings and cathedrals in early Europe so the competition wouldn't learn them. Nowadays, they mostly work to help people in need, like you, and help our country's government stay on the straight and narrow. Half of all U.S. presidents were Freemasons including most of the founding fathers like Washington, Jefferson, Ben Franklin, Paul Revere and John Adams. President Franklin Roosevelt was a Mason. Our former president, Harry Truman, is a Mason of the highest order. It's called the thirty-third degree. His ring like this has a number thirty-three on it."

"Is President Eisenhower one?"

"No, he was busy being a soldier and a general during the Second World War."

"What do you have to do to become a Mason, Les?"

"Well, you have to be willing to serve other people and help them when they really need it."

"Do they take kids? If they do, I'll join and help out."

"Well, Clay, when you're a little older, if you still feel that way, I'll help you join. There is a chapter in some larger cities called the DeMolay that is especially for young teens. Our lodge in Somerset doesn't have one, but there's a group in Cumberland."

"Cool. How can your Mason friends help me?"

Les paused and looked directly into Clay's eyes. "I want you to listen very carefully to what I'm about to say. It's about the most serious thing I've ever thought about doing. For some reason, something is telling me it's the right thing to do, but you have to understand it completely and be willing and comfortable with what I'm planning to ask of those two men."

"Okay, Les. What is it?"

"Clay, I'm going to ask the judge to act on your behalf and sever your ties to your uncle and aunt. I want to take you to see him today and show him your bruises. That alone will show him the kind of danger you could be in if you're forced to go back to them."

"Where will I have to go if I can't live there? Please don't say the orphanage."

"Oh no, Clay, I'd never do that. I've heard stories too. Look at me, Clay. Look right into my eyes." Les took a deep breath before continuing: "I'm going to ask the judge to appoint me as your legal guardian. That means I'm going to ask him to let you live here with me."

Clay's eyes begin to blink and water and suddenly he threw himself at Les and hugged him tightly, kissing him on the cheek and sobbing as he said, "Oh Les, I love you and want that so much. You can be my dad that way. I'll be so good and help out around here and do everything you say. I'll do your laundry and keep Debussy's sandbox clean and..."

"Whoa! I'm not looking for a housekeeper, son. I'm looking for someone who needs me as much as I need you. I'm never going to be married and I want a son so much. This will be the answer to both of our prayers. Neither one of us has to be lonely anymore if this can come about. Let me call the judge right now and see if he can see us today. I want him to see the bruises and talk to you. I'll also call Reverend Brooks. I'd like him there as well; he's known me since I was a little boy."

"Wow. That's a long time. I think you told me once, but how old are you?"

Les chuckled, "I'm positively ancient; I'm thirty-three."

"Just like Truman's ring."

"Huh? Oh yeah, I understand. At least until October first, then I'll be thirty-four."

"That's about how old my real dad would have been, I think. Oh, Les, I sure thank you for wanting me. I hope those men can make me your son. I'd like that more than anything else in the whole world."

"Me too. You gather up the breakfast things and I'll try to reach Judge Brand."

"Les?"

"Yes?"

"Is it okay if I hug you once in a while? I love it when you hug me. Some teenagers, like my stupid cousins, don't like to hug unless it's their girlfriend or something, but I'm not like that at all. I've been saving up a lot of hugs for a long time, ever since my family died."

"Oh, Clay, you bet you can hug me. I like hugs too. Anytime you want."

Clay embraced him like before and Les kissed the top of his head. Both were happier than they'd been in a long time.

The judge and the minister were both free, so as soon as possible, they locked up the house and climbed in Les's old Buick for a trip north to Somerset, the county seat, less than twenty miles away. Les turned on the car radio and found a Somerset station. He was mainly listening for any report of a missing or runaway boy, just in case, Clay's family had called the authorities. He figured they would wait a while thinking Clay's bruises would have time to heal. An announcer gave the daily news report, but there was no story of a missing teen.

Les asked, "Clay, the judge is going to ask you a lot of questions. He asked me a few on the phone, but I suggested we wait until you can tell your own story. One thing he asked and I'm going to ask you ahead of time. Do you want him to have your uncle arrested for criminal assault of a child?"

"What does that mean exactly? Would he have to go to jail?"

"Probably."

Clay thought hard for a few minutes and then said, "I don't want him to go to jail, but I think the judge should tell him to quit drinking and if he doesn't he might have to pay a fine or something. He beats on Peter and Paul sometimes too and could hurt them. Peter's moving out, but Paul will still be at home. I don't know what made him so mean, but I know the whiskey makes it worse. Maybe someone beat him when he was little and he doesn't know any better."

"Might be. That's the way it is sometimes. Your parents were nice to you and loved you and that's what you've learned. If you had

93

to stay around Warren much longer, you might turn mean yourself. I'd sure hate to see that. I swear to you right now, Clay, if this works out, I will never raise my hand to you, or willingly hurt you."

"I know, Les. You're too nice a man to do something like that."

"If I do become your parent or guardian, and you do something wrong, I'll talk to you about it and we'll work it out. If I feel you need a lesson, I'll take away some privileges for a while, but I won't ever hit you. I might make you go without hugs for a week or two though," he said with a smile.

Clay smiled back, slid across the seat, and gave Les a small hug as best he could while driving. "I'm gonna get a few hugs now in case that happens. It's like putting money in the bank for a rainy day." He giggled and stole another one.

"Oh gosh, I forgot in all the excitement this morning. I have that surprise I promised you from Saint Louis."

"Oh wow. What is it?"

"That's the same thing you asked last time. It won't be a surprise if I tell you. When we get back, I'll show it to you."

"Can we play twenty questions and if I guess right, you'll tell me?"

"No."

"Oh, poop. Here you're about to be my new dad and the first thing you say is 'no'."

"That proves I'll be a good parent. I know when to say no. You won't be spoiled. Well, not too badly."

"Les, you said you won't ever get married. Is that because you had a girlfriend and she dumped you and now you don't want anything to do with women?"

Les laughed and said, "Where did you come up with that idea?"

"There was a movie that Albert's mom took us to see and the guy in the movie said that's what happened to him and he'd never get married, but the woman who worked with him, and wanted to marry him, finally changed his mind."

"Life's a little more complicated than the movies. That's not what happened to me at all. I'm just one of those guys who never wanted to get married. I've always liked being free of responsibilities and obligations that being married would require."

"Looks like you're gonna have responsibilities and ob-la-watch-a ma-call-its anyway with me coming to live with you."

Les applied the brakes and stopped the car after checking the road behind them. Clay looked puzzled and said, "What's wrong?"

"I heard what you just said and I'm turning around. That makes sense. If I take you in, I'll never have a moment's peace."

Clay was looking completely perplexed; he was beginning to frown as his voice broke and he said, "Noooo!"

Les couldn't hold back any longer and laughed. He started forward once again.

Clay said while shaking his fist, "I didn't promise to never hit you. Don't scare me like that. I'm still getting used to you. I almost had a heart attack, Les."

"I wish you could have seen your face. I'm sorry. I'll warn you now, son, I tease the people I love sometimes, but I do it in a fun way to make them laugh."

"Okay. I'll forgive you especially since you said two magic words."

"What were they?" Les said with a puzzled look on *his* face this time.

"You called me son and said you love me."

Les's eyes were filming over and he almost had to stop the car again but sniffed and wiped his eyes. "I do love you, son, and always will."

They arrived in Somerset a few minutes later and parked near the county courthouse. Les led Clay through the building and up a flight of stairs to the second floor. There they found a carved oak door labeled:

Lucius T. Brand
Chief Judge

Clay was looking a little apprehensive, so Les put his arm around the boy's shoulders and said, "Take it easy, Clay. Judge Brand is a nice man and loves kids. He's had eight of his own."

"Wow! That's a lot of kids. How does he feed that many?"

"Judges make a lot of money, I guess. Most don't live at home anymore. Two are lawyers themselves."

"Oh."

"You ready?"

"I suppose."

They entered and a young lady greeted them and asked how she could help them. After giving their names, Les and Clay were shown into the judge's office. He was an older man, maybe sixty, who stood and shook their hands and introduced Clay to another gentleman, Reverend Brooks. He was dressed in a black clerical suit with a white collar and looked to be in his sixties as well. The judge then invited everyone to have a seat.

He smiled at Clay and said, "Young Mr. Parker, Les here has told me about what's been going on at your uncle and aunt's house and I'm very disturbed by what he's had to say. Has your uncle hurt you while drinking?"

"Uh, yes sir, he has."

"Hummm. It's a very serious thing for a grown man to hit and hurt a boy your age and I won't put up with it in Somerset County. Les told me about what happened to your folks and little brother. The Reverend and I both want to say how very sorry we are that you had such a loss at a young age. You were injured pretty badly too, I understand."

"Yes sir, I was burned on my left arm, chest, stomach and legs."

"I'm glad you recovered from that, but I'm sure it was a difficult time for you."

"Yes sir, it was."

"Mr. Mills is a very good and honest man and I have been privileged to know him for a number of years. The Reverend here has known him since he was eight, I believe."

"That's true, Clay. I'm here to help too. The judge and I trust Les and feel he will make a very fine guardian for you if you're not able to live with your relatives. Do you trust him?"

"Oh yes, Reverend. He's been a good friend and I love him already. He cares about me and, well, up until now, no one else ever has cared much since Mom, Dad and Timmy died. He even cries if I'm hurting."

"Does he now?" The judge smiled and Les looked a little sheepish. Judge Brand said, "A man who can feel sorrow and show it for a hurt child is the very best kind of man there is. Remember that as you grow up, Clay and try your best to be a man like Les."

"I will, sir. I promise."

"Son, do you think your uncle should go to jail for what he did to you?"

"I thought about that on the way here. No sir. I just don't want to have to live there anymore. He drinks and that helps to make him meaner. He hits my aunt and my cousins sometimes too when he's like that. Maybe he can go back to that group of men who helped him stop drinking before and have a second chance. But, please, Judge, fix it so I can live with Les. He loves me and will be a real good dad, and that's what I really want and need right now. I know he's not married, so I won't have a mom, but as long as I have a dad as good as Les, I won't need a mom like younger kids might."

The judge smiled and said, "You're very wise for your age. I'm going to have you see a doctor today, Clay. He will look you over and take a few X-rays. I'm sure with all the time you spent in the hospital you know about X-rays and that they don't hurt a bit. I want to make sure you don't have any tiny breaks in your bones. Also, I'm going to ask a favor of you and I'm hoping you aren't too shy. Would you mind showing the Reverend and me those bruises? That way, we can sign papers saying we saw them; I'm also going to have you swear to me that everything you've been telling us is the gospel truth."

"I won't mind showing you, Judge, and, I swear to tell the truth, the whole truth and nothing but the truth, so help me God."

The adults all chuckled and the judge said, "He's been watching too many movies, Les. He's got that memorized. Sometimes I get it balled up and say it wrong, but I'm getting old."

Clay grinned as Les ruffled his hair. "Show them the bruises, Clay." So he did and like Les, they were both shocked and angry.

"All right, you fellows go see Doctor Whitehouse, just across the street. I'll call, as he's expecting you about now. Come back after lunch and I'll have my secretary draw up all the documents for this process. Les, I'm going to name you as provisional guardian for a year. At the end of that time, or maybe earlier if all goes well with you two, which I'm sure it will; I'm going to do something I don't often do for a single man. I'm going to grant an adoption and make you Clay's father. Are you up to that, Les?"

"Oh, yes sir. Nothing would make me happier."

"How about you, Clay, you want this fellow to be your dad?"

"Oh, yes sir. Thank you, Judge and you too, Reverend. I'll be the best son in the world."

"Good. Go see the doc and I'll see you fellows back here at say, two o'clock."

After a visit to the doctor, Les took Clay to a restaurant in Somerset to celebrate their becoming a family. Les drove past the Masonic Hall in town and told Clay that someday soon he'd take him inside and show him some of the memorabilia the local Masons kept on display there.

The judge was true to his word. When they returned, he told them he was having Warren and Martha summoned before him to inform them that Clay was being removed from their custody, effective immediately. The judge wanted to hear no objections from them, or he would sign an arrest warrant on the spot and have both of them jailed. They were to allow Clay to gather his belongings and were not to threaten or harass Clay or Les in any way, or they would face charges. Any belongings of Clay's parents were to be given to him as well.

Chapter 10

Upon returning home, Les asked Clay which of the two bedrooms he wanted as his own. "I think I'd like the front bedroom as it has more windows and is closer to your room."

"Okay. That used to be my bedroom when I was a boy."

"Cool. I'll straighten up the back bedroom where I slept last night."

"Okay. Tell you what, I'm going to need some private time to get your surprise ready, so you do that while I take care of the surprise." Les grinned as Clay smiled and said okay.

Les went off to the little guest house in the backyard with his packages from Steamboat Hobbies. He'd not only purchased Clay's locomotive but several other items for use on the HO scale, model railroad. Once in the building, he went through the kitchenette and unlocked the door to the train room. It was a fifteen by nineteen-foot room and three sides were devoted to the massive train layout he'd created gradually over a number of years. He put away the miscellaneous supplies in a cabinet beneath a worktable and took out the box containing the B&O Mallet locomotive.

It was a handsome model, faithful in scale detail. He dropped a smoke pellet into its stack and placed the locomotive on the rails not far from a tunnel entrance. He re-located several freight cars already in place on the layout and made up a train of seven cars and a blue, B&O caboose. Once the train was assembled, Les switched on the electrical power and slowly backed the train into the tunnel until the engine was at least three feet inside the portal. He threw an electrical switch so whenever the train was next powered, it would run forward, instead of in reverse.

He left the main power on and threw several other switches that turned on tiny lights in the buildings scattered around the layout. He adjusted the room lights until everything was bathed in dim blue light, to simulate a night scene. It was perfect. *Now, all I lack is Clay, my son.* At that moment, the reality of what he'd just thought hit him. Tears of joy gathered in his eyes as he felt happiness such as he'd not felt in many, many years. He closed the train room door and left the guesthouse, drying his eyes with a handkerchief as he made his way toward the main house. Before he reached it, however, he heard a call from above and looked up to see Clay waving from the back bedroom window.

"Should I come down now?" the boy asked with a beautiful smile on his handsome face.

"I'm all ready for you. Meet me right here." Les had been running on reserves all day after coming home tired and having no rest after finding Clay in the bedroom. After Clay received his surprise, he had to get some sleep. He sighed and looked around the backyard thinking how very lucky he was. He owned a fine, debt-free home --- the one he'd grown up in --- he had a good job with the B&O that was soon to get even better after he completed conductor training and now he had a family --- a fine son. Even though his life had been difficult at times because of his sexual nature, he felt blessed in so many other ways.

He heard the back door open and saw the boy running across the lawn to meet him. Debussy ran along behind the lad. Les opened his arms inviting a hug and wrapped his boy in a fierce embrace. Clay snuggled against him and he kissed the top of the boy's head. Clay looked up and Les gave him another kiss on the forehead. He felt complete for the first time in his life.

"I love you, Dad."

"I love you, Son."

Nothing else needed to be said and for nearly a minute, the two stood in place holding on to one another, preserving the moment in their memories forever. Debussy seemed to sense the intensity of their love and wove an intricate pattern in and about their ankles, rubbing against them and sharing in the special moment. He mewed several times to make sure they knew he was there too. Finally, they let go and Clay bent and picked up the animal and nuzzled his soft fur as together he and Les walked to the guesthouse.

Once inside, Les said, "Now, before I take you to where your surprise is, I want you to close your eyes and promise not to peek. Can you do that?"

"Sure. What is it? Is it a..."

"A surprise! Now, shut up and close your eyes, or I'll have to blindfold *and* gag you."

Clay giggled and said, "I'll behave, now please show me." He closed his eyes and Les led him through the building past the small kitchenette and into the train room. Les closed the door behind them so Clay would see the layout in its moonlit glory. He guided Clay over to stand just in front of the control panel.

Les leaned close to Clay's ear and said, "Don't open your eyes until I tell you. I love you very much, Clay and promise to be the best father I can be. This is something we can work on together and share over the coming years. On the count of three, open your eyes. One --- two --- three." Les moved the throttle control forward until he heard the train move inside the mountain.

Clay opened his eyes to a miraculous world of wonder and whispered, "Oh my God, Dad! Oh, my God! It's beautiful!"

The new B&O Mallet and its train of cars left the tunnel and steamed toward them, little puffs of smoke beginning to leave its stack.

"It's a Mallet; a B&O Mallet!"

"The Mallet's all yours, Clay, that's your surprise gift. I knew they sold them in Saint Louis at a hobby shop there and that's what I wanted you to have. It will be your first addition to our family railroad. Let me show you how to operate the controls."

Les was nearly knocked over by the exuberant lad as he hugged, kissed and pawed at Les, saying how much he loved the train and his new dad.

Les spent a half hour with the boy teaching him how to handle the equipment and controls of the railroad. Les then said he'd be nearby on the sofa in the front room sleeping.

"I've been up since about this time yesterday and a lot has happened, Clay, so I have to get some sleep. Wake me up at five or so for supper. Keep Debussy in here with you, or he'll want to sleep on my chest and paw push me to death. Oh yeah, make him stay off the railroad. He knows it's not permitted and there's a basket over there for him to sleep in. There's a lot of kitten left in that rascal and he likes to tackle and bat at moving things too much. Have fun, son. I love you."

Les was off for the next four days and during that time, he and Clay made a somewhat uncomfortable visit to Clay's former house to pick up his belongings. Fortunately, his uncle was working a train that day and only Clay's aunt was there. His cousin Paul was off with some friends. It didn't take him long to gather his things as he really didn't own much besides the bicycle equipment Peter had given him, clothing, his photos and some bathroom products. There were a few pieces of his mother's jewelry and his dad's pocket watch Clay always kept in his dresser. They had survived the fire in a small home safe; he packed them carefully along with his other things.

Just before they were ready to leave, his aunt asked if she could have a private word with her nephew. After Les stepped outside on the front porch she asked in a lowered voice, "Clay, are you sure you want to do this? We're your family. That man is an unmarried stranger. He hasn't done anything unnatural to you has he?"

"Unnatural? What do you mean?"

"Has he ever touched you the wrong way?"

'What do you mean?"

"Well, has he tried to play with your private parts?"

Clay's face was drawn in disgust as he saw where her thoughts were going. He answered, "That's just sick, Aunt Martha. The answer's no. He's done nothing wrong, so don't even talk about him that way. Think about what I've had to put up with my so-called *family*. Uncle Warren never played with my private parts, as you put it, but he beat me, kicked me, cussed me and never did a single thing to show he cared about me as a person. You weren't much better. You never gave me a hug or a kiss when I was younger and came home from the hospital all scarred and sore. It was like you were afraid, or too disgusted to touch me. You never wanted to help me with the burns; you wouldn't even buy the medicine the doctor said I needed to make the skin stop hurting.

"There's no love at all in you. I feel sorry for you and wonder how in the world you could be Mom's sister. She had so much love in her. You have nothing inside but bitterness, like an old persimmon. Les will love and take care of me. He'll love me like a father should. He's gonna *be* my father. Uncle Warren might have come home drunk one of these nights and killed me. He's crazy when he drinks; you know that. I've seen him hit you, Paul and Peter. If you're crazy, or cowardly enough to want to stay here with him, that's your business, but I'm free of both of you now."

And with that said, Clay walked out the door and left his former life behind forever.

Les hadn't intended to listen in, but Clay's angry voice carried through the open windows of the front room, so he heard the whole speech. He was proud of the boy and realized how accurate a grasp he had on reality. At times, Clay seemed like a carefree child, filled with joy and the exuberance of youth. However, he'd toured the outskirts of hell in his young life; he knew of life's darker side.

Les hugged the boy close as he stepped beside him. "I heard through the window what you said in there, Clay, and boy I'm proud of you. She needed to hear that. Let's put your things in the car and get the hell out of here. This place gives me the creeps."

Les had one concern and decided to have a talk with Clay the last night of his lay off. He was scheduled to work local freights over the next few days and therefore wouldn't have any long hauls that would keep him away from home for days at a time. He trusted the boy completely, but to leave him alone for several days in a row was of some concern to the man. He planned to talk to the dispatcher and request short runs as a regular thing until he started conductor training. At least until school started in the fall, if he ended up working a long-haul passenger train as he'd done on his trip to Saint Louis, he could take Clay along. If working a freight train, however, the same option wasn't possible.

"Clay, I'll be going back to work in the morning. I have two runs back and forth between Cumberland and Sand Patch on a helper engine tomorrow, probably a Baldwin Mikado, number 63 or 108."

Steam locomotives were classified by their wheel arrangements. A Mikado was a 2-8-2, meaning it had two leading wheels, eight drivers --- the big wheels that did the work --- and two trailing wheels just beneath the cab. The Mallets, also called Big Boys, were 4-8-8-4.

"I wish I could take you along, but that's strictly forbidden for safety reasons. Will you be okay here by yourself?"

"Uh huh, I'll be fine."

"You're fourteen and a half and I trust you one hundred percent. My only concern is your safety in case of an accident or emergency. How do you think we should handle this?"

"I'll be careful, Dad." Clay had started calling Les Dad most of the time now and every time the man heard the word, he felt a surge of love and affection for his new son. "If anything happens, I can use the telephone and call Albert's folks or even the sheriff's office in an emergency. Once Albert gets back from his grandma's house, I can spend time at his place or, if it's all right with you, he can come over here with me. He's a good boy and never gets into trouble."

"Yeah, I trust him too. I might ask his folks to let you stay overnight occasionally if I get assigned to a long-distance freight. By the way, once I'm a conductor, if I work a passenger train this summer as long as school's out, I'm going to take you along. Would you like that?"

"You bet. That would be great. Where does the crew ride on a passenger train? They don't have a caboose."

Usually in the baggage car, there's a partition and behind it is a couple of tiny, and I do mean tiny, bunks stacked three high. I hate using them; it's like sleeping in a coffin. Your face is only about twelve inches from the bottom of the bunk above and it's damn near impossible to turn over. The bathroom is a small commode behind a curtain. In our case though, if you're along, I can get space in a sleeper coach and if the train isn't sold out, I might even arrange a Pullman roomette we can both use. I have a rail pass for myself and family, but I can't use it to take a roomette that normally would make money for the railroad. I can always get us in a sleeper coach though. I'll talk to Ed Lake, my boss and chief dispatcher; he'll make sure to work it out for us. He's a close friend and a good man to work for. He's a Mason too and we help our own."

"Just how many Masons are there?" asked Clay with a laugh.

"Quite a few, kiddo, quite a few. Oh, and in August, we'll both be going to Hagerstown for two weeks."

"Why's that?"

"I have to go to school. I may have mentioned that I have to take classes to become a conductor. Once I do that, I'll make nearly twice the money I'm making now and I hope to get on a permanent train cycle, say from Cumberland to Pittsburgh and back, or Cumberland to Baltimore or Washington. The railroad tries to place family men on short runs and all of the sudden I find myself a family man and I love it."

"How come you never got married, Dad?"

Les had evaded that question once before, but now that things had changed; he eventually was going to have to make a decision about how to talk with Clay concerning his reasons for bachelorhood. For now, he'd stall a bit longer.

"I'm kind of shy and awkward around women, Clay. As I was

growing up, all my friends found it easy to mix-in with girls and go out with them to dances and that sort of thing. I was made fun of a lot because I loved music and took piano lessons and liked to paint and do things that the other boys found un-manly, I suppose. I was happy though and didn't miss that sort of thing. Most of the girls liked boys who played ball, took them to dances --- that sort of thing. I just didn't fit in, I suppose, so I became a confirmed bachelor."

"I see. I'm kind of like that too. I don't like baseball or basketball. I like to swim though and I'm a great runner. I might try out for track and field in high school." Clay chuckled and added, "Uncle Warren taught me how to run."

"He did? Well, I'm surprised he cared enough to help you practice running. What did he do, measure out a track and time you, or..."

Clay started laughing. "No, Dad. I got lots of practice running away from the old devil when he was drunk and trying to catch me to give me a lick'n'." Both started laughing as Les figured out what his boy was saying.

"I bet once you get to high school you'll find a girlfriend, Clay. You're a good-looking young man."

"Yeah, until I take my shirt off or wear shorts," Clay said with a laugh. "I don't think a girl would think I'm very handsome then."

Les was surprised the boy laughed it off so easily. There might be some hidden emotional problems he'd eventually have to be dealt with.

"I'm like you, Dad. I'm a confirmed bachelor too. I'm happy with things just the way they are."

"You never know; guys your age are going through a lot of changes. You might start having different thoughts about the young ladies. I'm sure Warren didn't have the courage to have a talk with you about the facts of life, so if ever you have questions, I'm here now and I'm not ashamed to talk about those things. Birds and bees kind of things, you know."

"I know. I'll ask if I have anything I don't understand."

"Good. That's part of my job as a dad now." They were in the parlor having this talk and Les walked over to the grand piano, raised the top and propped it open. He sat down, lifted the key cover and started playing. Clay stood beside him and watched as Les's hands glided over the keys and beautiful music flowed from the strings. Les looked up at Clay and smiled.

"What's that song you're playing, Dad?"

"It's part of a suite of music by Alexander Borodin, a Russian composer. This piece is called *The Maiden's Dance*. It's one of my favorites from the *Prince Igor Suite*. Borodin never finished the whole suite, however, and it's truly a shame. He was a very gifted composer."

"It's very pretty. Did the guy die before he finished."

"No, his real profession was as a chemist and he wrote music as a hobby. He just never got around to finishing the entire composition."

"That's a shame. It's beautiful." Les continued to play while Clay sat beside him on the bench and snuggled close.

"Usually it's played by a full orchestra, but I've memorized an adapted piano score for *The Maiden's Dance*."

"I love it. It reminds me of music from a movie I once saw."

"Oh? Do you remember the movie?"

"It was from the Arabian Nights; the story of Sinbad, the Sailor."

"Okay. That makes sense; Borodin was writing this about Mid-Eastern girls. It's in a minor key like a lot of music from that part of the world. You have a good ear, Clay. Music can speak to you and paint pictures in your mind if you let it."

"I know. Sometimes, when I hear certain pieces, I think of different things like sitting by a river or looking out over the mountains. If I close my eyes while I'm listening, I can almost imagine I'm right there. I used to listen to our record player a lot at home before the fire. Mom and Dad had a lot of music like the kind you play."

"I have a pretty good record collection and it's yours now too, so feel free to listen on our record player."

"Thanks, I will."

"Also, if you ever want to learn to play the piano, let me know. I'd be happy to teach you."

"Okay. I'd like that a lot."

"It would impress the ladies if you ever change your mind about having a girlfriend."

"Yeah, maybe it would." Clay said no more while he sat quietly and enjoyed Les's playing.

Lying in bed that evening, Clay did some deep thinking. He was pondering the sort of things that usually led to masturbation, but before getting too involved, he thought, *I wonder what Dad would think if he knew the truth about me? Would he still love me if he knew I'm never going to have a girlfriend and that I dream about doing things with other boys like Albert? I'd tell him if I thought he would still love me because I have a lot of questions about why I'm this way. Maybe he knows a way I can change and be normal.*

His thoughts along those lines led him to decide to wait a while and get to know Les better before he brought up the subject. Was Les one of those men who thought queers were bad and sick? He sure didn't want Les to stop loving him.

Clay pulled out his photo of young Roddy and felt the usual reaction below. *I wonder what Dad would say if he knew I look at a picture of a boy in a movie and play with myself? I'm pretty weird.* He almost decided to put away the photo, but if he did, he would just think about it or Albert anyway. Something down below was pleading for his attention and he finally gave in and did what he enjoyed so much. Someday soon, he'd have to take a bike ride back to the millpond and sit in that V-shaped crack in the weir and...

A room away, Les had just settled into bed himself. He too had a number of questions on his mind. *Someday, when that boy is older and wiser, he's going to ask me again why I'm not the marrying kind and I won't be able to avoid it any longer. How do I tell him his new dad once fell in love with another man? That could wreck what we have going as father and son. I sure don't want him to hate me someday for keeping it a secret. I'm going to have to find out just how much he knows about the facts of life too, so I have some idea how he might feel about homosexuals. God, I love him and surely don't want him to be hurt by anything I do, or by what I am.*

107

Chapter 11

One thing about Clay that pleased Les was that the boy certainly wasn't lazy and was ready, willing and able to pull his weight around the home and property. He asked Les what chores he wanted him to do and between them, they worked out a schedule suitable to both. Les owned a Ford tractor with an attachment to mow the large lawn. He would continue to operate it, however, until Clay was a little older and learned how to operate it safely. Clay would handle the laundry, the dishes and much of the housekeeping. Clay also took over care of Debussy who now followed him around everywhere and often slept in his bedroom.

Les told Clay he would receive a weekly allowance of five dollars a week for his work, something Clay was completely unfamiliar with while living with his relatives. In 1953, that was a very generous stipend for a fourteen-year-old. Les suggested, however, that Clay set aside half of that each week in savings for the future. He said that if Clay did that for a month, he would increase his allowance to six dollars a week. Clay started making a chart right away to keep careful track of his earnings and used a small metal box he found in their garage to store his money.

Les was lucky to have such a great dispatcher, for he worked out a schedule for Les that kept him on what his boss called a *Family Man Schedule*. Les would likely be gone in the morning when Clay woke up, but would normally arrive home by five or six. Due to union rules, his workweek was only four, ten-hour days, unless he was called upon to work overtime occasionally and time and a half pay. Soon, conductor training and a change of job might alter his schedule somewhat.

Clay was free to ride his bike around the area during the day after he finished his chores and on several days after Les started back to work, he biked to the old millpond and enjoyed the water (in more ways than one). He was anxious for Albert to come back and join him at the pond, but of course; he'd not be able to utilize the V-seat as he'd started calling it. He was especially anxious to see Albert this summer while skinny-dipping, as he hadn't seen him in the buff since late last summer.

He secretly hoped that Albert would continue to be uninterested in girls. When they were both with Toby, Albert said things like,

'There's a girl I talk to once in a while', or 'I plan to wait until high school before finding a girlfriend'. These were the same sort of phrases Clay often used to cover his lack of interest. Maybe Albert was like him. He sure hoped so, because Albert certainly featured in Clay's imagination every night. Less and less, he was pulling out the photo of Roddy and more and more he could close his eyes and imagine all sorts of interesting things he and Albert might do.

The Sunday finally arrived when Albert returned home and Clay could hardly wait until Monday morning to tell Albert of all the wonderful changes in his life and especially show his best buddy his new home and the train room. Albert and his family knew Les, of course, since they were relatively close neighbors, living about a fourth of a mile apart, but Les had never mentioned or shown Albert the train room. Clay asked Les if it was all right for him to invite Albert over to play and enjoy the model railroad, and Les assured him this was now his home and he was welcome to do whatever he wanted as long as he let Les know in advance. His only rule was that Albert's folks should know when he was visiting so they knew where Albert was in case of some emergency or need. Les had already talked to Mr. and Mrs. Stiles, so they knew about the guardianship and said Clay was always welcome to stay over if Les was assigned to a two or three-day train trip.

Right after Les had called and talked to Albert's folks, Clay called and asked his parents to keep it a secret that he now had a new home and a dad. He wanted to be the one to break the news. They agreed and he could hardly wait to see Albert's face when he told him.

Albert was somewhat surprised to get a phone call from Clay on Monday morning, just before eight o'clock.

"Hey there, Clay, I sure have missed you the past two weeks. Your aunt and uncle letting you use the phone?"

"Uh, no, they don't know I'm calling you." Clay figured that was the truth and still avoided telling Albert where he really was.

"Can you meet me at Hickory Esso on 160 in fifteen minutes?"

"I have a few chores to do before I'm free. Can I meet you there in an hour?"

"Sure. That'll be fine. Uh, we'll meet at nine, okay?"

"See you then. Whatcha been up to lately?"

"Uh, I'll tell you later. I don't want to talk too long right now."

"Oh yeah, your aunt and uncle. I'll see you in an hour. I've missed you as much as I've missed my parents."

"Me too, see you soon. Bye."

Les was off that day and would be mowing the seven acres of grass that was growing fast now that summer rains were frequent. He told Clay to go and have fun with his friend.

"Once you're done swimming, why don't you invite Albert over for lunch?"

"Thanks, Dad. I won't tell him about you adopting me until we get here. I want to surprise him." Clay gave Les a warm hug and a kiss on the cheek.

Clay had no compunctions about showing affection and Les was eating it up anyway. *What a sweet kid I have*, he thought as Clay explained exactly where they were going to swim.

Les knew the place well and said, "I used to swim there with a friend or two when I was your age. The mill had only been closed about twenty years then and we used to climb all around inside the building. We used to think it was haunted because a man was murdered out there. Did you know that?"

"No, really?"

"It happened to the miller. He got into an argument with a customer and the two of them fought. The guy had a knife and stuck the miller in the chest and he died. The man was caught, because the miller's son, a lad of about seventeen, saw the fight and ran to a coal mine nearby and reported who did it. The miller's wife had died several years before and the son tried to make a living with the place, but simply didn't know how to run a business. The mill closed down and gradually fell apart from lack of care. By now I'm sure it's in even worse shape than it was the last time I saw it about ten or twelve years ago."

"Think it's really haunted?"

"No. That was just us kids making up stories to scare one another. Be careful around the inside of the old place though; it had a basement and the floor could cave in on you if you go stomping around in there. The pond's pretty safe. I don't think it's much more than seven or eight feet deep and has a sand and pebble bottom. Don't try diving though; it's too shallow for that. We used to slide naked in the millrace until we reached the end and shot out over the pond."

Clay giggled and said, "Yeah, we do that too. It's about a hundred feet along the whole millrace and you get going real fast."

"Just be careful you don't cut your bare bottom on a sharp stone or a piece of glass. One hole back there's enough." Clay giggled and felt glad his new dad had a good sense of humor.

"Do you ever go swimming now, Dad?"

"I haven't lately. I swam at the YMCA pool in Cumberland a few times with a friend of mine, and at the public pool in Constitution Park, but that's been years ago. We used to go down to Deep Creek Lake west of Cumberland and swim there." He looked at Clay and grinned. "Tell you what; someday soon you and I will go to the millpond and have a swim together."

"Oh, Dad, that would be super. I'd love us to do that. Will you skinny dip?" Clay asked with an impish grin on his face.

Les answered in a conspiratorial whisper, "I just might. Everyone has to act like a kid once in a while. We'll see. You better get ready to meet Albert. Be careful, but have some fun while your poor old dad sweats and slaves away on the tractor."

"I love you, Dad. We'll be careful." Clay checked the clock and headed for his bike on the front porch. Within a few minutes, he was cruising down the road toward Hickory Esso.

Clay beat Albert to the Esso station by about twenty minutes. He planned it that way so Albert wouldn't catch sight of him passing his house and wonder why he was coming from somewhere north of his home. He wanted to wait until lunchtime to share the good news. Albert arrived around nine wearing an old pair of blue jeans and a short sleeve shirt. Clay was wearing a short sleeve shirt too. For some reason, since he had a new home, he felt less bothered by his scars. They were his for life anyway, so he might as well accept it.

Albert pulled up beside him and immediately asked, "Where did you get the bike? It's nice."

"Yeah, it was Peter's. He gave it to me when he moved to Eckhart to work at a coal mine; he's got an old car now. I could hardly believe it."

"We can go a lot of places now. Have your uncle and aunt been any better since summer began?"

"Oh, they're no trouble at all now. I'll tell you more about it later. Right now, I'd like us to go for a swim at the old mill. How's that sound?"

Albert grinned and said, "I didn't wear my bathing suit."

"Neither did I, but we've never let that stop us before."

"Yeah, no one goes out there much and I don't mind skinny dipping with you."

Clay asked as they left the station and began peddling along the road to the mill, "Have you ever gone skinny dipping with anyone else besides me?" Somehow, that was important to Clay.

"Just the time or two Tony was with us when we were younger, but I've never done it alone with anyone but you. I'd be shy around anyone else, especially since I'm more grown up and have hair down below and everything. With you, I'm not shy. I don't think I'd even do it now if Tony was along. He might make fun of me."

"Why would he do that?"

"I don't know. But I think I'd be shy around Tony."

"With all my scars, I should be the one who's worried about being shy."

"I'm not bothered by them. I just feel bad you had to hurt so much back then and lost your family. I wish you had a better family and a nicer place to live, Clay. You deserve to be in a better home."

"Thanks for saying that, Albert. It means a lot more than you think. You're my best friend you know."

"Thanks. You're mine; that's for sure."

"Good. That's very important to me too."

They rode in relative silence for a while listening to the incessant buzz of cicadas and occasionally seeing a rabbit or squirrel along the road. Clay often glanced over at his friend. Albert's blond hair was longer than he wore it to school and fluttered in the wind. Clay thought Albert was the best-looking boy he knew --- even better looking than Roddy and of course a real person. Roddy was real too, but now in his mid-twenties and much too old for Clay. McDowall probably lived somewhere like Hollywood, California with a wife and a bunch of kids.

Before long, the ruins of the mill showed through the trees and they pulled to a stop at the footpath to the mill and pond. As usual, no one else was around. Clay had bought them each a box of Cracker Jacks and a bottle of pop at the Esso station which doubled as a small store for snacks and drinks. Albert was surprised to see Clay with some money. He was usually the one to treat, but today, Clay said it was time for him to start catching up. He'd also bought a bag of chocolate cookies and some jawbreakers, for later. Les had given him some "spending money" for the trip today, so he wouldn't have to use his allowance. Les said he wanted Clay to get himself and Albert something to eat and enjoy --- the treat was on him. Clay would tell Albert later who had sprung for their snacks, but not just yet.

He also planned to return the money and belongings he'd borrowed from Albert's backyard shack once he'd sprung the surprise about his new home and told him everything that had happened since the day he ran away. Albert hadn't said anything about the IOU note he'd left on the plywood cover, so he probably hadn't been to the shed since returning home.

Clay and Albert sat down on the flagstones along the millrace to enjoy their treat. It was so quiet and peaceful with only faint insect sounds and the chirping of some songbirds. Clay pulled off his shirt exposing his scarred chest. Albert did the same and they soaked up the warm sunlight. Both were still a little pale from earlier months spent in school and indoors, so started working on their summer tans. Clay went a step farther after a few minutes and took off his shoes, socks and pants leaving on only his boxer shorts. He waited to see if Albert would do the same.

He wasn't disappointed when Albert started untying his tennis shoes and removed them and his socks before pulling off his jeans. There was a difference though. Albert wasn't wearing boxers like he did last summer. He was wearing white briefs like the ones Les wore. Clay had mentioned to Les that when they bought him clothes soon he would like to try wearing briefs instead of boxers. Les said they were better for boys his age anyway without explaining why. He might have to ask about that.

Clay was a bit excited, as Albert had obviously grown. The briefs surrounded a most interesting shape that had Clay wiggling a bit as his own parts shifted, seeking more room. He knew he was going to have a problem as soon as they stripped to swim, but he'd get in the water quickly and maybe Albert wouldn't notice.

And then he thought, *I really wouldn't mind if he did notice though. Maybe that would tell me if he likes to look at me down there.* Then Clay had an interesting idea. He'd shifted himself in such a way as to hide his crotch, but now he wiggled around a bit and raised one leg in just the right way to allow his baggy boxer leg to fall open along Albert's line of sight. If Albert was interested, maybe he would peek in there and Clay could catch him at it.

At the moment, Albert was in a busy battle with his Cracker Jack box. They always were hard to get open with all the wax and wrappings to keep them fresh. Albert, like most boys in those times, knew that you had to open the Cracker Jacks from the bottom of the box to find the surprise toy first, as they always seemed to be in the bottom.

Clay was getting impatient, as Albert seemed to have no luck whatsoever in getting the damned box open. Because Albert bit his fingernails, he was using his front teeth to try and gnaw open one corner of the box. Clay felt his hardness failing and was hoping it would stay a little hard for Albert to notice. Finally, his friend got the bottom opened and started shaking the box while peering inside, hoping to find the prize. He smiled as he located the small package and picked it out of the box.

Albert shifted position and crossed his legs sitting Indian style in such a way that Clay had a nice view of his crotch. That helped re-inflate Clay's sagging anatomy. Albert tore open the prize wrapping and inside was a small tin-plated whistle. He blew it twice and grinned. He put it in the pocket of his folded jeans for later, dumped a few Cracker Jacks and peanuts into his hand and tossed them into his mouth. He smiled and looked toward Clay.

For just a moment, Albert's eyes glanced along Clay's raised leg and his eyes opened a bit wider as he realized what he was seeing. Clay saw him blush and divert his eyes. Albert looked at his face instead and smiled as though he'd noticed nothing. Clay knew he'd had an eye-full and he could feel himself growing even longer due to his excitement. He'd have to soon shift his position again or risk growing beyond the hem of his boxers. Just as he was about to do that, he saw Albert's eyes take another quick glance down below and blink in surprise before looking away again. Clay moved and the show came to a close.

Now Albert started chatting about what they could do the rest of the summer, and while he talked, Clay listened but noticed that the bulge in Albert's briefs had gotten considerably larger for some reason. Clay smiled and thought, *He noticed and it made him get hard too. Maybe we're alike. I sure hope so.*

A little after they finished eating their snack, Clay said, "Well, I'm ready to take a swim. I'm getting hot sitting here in the sun, how about you?" Clay stood up and stretched. His boxers were protruding quite a bit and Clay saw Albert gawk once more and blush.

Albert said, "Yeah, I'm getting hot too."

Clay slipped off his boxer shorts and watched Albert's eyes. Albert was more guarded and turned away before pulling off his briefs. He laid them to the side and walked to the edge of the stone ledge, sat down and slipped into the water. Clay followed suit and soon both were treading water after swimming to the center of the pond. Clay suggested they take a ride in the millrace, so they swam to the side once more, got out and began walking along the stone path that led upstream to the head of the flume.

As they walked side by side, Clay glanced from time to time at Albert admiring his friend's bare body and several times thought he saw Albert doing the same to him. Neither had any reaction and soon arrived at the beginning of the flume. Both carefully stepped into the race and sat down on the slippery, algae-covered bottom holding onto the raised sides until both were ready to let go and take off along the hundred-foot-long channel. Albert was seated just ahead of Clay and counted, "One, two, three." On three, they let go and both began the slide along the slick bottom.

The fast current whisked them away as each let out a whoop. At one point, Clay caught up slightly with Albert and rather than try to pass him in the four-foot wide channel, he boldly opened his legs enough to slide right up against Albert's backside. He grabbed his friend's shoulders before they got too close and both laughed as they gained speed while positioned like two bobsled riders. Both squealed with delight as they shot off the end of the race and splashed into the millpond below. For the next half hour, they made a number of similar trips down the slide. Clay was pleased that Albert seemed to like sliding closely together. First he and then Albert took the lead position. Clay especially liked holding on to Albert's shoulders and on several occasions, he held Albert by the waist. Albert did the same and Clay enjoyed his friend's touch.

After riding the flume, they swam and played in the cool, refreshing water for nearly an hour. Occasionally, as they romped, Clay opened his eyes underwater to take a guarded look at Albert and was happy with what he saw. Albert had grown about an inch or maybe two over the past year and Clay wasn't noting his height. Albert's pubic hair was a golden puff of silky-looking strands that Clay wished he could run his fingers through. During their horseplay, Albert --- as far as Clay could tell --- had not gotten hard although Clay certainly did from time to time.

Clay showed Albert the break in the weir wall and dared Albert to sit in it and try to plug the leak. Albert did and laughed as the water found its way beneath him and over his lap in spite of what way he sat to try and stop it. Albert wiggled a bit and giggled as his privates fluttered about. His expression suddenly changed and he quickly moved away from the break in the weir and slipped deeper into the water.

"You try it," Albert said as he floated nearby. Clay lifted himself into the flow and as usual started to harden as the water did its work, wiggling him about. He was watching Albert's eyes and saw him taking note of what was happening. He watched just long enough to see Clay fully aroused and then he paddled back a bit and averted his eyes.

"Your turn; try it again," prompted Clay.

"Maybe later, I want to swim some more."

He's shy. I think he knows what'll happen, thought Clay.

They swam some more and again rode the full length of the flume a couple of times. It was nearly eleven o'clock, as best the boys could judge by the sun's height when they dressed and gathered their things to head back. As they walked to their bicycles, Clay said, "I have a surprise for you today. There's a place we can go and have lunch. I already asked your mom if it was okay and she said it was. I wanted to surprise you. We're always eating at your house and today it's my treat."

"We're not gonna eat at your aunt and uncle's place, are we?" Albert asked with raised eyebrows.

"No, another place. I eat there a lot now. It's a whole lot better than Aunt Martha and Uncle Warren's house."

Albert frowned as he tried to come up with some possible answer to what Clay was talking about. He finally asked, "Where is it?"

"You'll see. If I tell you now, it won't be a surprise. You'll just have to trust me."

"I trust you, but I gotta say, you're acting mighty mysterious all the sudden."

Clay grinned and nodded saying only, "Yep."

Albert went on in another vein, "I enjoyed our swim today. I thought I might be a little shy to undress in front of you since I've kind of grown up some, but I got over it. You've grown a lot too."

"I'm just glad you don't mind being with me with all the scars and stuff. I think they bother Toby sometimes."

116

"Maybe, he said so once, but it's not like he doesn't like you because of the scars. He said it makes him feel funny to think of how much you must have hurt to get burn scars like that. He said you must be really brave to have gone through that."

"That's nice to hear. I know he always tries to look away and I wasn't sure how he felt. I'm glad you told me."

They'd reached the bikes and headed up the road. As they peddled, they chatted some more.

Albert asked, "Have you ever noticed that all Toby seems to talk about now is his girlfriends? I think he has two of 'em."

"Yeah, he never shuts up about 'em. One of these days they're going to find out he likes 'em both and there's going to be a cat fight." Clay snickered as he looked across at Albert.

"Yeah. That or they'll team up and beat the crap out of Two Timing Toby." Both laughed at the mental picture.

"Do you have a girl you like, Clay?" Clay glanced at Albert and saw his friend was watching him more carefully than he was the road.

"No. I'm not interested in girls at all. I'm going to be a confirmed bachelor."

"What's that mean? I know what a bachelor is, but what's a *confirmed* bachelor?"

"Uh, it means you've decided that for the rest of your life you won't get involved with women and get married." Clay was explaining it the best he could since he wasn't completely sure what it meant himself. He was only repeating what Les had said. Confirmed sounded pretty determined and permanent. *Maybe I should ask Les exactly what it really means.*

Albert was silent before saying, "I'm the same way, I guess. I think I'd like being a confirmed bachelor too. Girls seem to get boys in a lot of trouble; especially high school girls."

"What do you mean?"

"You know that older kid who lived just past Hickory Esso on the way to town, uh, Bill Rivers?"

"Oh yeah, I remember something about him getting into trouble, but I never found out what it was. His folks sent him off to live with a cousin or something."

"Yeah, they found out he got his girlfriend pregnant."

"Really? Gees! Why would they make *him* leave town?"

"His daddy had to pay for some kind of illegal operation for the girl so she wouldn't have the baby and the girl's folks said if Bill didn't leave town, they'd have him put in jail. He was eighteen and she was only sixteen. It was supposed to be a big secret, but one of the girl's girlfriends blabbed it all over the school. The parents had to send her away too. It caused a lot of problems for everybody."

They were nearly to Hickory Esso by now, but Clay wanted to know more. "Why was Bill stupid enough to make her pregnant?"

"That's what girls do to a boy. They get him all worked up and anxious and then they go to kissin' and touchin' each other and before you know it, they both take their clothes off and do it and she gets pregnant."

"Why did Bill just *not* do it?"

"I don't know. I'm real glad I'm not interested in girls. I sure don't want to be a father at my age. I'd rather be a confirmed bachelor like you."

"Wouldn't you like to have a home and a wife and kids someday though?" asked Clay watching Albert's reaction carefully.

"I want to have a home, but I'd rather live alone or maybe with a close friend like you. I wouldn't mind that so much."

"I'd like that too. Maybe when we grow up, we can share a house."

"Yeah, I bet you sure want to move away from your uncle and aunt."

"I've kind of solved that problem already."

"Really? How?"

"I'll tell you right before we eat lunch."

"Why wait 'till then?"

"I have my reasons."

"Gee whiz! You're acting weird. What's going on with you? I can't figure you..."

Clay interrupted, "There's the Esso ahead. We have to stop in so's I can get the four cents back for the soda bottles."

"Oh yeah. How far do we have to go before we get to the mysterious place where we'll have lunch? Are you talking about the soda fountain at the drug store in town? I'm getting hungry again. Swimming always does that to me."

"Me too, no, it isn't the drug store or any place in town. We have to go north, past your house a little way."

"What's up there? There's only a few houses between there and the bridge over the creek. The only people I know of up that way are

118

that old couple who used to raise goats, Doctor Foose, the veterinarian and Mr. Mills. Is it the vet, or Les Mills?"

"Be patient. You'll see."

"All right, Mister Mystery."

After visiting the Esso store and getting his deposit back, Clay used the four cents and bought each of them a couple of cinnamon-flavored candy sticks to suck on as they pedaled north toward his new home. They passed Albert's house and just beyond, Albert said, "I need to stop and take a leak."

They pulled to the side and both stepped into the woods far enough to find some concealment. Clay made sure he was standing where Albert could see him as he opened his pants and peed a stream into the dirt. He noticed that Albert took a few furtive glances before turning a bit, as he also relieved himself. Clay felt himself becoming hard and thought Albert noticed that as well because his eyes lingered there as Clay tucked his somewhat longer self back into his pants. Clay was being reckless and surprised himself with his boldness, thinking, *I hope I'm not bothering him doing this, but I just want to know if he likes looking at me. So far, it seems like he does.*

It wasn't long before they came to Clay's new home and he turned in at the driveway. Albert followed and said, "Are you sure it's okay to come here? Mr. Mills is a nice guy, no matter what Toby says, but will it be okay to disturb him?"

"Oh yeah, Les is great. I love him a whole lot."

"*Love* him?" Albert was wide-eyed as he watched Clay dismount and stroll toward the porch.

Clay didn't answer right away. As they mounted the steps, Les opened the door and stepped out. Clay ran to him and gave him a warm hug and a kiss as Albert stood with an open mouth staring.

"I really do love him, Albert, and he loves me." Les was grinning, had his arm around Clay's shoulders, and was nodding at Albert. "He's my new dad. I live here now."

"Huh?"

It took about a half hour to tell Albert all that had happened in the last week or so. He was amazed as well as happy for Clay. After lunch, the rest of the afternoon was like a dream come true for Clay as he proudly showed Albert his new bedroom, introduced him to Debussy and was especially thrilled to show him the train room. They played for hours there until it was nearly time for Albert to go

119

home for supper.

They were in Clay's room when Albert said, "I'm real happy for you Clay. Mom, Dad and I often talked about how crazy your uncle was and Dad even said he was afraid for you living there. I'm glad you're here and have a new dad who loves you. Les is great. I can't wait to tell Toby how wrong he was about Les."

"Yeah, Albert, before you go I want to tell you again that you're my very best friend. I love Les now and I want you to know that I love you too as my closest friend." Clay was staring intently into Albert's eyes and saw him smile.

"Yeah, I love you as my best friend too." Albert extended his right hand, as though inviting Clay to shake it, but Clay went farther and hugged the surprised boy. For a moment, Albert tensed in surprise and then suddenly he gripped Clay tightly and hugged him back hard.

Clay felt Albert's soft blond hair brushing against his cheek and whispered directly in the boy's ear, "You really are special and I'll always love you as my closest friend. I hope someday we *can* live together as confirmed bachelors. That's my wish."

"Me too," he heard his companion whisper. Clay was nearly as happy at that moment as he was when the judge made Les his dad. Debussy, as usual, seemed to sense their mood and he too oozed around their ankles wanting to be included in their love and friendship.

Chapter 12

On Wednesday of the first week after the Fourth of July, Les took the boys on a rail trip to Harper's Ferry, West Virginia where the Shenandoah River joins the Potomac and three states, Maryland, West Virginia and Virginia meet. It was a historic old town, well known for the infamous raid on the Federal Arsenal there by the abolitionist, John Brown, shortly before the start of the War Between the States. They visited historic sites and several museums in the small, quiet town.

Les had known ahead of time that the local passenger train serving the Potomac Valley that day would be pulled by a Mikado steam locomotive. He also knew in advance that the engineer, brakeman, fireman *and* conductor were all close friends of his. Things worked out just right and he was able to take Clay and Albert in the locomotive's cab for the short run between Martinsburg, West Virginia and Harper's Ferry. They boarded a few moments before the train pulled out of Martinsburg and stepped from the cab just after the train stopped at Harper's Ferry to avoid being seen by the stationmaster or a railroad policeman.

Both boys were ecstatic as they finally got a chance to ride in a real steam locomotive and even blow the whistle occasionally for crossings after the engineer told them it was two long, a short and a long toot. Each boy got to keep a real B&O engineer's cap, Les had bought them. The trip back was on a different westbound passenger train pulled by an F7, General Electric, diesel locomotive and helper unit, with an unknown crew, so Les and the boys rode the entire way

121

home in a passenger coach.

Several times during July, Albert was invited to spend the night at Clay's new home and several times Clay stayed over at Albert's place. Albert's room had a bunk bed, but at Clay's home, his bed was a wide, antique, four-posted, double bed. It was during one of these sleepovers, in late July, when something happened to give Clay much food for thought.

The two boys had played hard both outdoors and indoors that afternoon and evening and were pretty much worn out by the time they each took a bath and dressed for bed. Albert was yawning as he pulled his pajamas on over his briefs. Clay had recently given up boxers and was wearing briefs too. Usually, he either slept in his briefs or just his pajamas, but since Albert wore both, he did the same as his buddy.

There had been several times when Clay had experienced the urge while Albert was sleeping to kiss him or snuggle close. Fear of discovery kept him in check, however, and it wasn't unusual for him to masturbate carefully once he heard Albert fall deeply asleep, start breathing heavily or snore.

A very unusual event, however, took place that night in late July, revealing much about Albert's interests. Clay was nearly asleep ten minutes or so after they crawled into bed when he heard Albert whisper, "Clay? Are you awake?" He was about to answer but decided not to for some reason. He'd detected an unusual note in Albert's voice and something told him to pretend to be asleep.

A few minutes later, Albert asked, "Clay? Can you hear me?" Clay maintained his silence. He was resting on his back and the excitement of the moment had caused him to become hard. He knew that Albert was resting on his right side facing Clay. Albert was left-handed, while Clay was right-handed.

Albert next said, ever so quietly, "If you're awake, Clay, please tell me." Clay said nothing. Then he felt Albert snuggle close and was thrilled as Albert gently put his arm around him and hugged him. He also felt Albert nuzzle against his shoulder and heard him say, "I just want to be close to you tonight. If you're awake, I just want you to know that I feel like being close to someone I love and I really do love you."

Clay was feeling things he'd never felt before. He mumbled something as though he was talking in his sleep and shifted his right arm until his hand fell upon Albert's upper arm where it rested

122

across his chest. Albert skooched even closer and Clay could now feel his friend's hardness pressing against his left outer thigh. Clay's penis was painfully hard and he knew he was becoming wet from excitement. He wanted so much to masturbate at that moment, but couldn't. He wanted even more for Albert to take him in his hand and do it. He settled instead for simply enjoying Albert's affection and closeness.

Albert nuzzled against his shoulder and pushed against him harder. Clay squeezed Albert's arm where his hand rested and turned his head to the left and pushed his nose and lips against Albert's face. He almost opened his eyes and kissed the boy, but was still too afraid to act. Both remained very still and eventually fell asleep.

In the morning, Clay found that he'd had a wet dream and his briefs were soaked. When he felt the wetness there and sniffed his fingers, he could smell the exciting odor of semen. He wondered if Albert had experienced the same thing as the boy turned away and changed his underwear just after getting up. They had been clean the night before after his bath, so he probably had. Clay watched Albert as he changed and wanted so much to touch his butt as Albert raised one leg after the other to pull on his fresh underwear. Clay made sure that Albert was watching him as he pulled off his clothes and changed into fresh underwear too. He even let Albert see him feel the wet front of his underpants; he left them on the bed before smiling and running off to pee.

When he got back, he noticed that the briefs had been moved a little, so Albert must have handled them. Albert went off to use the bathroom and Clay reached in his friend's duffle bag and located the briefs he'd just changed out of. He brought them to his nose and, sure enough, they were damp and smelled strongly of semen. Instead of putting them back, however, Clay took one more deep sniff and then stuffed them into his nightstand drawer hoping that Albert wouldn't notice them missing once he got home.

But then he had an inspiration. Before Albert could return from the bath, Clay grabbed his own damp and soiled briefs and stuffed them into Albert's duffle bag. His were a different brand and had his name written on them with a laundry marker. He *wanted* Albert to find them and know what had happened. He *wanted* him to have them and be able to hold them and do whatever he wanted with them. He *wanted* Albert to know that he loved him in more ways than simple friendship. And most of all, he *wanted* Albert to know

123

he too had enjoyed a wet dream while his arms were wrapped around the boy he loved.

During the final week of July, neither boy said anything about the briefs, but Clay noticed that Albert was more affectionate and would wrap his arm around Clay's shoulder more often and wanted to roughhouse and wrestle with him playfully, brushing occasionally against more private parts of Clay's anatomy. He was more than happy to do the same. Both boys would grin sheepishly after doing things and snicker.

August began before the boys could spend another night together. Les and Clay were preparing to move temporarily to Hagerstown where the B&O Training Center was located. There was a well-known summer camp operating in the Catoctin Mountain area just east of Hagerstown and Les arranged for Clay to spend two weeks there while he attended school. It would be good for both of them as Les didn't want to leave Clay stuck in a hotel room every day for two weeks. He knew the boy would enjoy and benefit from the camp experience as well.

Clay was a little apprehensive about going alone and asked Albert if his parents might send him along too. Albert told him, however, that the family was planning a trip to Philadelphia for two or three days to visit his mom's brother's family during that time and he wouldn't be able to make it. Clay was disappointed but took it in stride. Les told him it would be good for him to meet new friends and learn new things at the camp. Les also hired Albert to stop by and take care of Debussy for the two weeks while they were gone, once he came back from Philadelphia.

On Sunday, August second, Les and Clay drove to Hagerstown. Had Les been going alone, he probably would have taken a train, but he would need the car to take Clay to Camp Cunningham, located near Cunningham Falls on the west slope of Catoctin Mountain. After driving east, on the Baltimore Pike or Route 40, they arrived in Hagerstown a little before noon. Les checked into the railroad hotel and he and Clay had lunch together in a nearby Pennsylvania Dutch restaurant Les was familiar with. After eating, Les drove his son into the mountains; after a fifteen-mile trip through beautiful hardwood forests, they arrived at the camp.

Les had bought Clay a set of required camping equipment including a four-man tent. Les figured Clay and he could use it in the future to go camping on their own and take Albert along, so buying the larger tent made sense. Clay had a new sleeping bag, mess kit, compass and several other items required by the camp.

The central camp area featured a number of log cottages and buildings. As they arrived, a small hoard of other boys and young teens were moving about and settling in. Les checked in with the camp office and paid Clay's fees, sixty dollars, for the two-week program. Clay was shocked at the cost and asked Les, "Are you sure we can afford this? That's a fortune! I could stay at the hotel if you want to save the money. It's already paid for by the railroad."

"Hush, Clay. We're doing fine." Les noted Clay's troubled expression. "Are you a little worried about being on your own for a while?"

"Maybe a little."

"All kids feel the same way the first few days of camp. After that they're so busy having fun they forget all about their parents and home. You'll see. I bet you'll forget what I look like by the time I pick you up in fourteen days."

"I will not. I'd never forget you, Dad. I love you too much." There were tears in the sensitive boy's eyes and Les figured it was just about time to get lost. He gave Clay a quick hug. With other boys around it was more father-like to do, even though he could see Clay wanted a kiss too. He ruffled the boy's hair and left.

Clay looked lost with his gear piled around his feet. An older teen --- maybe seventeen or eighteen --- approached with a clipboard and asked, "Hi. Are you Clay Parker?" When Clay nodded yes, the youth said, "Good, I'm Jerry, and you've been assigned to my cabin. I'm the junior counselor for Cabin D. Grab your gear and follow me. Do you need a hand?"

"Uh, maybe a little. If you can grab my duffle bag, I can handle the rest. Thanks, Jerry."

"Cabin D is Dragon Squad, so for the next two weeks, if you hear the loudspeaker call for Dragons, that's you. How old are you, Clay?"

"Fourteen. I'll be fifteen in January."

"You won't be here in January," Jerry laughed. "That is unless you get lost in the woods. I sure wouldn't want to be here then. These mountains are cold as a well digger's ass, in January."

Clay chuckled, as he'd never heard the expression before. "What all will I be doing while I'm here?"

"A lot. Hiking, swimming, canoeing; the colonel will tell you all about it when he tells the whole camp at four o'clock this afternoon." He checked his wristwatch and said, "It's two-thirty now. You'll have until four o'clock to settle in your bunk and make your bed. Dragons run a neat and clean cabin, Clay, so if you're a messy guy at home, get over it right now. There's a competition for best cabin and I want to see Dragon squad take the lead as the days pass. Anyone who gets us more than ten housing demerits gets run through the gauntlet."

"What's the gauntlet?"

"I'll tell you about it later. You won't like it. Everything else here is pretty fun, but not the gauntlet."

Clay felt a sense of alarm as he tried to imagine what the gauntlet was. Was it some kind of terrible punishment machine? He'd always thought a gauntlet was some sort of metal glove knights used to wear but wasn't completely sure. He was glad he was neat at home and swore he wouldn't be the one to earn a demerit --- whatever that was --- and have to experience the gauntlet.

They arrived at Cabin D and stepped inside. Clay found himself in a common room with a large stone fireplace and a number of chairs and puffy sofas arranged around the room. Two open doorways led off left and right. A wide hallway led straight ahead past two doors along the way to another larger room farther back in the rear of the large cabin.

Jerry talked and pointed, "The door to the left is to bunks 1 through 12, the right-hand door is 13 through 24. You're fourteen so you go left. Thirteen-year-olds go right. The center hall ahead leads to two offices and single rooms for counselors. My office and room is on the right. Our cabin's commander is Mr. Biggs. He's an adult and his room is on the left. If you need an appointment to see him, see me and I'll arrange it. Always knock and announce yourself before you open either counselor's office door. Wait to be invited in. It's common courtesy. Have you got all that?" It was obvious the young man had given this speech a number of times.

"Yes, sir."

"Uh, relax, Clay. You don't have to call *me* sir, but you should use sir with Mr. Biggs. He's a nice guy and we're lucky to have him in charge of D Cabin. Be glad we don't have Freedman. He's a dick."

Clay snickered at the blunt reference.

"Don't cross Freedman, whatever you do. He loves to run kids through the gauntlet for the least little thing. I'll point him out to you, soon as I get a chance. Let's see, where was I? Oh, yeah. The hall just beyond our office doors leads to the toilets and showers. There's laundry tubs and a hand wringer in there too for small washing needs. A back door leads to the clotheslines behind the cabin. For large washing loads, there's a laundry room with machines not far away. Showers are mandatory after sweaty activities and before bedtime. I can smell a sweaty camper from twenty feet away, and if you don't bathe, I'll do it for you with a toilet brush and lye soap. It hurts, but by damn, kids only skip their shower once."

"I'm clean. I bathe every day at home."

"Good. A few unwritten rules: Uh, if you jack off, do it under the covers and not out in the open. If I see your dick while you're doing it, I'll send you through the gauntlet myself. And don't tell me you don't do it, 'cause I don't like liars."

Clay grinned sheepishly and nodded.

Jerry continued: "No sex with other boys in the cabins or anywhere else where you might get caught." He gave Clay a careful scan before saying, "I don't care if you're queer or not. A lot of the older boys experiment while they're here. Just do it in your tent during a campout or in the woods or something." Clay was surprised to hear Jerry speak so casually about sex. "No alcohol and no smoking. If you brought along booze, cigarettes, chew or snuff, flush 'em down the toilet right now. It's two trips through the gauntlet if you're found with tobacco and three for alcohol."

"I don't smoke or drink. I had an uncle who beat me when he was drunk, so I hate the stuff."

"Good man. Where are you from, Clay?"

"Sand Patch, Pennsylvania."

"Sand Patch? Never heard of it. Don't tell anyone else that, they'll make fun since it has an odd name. Pick a nearby town with a common name. Try to blend in and not stand out. It's better that way. You're a nice kid and I can tell this is your first time at camp. If you have any problems, come see me. I'm here to help you adjust and have a good time. Any questions?"

"Uh, I don't think so. Maybe after a bit, or once I hear what the colonel has to say at four."

"Okay, Clay. Go in there and pick out an empty bunk. There's about seven left. Blankets, sheets and towels are on the beds. Make the bed as neatly as you can today. Tomorrow I'll show you the way to do it so they all look the same. Have fun, kid. I'll see you later."

Clay was still reeling from the shotgun lecture; he hoped he could remember everything Jerry had said. He went through the left-hand door and saw four other boys standing in a group talking. They stopped their conversation and looked him over. One was a tall, slender boy with black hair and light brown eyes. He looked Clay over from head to toe, nodded and smiled. Clay smiled back. Beside him was a redheaded boy with so many large freckles he looked like he was polka dotted. He frowned a bit while looking Clay over with a critical gaze. Another boy was slightly overweight and short, but grinned and said hello. The fourth boy was even thinner than the first boy and had pale blond hair that was nearly white; he nodded and seemed friendly.

"Hi," said the tall boy with brown eyes and black hair. "I'm Randy Meadows. This is Ed Bigalow," he pointed out the freckled, redhead, "this is Mack Ford," the white-haired kid, "and this is Sam Walden," indicating the chubby, short lad.

"I'm Clay Parker from near Somerset, Pennsylvania. It's good to meet all of you. What bunks aren't taken yet?"

Randy stepped over close, put his hand on Clay's shoulder, and said, "Any bunks that still have stacks of blankets and pillows, are up for grabs. It's up to you if you want an upper or a lower, but there's a good lower bunk over here. It's in the corner and more private and quiet." Randy led him toward the back corner of the room and pointed out a lower bunk. The bunk above was already taken and neatly made.

"This will be fine, I guess," said Clay as he set down his duffel bag and gear.

"Cool, I'm your upstairs bunky," said Randy and offered Clay his hand and they shook. Once they returned to where the other boys were still talking, Clay made the same gesture and offered his hand to the other three boys who seemed friendly and accepted him without any problem. They went back to their conversation and from what Clay could gather it was about a nearby girls' camp called Camp Dogwood. Randy, on the other hand, seemed uninterested and suggested they go back to their bunk and asked, "Can you use some help unpacking and settling in, Clay?"

"Yeah, thanks. Uh, Jerry said there was a special way to make a bunk. Have you been here before? It's my first time at camp."

"I was here last year and had a great time. I'll show you how they want it done." After returning to their corner bunks, Randy set about showing Clay how to make a bed with military corners and a line-folded collar. Clay said it looked very neat and thanked him. Next, the boy helped Clay unpack his duffel bag and put his belongings in a locker beneath the bed. He said his locker was the one beside it. It had a lock on it and Clay was concerned.

"I didn't bring a lock."

"It's okay; just see Jerry and he'll issue you one. All of the locks belong to the camp and they have a master key if you lose yours. The keys are on a double chain so you can wear it around your neck. If one chain breaks, you still have your key. Is that your tent?" He pointed to a canvas bag labeled: **Sears Campmaster 4**.

"Uh huh, it's brand new. I've never even set it up yet. My dad bought it in Cumberland and we didn't have time to use it."

"It's big. Mine's a one-man pup tent. A few other boys have large tents too, so it's okay."

"Why do we need a tent when we have the cabins?"

"We'll be going on one or maybe two overnight hikes. That's when we'll need the tents. You're going to have a heavy load with that thing and your other stuff. Hope you have a strong back."

"Uh, Randy, if you want, we can share the tent when we go on the hike. It's big enough for four, but I wouldn't want any more than one other kid to share it. You've been a big help, so if you'd like to share, let me know."

"I just might. It's allowed. My tent's so tiny if I fart I'm liable to die from poisoned air."

Both boys laughed at the joke before Randy added, "One of us can carry the tent and the other can share the rest of the load. We'll even it out and that'll be better for us both. Do you have a girlfriend?"

The sudden change in topic threw Clay for a second, but he said, "Uh, no. I'm gonna wait until I'm well into high school before I start thinking about stuff like that. How about you?"

"Naw. I'm a loner most of the time. I have just a few close friends and don't mix well with other kids in school. Girls just get you in trouble. I talked to a girl about a homework question once in school this past year and she had a boyfriend who thought I was making time with her."

"Uh oh," said Clay with a smile.

"Yeah, he caught me after school and roughed me up pretty bad. I told him I wasn't after his girl, but all he said was that he was making sure I remembered that. He was wearing a ring and chipped my tooth when he hit me, see." Randy opened his mouth and sure enough, one of his upper front teeth was missing a corner.

About that time, several other boys arrived and began to select bunks and make them. Soon, all were taken but one. Randy and Clay worked together and helped some of the other boys do the beds right.

One boy, however, took offense to their offer of help and said, "Tend to your own business. I know how to make a fuckin' bed." It was unfortunate, but he had tossed his gear on the lower bunk right beside Clay. The upper bunk above him hadn't been claimed either and was the only remaining cot. He made no effort to start making his bed. They left him alone; Randy rolled his eyes at Clay and wrinkled his nose.

At ten minutes till four, a loudspeaker began playing a bugle call of some kind. Randy said, "That's assembly. We all have to go to the amphitheater. If the weather's bad when they play assembly, we go to the chow hall instead."

"What's the amphitheater?"

"Follow me and I'll show you. It's easier to see it than describe it." He led Clay past the other cabins and over a rise. Just below, along the slope leading down to the lake, Clay saw a bowl-shaped area with wooden benches arranged in several half circles facing a flat cement platform where some adults and the junior counselors were milling about.

Altogether, about seventy boys eventually assembled. The benches were painted in different colors and labeled by cabin names; Randy showed Clay where Dragon Squad was supposed to sit on red-colored seats. After all the campers arrived, a man in a neatly pressed khaki outfit stepped to a portable lectern and spoke into a microphone. Two, horn-shaped speakers, mounted on elevated poles squealed and hissed until a lady --- the only one Clay had seen all afternoon --- adjusted a metal box nearby and the racket stopped.

The man started speaking, "Hello campers! I'm Colonel Matthew Lincoln, camp commander and I'd like to welcome all of you to Camp Cunningham here in the beautiful Catoctin Mountains of Central Maryland. I'm going to tell you a few things about the camp that everyone here needs to know and then we'll head to the chow hall for supper. I'm sure you'd rather eat than listen to me anyway, so I'll keep it short."

He went on to share general rules and talk about all of the activities planned for the next two weeks. From what he said, half of the campers were on a one-week stay and would be replaced by another one-week troop in a week. Clay and all the boys in his cabin were on the two-week cycle. From what the man described, Clay thought it would be an interesting *fortnight*; a word the Colonel used for the two-week campers or *fortnighters* as he called them. He seemed to be a jovial man and told a few jokes during the speech that everyone enjoyed. He didn't say anything about the dreaded gauntlet. Clay wasn't sure if that was good or bad. He made a mental note to ask Randy what it was.

After the speech, everyone was herded toward a large nearby building with many screened windows labeled **The Trough** on a carved wooden sign over its door. Clay chuckled because the string of hungry boys did resemble a herd of cattle, or perhaps pigs, on their way into a barn for feeding. Supper was spaghetti with meatballs and wasn't half-bad. There was a salad, plenty of crisp garlic bread and cold iced tea to drink. The helpings were generous and he saw some boys doing some food trading. Dessert was fruit cocktail served in paper cups. The tables were open to anyone and the boys were not required to eat with their cabin mates. The colonel said that was to encourage interaction and friendship between the various campers.

The ages of the boys ranged from nine through fourteen. One little boy sitting near Clay was picking at his food and snuffling; several other boys were teasing him unmercifully. It seemed, from what Clay could tell the child was homesick. He and Randy invited the boy to sit between them and that helped to end the teasing. They told him everything was going to be all right and soon had calmed the boy somewhat, although tears still lurked near the surface.

After the meal was over, the younger boy, whose name was Mark asked if he could go with them to their cabin, but they explained that wasn't allowed. About then an older teen came over and collected the boy and thanked Clay and Randy for their help. "I was watching what you did and you both just earned your cabin four merits."

Clay panicked as he misunderstood the boy and thought he had said *de*merits. The older counselor set him straight and explained that merits canceled out demerits for the final tally at the end of the weeks. He also added, "You both have what it takes to be counselors. After you finish your two-week session, if you want to be considered for jobs here next summer, come and see me and I'll introduce you to my dad, Colonel Lincoln. I'm Todd Lincoln, counselor for Fox Cabin. We have the younger guys and they often get a little homesick."

He shook their hands and then said to Mark, "You feeling better, big fellow. These guys were right. As soon as you start doing things tomorrow, you'll feel better. If you get to missing home, or if anyone teases you too much, you come and see me and I'll make sure they leave you alone. How about you and I walk together to Fox Cabin; I have something I need help with there and I've been looking for a special helper." Mark smiled and followed the older boy who looked back and winked at Clay and Randy.

"Wow!" said Randy. "We could get summer jobs here next year. That would be great. I wonder how much it pays?"

"Maybe we can ask Todd tomorrow. He sure seems like a nice guy. He was great with that little boy. Say, Randy, I have a couple of questions for you as we head back. First of all, where's your home at?"

"I'm from Harper's Ferry, West Virginia."

"Oh wow, I was just there with my dad and best friend a week or so ago. We went to some of the museums. My dad works for the B&O and I can travel on a train anytime I want for free."

"Cool! My house is on a hill real close to the B&O station, just six streets away. I can see one end of the station platform from my bedroom window."

"Super. Maybe I can visit you this year after camp's over. I'll bring Albert along. You'd like him. He's my best friend and I love him like a brother."

Randy smiled and said, "I have a close friend like that in Harper's Ferry. His name is Claude De Mer. He's from France. He grew up in America though; he speaks English as well as he speaks

French. He has a little accent, but not much. You'd like him too. He almost came with me, but broke his leg last week and will be in a cast until school starts. It's bad luck; I really miss him. He's like a brother to me too."

"It's a shame he got hurt. I wanted Albert to come along, but he had to visit some cousins in Philadelphia for a few days and couldn't be in both places."

Randy smiled at Clay and tilted his head slightly as he said, "You said you love your friend. Most boys won't say things like that, but I know what you mean. I love Claude and he loves me --- just like brothers. I *had* an older brother, but he got killed in the war in a place called Iwo Jima. It's an island in the Pacific Ocean. He was fighting the Japanese. I just barely remember him, but Mom and Dad still miss him something terrible."

"I'm real sorry about that, Randy. I lost my little brother and my mom and dad in a fire when I was ten."

"Oh my god, Clay, that's awful. I'm sorry too. You were talking about your dad and I thought..."

"He's my adopted dad and he's wonderful. He's the kindest man I've ever known and I love him so much it hurts sometimes. I even get a little homesick like Mark when I think about him. He's in Hagerstown right now taking classes to get promoted to be a railroad conductor, so while he's there in school, I'm here at camp. He said he'll be here for Parents' Day on Sunday, so you can meet him."

"That'll be great. You can meet my family too. I have a little sister named Sara. She's ten and pretty nice. I love her too, but sometimes she gets on my nerves."

They arrived at Dragon Cabin and went inside. The common room was filled with thirteen and fourteen-year-olds but was somewhat noisy, so Randy and he went to their bunks to talk.

"So, Clay, exactly where are you from?"

Clay went on to tell his new buddy where Sand Patch was and as much as he could about his home including Les, the model trains, Debussy and especially Albert.

After sharing other things about their lives, Clay remembered one other question he just had to ask. "Randy, what in the world is the gauntlet?"

Randy laughed and said, "You'll get to see tomorrow morning. You know that nasty, smart-assed kid who was going to bunk right there?" He pointed to the bunk beside Clay's bed which was now empty. "Well, he has to run the gauntlet in the morning. He sassed Mr. Biggs earlier today and I just heard he was moved to Freedman's cabin where they put all the goof-ups. You'll love what happens to him. It's harmless, but embarrassing as can be. You have to crawl in your bathing suit along the beach, through a line of senior campers --- those who have been to camp at least two years before --- they get to make fun of you, slap your butt, but not too hard, pour ice water, mud or pondweeds on you until you reach the end. Last year one guy found a load of frog eggs and dumped them on a boy no one liked."

"Gees, that's pretty nasty," Clay wrinkled his nose.

"The whole camp gets to watch and your name gets posted on a list. If you don't run the gauntlet, your cabin automatically gets twenty demerits and then you have to face your cabin mates after lights out. Believe me; it's easier to do the gauntlet."

"Have you ever had to do it?" Clay said with a grin.

"Almost, I got caught peeing behind a bush by, of all people, the colonel's wife. She's the nurse here too, so it wasn't like she's never seen a boy's dick. She let me off with a warning, gave me three demerits and told me to use the restroom next time."

"Was that the woman who had to fix the speaker?"

"That's her. She's the only lady in the whole camp. She's Todd's mom, I suppose."

"Is the Gauntlet the only punishment other than demerits?"

"Yeah, for anything worse, they just call your parents and you have to leave and never come back."

"Well, I'm gonna be good, because I'd like to work here next summer."

"Yeah, me too."

Chapter 13

There was an optional sing-along at the amphitheater, but Clay, Randy and a few other boys decided to stay inside and get their showers early before the bedtime rush. Two of the first boys he'd met stayed behind. One was Mack Ford, the white-haired boy and the other was Sam Walden, the heavy kid. Their bunks were not far from Clay and Randy's. The bunk beside Randy and Clay's was now completely empty since the belligerent kid had been moved out. Clay secretly hoped it would stay that way. There was less chance someone would see him if he chose to masturbate under the covers at night.

Clay knew that with showers looming, the moment of truth was coming when he'd have to explain his scars to the other boys. He was dreading it but suddenly had an inspiration. Instead of having them be surprised by his appearance in the shower, he called out to all the boys in the bunkhouse and asked to speak to them. They all looked surprised at having another boy call them to a meeting, but they joined Randy and him. There were a number of other lads he hadn't met as yet in the group that gathered.

"Uh, I wanted to tell you all something rather than have to explain it over and over. You guys can spread the word for me too and that won't bother me. When I was ten, I was in a bad fire that killed the rest of my family. I got burnt pretty badly too." Most all the boys expressed their sorrow, but Clay went on: "I'm not telling you all this to gain your pity, but I do appreciate what you all just said about losing my family. I only wanted to tell you that I have a lot of ugly scars on me that will be easy to see once I undress for a shower. It's easier for me this way to tell you all in advance. If any of you have questions, I'll be glad to answer you."

The Ford boy asked, "Do they still hurt or anything?"

"Sometimes they kind of prickle and sting. The ones on my legs do especially because I'm growing faster than the scars can keep up and that makes the skin sensitive and hurt a little as it stretches. Feels like ants crawling on me sometimes. It's nothing like it was during and after the fire, though. I was in the hospital for over six months and they had to give me medicine that made me real dopey and sleep a lot. They had to take me off the medicine gradually; it was the kind of medicine people get addicted to. One drug they used

135

at first was called morphine. It's good stuff, but you have to keep taking bigger doses and it's hard when you can't take it anymore."

"How come there are no scars on your face?" asked one of the un-introduced boys. "My name's Mike Deal, by the way.

"Great, I'm Clay Parker." They shook hands. "Well, Mike, I only got burned where my pajamas were touching me. They were made out of a cloth called nylon. They don't use it for kid's pajamas anymore because it burns real fast and sticks to your skin as it burns. I had on underpants and I didn't get burnt down there. Thank heavens the cloth didn't catch on my back. I just got lucky with my face. My belly and chest got the worst burns, see." Clay shrugged off his long sleeve pullover shirt and the boys moved closer to have a look. A few gasped and one even turned away and shivered. A few more boys had joined the group by now and were brought up to date by the others.

"My leg burns will have to wait for the shower. I'm not going to take off my britches and have a bunch of boys gathered around me gawking in case Jerry or Mr. Biggs walk in." Everyone laughed and that helped to break the tension.

There were no more questions so Clay said, "Okay. Thanks for listening. I just thought it would be best to do it this way. I'm glad to meet all of you and look forward to having fun with you the next two weeks. I'm ready for a shower."

After that, Clay had no trouble with teasing or whispers about his scars. The word spread in the right way, the truthful way, and other boys all over the camp started saying they were sorry about his folks and his burns and made friends with him easily. He planned to do the same when high school started in the fall.

After showers, just before lights out, he and Randy sat on his bunk since it was the lower one. They had played cards there for nearly an hour, but now were talking a bit before bedtime. They'd been given the next day's schedule of events and found they would have little time to be bored. Swimming and diving lessons were first on the agenda. The camp wanted to make sure every boy could swim and swim well. Those who proved themselves could move on to other water sports and activities. Those who needed swimming lessons or practice would spend more time on basics. Randy said he was a great swimmer as was Clay, so they were looking forward to canoe lessons and a canoe ride.

When Mr. Biggs announced five minutes until lights out, they began to say goodnight. Randy said, "I'm sure glad we met, Clay. You're every bit as great a guy as Claude and it helps me not miss him as much. For some reason when you came in the cabin today, I felt I should get to know you. You looked at me and smiled and that was nice. So many boys act tough and strut around as if they're super important."

"Yeah, I know kids like that and don't like being around them much either."

Randy continued: "You didn't and I like that. I think it's super too that you can ride the train free and might come to visit me at Harper's Ferry. I want to meet Albert too because he sounds like a nice boy. You'll love Claude. He's kind of quiet, shy, and blushes a lot. He's tall and thin like me and has thick, curly, black hair. It's darker than yours and almost looks blue in the light sometimes."

Clay described Albert in detail. The way Randy was talking about Claude made Clay feel he might be queer too. He described Claude as though he was fascinated with his looks and personality. Most boys would never do that. Clay realized he was doing the same thing with Albert. He would have to watch and see if Randy showed any other signs of being queer. It would be great if he and Albert were that way and had two friends who were also like them, even if they lived at a distance.

At that moment, Clay realized Randy was sitting very close beside him. The boy had gradually shifted until they were pressed close together, shoulder-to-shoulder and hip-to-hip. As he thought about it, his body started reacting. He had on only his pajamas without briefs, so he would have to be careful or something might pop out of his fly opening. He tightened his inner thighs and pinched his growing erection between his legs to prevent an escape. He looked over at Randy's front and couldn't tell for sure, but he thought he saw a lump there.

Just at that moment, the lights went out and it was completely dark in the room. He heard Randy whisper very close to his ear, "Clay, I really like you. Would it be all right if I hugged you goodnight? The lights are out, so no one will see me do it. Claude and I always hug before bed when he stays over and I miss him so much. Will it bother you?"

"No, I don't mind. I like to hug too. Albert and I do it. Let's do it quick though before everyone's eyes adjust to the dark. I can see a little light at the windows already. He felt Randy's arms go around him and he reciprocated. His erection escaped the vice of his legs and he was very glad it was dark. Randy hugged him tightly and nuzzled against his neck. Clay thought for a moment he felt Randy's lips brush over his ear and hair. He leaned into the embrace and felt his lips and nose against Randy's neck. The boy's skin was so soft and he smelled good from the soap he'd used in the shower. They hugged for what must have been a half minute or so; he felt a little light headed as they separated.

"That was nice," whispered Randy.

"Yeah, I liked it too. I wish we could hug longer, but I don't want us to get caught. I don't think many of these boys would understand that it's only a strong friendship."

"Maybe we can do it again tomorrow night."

"Sure. I'd like to. It felt special. I kind of felt light-headed like I used to feel when they gave me those shots for pain." Clay giggled.

"Me too, my whole body was tingling; every single part of me." Clay gave that some thought and wondered if Randy intended it to mean what he thought it might mean. Randy was a bright kid and Clay believed --- or wanted to believe --- the boy meant exactly what he'd said.

They had been sitting very close, with faces side by side, whispering in each other's ears, but it was time to stop, as the room was growing quieter.

Randy's left hand found its way to the center of Clay's chest and he whispered in Clay's ear. I love you almost as much as I love Claude." Clay felt him kiss his cheek and gasped at what had just happened. Randy giggled and leaned away. Before Clay could do anything else --- and he really wanted to --- Randy said, "Goodnight," and scampered up the side of their bunk bed and crawled under his sheets. Clay whispered goodnight as well and stretched out pulling the sheet over himself as well. His penis, now out of his fly opening, was rock hard and oozing wetness. He reached beneath the sheets, took it in his hand and shivered at the intensity of his own touch. He pushed his forefinger inside his foreskin and rubbed the moist areas within. As usual, during his shower, he hadn't washed away all of the natural odor that lurked there; he liked the smell and used it to heighten his mood and pleasure. He'd noticed while bathing, that Randy was circumcised like Albert and tried now to remember exactly what he looked like in the shower.

He raised his knees enough to make a small tent over his privates, un-snapped his pajama bottoms, raised his shirt and within a few minutes brought himself to the peak of pleasure and over its summit. With several powerful surges, his loins expelled his seed. Clay caught it with his left hand and, after the orgasm ended, brought it to his nose and smelled its earthy aroma. As he rested there, very still, he felt the bed moving just a little bit and as it intensified, he heard a low moan of joy from above and knew that Randy was feeling the same blissful joy he had just felt.

His last thoughts, just before sleep overcame him were, *I wonder what might happen when Randy and I share my tent on the overnight hike.*

Morning literally came with a bang. Every morning at six o'clock, Colonel Lincoln, or one of his assistants, fired an old civil war cannon --- without a cannonball of course --- as the signal to begin the day. Just after that was a rendition of revile via the loudspeaker system played live into a microphone by one of three camp buglers. Clay sat up rapidly and tried to figure where the heck he was. *Oh yeah, camp.* He swung his legs over the edge of his bed to get up, but suddenly found two, thin and somewhat hairy legs on either side of his face as Randy did the same.

Clay had enough presence of mind to grab hold of Randy's calves and kept his new friend's heels from hitting him. Feeling someone grab his legs Randy yelled; but was promptly shushed by several other sleepy campers. Clay was still hanging on as Randy peered down between his knees and smiled at Clay who was looking up and grinning. Clay turned his head and bit Randy's right calf just enough for him to feel it. The boy above laughed. Clay slid his hands down along Randy's legs until he had hold of his feet and squeezed his toes. He nibbled again at Randy's calf.

"You must be hungry," whispered Randy as Clay finally let go. "I'm not on the menu, sorry."

"That's a shame. You taste kinda good. You're a little hairy, but good. You have very fuzzy legs. I thought I was holding Debussy, my cat."

Randy giggled, turned and slid down beside Clay. It was obvious that Randy was a bit stiff as his bulging pajamas were right in front of Clay's face for a moment. *I'd like to bite that,* he thought. His own penis was at attention as well and he'd already had to make sure it was tucked between his legs. He'd wear briefs at night from now on. If Randy hadn't been wearing his... Well, the possibilities were worth thinking about. Randy landed on the floor and scampered off for the restroom followed closely by Clay.

They located themselves side by side at the bank of six urinals. Both giggled, as they had to force their erections down while they drained themselves.

Randy whispered, "Can't keep a good man down."

Clay laughed and said, "You're terrible, and not at all shy, that's for sure."

"How proudly it waves," he said as he shook off.

"That's worse than the last one."

They padded back to their bunks and got dressed. Both were taking liberties with their glances and neither tried to hide it either. Randy had a mischievous grin the whole time. "I think we're going to get along just fine," he said with a smile as he gave Clay a quick pat on the rear end as he walked past him and started making his bed. Clay felt unusually bold and when no one was looking their way, he gave not a pat to Randy's rear, but a gentle caress as he ran his hand down and over his new friend's butt. Randy only turned and smiled. After checking to make sure no one was looking, he gave Clay a quick side hug and whispered, "I thought you and I might be alike in certain special ways. If you want, we can have a lot of fun at camp this summer."

"It's okay with me," Clay whispered, feeling warm and flushed as he fully realized what they'd just agreed to do.

"We'll talk about it later. Let's get these bunks done for inspection. Mr. Biggs is due to come through in about five minutes."

Both boys passed inspection and soon were off for The Trough and breakfast.

After a big meal of bacon, scrambled eggs and toast, everyone was expected to help clean up around their cabin, both inside and the grounds outside. Clay and Randy were assigned two toilets each to clean and sanitize. Duties rotated, so the toilets were not a permanent task.

Clay was looking forward to seeing the nasty-tempered kid go through the gauntlet, but Jerry informed them, when they asked, that the boy chose to call home for pickup by his father. At least his cabin wouldn't be given demerits that way.

The first activity of the day was swimming trials at the lake. The evening before, every boy had been given two pairs of shorts, three tee shirts and a form-fitting bathing suit, all with the camp logo on them. The clothes were also color-coded for each cabin. Dragon Squad's outfits were bright red. Clay especially liked the way the bathing suits looked on all the boys, leaving little to the imagination as to what they were supporting inside.

Four small tables had been set up near the docks and after each boy visited a table, he either left and jumped into the water, or was sent to another area for instructions. Each station was staffed by an adult counselor. Dragon Squad was told to go to table 4. An unpleasant-looking man was seated there with a stack of files. Randy whispered to Clay, "Freedman, The Terrible."

When Clay, who was ahead of Randy in line stepped close, Mr. Freedman asked his name before thumbing through his files and pulling out one with **Parker, Clay** written on it. "Can you swim, Mister Parker?"

"Yes, sir."

"Prove it. Jump in and swim out to the float and back for Mr. Biggs, who's manning the dock and prepared to rescue any liars."

"Thank you, sir."

"Wait just a minute." Freedman was scanning Clay's file and asked in his slow, irritating voice "It says here that you received two *merits* yesterday for assisting a junior level camper who was --- *homesick*." He said the word as if it was a disgusting disease of some sort. "It seems unusual for a camper to earn merits before camp officially starts. I see it was given by Colonel Lincoln's son. Interesting. We'll have to keep a sharp eye on you, Mr. Parker. I don't like gold-diggers. Go and prove you can swim. If you were lying, it will be ten *de*merits and a trip through the gauntlet." He handed the file to Clay to carry along to Mr. Biggs's table.

Clay walked along the dock, checked in at the table with Mr. Biggs and easily swam the thirty or so feet to the float and back. Mr. Biggs said with a smile, "Good job, Clay. You're all cleared for water activities. Have fun."

What a difference from Freedman thought Clay. He waited nearby for Randy to return from his swim and get clearance.

His friend joined him, still dripping, and said, "Did Freedman give you grief about the merits?"

"Yeah, you're right, he is a dick."

141

"He told me he thought there wasn't anything in the rules that allowed a camper to earn points before camp officially starts. It would be just like him to have them removed too. Luckily, the colonel's son gave them to us. He probably won't do anything, but we're in his gun sight now, so we'll have to watch ourselves around him."

Since they qualified for water activities, Clay and Randy opted to sign up for canoe lessons, snorkeling and water skiing; over the next few days, they would be scheduled for those activities. Campers were permitted to list another camper as a partner in most activities, so Clay and Randy listed each other in the partner space.

They had nearly two hours to kill. They would have gone swimming, but that part of the lakeside was reserved for swimming classes for the boys who needed to learn or improve their skill.

Camp Cunningham had a number of nature trails, so they decided to walk one of them. The lake the camp was located on had a six-mile perimeter. Their location was along one small part of the southwestern shore. At the south end of the lake was Cunningham Falls, a twenty-foot drop in the river that cascaded along a step-like series of rocks. The trail they chose was the one to the falls. Randy said it was about a two-mile trek, round trip. They wore their red shorts over their bathing suits as Randy said there were a few places along the lakeshore where they might want to swim and cool off. He also said it was fun climbing over the rocks of the falls itself, as there was little danger there.

It was to Clay's advantage that Randy had been to the camp the previous year, knew all the trails and locations by heart and was now happy to share them with Clay.

At one point along the path, where one could see the entire lake from an elevated rocky ledge, Clay said, "This is a really pretty place. The lake's about three miles long and maybe a mile and a half wide, I'm guessing."

"Yeah, there's a girls camp on the eastern side right across from our camp. If you look across at night, you can see the lights. That side's off limits for us though."

"I'm not that interested in girls anyway," ventured Clay with a smile.

"Yeah, after last night, I kind of figured that out. I'm looking forward to us having some fun with one another."

"Yeah, me too." Clay started wondering what Randy might have in mind.

It was nine-thirty when they'd left and headed south along the falls trail. A few other boys were hiking the trail that morning too, but none was walking with them. They passed a few slow walkers; but were passed by boys who were jogging or running. At one point, about a third of the way to the falls, Randy led them off the main trail and down a narrow path that descended to the lakeshore. At one point along the way, they passed through a thicket of wild holly bushes that blocked their view completely from the trail ahead and behind. Randy stopped and said, "Let's stop here for a few minutes. It's not far to the lake from here. Listen carefully. Do you hear any other campers coming or going?"

Clay and Randy both stood quietly and listened. All they could hear were a few buzzing cicadas, songbirds and a distant motorboat on the lake somewhere to the northeast. There was no sign of voices, or people walking the trails nearby.

Clay said, "I can't hear anyone. Why stop here?"

"Because I wanted us to be able to do what we did last night before we got in bed and I wanted to make sure no one sees or hears us."

"Oh, okay."

"Is that all right with you?"

"I don't mind. It was kinda nice last night. I was surprised when you gave me a kiss though."

"You're not mad are you?"

"Nope, it didn't bother me. It was nice."

"Claude and I do that a lot because we love and trust each other. I trust you and I want you to know that you can trust me. It was nice this morning when you touched my backside. Claude does that and I don't mind; I like it. Can we hug now?"

"Sure." The two embraced tightly and held on. Clay felt Randy push himself closer and was excited as he felt the boy's hardness growing and pressing against his own body. Clay's body was reacting too as Randy pressed and shifted back and forth against him; Clay knew he would soon be getting wet.

This is so cool, he thought as he closed his eyes and nuzzled against Randy's thick black hair and brushed his lips over the boy's neck and ear. He felt Randy's right hand slide down and over his backside, so he did the same and could feel the divide between the boy's narrow hips.

"This is so nice," said Randy in a whisper. "I love doing this, Clay. I was hoping you were like me. Claude is the only other boy I know who likes to do this."

Clay whispered back, "Yeah, it's great. I've never done anything like this yet with Albert, but he's hugged me and gotten hard against me in bed. As soon as I get home, I want to see if he wants to do stuff like we're doing. That doesn't bother you and make you jealous does it?"

"No. I think it'll be nice if we each have a boyfriend at home and maybe when we visit each other we can all hug and do stuff."

Clay whispered, "That would be something." All the while, they were still embracing and pressing against each other while listening for others. Clay's heart was pounding and he felt flushed and warm. He could hardly believe what was happening and was amazed at how easy it was now to talk about the things he'd kept a secret so long. Randy was so open and unreserved about his feelings. Clay moved his hand upward from Randy's butt and slid his hand up, under the boy's tee shirt, and along his warm, smooth back. He could feel every vertebrate and loved each one of them.

Randy followed Clay's lead and explored his back the same way. As they did so, Randy pulled his head away from Clay's neck and then gently and briefly kissed Clay's lips. Clay felt a bit dizzy and his erection became painful, as his penis was twisted to one side straining to point upward. He pushed himself forward against Randy and kissed him more forcefully keeping his lips on his companion and sucking at his full, puffy lips.

Randy moved his hand down along Clay's back until he came to his waistband. Clay did the same to him, but slid beneath the shorts and the tight bathing suit and slowly slid downward along the boy's fissure. He felt moisture there from sweat and could scarcely believe he was doing what he was doing. He felt Randy delving into his secret places the same way as they pushed against each other and kissed more and more forcefully. Clay felt himself losing control down below, so he pulled away and said, "Whew! I'm sorry, but I have to rest a minute. It was about to happen."

"Me too! Mine hurts and I bet I'm getting wet and slippery. Are you?" They each still had their hands down the back of one another's swimsuits.

"Yeah, super wet. I love doing this. I've had dreams about doing stuff like this with Albert. Why do some boys like us not want to be with girls?"

"I don't know, but I try not to feel bad about it. I don't think we'll ever change, so I've decided to be myself and enjoy things if I can. I figure God made me this way and maybe there's a reason."

"You think so?"

"I hope so." Randy kissed the tip of Clay's nose as he continued: "I love touching you and feeling you get hard against me." He leaned forward without thrusting below and they kissed again and again. Randy continued to feel along Clay's crack and Clay was now exploring the most secret and warm part of Randy's cleft. He felt his warm opening and played over it with his fingers as Randy did the same to him. Clay could feel his heart pounding and felt light-headed and more excited than he'd ever been before.

Randy giggled and Clay felt his tongue push past his lips and brush over his teeth. He did the same and felt the chipped tooth Randy had shown him the night before. He pulled his hand from Randy's pants, planning on exploring beneath his waistband in the front when they heard the laughter of someone approaching from the main trail.

They both pulled away from one another and moved quickly along the path in the direction of the lake, away from the approaching hikers. Both were still painfully hard, but the fear of discovery soon took care of that. By the time they left the woods and saw the lakeshore a few feet away, both were losing their erections, but their loins still ached from the intensity of their excitement and their young hearts were still racing. Clay raised his hand to his face and breathed in the musky, exotic scent of Randy's lower secrets. He barely could believe what had happened. He looked at Randy and saw that his companion was doing the same with half-closed eyes and an angelic smile upon his face.

Clay was finally able to speak and said, "Let's start back as though we just came from the lake. Walk slowly and we'll soon be back on the main trail."

"Yeah. Whew, I never heard them coming until one of them laughed. I thought we were in for it. They sounded close; yeah here they come. Start walking back."

A group of six boys, younger than twelve, came skipping along the path laughing and horse playing as they walked. One was trying to trip another until they saw Clay and Randy.

"How's the water," the tallest of the boys asked.

"We didn't go in. We were just looking," said Randy as they passed the six. All of them were wearing the brown bathing suits for Bear Cabin and apparently were planning on going for a swim. "Be careful," he added. "A boy almost drowned down there last year. If you go swimming, don't go out too far. There's a drop-off."

"Okay, thanks," one of the boys said.

The two moved along the path and said nothing until they were back on the main trail. As they turned toward the falls, Randy giggled, looked around and gave Clay a quick kiss before starting back down the trail. The walking helped and soon they weren't aching below as before. Within a few minutes, they reached the falls and decided to do some wading and walking through the splashing water as it cascaded down the layers of sandstone. Each took off their shorts, socks and shoes leaving on only their bathing suits. There were several other boys around, so they did nothing intimate while playing in the water.

By eleven thirty, they'd returned to the camp for lunch. Both were famished and tucked in with gusto. After the meal, they were scheduled for a nature walk with one of the adult counselors. He was a high school teacher from Baltimore, named Arthur Wills, who worked during the summers at the camp. Clay and Randy were both looking forward to the walk as they loved natural history and science, but several boys said they expected it to be boring. Mr. Wills soon changed their minds, as the man really knew his subject. Before long the entire group of twenty boys, mostly thirteen and fourteen-year-olds, were actively turning over logs and rocks, seeing things they'd never noticed before on the forest floor. Mr. Wills had led them along one particular nature trail that was kept closed to any other activities to protect it from damage so other students of nature could long enjoy its secrets for years to come.

Chapter 14

By four o'clock, the nature class was over and the boys returned to camp. The swimming area was free now. Most of the campers had worn themselves out swimming earlier in the day, so the lakefront was nearly deserted. Clay and Randy preferred it that way and chose to swim until suppertime. As they headed for the water, Jerry, their cabin's junior counselor, asked them to coach and watch out for two boys from their cabin who were still intermediate level swimmers. He asked them privately so they could decline if they didn't want to be bothered. Both said they would stay with the younger boys and make sure they were safe. Jerry smiled and thanked them before introducing the other fellows. They were thirteen-year-olds even though both looked somewhat younger. There was a lifeguard on duty in case of an emergency; his elevated bench was on the shore, about a hundred fifty feet away.

One of the boys was Sajid Mahoud, a dark, round-faced, olive-skinned boy from India. His English was excellent but heavily accented. He was small for his age, round-faced, intelligent and looked eleven. He had a bubbly personality and giggled a lot. The other, Henry Winters, was a cute, blond-haired boy with sparkling hazel eyes and a winning smile. He was quiet spoken and timorous at first but thanked Clay and Randy politely for spending time with Sajid and him. Soon he became more playful and at ease. Henry was also blessed with a good sense of humor and a teasing nature.

Clay found an odd-shaped, colorful rock and used it to invent a game for the boys to play in which they tried to be the first to dive in shallow water and find the odd stone before the other did. It was a fun activity and gave them practice swimming and diving beneath the surface. Both could swim well enough to play, but neither was ready yet for deeper water or long distance swims. Randy and Clay would throw the rock while the younger boys closed their eyes and turned around slowly to confuse where the sound of the splash came from. Once the rock was in the water, they set off looking. While they hunted, Clay and Randy could talk and still watch them at the same time from near the dock where they paddled about and chatted.

As the younger boys played, Randy had been talking about one of last year's campouts, but suddenly asked, "How close were you to having it happen, Clay?"

"Uh, what do you mean?" Randy was good at rapid changes of subject and it took a moment for Clay to figure out what he meant.

"You know, on the path when we..."

"Oh, I know what you mean. You threw me for a moment. Uh, I was real close. That's why I had to pull away. Just pushing against you while we were kissing and stuff was making me crazy. I was leaking too. How about you?"

"Same thing, I didn't want to stop. I was about ready to reach in your pants right before the other kids came along. I thought for a moment they were about to catch us. Bear cabin kids are all ten and eleven. How old were you the first time you made sperm?" Another quick subject change.

Clay went on to describe his discovery earlier in the spring.

"Wow, that wasn't long ago at all. I was nine when I felt it the first time."

"Nine? A nine-year-old can make sperm?"

"No, nothing came out, but it still felt good. I think any boy can get the feeling."

"How did you learn how to do it?"

"Another boy did it to me. He was twelve and did it with his mouth."

Clay looked at Randy, surprised, "His mouth? What do you mean?"

Randy grinned and said, "He sucked on my thing and moved up and down and all of the sudden I got real hard and it happened. He used to visit me at my house a couple times a week and we'd go up in the attic, where I had a playroom, and do it just about every time. Mom wouldn't come up because she hates climbing a folding ladder. If Dad was home, we had to be more careful. I did it to Luke; he's the boy who helped me feel it the first time. I did it to Luke by hand at first because I was squeamish about putting his dick in my mouth, especially after I saw sperm shoot out. Back then, I thought the sperm was gross and nasty. I still liked to watch it happen to him, though and wondered how long it would be before I was able to

148

come."

"Come where --- his House?"

"No! Come! You know, squirt out sperm. That's called coming."

"Oh. Sorry. I've never been around other boys who told me all these things."

"Oh, okay, I can understand that. I had Luke's help learning all the words and stuff. I was too young to understand everything or start falling in love with him, but I sure liked doing it and the way it felt. He'd hug me from behind and kiss my neck and hair as he did it to me too; it made me feel good inside to know he loved me enough to kiss me."

"It didn't bother you?"

"Nope, somehow I knew it was okay. I knew boys aren't supposed to hug and kiss, but I was different, I guess. I was queer from the start and now it doesn't bother me."

"I think I was too; I just didn't know about it until I started to change. How old were you started, uh, coming?"

"I was eleven and almost twelve. By then, Luke had moved away and I was doing it myself with my hand. Shhh, they found the rock." He said loudly, "Sajid gets a point."

Clay retrieved the stone and started the process all over again. After the boys took off on their search, Clay said, "Just now as we were talking about things, I got hard, did you?"

"Yeah, thinking or talking about this stuff always makes me hard. I bet I'm real full too since we did that stuff this morning and couldn't come. There I go, I'm getting hard again."

"Me too," Clay said and giggled. "Would it be all right if I feel yours? You can feel mine if you want."

"Sure. Stay close to the dock, stand right beside me and keep an

eye out for anyone coming out on this wing of the dock."

The dock was a long one with a number of T-shaped cross arms for diving and launching the canoes, which were otherwise stored in racks on shore. They

149

had chosen to stand along a section that would hide them from the lifeguard. All he could see, for the most part, were their heads and shoulders. Standing on the bottom here, the water was up to their armpits.

Randy added, "Make sure and keep track of where the kids are. We don't want our rock hunters to swim close enough to see what we're doing."

After looking around, Clay reached out and felt Randy's bathing suit. His penis was semi-hard and pointing upward. He felt its shape and gently squeezed as Randy did the same to him. Clay's was pointing downward, so Clay reached into his own suit and turned it upward, telling Randy what he was doing.

"It feels better if you touch it on the underside. Yeah. That feels good. Keep doing that."

Randy was lightly stroking Clay's shaft through the bathing suit fabric with his fingertips. Clay started doing the same to him. Both shivered from time to time from the stimulation.

Less than a minute later, Randy hissed, "Shit! The rock collectors are coming back." Aloud he said, "Sajid gets another point." Clay collected the rock and threw it once more as Randy turned the kids around. They took off on their search once more.

Both had lost their erections but were discovering that the on again, off again, sexual play was making them much more sensitive than usual and both were enjoying themselves more than expected. It only took seconds before they were again aroused, feeling good and climbing once more.

Randy asked, "Are you wet?"

"Yeah, I'm standing in a lake, Randy." He giggled at his own humor.

Randy laughed and said, "Smart ass; I mean, can you feel your slippery stuff flowing out once in a while?"

Clay thought about it and said, "I think so. It's hard to tell with your hand running up and down over it."

"Let me try something, okay."

"What?"

"You'll see and you'll like it."

Randy used one hand to pull down Clay's bathing suit enough to free his erection. He next milked along Clay's shaft until he reached the top. He pushed his finger inside the boy's foreskin and could feel the slipperiness of the mucus.

"Whew. You're super slippery. It's a shame you're underwater. I could really make you feel good with all of that goop."

"Yeah, that's for sure."

"I'm looking forward to trying all kinds of things. I'm glad you still have your extra skin, too. So does Claude. Does your dick smell funny inside the skin sometimes?"

"Yeah, if I wash it often it doesn't, but I'd have to wash several times a day, so it most always has that odor."

"Well, don't wash under there when I'm around. I like to smell that stuff. Claude gets smelly real fast and I love to sniff it. It makes me super hard."

"Yeah, I like the smell of my own stuff too. We're both kind of weird, I guess." Clay snickered and gave Randy a squeeze through his suit. "Better stop down there for a bit, I'm getting kinda close." Randy stopped and Clay pulled his suit back up and over his erection.

"I'd like to smell yours sometime, Clay, but with us swimming so much at camp, I may not get the chance."

Maybe we can find someplace private when we haven't been swimming and you can touch me and see what it smells like. I'll make sure and check so I can let you know when it's got that smell. Can I feel you now before the kids get back? They're looking in all the wrong spots anyhow."

"Oh yeah, just go slow. I like it better slow."

Clay pulled Randy's suit down until everything was freed. He felt through Randy's puff of soft pubic hair, fondled his tight wrinkled sack and firm balls for a moment and then slipped his hand up and over the head of Randy's penis. He looked down through the still water as he played with it. Randy's penis was thick and long, maybe four and a half inches. His tip was smooth and firm and, having lost his foreskin, was pink and puffy. Clay squeezed along his shaft slowly and felt a rush of mucus as he reached the tip. For only a second he felt how slippery it made his friend's penis feel before it mixed with the lake water.

Randy hummed with pleasure and ran one hand over Clay's chest and belly as he whispered, "Oh gosh, that feels great. Keep going until it gets close. I'll warn you in time. Watch for the kids, too. They're close to the spot. Mmmm, gosh that feels... Oh, stop, stop! Shit! Whew! That was too close. It came up so fast; I almost lost it. I'm gonna pull up my suit and let it rest a bit. The kids have the damned rock anyway." He announced loudly that Sajid just won a third point, but whispered to Clay, "I'd like to throw the damned stone halfway across the lake and keep 'em busy longer." They both laughed.

The younger boys said they were going to make this the last rock hunt. Sajid was too far ahead in points anyway. After they took off, Clay said, "What do you think we should do?"

"What, about the kids or us?"

"Us, I want to make it happen and I bet you do too. I can't hold it back much longer and I'm afraid it'll cut loose when you're not holding it. I really want to feel it come while you do it to me."

Randy agreed, "Me too. I'd really like to do you with my mouth, but that might be hard here with the kids around."

"Wow! You'd do that? I thought you said you couldn't do that to the other boy who taught you everything."

"That's when I was nine. I'm fourteen now and I love doing it. Claude loves it that way too. That's the way we most of the time now. I'd really like to do you that way too."

Clay looked around and said, "Let's just do it by hand today, but let's hurry. The kids might soon spot the rock and come back. Just do it by hand and maybe we can both feel it at the same time."

"Okay. I wish we could kiss while it happens. It makes it so much better that way, but with the kids and the lifeguard, we can't."

"Yeah, it's too risky."

"We'll do it by mouth out in the woods sometime soon. I know places where no one ever goes." Randy pulled down his suit and Clay did the same.

Clay felt such excitement as Randy fondled his scrotum lovingly and played in his pubic hair. Randy started stroking and squeezing him tightly, sliding his foreskin up and down. At one point, he pulled the skin back, left it that way exposing the sensitive, swollen tip and started rubbing Clay hard and slow. Clay was doing the same to Randy and both were climbing fast. He soon had to warn Randy to be cautious and ready to stop. They stared into one another's eyes and shivered occasionally from the nearly unbearable sensations.

"I'm awful close now too, Clay. Go slow and barely touch mine to keep me just at the edge. Tell me when you're about to come and then you can tighten your hand and we'll come together for sure," panted Randy, barely able to speak.

Somehow they both knew the moment had arrived as each

leaned slightly closer to one another. Randy turned his body more directly toward Clay below. Their hands slowed and tightened as they stroked and groaned as nature granted them blissful relief.

Each felt their inner muscles drawing back, more and more until the dam suddenly broke. Both looked down into the clear water to see silver jets of semen bursting from one another. Randy's free hand was reaching below Clay's scrotum and pressing upward where he could feel the powerful contractions as the semen raced along to his opening. Clay had clutched the base of Randy's organ and was squeezing as though to stop the unstoppable flow from within. Randy was jerking and twitching as pulse after pulse wracked his young body.

"Oh my god!" hissed Clay as he felt the most powerful orgasm of his life to that point. He wanted more than anything else to lean forward and kiss or even bite at Randy's lips but had to resist the urge.

"That felt so good," hissed Randy as he let go of Clay's penis and ran his hand lovingly up and over his new friend's belly and chest. Randy didn't seem to be bothered at all by the scars. Clay shivered from the meaningful touch.

He would have done the same to Randy, but just then Henry Winters squealed that he had finally found the stone.

Both tucked themselves back in quickly and prepared to greet the kids as they returned with the rock. Both smiled conspiratorially as the two younger boys joined them. Randy managed to say, "Uh, great game, fellows. You're both swimming much better already. We'll buy you each a candy bar at the camp store tonight. You earned it."

"How come you guys were just standing around talking?" asked Henry. "Don't you get bored just talking and not swimming?"

Randy grinned and tousled the boy's wet hair. "We had a great time getting to know each other better. We talked about several things; some were hard things to talk about with just anyone. A good friend, like Clay, is hard to find. You have no idea how uplifting our day has been. We're so glad we both came."

Clay rolled his eyes and nearly choked with suppressed laughter at the double meanings Randy was tossing about. He finally had to duck under water and expel a blast of air.

All four boys were shivering, ready to leave the water as their hands were wrinkled and their lips tinted blue from staying in the cool water so long.

Sajid and Henry ran ahead while Randy and Clay walked slowly together along the beach toward the boardwalk path to the cabins. It was only five-thirty and supper call wasn't until six. Clay whispered sarcastically, "A good friend is hard to find? I thought I was gonna choke when you said that, geez!"

Randy giggled and said, "I wanted to say a hard friend is good to find, but I couldn't. They might have figured that one out." Both boys shared another laugh.

As they walked, they saw Jerry coming from near the lifeguard tower. He waved and asked them to join him on several wooden chairs beneath a pavilion. They sat down and wondered what he had in mind.

"Fellows, I saw, from time to time, what a great job you did with the other kids today. You got them involved and made up a game on the fly. That shows initiative. You know what initiative means?"

Clay said, "I think it means you go ahead and do things on your own even though you don't have to."

"You're smart too."

"My dad said I was like that because he doesn't have to make or remind me all the time, to do my chores."

"Good. The colonel saw you as well and told me to issue you each five merits for coaching the boys." Randy and Clay looked at one another and smiled, considering their success.

"Cool," said Randy. We're seven ahead already, Clay. Oh, by the way, Jerry, How much would we get paid if we got counselor jobs here next summer?"

"Twenty dollars a week; plus everything else is included; meals, clothing, free snacks, your own room. It's a great summer job for ten weeks as the camp opens in mid-June and doesn't close until late August."

"Wow, that's two hundred dollars! I sure hope we can do it next summer," said Clay.

"Good. Now, fellows I have something else I want to talk with

154

you about. I was watching you pretty closely as best I could while doing my work and saw some of the other things you were doing while the kids played their game." Both boys felt their faces flush as Jerry gave them a critical eye.

"Remember I said to you guys when you arrived that I didn't care if you were queer or not. I sort of have a knack for spotting boys like you. Your eyes give you away every time. Randy, you always smile at Clay and your eyes often go right to his crotch. Clay, you do the same thing and like looking at Randy's butt when he turns around."

The boys were looking panicked by now so Jerry said, "Relax, I'm not going to tell. Anyone else would have had no idea what was going on beside that dock today. I just wanted to warn you to be very careful. You could have been spotted by someone *else* who *could* figure it out. Apparently, you two went for each other on sight. It happens sometimes at camp. You're here for a few weeks, experiment a little, go back home and go your own way. It's okay. I understand."

Randy was snuffling and said, almost sobbing, "You won't write it down or anything and tell our parents will you?"

"No, I won't tell. I know what you're going through and feeling. I only wanted to give you a warning to be very careful --- especially with Freedman. He's asked questions about where you guys are from and why you got those two merits the first day. That really twisted his dick for some reason. He's irrational sometimes."

"Why doesn't the colonel fire him?" asked Clay.

"Freedman's his brother-in-law. His wife won't let him. Freedman doesn't much like the colonel, even though he has an automatic summer job here. He's a teacher during the year and isn't paid well so he needs the work. A lot of the adult counselors are teachers working the summer months. Most are damned good with the kids too, but not Freedman. He's a junior high school gym coach in Frederick, Maryland. A few of his students have come here and told tales of what a horse's ass he is there too." Randy and Clay chuckled.

"But, back to you young lovers. Please be careful. If you really need some private time and can't find a place, let me know and maybe I can help you out."

Randy asked in a suspicious way, "Why would you do that?"

"Because, young Romeo, I'm as queer as the two of you. My

boyfriend's here too."

"Really," said Clay, wide-eyed and amazed. "Who is he?"

Jerry hesitated for a few moments before grinning and saying, "Todd Lincoln."

It took a few seconds before both boys realized who he'd just named.

"The colonel's son?" squealed Randy and Clay in unison.

Jerry laughed and said, "Yeah. He and I met here as campers about six summers ago and fortunately live close to one another. You two live apart so prepare yourself for that. In two weeks, you can get very attached to someone. I believe you guys were rather attached underwater today as a matter of fact." Jerry snickered, as did the boys. "You're both going to be heartbroken at the end of camp."

"I have a boyfriend back in Harper's Ferry called Claude, so I'll be okay."

"You're cheating on him?" Jerry asked with a degree of criticism.

"No, he's French," as if that explained everything, "He's told me to feel free to play around with other boys like us. He's done it too, but we still love each other. Clay has a friend back in Sand Patch, Pennsylvania he's just starting to love. We all plan to get together too. Clay can ride the trains for free."

Clay said, "My dad works for the B&O and is about to become a passenger train conductor."

"I'll be darned. You guys are planning to get a four boy thing going?"

"Uh huh." they both said with matching grins.

"Good luck. It usually doesn't work. Todd and I once involved a third friend and both he and I got jealous and worried about each other sneaking around. It almost broke us up, so be careful. Love can make people get crazy and sometimes even mean. Tread lightly."

Clay asked, "Does Todd know about us?"

"No, but with your permission, I'll tell him. That way he can help protect you if he sees you're about to get into trouble. Homosexual activities will get you tossed out of camp for good, so be careful. The colonel knows about Todd and me, but if it got out, he'd have to let us both go. You guys look great together, by the way. I see a lot of love between you already. I just hope you don't hurt your regular boyfriends. People like us have to be so very careful. In some parts of the country, the Ku Klux Klan will string you up for loving another guy. Maybe not when you're a kid, but once you're older you'll need to be careful. Keep a low profile and stick with your partner."

"We will. We're looking forward to telling our other boyfriends about us and what we did here in camp," said Randy.

"I hope they're open-minded. Hey, it's almost suppertime and I have to go and round up the rest of the dragon boys. Remember, be careful."

Clay said, "We will. And thanks, Jerry, for being such a great guy. Give our regards to Todd tonight."

Randy added, "Yeah, give him a kiss for us too."

Jerry laughed and said, "I will. See you guys after chow."

Chapter 15

Over the next three days, Clay and Randy were kept so busy, they had little time for anything more intimate than a few touch and feel sessions and a little kissing in the woods or just after lights out when no one was around.

Friday, however, was their overnight hike and campout and both were looking forward to breaking in Clay's new tent in more ways than one. The excursion would take them to a campsite called Fiddler's Bald near one of the highest ridges of Catoctin Mountain.

Sajid and Henry, the two thirteen-year-olds from Dragon Cabin, had been following Clay and Randy around like puppies all week, begging to share their tent too, once they learned how big it was. Jerry stepped to Clay and Randy's rescue telling the two younger boys that four to a tent was too many and encouraged them to share Henry's tent which was big enough for both.

Clay and Randy sighed inwardly with relief and thanked Jerry for his intervention once the two kids moved off.

Jerry laughed and said, "I'm not positive, but I think those two might be like the rest of us."

"Really?" asked Randy. "What makes you think so?"

I saw them wrestling and playing in the water yesterday and Henry definitely had a boner you could see from thirty feet away. I'm not sure about the Indian kid though. Maybe they need a night alone in their own tent to experiment a bit."

"Are there usually this many queer boys at camp?" asked Clay.

"Sometimes; most of the kids we get are boys that aren't good at sports or don't socialize well, so their folks send them here to force them to mix in while learning about things that interest them. You might have noticed, we don't stress rough and tumble team sports like football and basketball at Cunningham and most activities are geared for artistic, studious and quiet kids."

"Yeah, I wondered about that," said Randy. "I like it better that way."

"We offer activities where boys can challenge themselves and conquer their own fears and problems rather than compete all the time. The camp is advertised that way in area newspapers and magazines. Some competition is okay, like the canoe races and the track and field events, but a lot of the boys we get are often the weak ones on a team, or the ones who are different and don't get picked for teams at home. "

"Yeah," said Randy, "I've had that happen a lot."

"A lot of guys like us are that way to begin with, so we often have homosexual boys even though some of them haven't figured out what they are just yet. Some learn more than hiking, swimming and basket-making at camp," he said with a smile.

Clay said, "I'm kinda that way. I got left out of a lot of things because of the scars. I was never fond of team sports either for some of those reasons. After the fire, I had to learn all over again how to walk, let alone run, because of the tight scars and weak muscles from being in bed for so long. Now that I'm older, I can run pretty well. I might try out for track and field next year in high school."

"Yeah, I don't like rough sports," agreed Randy. "I'm clumsy with a baseball or basketball. I think I'm soon going to need glasses too. Things are a little blurry in the distance and I have to squint sometimes. Dad and Mom said as soon as I get back from camp, I'm going to see an eye doctor, before high school starts."

"My friend Albert's the same way. He's been dreading it, but I think he'll be getting glasses before high school too. I won't mind. I kind of like the way they make a boy look studious and smart."

"Todd's farsighted and needs glasses to read," said Jerry. "Well, I have duties to perform, so I'll see you two lovebirds later. Make sure all your stuff is packed before eight this evening. Lights out will be at nine instead of ten, so everyone's ready for an earlier start to the day. We get up at five tomorrow and board the buses right after an early breakfast." Both boys groaned, at the early wake-up time, but were still excited about the hike and campout.

That night, just after the lights went out, Randy, after running his hands inside Clay's pajamas for a quick squeeze, jumped up on his bunk and stretched out. Clay stood beside his bed and gave him a quick feel beneath the covers. They'd been doing this the last few nights as their special way of saying good night. It got them both in the mood for self-entertainment once they were under the sheets. Randy wanted to take a chance and see if they could get close, then sit on one bunk and finish up, but Clay said he didn't want to risk getting caught as some of the other boys in the cabin had already teased them about how they were always together.

After an early wakeup, without the usual cannon shot, the boys ate a big breakfast, gathered their gear and boarded camp buses that carried them several miles to where the trail to Fiddler's Bald began. It was about seven when they started along the four-mile trek to the ridge-top. For the most part, the trail was easy for the first two thirds of the way, but after that, the climb was steeper and by the time they reached the camping area near the summit, it was nearly eleven o'clock and some of the less fit boys were ready to drop.

Clay's calves were aching a bit, but otherwise, he and Randy had done well. Both had good, comfortable hiking boots. Clay's were brand new though and he discovered a couple of small blisters when he pulled them off to wash and cool his feet in a small stream that ran from a spring near the campsites. The top of the ridge was still another hundred feet above, but the camping area was on a level section of the slope, near the spring and stream.

Randy said, "While you soak your feet, I'm going to try and find a spot for our tent and lay claim. Once you finish, find me and bring the tent. I'll take the rest of our stuff with me. We'll set it up, or at least start, before lunch. I want to find a level spot a little distance from the rest of the crowd, but not too far from one of the latrines."

"That'll be good," Clay agreed.

"There're three outdoor toilets around the area, back in the woods. They're a little smelly and loaded with granddaddy long-leg spiders, but it beats squatting in the bushes."

Clay soaked a few more minutes before air drying his feet and putting on fresh socks. As he sat there, he washed the socks he had worn and wrung them out. He'd dry them at their campsite once Randy found one. Les, when he bought Clay's camping gear, had told him the importance, when hiking, of wearing fresh, clean socks to avoid foot problems. He missed Les and wished he was with them too, but of course, he wouldn't be able to do things with Randy if his new dad was along. Les had told him he would take Albert and him camping for several days before the end of the summer. That was something Clay really looked forward to.

Clay left the stream, grabbed the backpack with the tent and headed off in the direction he'd seen Randy go. Fiddler's Bald, the relatively flat area where they were camping, was what was called a laurel bald and, instead of woods, was covered with mountain laurel, rhododendron bushes and fields of wild grasses and wildflowers. Here and there among the laurel were clear grassy areas perfect for camping. The trails through the laurel were like a maze, but one could easily see over the bushes in most places. It wasn't long before he spotted Randy's head in a small clearing right next to the edge of the woods on the upslope side of the bald. Randy caught sight of him and waved him over.

The site Randy was guarding couldn't have been better. Due to the shape of the woods there, a small cove of flat, clear ground was surrounded on three sides by a dense wall of spruce trees. A single path through the laurel led to it, so they would not have any neighbors even though there was room for two tents in the area.

As soon as Clay joined him, Randy said, "Listen, I want to make sure we don't have any assholes setting up here with us, so you guard the stuff. I'm gonna find Sajid and Henry and invite them to set up their tent beside ours. Hold the spot for them while I'm gone. Jerry thinks they're like us and they're good kids. I'd rather have neighbors I know and trust than strangers who might say things about us later."

"Good idea. I passed them over that way," Clay pointed. "They were looking lost as usual and probably have no idea where a good site would be. Go find them, I'll unpack the tent."

Randy took off at a trot and within five minutes returned with two grinning kids who were positively ecstatic that their two heroes had invited them to share the site.

After shucking their packs, Henry flew to Clay and gave him a hug and a little kiss. Sajid hugged Randy, babbling how happy they were to be invited to camp with them. Their exuberance surprised both boys who grinned as they were squeezed by the younger boys. This could be another sign of their nature. After the initial hugs, Clay and Randy were again embraced as the kids traded hugging partners.

Randy said to Clay as soon as they were turned loose and alone. "Darn! I think we have two buddies for life. I thought Henry was gonna kiss me there for a moment."

"He probably was, 'cause he did give me one and then giggled. It's hard to believe they're thirteen. Both look a lot younger, maybe eleven. I'm not sure about Sajid just yet, but I think Henry's queer. He's always staring at Sajid's crotch when they go swimming. He likes watching bathing suits, especially the tight ones the camp gave us."

"I do myself, especially yours. But, yeah, I've noticed him. Henry often gives us a look too and I've seen him pulling at himself a couple of times and getting hard. He's queer and just trying to figure it out."

"They're both nice kids. I'm glad we asked them over. They'll probably be needing help setting up their tent and the other kids would have just teased them instead of helping. They're both pretty green when it comes to camping. In a way I am too, I guess. When's lunch?"

Randy checked his wristwatch and said, "We have about a half hour, it's cheese and bologna sandwiches and won't take long to pass out. Our meals up here, after that, will be camp-made stew, canned beans and vegetables, baked potatoes, corn and that sort of stuff."

Clay was puzzled. "How did they get all the food and stuff up here? I didn't see anyone toting any of it in."

"They cheat. There's a fire road nearby and they use a jeep and a trailer to bring the stuff up ahead of time. They take away the garbage after we're done the same way. I think the road's over that way. They keep the jeep handy in case someone gets hurt too." Randy pointed westward into the woods. "One of the outdoor toilets is over that way. That's the closest one to us."

It took Randy and Clay most of the half hour to set up their four-man tent and tell the other two boys how to get theirs set up. They did the best they could, but their tent was slightly lopsided. After chow, Clay and Randy would help them set it right. A bugler called assembly and they trotted off for lunch. By the time they got back and helped the boys finish their set up, it was about two o'clock and they had the rest of the afternoon to explore the area and do whatever they wanted. In the evening, there would be a communal campfire and some sort of Indian ceremony presentation by a guest visitor who was part Seneca Indian. All the boys were given a package of special clothes they would be wearing for the event.

Clay opened the pack and blinked at what was inside. There was a note that after the ceremony the "clothing" would be collected, as it was property of the camp.

"We have to wear this?" asked Clay holding up a simple cloth and leather device that would be tied around their waist. It was designed to cover their backside and front side with nothing more than a flap.

Randy laughed and said, "Yep, that and nothing else. No underwear or bathing suits allowed."

Clay said, "You're kidding. You mean we just hang out

underneath and behind this thing and hope no one peeks?"

"Not only that, but you have to sit, Indian-style, with your legs crossed and believe me, that little flap doesn't do much to cover your boy parts." He half whispered, "It's especially nice for guys like us though. Everyone sits in a circle around a really bright campfire while some boys jump and dance in nothing but war paint."

"Nothing at all --- naked?"

"Yeah, and believe me, as they jump and dance, all kinds of things flop around and wiggle. You'll love it."

"I'm just glad I'm not one of the dancers," said Clay. "All that shaking around with other naked boys would probably make me get hard."

"Welllll," said Randy with a grin. "You might end up being a dancer. They're chosen at random by the Indian guy who does the ceremony. He passes around a gourd with grains of corn in it. Most are yellow, but twelve are blue. Each boy takes a grain and if you get a blue one, it means the Great Spirit has chosen you for the dance. I hope we both get a blue corn, because it will give us an excuse to dance naked with one another and get away with it."

"You're crazy," said Clay with a laugh. "I hope we have corn on the cob for supper, 'cause I'm gonna hold back a few seeds so I can get out of dancing."

"The corn the Indian guy has is dried corn, so there's no way out of it, Clay. I'm hoping for blue corn for you and me both. We can help paint each other with war paint too. That should be fun in itself. I'm gonna paint two eyes on your dick and color the rest of it red, like a dragon, for Dragon Squad. Everyone will get a thrill when the dragon *comes* to life and rears its scary head." Randy started laughing and could hardly stop.

Sajid and Henry came over about that time and Henry asked, "What's so funny? Was it a joke? Tell us too."

Clay said, "Never mind. It's just Randy being silly."

Randy got himself under control and finally said, "No, no, it's a great story, fellows."

"Tell us, please," said Sajid.

"Okay. Once upon a time, there was a guy named Clay who had a dragon he was really attached to. One day the dragon felt real sad and just hung around Clay, but wouldn't do anything or say anything."

"Shut up, Randy," said Clay, turning red.

"No, tell us the rest," said Sajid. "I like stories about dragons. They are very, very beautiful and strong." Randy burst out laughing at that comment, but Sajid rattled on, "Was it a red dragon and could it breathe fire, Randy?"

Randy grinned like an imp, looked right at Clay and said, "Oh, no. Clay's dragon was pink and it didn't breathe fire. It spit white sticky stuff at..."

"That's enough, you idiot." Clay grabbed Randy, rolled him on the ground while laughing and said. "The story's over, guys. Randy's just making fun of me. It's a private joke. Go do something. Hunt for wild mushrooms, or fossils, or whatever. I don't want any witnesses when I strangle this fool." Clay was tickling his buddy's ribs and belly and Randy was laughing so much he could hardly breathe and was struggling to say something, but couldn't get it out.

Finally, he managed to say, "Oh, god, Clay, let me up. I've pissed myself."

"Huh?" Clay had straddled his buddy so his crotch was right against Randy's. He looked down at his and Randy's shorts and sure enough, both Randy *and Clay's* fronts were soaking wet. Tears were streaming from Randy's eyes and he was beginning to choke on laughter again.

Sajid giggled as he said, "Oooo! Randy has pissed on you, Clay. That is very, very bad. You will have to change your clothing now, or begin to smell odd."

Henry was rolling in the grass; holding his sides and laughing louder than anyone.

Clay got up, pulled his sodden shorts away from his body and said, "If any one of you guys says anything to anyone, I will sneak into your tent tonight and pee all over *you.* Got it?"

"Yes, Clay," said Sajid, still giggling. Randy was getting up and looking sheepish as he too pulled at his wet shorts.

Shy, quiet, Henry surprised everyone though when he said, "Clay, if you decide to pee on anyone for telling, can I watch?" He smiled and went over and crawled into his and Sajid's tent.

Randy, Clay and Sajid looked at one another speechless, until Randy laughed and then they all did.

Randy and Clay had to make a trip to the stream a little below camp to wash themselves and their clothing. The water at this elevation, having just come from a spring farther up-stream was icy cold and they certainly didn't stay long enough to do much of anything other than clean up. Both of their "pink dragons" went into hibernation in the chilly water and neither had any urge to wake them up.

Unbeknownst to them, Sajid and Henry had followed along behind and waited until Clay and Ray were both squatting naked in the stream washing themselves and their soiled clothes, before coming out of hiding and running off with their dry clothes.

Randy yelled, "This is war, you weasels! We know where you'll be sleeping tonight."

They ended up returning to the campsite in the wet, but clean clothes and found their dry things decorating an oak tree near the tents. One of the culprits had erected a crude flagpole using a sapling. Flying from it was their underwear.

Clay collected his clothes and after they went in their tent to change, he asked Randy, "Hey, do they tell anyone in advance about what they have to do if they get a blue corn seed?"

"No. Guys who've been here before keep it a secret for the most part. The Indian guy passes around the gourd at the beginning of the ceremony. After everyone gets a seed they ask who has the blue corn and those boys are led off for instructions and the war paint."

"Great. I know how to get back at our little clothing snatchers." He whispered his idea to Randy who roared with laughter and said Clay's idea was brilliant.

Clay and Randy called to the boys who approached warily, expecting revenge. Clay set them at ease by praising them on their clever prank at the stream. He then told them, "Hey fellows, we really like you guys. You're a lot of fun to have along and we wanted to clue you in on a secret. Tell 'em, Randy."

"Tonight there's this Indian ceremony called the Corn Dance, where they pass around a gourd with dried corn in it. In the gourd are twelve blue corn seeds and the rest are all yellow. The lucky boys who get the blue grains get all kinds of neat Indian artifacts to take home: arrowheads, bows, arrows, and all kinds of Seneca stuff. They get to dress up like Indian braves and dance around the fire in war paint for everyone to enjoy. They don't tell anyone ahead of time, so we wanted to help you guys win the prizes."

Clay picked up the conversation: "We're going to give you guys each two dollars you can use to try and buy a blue corn each from the kids who get them. You'll have to do it as soon as you see

165

another kid get blue corn, though, because once the leaders tell what it's for, no one will want to sell. If one of us gets a blue corn, we'll give it to one of you and you can keep the money we give you for something else. You interested?"

"Oh yes," said Sajid. "I am already Indian, but not the American kind," he giggled. "I would like very, very much to have American Indian things for my bedroom."

"Me too," said Henry. "Won't we owe you back two dollars though?"

"No, this will be our treat. Seeing you boys after you get your prizes will make our evening," said Randy. "You guys will look great in Indian make up. Here you go." Randy handed each boy a crisp, two-dollar bill.

Henry said, "Wow, a two dollar bill. One of my friends at school said that two dollar bills are unlucky for anyone who spends them."

"Not tonight, fellows."

"Yeah," said Clay. "I wish I had a camera, because I'd love to take a picture of you guys after you're dressed like Indians for the corn dance."

The younger boys ran off to their tent happy with their good fortune. Clay and Randy laughed for several minutes and could hardly wait for the evening's ceremony.

Jerry happened by, stuck his head in their tent and asked what was so funny. After telling him what they were planning, he grinned and shook his head, "You guys deserve the Gauntlet for a stunt like that. That's just plain cruel taking advantage of those two babes in the woods."

"Hey, we're just getting even," said Randy and told Jerry of the youngsters' earlier prank.

"You're not getting even, you're escalating the war." He grinned nevertheless and said, "Hummm. It should be fun to watch."

After dinner, the camp was abuzz with the evening's upcoming event. It was a tradition for more experienced campers to keep silent about the Corn Dance and so there was little chance that Henry and Sajid would discover what was really about to befall them.

Just before dark, everyone was told to dress in their loin covers and report to the campfire area. Clay and Randy were having fun helping each other change into the very brief outfits and both had problems with physical reactions as they helped each other tie on the outfits using the attached leather thongs. When finished both boys had to keep pushing down on their front panel; for some reason they wanted to rise, even though there was no wind blowing. They finally got themselves under control and left the tent. They found seats side by side as soon as possible and did the best they could to sit Indian-style and still keep their better parts covered.

Clay was pleased to see that many of the other boys seemed unconcerned and did little to guard the family jewels from roving eyes like Randy's and his. As they gazed across the fire pit, they whispered back and forth making comments about one boy or another as to who they found to be interesting. Sajid and Henry finally showed up looking sheepish as they too tried their best to keep themselves covered. Both had brought along their two dollar bills and held them folded and hidden in their hands. All of the seats on either side of Clay and Randy were taken, so the younger boys had to settle for a spot farther around the circle from their friends.

Sajid was less preoccupied with looking around at other boys, but quiet and timid Henry's eyes were wide open and gawking everywhere. Clay laughed and said to Randy, "Look at Henry. He has to keep mashing down on his front cover. Poor kid; he's got it bad."

"Yeah, Sajid comes from India. I think going without clothes is less of an issue over there. I've seen pictures in the National Geographic and kids in that part of the world run around naked all the time."

"I still think he might be like Henry and us, though. I wonder if they've done anything with each other yet."

"I don't know. I'd like to be a bug on the wall of their tent tonight. We better stop whispering, It's about to begin and the gourd will soon make its rounds."

Colonel Lincoln dressed in a buckskin outfit stepped into the glare of the giant bonfire that had flared up as a number of the junior counselors tossed bundles of fresh pinewood on the pyre. Clay felt a little uneasy as the flames doubled in height and the heat reached out toward him. He scooted backward about six inches as he told himself, *It's okay. It's safe and I'm far enough away from it to be safe. I'm almost fifteen and like Uncle Warren said, I have to get over this.* It was about the only good advice the man had ever given the boy, although he did little else to help Clay conquer his fear of fire.

167

The colonel introduced their guest for the evening, a man named Sam Starshadow, who was half Seneca Indian. He talked for a few minutes about his people and their history and said that this evening he was going to teach them about a dance his people once performed to celebrate a good harvest, and to call for continued good fortune. It had become a tradition for all boys at Camp Cunningham to participate in the rite.

"Some of you boys will be honored and invited by the Great Spirit to dance this evening for the entire troop of boys. To choose, I'll pass around the great circle with a gourd that contains many seeds. There's one seed for every boy here. Twelve of the seeds are special and the Great Spirit Himself will decide what boys find the holy seeds. Reach in and take only one. Do not show it to any others as you look at it cupped in your hand.

"After all have taken a seed, I will tell you which seeds are the ones Tei-che Man-nit-to --- the Great Spirit --- has chosen to be his dancers. It is a great honor to dance for Tei-che Man-nit-to, and preserve the old ways, lest they be forgotten. You need not be embarrassed to dance for him and his glory. Only twelve will be chosen; only twelve will honor the Great Spirit of air, earth, fire and water."

The man slowly walked around the circle as a number of other boys began pounding a large drum slowly and softly while another played a haunting wooden flute of some kind. An Indian boy, or maybe one dressed as one, threw a handful of ground leaves on the fire, it suddenly flared up, and a wave  of scented smoke filled the area. It was sweet and reminded Clay of the sage he'd used when cooking at home. From time to time, the youth with the powdered leaves tossed more on the fire until the sweet, exotic scent was everywhere.

He saw the gourd pass the two boys. Sajid, peeked into his hand and looked disappointed, but Henry grinned as he opened his hand. Apparently, he had gotten lucky and gotten a blue corn seed. Sajid started whispering to nearby boys and Clay and Randy were pleased to see that the third boy he spoke to looked around to make sure he wasn't being watched and then exchanged his seed with Sajid as Sajid handed him a two-dollar bill. The stage was set for their little plan.

The gourd came to Clay and he reached in and retrieved a seed. Randy did the same. Both peeked into their palms and were surprised to see they each had blue seeds.

"Oh crap!" said Randy. "I got one."

"Me too, darn it. We have to trade them off for a yellow seed."

They started frantically asking if any boys near them had a yellow seed. Clay found a boy nearby who did. Clay told him he would give him two bucks later if he would trade. The boy agreed and the seeds changed hands. Poor Randy was frantic and, because he couldn't get up and walk from where they were seated, he passed the word along, saying he would pay anyone five bucks when they returned to the tents to trade a blue corn for a yellow one. Six boys down he found a taker and just before Mr. Starshadow reached the last of the boys in the circle, the seeds were traded.

Both Randy and Clay looked at one another and collectively sighed with relief. "Whew! That was close," said Clay.

"Yeah, now the fun begins. Those two both have blue corn. Any minute Chief Starshadow's gonna call for the blue corn."

The Seneca gentleman set the now empty gourd on the ground and chanted something in his native language as the whole crowd became very quiet. He threw something into the fire and blue flames shot up and for the next few minutes, the entire fire glowed blue.

As the flames gradually turned back to yellow, Mr. Starshadow said in a quiet and ominous voice, "Tei-che Man-nit-to has chosen. Within your hand, you each hold the seed of his choice. Tei-che Man-nit-to has spoken; he has told me that this night was to be special and different. He told me that the yellow corn would mark his choice. Will all braves with yellow corn please stand up and gather with me here before the fire."

Ten boys around the circle stood and moved toward Starshadow. Two other boys felt their world spin off kilter as they realized what had just happened.

"There are two more somewhere. Tei-che Man-nit-to has chosen twelve," said Mr. Starshadow. "Who are the other two? Please stand up and join us before the fire."

Two sheepish lads gritted their teeth and stood. Across from them, Sajid and Henry were looking hurt and angry, thinking they'd

169

been cheated by their heroes. Clay and Randy joined the chief who told them to follow another Indian youth.

As they passed by Jerry, they heard him whisper, "It's really wrong for an older kid to pick on younger, innocent kids, but I did it anyway. My uncle, Sam Starshadow, owed me a favor."

Chapter 16

It must be said, the two would-be pranksters took their *medicine* well. They striped, they donned their war paint --- without any creative dragon art --- and danced around the fire with their other ten sufferers, one of whom was Mack Ford, the boy from Dragon Cabin with the pale white hair. Neither Randy nor Clay were prone to unwanted erections throughout the spectacle for they were much too embarrassed to even think about sex even though Clay privately thought Mack had a cute rear end as he was dancing right in front of him the whole time.

After the ceremony, they settled their debts with the two boys from whom they'd bought the yellow corn. It was no wonder both of them got blue seeds to begin with, as all but twelve of the seeds in the gourd were blue. The boy Randy arranged to pay five dollars to, had a hard time figuring out why Randy and Clay wanted to dance naked in front of sixty other boys, but was glad to give up the yellow corn for a five and went so far as to thank Randy for bailing him out. Randy smiled, but secretly felt an urge to hit the boy.

The rest of the evening was spent playing flashlight tag in the laurel maze for nearly an hour before getting ready for bed. By now, Henry and Sajid had figured out what had happened and the ribbing the older boys got from those two was nearly unbearable. Clay and Randy swore an oath to one another that somehow, before the fortnight sojourn at camp was over, they would get even with Jerry for his well-executed prank. They both agreed it would be best to wait until the very last day to do it though, to reduce their chance of being retaliated against before their folks carried them safely away from Camp Cunningham and Jerry.

By ten, all four boys were growing weary and, right after a camper count to make sure all boys were present and accounted for, they returned to their two tents. Just before he followed Sajid into their tent, Henry stepped over to Clay and said, "Even though you guys tried to trick us into dancing naked tonight, I still like you a lot. Along with Sajid, you're about the best friends I've ever had. I'm going to miss you guys so much next week when we have to go home." There were tears forming in the sensitive lad's pale, hazel eyes.

"We'll miss you too, Henry. Do you live near Sajid?"

"No. He lives in Rockville, Maryland, near Washington D.C. and I live in Cresaptown, Maryland, a little south of Cumberland."

Clay said, "Well that's not so bad then. I live just north of Cumberland in a little town called Sand Patch, Pennsylvania. I'll have my dad drive me down to see you sometime. Maybe you can come to visit me too. I know you like Sajid, but Washington is a long way to travel."

"It would be really nice to visit you. Sometime after we get back to the camp, Clay, I want to talk to you about something. It's real important."

"Is it something you need to talk about now?"

"No, it can wait. I'm kinda sleepy now anyway. I love you and Randy too as my best friends and I trust you especially to give me an honest answer about something. I'm always so darned shy, but I feel good talking to you. You and Randy tease, but you do it 'cause you're my friends."

"You bet we are, Henry. I'll see you in the morning. Goodnight." Clay reached out to give the boy's shoulder a squeeze, but as usual, Henry hugged him and kissed his cheek gently. Clay leaned forward, kissed the boy's forehead, and told him to sleep well.

Clay told Randy what had happened, and Randy smiled and said, "I bet he's going to ask you about being queer. He might have figured us out too. He's a nice kid. He looks about eleven, but he's growing up."

Clay agreed, "Yeah, he's pretty long and real fuzzy down below already."

Randy giggled and said, "Sajid looks like he's wearing a black, steel wool pad between his legs and under his arms. He's even got a mustache too, but still looks like an eleven-year-old. Maybe Indian boys grow up differently. Both are great kids."

Once inside the tent, Randy looked at Clay and Clay stared back at him with a smile. The tent was lit by a large, three battery, flashlight Randy owned. While Clay talked to Henry, Randy had arranged their sleeping bags side by side on the canvas floor of the tent. He had a sheet and a blanket spread in such a way for both of them to cover up with. Neither intended to sleep apart, and seeing the bed made this way made Clay feel nice inside. It also made him feel somewhat guilty. He missed Albert and remembered how his best friend had snuggled against him the last time he slept over in

Clay's bed.

He enjoyed what he and Randy had done this past week and was sure he'd enjoy what they were about to do here this evening. Randy kissed him and touched him, but he got the impression that Randy loved the sex more than anything. He was very physical and was fun to be with, but with Albert, Clay felt a deeper kind of attachment. Albert loved him first and foremost as a special friend. The sex would maybe come soon and be wonderful. With Randy, the sex seemed the driving force in their friendship. It led to a kind of love, but was it the very real, deep kind that Albert had shown him for years, long before either of them had felt the powerful sensations of sex?

Clay was thinking some truly grown-up thoughts that evening as he prepared to have sexual fun with Randy. He felt better about it knowing that Albert was special and would always be there. Randy had Claude and Clay was sure the boy loved his French buddy much the way he himself loved Albert. Clay was young and trying out his wings, so to speak, with Randy. He looked at the tall, good-looking lad who had striped to his underwear and was lying on the sleeping bag already sporting an erection beneath his briefs.

Clay felt himself hardening and started taking off his clothing. As he crawled along and snuggled beside Randy, his buddy switched off the flashlight and they moved close together. Clay felt Randy pulling off his briefs, so he did the same. For a while, they lay on their sides and pushed themselves close together with their genitals pressed hard against their pubic areas. After a few minutes of this, as both became aroused enough to feel moisture, Clay felt Randy shift downward, take hold of him and soon felt the boy's warm lips kissing and then enveloping his sex.

That night they made love several times trying new things and feeling new sensations as they built memories that would last a lifetime. It was Clay's first time experiencing oral sex and he hoped the day would someday arrive when he and Albert could love each other in this new exciting way. Afterward, both were nearly spent and Clay just managed to throw the sheet and light blanket over them before both drifted off to sleep curled together like two puppies. Dawn found them much the same way and before leaving the tent, they coupled again quickly. Shortly thereafter, they heard the bugle call reveille.

Morning and afternoon on the mountain was spent hiking to and exploring a small cave and visiting a vertical rock-face where very nice fossils could be easily located and removed from the soft limestone. Clay found a beautiful, three-inch wide, crinoid "flower"; actually the head and mouthparts of a long-stemmed echinoderm --- a starfish relative --- that lived in the Ordovician Period of earth's geologic history, roughly four hundred, and fifty million years in the past. Randy found several, four-inch-long, belemnites --- primitive, squid-like mollusks that resembled black, three-inch-long cornucopias. The naturalist instructor who led the fossil hunt identified everything they found.

By three o'clock, it was time to break camp and hike down the mountain trail for pickup by the camp buses. All the campers were tired, but happy, as they boarded and rode back to Camp Cunningham. Supper was ready by the time they arrived. After chow, everyone pitched in and spruced-up the entire camp in preparation for Parent's Day. Clay could hardly wait to see Les, and Randy was anxious to introduce Clay to his mom, dad and younger sister.

About an hour before lights out, Henry asked to speak privately with Clay. He didn't mention including Randy, but Clay let Randy know and he wasn't bothered by the request. In fact, Randy said, "He's probably going to ask about sex stuff and feels a little shy talking to two guys instead of one. I think he takes to you more anyway, Mr. Hero." Clay blushed slightly and scoffed at the title.

Clay walked a little way from the cabins with Henry until they came to a small covered picnic table under several tall oak trees. A single light on a pole nearby lit the area. "So, Henry, what's up? How can I help you?"

"Henry was silent for a few moments and gazed at the ground before saying, "Clay, I need to talk to someone I trust a whole lot. You and Randy tease us some, but I trust you both. I would have asked him along too, but I was kind of shy. Also, you live near me and I might see you again sometime if our folks are able to drive us to see each other. I know you're a year older than me and I'm kind of small for thirteen, so I guess to you I seem like a little kid, but I'm not."

"I don't think of you that way. Everybody grows at a different speed. I bet you've been growing a lot lately since turning thirteen." Clay thought he'd bring up the subject and perhaps give Henry a starting place.

"Uh huh, a lot of things have been changing and I'm confused by some of the crazy thoughts that go through my head." He paused a moment before adding, "Clay, I'm afraid."

"What are you afraid of, Henry?"

"I think I'm going crazy. I'm afraid my mind is sick. I have an uncle that had to be put in a home because his mind was sick and... Oh, god, Clay! I don't want to be put away like that." The boy started sobbing, leaned against Clay's side, and began to bawl as his body shook with emotion. He sobbed, "Mom said they had to put wires on my uncle and shock him with electricity, trying to make him well." Henry's hands were trembling and he started biting one nail on his right hand.

Clay put his right arm around the kid and said, "It's okay, Henry. Now, tell me what's got you so sure you're going crazy. I don't believe it, myself. I haven't seen any signs of insanity. You're a very nice boy. You're kind of quiet and sometimes shy, but I like you that way. I'm that way myself sometimes. We're buddies now and you can tell me what's eating at you. Come on."

It took a few minutes for Henry to get over his cry. Clay loaned him a clean handkerchief to dry his eyes and smiled as Henry blew his nose loudly, then offered the handkerchief back. Clay smiled and told him to keep it.

"I'm sorry, Clay. I'm just so mixed up about things. I have weird dreams and I think about stuff during the day that's just not normal. I'm afraid I'm not going to be like other boys and it makes me scarred."

Clay was beginning to see Randy and he had been right about what was going on with the boy, so he gave him another hug. "Henry, I bet I know what's wrong. I've been watching you this week and I want you to know that I believe I understand what's bothering you so much."

"You do? I'm not sure how you could know what's really wrong with me."

"Tell you what. I'm going to whisper it in your ear and you tell me if I'm right or wrong. Okay?"

"Okay."

"Lean over here, buddy." Henry did and Clay whispered, "I think you are all upset because you like boys instead of girls."

Henry sat up straight and gazed at Clay open-mouthed, as if he was a god. "How did you know that?" he said in awe. His eyes were moving all over Clay's face as Clay smiled and ruffled Henry's soft hair.

"A lot of boys, when their bodies start changing find out that not all boys like girls. Some boys are attracted to other boys and it's not because they're going crazy. Boys like that are called homosexuals and sometimes are called queer."

"Oh, please, Clay, don't tell anyone. I've heard other boys talk about queers and make terrible fun of them. Please don't tell."

"I won't, Henry. That's your secret and friends keep each other's secrets. In a few minutes, I'll tell you one of my secrets, so we'll both have a secret to keep. Okay?"

"Okay. But, how did you know?"

"Henry, I've seen you looking at Sajid in his bathing suit and I saw you peeking at all the boys around the campfire night before last. Randy and I saw how much trouble you were having keeping your penis from pushing up your Indian outfit."

"What's a penis?"

Clay just stared at the boy. "Wow! No one's ever told you anything have they?" A penis is that interesting thing between your legs that keeps getting hard every time you think about the interesting thing between Sajid's legs. Some boys call it a dick, a wiener, or a prick, but those are all slang words. The real word is penis. Understand?"

"I think so. Why is it that I can't stop thinking about them? I even dream about them. Mine's always getting hard and I'm afraid someone will see it and laugh. Did Randy laugh at me when he saw me trying to hold down my Indian pants? I hated wearing that stupid thing."

"Yeah, me too, but aren't you glad all the other boys had to wear one and you got to peek?" Clay said with a chuckle.

Henry had to grin and half whispered, "I guess so. Yeah, I did."

"What about the dance, Henry? Did you like seeing Randy and me making a spectacle of ourselves? I bet you had a good old time seeing us parading around with everything dangling."

"Oh no, Clay, I turned my eyes aside whenever you and Randy danced nearby."

"Henry! Just when we're starting to make progress, you go and tell a fib. Fess up, kiddo. I saw you looking at mine every time I passed. That's another reason I was able to tell you like boys. What did you think of mine?"

Henry was blushing and looked like he was about to start crying again, so Clay gave him a side hug and whispered, "I don't mind that you wanted to take a look at me. I'm flattered. It doesn't bother me. Randy wouldn't care either. We both understand. You ready to hear my secret now?"

Henry sniffed and said, "I guess. What is it?"

Clay leaned close once more and said, "I like boys too and so dies Randy. We're both the same way you are. Now, do you feel better? You're not all alone and you sure aren't crazy."

Henry was unable to say much of anything as his mouth was gaped open like a fish. Clay laughed, reached over, pushed his chin up, and said, "Careful Henry, you'll swallow a junebug."

Henry finally snapped out of it and said, "You mean that you like looking too?"

"That and even more --- so does Randy. It doesn't bother me that you wanted to look at me at the corn dance. Like I said, I'm flattered. So, what did you think about it?"

"Think about what, the dance?"

"No, my penis! Did you like how it looks? I've seen yours and it's kinda nice. Your hair down there is nice to look at too. It looks soft and fuzzy."

Henry was turning scarlet and Clay said, "I'm telling the truth, Henry. I'm trying to let you know that between you and me you don't have to be so shy and embarrassed. I know what kind of things go through your mind because they go through mine. I don't know why some boys turn out the way we do, but it happens. We can't change ourselves either. You won't grow out of it and you won't go to hell over it like some preachers will tell you. The best thing you can do, Henry, is to accept it and have fun once you find another boy your age who likes boys too."

"But how do I know if another boy is weird like me?"

"It's hard to do sometimes. What about Sajid? Have you ever seen him staring at you down below? Has he ever grabbed at your crotch when you guys wrestle or romp in the water?"

"No, he never grabbed me down there. He brushed against my butt once in the water a few days ago. And once he bumped into my front when I was all stiff and he giggled and said something in Indian."

"Did you ask him what he said?"

"Yeah, but he said he couldn't tell me."

"Did he touch you again?"

"Yeah, it happened once when we were swimming. But that time might have been an accident."

"He might be like you. Did he do anything odd in the tent last night?"

Henry blushed and said nothing.

"Come on, something happened. What was it?"

"He didn't do anything odd."

"Something just made you blush. I'm glad you blush, Henry, it always tells me when you're keeping something in here." Clay grinned and rapped on Henry's head affectionately.

"You won't think I'm weird or anything, will you?" Clay assured him he wouldn't. "Well, last night, when Sajid was asleep, I kissed him."

"That's all. Heck, you kissed me last night and I was awake. That's another reason I knew you were queer like me. Be careful doing that. It's kind of a dead giveaway."

"I know. I did it before I realized I'd done it. Somehow, I knew you wouldn't mind."

"So all you did was kiss Sajid?" Henry nodded but started blushing again.

"Oh, Oh, the blush-o-meter says you're hiding something. Fess up, Henry Winters."

"I touched his uh, penis thing too." Henry giggled. "But he was asleep, I think."

"And?"

"It got harder." It was already hard, but when I touched it, I felt it jump and get real hard. Mine did too."

"Was this touch from outside his clothes, or from inside?"

"Uh, at first it was through his underwear, then later it was outside his underwear. His thing just popped out."

"How'd that happen? Did you help it along a little? Might as well tell me before the blush-o-meter goes off."

Henry giggled. "Uh, I helped a little. His thing was pointing up along his belly and when I touched him and it stood up, I felt the opening in his underwear open up and I sort of guided his underwear up and over it, so it was outside."

"Weren't you afraid he would wake up?"

"Not too much. Sajid sleeps real sound and snores. His snoring never changed."

"So after you let his penis out for an evening stroll, what did you do?"

Henry giggled, "I looked at it with my flashlight. I have a little light my dad gave me on my key-chain."

"So, what did he look like?"

"He's real brown and wrinkled. He's like you with a ring of wrinkled skin on the end of his thing, but his whole thing is dark brown, almost like a colored person's skin. The wrinkled part was the darkest."

"Did you touch him then?"

"Uh huh. I couldn't believe how hard he was. I'd seen another boy once with wrinkled skin, but I didn't know it moves and slides around. How come some boys are born with extra skin and some aren't?"

"Oh, Henry --- that sounds like a candy bar --- Henry, every boy is born with the skin. A lot of parents have it cut  off right after you're born. That's what was done to yours."

"They had it cut off? My mom and dad had me operated on?"

Clay nodded yes and went on to explain the reasons and the process. Henry looked completely shocked and said, "Wow! I never knew that. I'm learning a lot from you tonight. Uh, talking like this makes my thing get hard, does it do that to you?

"Yep. Mine's hard right now. Bet yours is too, right?"

"Uh huh. Wet stuff runs out sometimes too. Do I have an infection or anything?"

"No, Henry. That's normal. Have you ever had white stuff squirt out?"

"No. Is it supposed to?"

Clay realized it was getting late and almost time for lights out. In fact, just then, the loudspeaker called for all campers to return to their cabins. "Lights out in ten minutes," said Clay. "Let's go. Tomorrow, you and I will talk some more because I have a lot more to tell you. You're going to learn things at camp this year you never thought you'd learn. You're a little behind in your education and I'm going to bring you up to date, so you'll better understand what being a teenager is really about. You're a nice guy, Henry and I like you a lot."

"I like you too, Clay. Can I give you a hug?"

179

Let's wait until we're out from under the bright light, but yes, when we get close to the cabin you can, as long as no one is in sight. I like being hugged as much as you do. Don't kiss me though unless we're completely alone, or we could both get into trouble. You're not a little boy any more and kisses mean altogether different things now."

"I love you, Clay."

"I know, Rascal. I love you too as one of my best buddies."

"Rascal?"

"Yeah; that's my new nickname for you since I know you feel on other boys while they're sleeping and do secret, midnight, flashlight exams."

Henry grinned and laughed.

"I want to know more about your late night explorations tomorrow too. It's best not to do that, by the way, until you know for sure another boy doesn't mind it. Here we are. A quick hug now and then head off to your room. Remember, Rascal, keep your hands to yourself tonight."

Chapter 17

Sunday morning arrived with the usual cannon shot. Clay no longer sprang from the bed as though a war was about to begin. He opened his eyes, yawned and stretched. After wishing Randy a good morning and giving his prominent front a careful squeeze after making sure no one was looking, he padding off to the restroom along with Randy and half the other boys in his side of Dragon Cabin to relieve themselves.

As he and Randy stood side by side at two of the urinals, Henry came in and stood on Clay's other side. He said with a cute grin, "Good morning. I was good last night."

"Morning, Rascal. Are you getting a visit from your folks today? I was going to ask you last night, but we ran out of time." Clay shook off and tucked in. He noticed that both Randy and Henry gave his efforts a glance as he did it. Somehow, it was nice to feel wanted and lusted after. He realized that he had taken two glances to either side himself, so he couldn't complain. *We all have it bad.* He couldn't help smiling as he stepped away from the porcelain and waited for Henry's reply. He saw the boy shiver as he finished his business and tucked in too.

Henry answered as they all washed their hands at a row of sinks, "Mom and Dad said they were coming when I called them on Thursday, so yeah, I think they'll be here. It's a long way to travel, but I think they'll come see me. Sajid's parents are coming if his dad gets back from India. He had to make an airplane trip there. Sajid says it takes about sixty hours to fly back home from there."

"I bet it does. India's half way around the earth," said Randy.

"I know. His dad does some kind of work for the Indian government and works in Washington, D.C. at an emmacy."

"Where *is* Sajid this morning?" said Randy looking around for the boy, but didn't spot him.

"He should be along in just a few minutes. He said he had to make a call home to remind his family about Parent's Day and see if they were coming."

By that time, the boys were in the main day room and Sajid entered through the front door looking very happy. He joined them and said, "I have just talked to my mother. She and Father are very, very well and will be coming today. You will all be able to meet them and my sisters. Father is back and has been assigned a permanent job at the Indian embassy, so now we will be able to buy an American house to live in instead of having to rent a stuffy, hot apartment."

"Good," said Henry. "I just wish you lived closer to me and we could see each other during the school year. I guess we might have to wait until next year and maybe see each other at camp if you decide to come back next summer."

"Oh I will. I will also ask my father to let me visit you at your home sometime this year. It is not too far to travel to Cumberland. I have looked it up on a map which told me Rockville is one hundred twenty miles from Cumberland. Father's job permits him to have a driver take him and family members places, so once in a while, if your parents say it is allowed, I will come to see you."

"Would they let you take a train?" asked Clay.

"I might be able to. The American trains are much safer than Indian trains that are very, very crowded and often run off the rails and crash. They are so crowded that people ride on the roof of the carriages, or hang on the sides."

"No kidding?" said Randy. "That's dangerous all right."

Clay continued: "The reason I ask, is that my Dad will soon be a conductor on passenger trains and if he's working a train that runs between Washington and Cumberland, he could watch out for you while you travel. Your parents wouldn't have to worry as much if he was watching."

"Oh, that would be very, very good. Maybe they can meet your conductor father and speak about that."

"Dad will be here today, so I'll ask if he'd be willing to help you out."

After breakfast and a final clean up of the camp for Parent's Day, the boys had the rest of the morning to do whatever they wished. All four decided to go canoeing. They had taken a brief class in canoe handling earlier in the week and Sajid and Henry were certified for water activities now that they had passed their swimming examination. They launched two canoes and headed northward in the direction of a small, wooded island easily visible about a mile from the shores of the camp.

Only campers thirteen and older were allowed to explore there without a counselor's presence. The island was as far as they would go on this trip, as they had to be back for Parent Day activities scheduled to begin shortly before lunchtime. Parents were encouraged to eat in the mess hall with their boys and chow would be served in two shifts to accommodate everyone. Dragon Squad boys were scheduled for the second meal shift, but all campers were to be in camp, and ready by eleven to greet parents. It was seven-thirty when the boys left for the island, so they had plenty of time.

They had a good time exploring and running along the island's trails. Most of their fun was due to the fact that they were the only four people on the small island that day. On the east side of the island was a small cove shaped like a miniature lake in itself as the two half-circle, spits of land that enclosed it, nearly touched. It was a great swimming area with a sand and pebble bottom. The water was no deeper than eight feet, and the four boys, at Clay's urging, decided to skinny dip instead of wear their bathing suits. Clay suggested it on purpose not only for Randy and his enjoyment, but for the other two. He figured maybe if Sajid was of Henry's persuasion, he might exhibit some behavior that would help Henry know where the boy stood.

Clay and Randy watched as Sajid and Henry romped and wrestled in the warm water; it was obvious that both had moments of arousal. Whether that was a result of sexual excitement, or due to simple physical contact, they couldn't be sure, but Sajid certainly didn't appear to be shy and was very physical with not only Henry, but with the two of them. Henry seemed to be a very happy camper and grinned at Clay from time to time, especially after Sajid had crawled all over him during their play.

They left the island by ten and headed back to camp. At Clay's suggestion, they switched canoe partners for the return trip. He wanted to ask Henry a few pertinent questions about what happened in their tent on the campout and what might have occurred at the hidden cove today.

Once they were underway, Clay asked, "Did you have fun swimming with Sajid, Rascal?"

"And how. Thanks, Clay. I've been wanting to swim naked with him, but was too chicken to ask. Besides, up to now, we haven't been anywhere that we could do it in private. He grabbed at me a couple of times and every time I was hard. I grabbed him back and it didn't bother him at all. He just laughed and grinned. What do you think?"

"I think you may have found a buddy who likes the same things you do. I don't think any boy who likes girls would grab another boy's penis especially if it was hard. I wanted to ask you something else, but we ran out of time the other night when we were talking outside."

"Sure. I don't feel as shy now talking to you. I was so glad to find out you were like me; that makes it easier to talk."

"Thought so. You said you gave his thing a little help escaping his underwear that night and looked it over with your flashlight."

"Uh, huh, Sajid's real dark-skinned down there. His hair is real black and thick too, like wool. I think the dark skin is because he's from India."

"Sure. Indians are often dark-skinned. Remember we talked about the extra skin boys are born with. How do you feel about the fact your parents decided to have yours removed?"

"I kinda wish I still had it, but I guess there's nothing I can do about it."

"After you looked Sajid over in your tent that night, did you do anything else?"

Henry grinned and said. "I touched him and watched it move and get harder. I reached inside his underwear, down below and felt his sack too. His sack is small and tight against his body. I could feel his balls inside."

"Do anything else?"

"No. I wanted to, but he groaned and moved, so I turned off the light and stayed real still. In a few moments, he coughed and rolled over on his side away from me. I waited, hoping he would turn my way with his thing still hanging out, but I was tired and next thing I knew it was morning."

"I was wondering if you pulled his skin all the way down and uncovered the tip of his penis. Did you?"

"Yes, just a little way though. I wasn't sure how far down it would go, or if it would hurt him and maybe wake him up. Does it pull down very far?"

"Yeah, it slides all the way down and over the edge of the rim. It'll stay there if you don't pull it back up."

"Wow, I didn't know. I'd like to see how that works."

Clay gave some thought to what Henry had just said as they paddled along. Apparently, Henry was deep in thought as well and from time to time pulled at his shorts and adjusted his bathing suit within. It was obvious he was having a serious erection. They were trailing well behind Randy and Sajid.

Clay said, "Listen, Henry, I know you're curious and I can see you're having a reaction to what we've been talking about. I'll keep paddling, so we don't fall behind. You stop paddling and come up close to me for just a few minutes. Yeah that's it. Careful; stay low so we don't get out of balance and tip over. Okay. That's it; squat there in front of me."

"What do you want me here for?"

"As I've said, you're curious and if you want, you can take a close look at me and see how my skin works."

Henry blinked with surprise. "You don't mind?"

"No. Pull my shorts and bathing suit to the side and take a look." Henry started to reach, but stopped. He was turning red. "Come on, we'll soon be back at camp. Do it. I'm sure you want to anyway, so go ahead, do it!"

Henry did it. Clay was hard, of course and Henry handled him as if he were made of fine glass. "You're so big!" he said and he felt along Clay's shaft with one hand and cupped his sack with the other.

"Pull back the skin." Henry complied. "That's it; see how it works?"

"Cool. There's a lot of slippery goop coming out of your opening. Mine does that too. I feel wet right now."

"You can rub it around on the tip if you want. Do you ever do that to yourself when you get wet?"

"Sometimes, but it makes me feel funny inside, so I stop. It feels better to do it off and on. Wow, your thing's getting even harder."

"Yeah, better stop, Henry. You and I will have to have another talk later today about this. See if you're real wet now too."

Henry did the best he could to tuck Clay back in, and then pulled himself out and squeezed along it. A rush of fluid flowed out. Clay stopped paddling just long enough to lean forward, feel Henry, and rub the liquid over his tip. Henry gasped and gritted his teeth from the surprising intensity of being touched by another boy. Clay didn't go any further, knowing how very close Henry was to his first orgasm.

"Now, Henry, I want you to promise me something."

"I won't tell anyone about this."

"No, that wasn't it. I know you won't tell. I want you to promise me you won't touch yourself like this at all until I can talk with you again in private and maybe show you some things you need to know. Maybe we can do it tonight, or if not, then tomorrow. Promise?"

"Okay. I promise. That felt good. What did you do? It's never felt that way with me touching myself."

"When we talk again, I'll share the secret with you. It's something you really need to know about, Rascal. You'll love it."

"Okay. Thanks, Clay."

"For what?"

"For letting me look at you and touch you. I've thought about doing that, but never thought I'd be able to. You felt nice."

"Thanks, Rascal. So did you."

After putting away the canoes, Clay did some more deep thinking. This trip to camp had opened up a lot of avenues of thought, it seemed. He was exploring many new aspects of his sexuality. Again, however, he felt guilty about doing these things with other boys instead of Albert, but his body and mind were telling him to enjoy himself and experience everything he could while here with several boys of similar nature. He wasn't completely sure Albert was homosexual anyway. He hoped he was because he still felt something entirely different for Albert. As Clay masturbated each night, it was Albert he pictured in his mind, not Randy or Henry. He hadn't thought about his photo of Roddy for some time either. Why dream about the impossible when he could enjoy reality.

His experiences at camp were freeing him to explore new things that later he could enjoy with Albert. Until Randy had talked about it, Clay never realized oral sex was possible. His first experience in the tent was terrific. He could hardly wait to do it that way with Albert once he and Albert started being intimate. The excitement he felt as he contemplated introducing Henry to the mysteries of sex kept him excited on and off the rest of the morning.

Eleven o'clock finally arrived and one after another, cars began to fill the parking area and road leading up to the camp. One grassy field had been staked off to make enough parking places for the anticipated number of cars. Clay watched anxiously for their old 1939 Buick, but as the lot neared the half way mark, Les's car had still not arrived. During a lull in cars coming up the road, he was standing with Henry, Sajid and Randy when he felt someone take hold of his shoulders from behind. He whirled around to find Les smiling at him. He threw his arms around his dad and kissed him with no thought of shyness.

"Oh, Dad, I'm so glad to see you. I've been watching for the car, but must have missed it. Gosh, I've missed you. These are my new friends." He went on to introduce his three buddies and describe where they lived and how he hoped to be able to visit them after summer. Les finally had to slow him down so he cold get a word in edgewise.

"The reason you didn't see our old Buick is because I traded it in and bought a new car in Hagerstown." Les pointed toward the parking area. "See that light green Buick over there with the white top? That's our brand new, 1953 Roadmaster. It runs  so smoothly you have to listen carefully to make sure the engine's running at all."

"Wow, Dad, it's really nice. How much did it cost?"

"Twenty-eight hundred dollars --- two hundred down and fifty dollars a month until it's paid off. With my new job, it won't be a problem. The old '39 was worn out and was about to cost two or three hundred for repairs."

"Maybe before you go back you can give me a ride."

"Maybe, if we have time. I believe one of your friends has spotted his parents. Henry was running toward a man and woman, threw himself into his mom's arms, and then hugged his dad. After that, he started pulling them over to meet his friends. No sooner had everyone been introduced when Sajid pointed out his family and what a family it was. It looked like he might be the only boy in a small village of sisters. Once introduced, Clay counted three older sisters and four younger sisters. He gave up on learning their exotic-sounding names. Mr. and Mrs. Mahoud were kind and loving. It was plain to see they loved the girls and their only son.

Clay thought to himself, *if Sajid is queer, Mr. and Mrs. Mahoud will have to depend on the girls for grandchildren.* Clay noticed

Randy was looking rather sad, so he stepped close and put his arm around his friend's shoulder and gave him a quick side hug saying, "There's still parents arriving, they'll be here, so don't feel bad, okay?"

"Yeah, thanks, Clay. I'm sure they just got a late start." Just as the group was about to walk toward the camp buildings, away from the parking area, Randy's expression changed and he said with a squeal, "There they are!" A few moments later, as Randy saw them get out of the car he yelled again. "Oh golly --- they brought Claude along!" A tall, dark-haired boy with crutches and a plastered leg was helped out of the car by Randy's dad and younger sister. Claude looked around until he spotted his friend and then waved.

Everyone waited until Randy's folks and Claude reached the group; introductions were repeated once again. Randy had to ask Sajid to introduce his sisters as he could scarcely pronounce, let alone remember, all the foreign names.

Clay felt strange as he watched Claude and Randy hug one another. Randy then stood with his arm around Claude's shoulders smiling and chatting to the French boy. Clay felt his face flush with heat and felt left out. Randy had completely forgotten about him and should have done a better job of introducing him to his friend from home. He just pointed Clay out and told Claude his name and nothing else. He didn't like the way Claude was looking at Randy and pawing all over him. *Stupid French brat; I bet he's spoiled and walks around with his nose in the air all the time!*

Les said as they walked toward the camp buildings. "You okay, Clay. All of the sudden you went from talking a mile-a-minute to a deafening silence."

"Oh, sorry, Dad, it's been a busy morning and I just ran out of steam, I guess."

"Well, that's one thing I'm good at. My job up until now was making sure my locomotive didn't run out of steam, so I'm going to stoke your boiler and cheer you up. Why don't you show me around the camp? We can join your friends later. They want to talk to their folks anyway just now. How come you haven't called me at the hotel? I gave you the number, didn't I?"

"I guess I got so busy, I forgot. I'm sorry, Dad. Camp's been a lot of fun and I just forgot. I'll make sure and call you next week as often as I can."

"That's all right. I figured you were busy." Les was looking around now that they had passed the amphitheater and were nearing the lakeshore. "This is a nice place. How about showing me the lake and telling me about everything you've discovered and done this week."

Some things I couldn't possibly tell you about, thought Clay as he considered what had just happened a few hours ago in the canoe and what he and Randy had done in the water and the tent. His thoughts of Randy brought his anger to the surface once more and he looked around for Randy and his *skinny, French bastard.*

Chapter 18

The first group to eat that afternoon was the one-week campers and their families. Right after the meal, they left for the amphitheater and an awards ceremony before gathering their things and leaving with their folks. While the first group ate, the two-week kids led their parents around the camp showing them the dorms and activity areas. Clay was so proud to have a parent now and managed to forget his jealousy for a while, although it flared up from time to time as Les and he passed near Randy, his folks and of course, *Claude the Cripple*, as Clay had started calling him in his mind.

After the fortnighter kids and their families had lunch, the parents started leaving, a few at a time, although they were told they could stay until four if they so desired. New one-week boys were beginning to arrive for the coming session. Henry ran over to Les and Clay as Henry wanted to ask Les for permission to visit Clay.

"Hello Mr. Mills, I'm Henry Winters, one of Clay's friends and I'd like to ask your permission to visit Clay sometime before the summer is over. I've asked my mom and dad and they said they would be willing to drive me to your house once in a while if you say it's okay. We live in Cresaptown, near Cumberland."

"That will be fine, Henry. I'll be happy to drive Clay to your house too, if your folks okay it. In fact, if we make plans in advance, since I'm probably going to be working out of the Cumberland area on passenger trains, I could pick you up and take you to Sand Patch for an overnight or weekend visit occasionally. I could bring you back to Cumberland when I come or go to work, if the schedules work out. We'll figure it out somehow. You're always welcome."

"That's very nice of you, sir. I like Clay an awful lot and it'll be nice to have a friend. I don't have any friends where I live."

"Why is that, Henry?" asked Les. "You're a nice boy, very polite too, and I'm sure you would have no trouble making friends."

"I probably wouldn't, sir, but where we live there's only a few houses nearby and the only kids I know are those at school. They live too far from me to see them after school much."

"Well, we'll do our best to get you two guys together once in a while." Les gave Henry a hair ruffle and the boy beamed and ran back to his parents.

"He's a nice kid, Clay. You're okay with him coming over aren't you? You didn't say anything while he was talking."

"Oh sure, he's more than welcome. I've told him about our house and the trains set and he said he plays the piano too."

"Oh, good, I'll look forward to hearing him play. He's welcome to use the Steinway."

"Dad, when we get home next week, I'd like for you and me to go camping together and invite Albert along too. I miss him a lot and wish he was here with me."

"Sure. We'll do just that and I'm glad you mentioned Albert. He called me at the hotel two days ago. I almost forgot to tell you. He asked for the camp address and said he was writing you a letter. You might get it tomorrow or Tuesday."

Clay felt so good hearing that and gave his dad a hug. "What's that for, kiddo?"

"Thanks for giving him the address. I really miss Albert a lot and it'll be so nice to get a letter from him. I'll start one to him tonight." Clay was wiping a few tears from his eyes, so Les asked him to have a seat on a nearby bench.

"Are you a little homesick, buddy?"

"Yeah, I guess so. I miss you and Albert both so much. I miss Debussy too. I'm glad Albert is taking care of him. Is Debussy okay?"

"Albert said he got in trouble on Thursday. Your cat's in the doghouse."

"What did he do?"

"Well, remember a few days before we left, I put that new brass planter in the parlor, just under the big front window and planted some palms in it?"

"Yeah, why is Debussy in trouble?"

"Well, he thought the planter was his new personal toilet and dug all through it and pooped. Albert told me he managed to rake a couple of pounds of the nice white sand I'd put in it, all over the Persian carpet. Albert walked in and caught him in the act. Debussy knew he was in trouble too. Albert said he took off and tried to hide in your bedroom. Poor Albert had to use our vacuum cleaner to clean up all the sand." Clay was laughing by now and feeling a little better.

I told Albert to get some mothballs from the basement and scatter some all through the planter to discourage him using it again. Clay, have you ever smelled mothballs?"

191

"Yeah, sure, Dad, they stink."

"How did you ever get their little legs apart enough to do it?" Clay just stared at Les, somewhat confused until it struck him how cleverly his dad had tricked him.

He rolled his eyes and said, "Ah, Dad, that's awful!" Both got to laughing and Les hugged his boy close and kissed the top of his hair.

"I love you so much, son. My life is so rich now and complete. God, I miss you too. I have a confession to make."

"It doesn't have anything to do with smelling moth-balls does it?"

"No." Les laughed. "On Wednesday, I got to missing you so darned much; I almost drove up here to see you."

"Why didn't you? I would have loved it."

"No, your friends might have teased you about your homesick daddy."

"I wouldn't care one bit. I love my dad and I'm damned proud of it. Sorry about the damn, Dad, but it's the way I feel."

"You're excused. I'm damned proud of you too. Even if you have been known to sniff mothballs once in a while."

Clay pushed Les backward off the bench into the soft grass and the two of them romped like kids for a few minutes. Neither cared who saw them.

After Les left that afternoon, Clay began to feel bothered again every time he saw Randy. He found himself avoiding the boy and spending more time with other boys. It all came to a head just after supper when Randy asked Clay if he wanted to go for a walk along a nature trail they hadn't yet explored.

Randy said, "If you want, we can do some stuff along the way. There's a place where we can go off the main trail to a special spot I know where no one can see us."

"Did you take Claude there? Is that what you guys did last summer?" Clay said with obvious rancor.

"Well, yeah, I already told you he and I messed around last summer. How come you're so mad? Did I say something wrong, or do something that made you angry?"

"Oh, nothing much except hang all over Claude all day. You never said a word to me or came over to see me and my dad. Did you guys go off in the woods to kiss or feel on each other while he was here?"

"No, of course not, he *is* my boyfriend though and I love and miss him." Randy looked confused and a little angry. "You're jealous, aren't you?"

"No, of course not."

"Yes you are. I thought you said it would be great for you, me, Claude, and Albert to get together sometime. If you feel that way because I spent a few hours with Claude today, then I doubt we'll all get along at all."

"It's not like that."

"Yes it is. You're real jealous. Hey, have I gotten jealous with you hanging around with Henry? Do I get mad when he gives you one of his little kisses? No, I don't. Henry's been all over you since the trip to the island. I didn't let that bother me. Now I ask you to come with me for a walk so we can have a little fun with each other and you puff up like a damned snake and strike at me. To hell with you."

Randy stomped off leaving Clay panting with a bubbling stew of conflicting emotions: a pinch of anger, aggression and confusion with a healthy dash of sorrow and a pound or so of guilt thrown in.

Clay ran toward the lake to get away from everyone. As he ran he began to think about what Randy had said, *'You're jealous, aren't you?'*

He burst into tears because he realized it was absolutely true. He *was* jealous and hurt and had no right to be. Randy had never made any promise to be anything more than a friend. The sexual experimenting they did was all done with the intention that they would each go back to their homes and other friends. Any effort to get together in the future was only speculation.

He next remembered Jerry's warning, *'Love can make people get crazy and sometimes even mean. Tread lightly.'*

Clay stopped as he reached the lakeshore north of the dock area. A few large boulders were nearby; he crawled up on one, sat down and started bawling almost immediately. *Damn! What have I done? I've ruined my friendship with Randy. He hates me now and called me a snake. Why was I so damned nasty to him? He had every right to spend his time with Claude. If Albert had been along with Dad, I would have spent my time with him and never given a thought to Randy. I'm a snake all right --- a low-down, stinking snake.*

He said aloud in a half whisper, "I have to apologize." As he climbed down from the boulder he thought, *I was so wrong. Now I have to hope and pray Randy will forgive me and still be my friend. I've got to find him right now, because if I wait, he'll just have time to hate me even more.* Clay dried his eyes, blew his nose on a pocket-handkerchief and ran back toward the cabins. He hoped that was where Randy had gone, but kept an eye out for him along the way.

Upon reaching Dragon Cabin, he crept inside and looked around the common room. There was no sign of Randy. He went into the fourteen-year-old side of the bunkhouse to the bunk he and Randy shared. Still no Randy. After returning to the common room he looked into the thirteen-year-old side and of course Randy wasn't there either. He saw Henry, however, and noticed the younger boy was laying face down on his bunk and crying. *Now what's wrong with him? It'll have to wait. I have to find Randy. I'll talk to Henry later. Maybe he's just homesick since his folks left.*

He ran from the cabin. It was nearly seven o'clock and would be getting dark within an hour and a half. Clay remembered the trail that Randy had mentioned and thought, *maybe he went on his own to walk off his anger.* He ran to the trailhead. Nearby were three boys from Dragon Cabin. One was Sam Walden, the chubby kid. Clay asked, "Sam, have you seen Randy?"

"Yeah, he went down the trail about ten minutes ago. He was all upset and crying. I tried to ask him if he was okay and he cussed at me."

"He cussed at you? That's odd. What did he say?"

"Uh, it was a really bad word." Sam looked around and whispered, "He told me to tend to my own *effing* business. I've never heard Randy talk like that. Did you and he get in a fight or something?"

"Just an argument; I have to find him before dark. If I miss him along the way somehow, and he comes back, tell him I'm looking for him and have to see him right away."

"Okay, I will."

Clay ran down the trail as fast as he could. He didn't want Randy to be mad at him one more minute than necessary. He cried as he ran, criticizing himself for his stupidity and meanness. *I'm lucky to have a friend who accepts and loves me. I've just got to find him and tell him how sorry I am.*

Clay soon came to a fork. One feature of this particular trail was that it split occasionally and took differing paths; some came back to the main path while others were dead ends. A sign pointed in two directions.

Which way would Randy go? Having never traveled this way, he had no idea what lay in either direction. He took a chance and called out, "Randy?" There was no answer. He chose the right hand trail to Stone Fort, wondering what it was. Randy had never told him what was along this trail, just that it had a lot of branching paths.

Again he ran. He wished he had his bicycle, but the occasional steps along the way and steep grades would probably have slowed him down. After a two-minute run, he saw the Stone Fort. It was a moss-covered, half-ruined structure with a stone stairway leading to an upper floor. He called out, but there was

no answer from Randy. The trail continued beyond the fort and all Clay could hope was that Randy hadn't gone to the Beaver Pond. Soon the trail to the fort rejoined the one from the beaver pond and again became the main trail. He continued jogging another hundred or so feet, but was confronted this time by a *three-way* fork in the trail. He called out for Randy once more and strained to hear an answer. Nothing.

"I'd like to kick the son-of-a-bitch who made this damned trail, square in the ass!" he said aloud, frustrated with the necessity of making another choice. This time a sign said:

^

Main Trail

< Hollow Oak Bridge	Gobbler's Marsh >
One-Way Trail	One-Way Trail

His eyes filled with tears and he was half-tempted to turn back, but he thought, *I can't, I have to say I'm sorry. He's the best friend I have here and he's just like me. I'm so damned stupid.* Aloud he called Randy's name again and said, "Please Randy. It's Clay and I'm sorry. Where are you?"

Still nothing.

He took a chance thinking Randy probably wanted to be alone

and get as far away from the camp and him as possible. Clay chose the main trail and ran even faster. He glanced at the new wristwatch Les had bought for him just before they went to Hagerstown. It was seven-thirty. About an hour was left before dark. *Maybe I should just wait for Randy to come back and talk to him then. He'll have to come back before dark.* He was slowing down and planning to turn back when he saw the next sign. It read:

<   Laurel Maze   Skeeter Bog   >
One-Way Trail   One-Way Trail

Apparently, these two choices led to the two ends of the nature trail. Randy was either at the maze or the bog. Clay remembered

how much fun they had playing flashlight tag in the other laurel maze on the mountain top and decided that maybe Randy would remember it too. He ran along the left fork until he topped a slight rise and saw a wide meadow overgrown with mountain laurel bushes.

Off in the distance, near the center of the meadow was a tall pole with the camp flag flying on it. *The flag must be at the center of the maze.* Aloud he said, "I hope I don't get lost and have to wander around trying to get there," he said aloud.

He leaned against a nearby tree, feeling utterly lost, but decided to try one more time and yelled, "Randy! This is Clay. I'm sorry. Please come out of the maze so I can talk to you. It's almost dark and I want to tell you how sorry I am. You're right. I am a damned snake; I was jealous, and I'm the one who was wrong. Please come out. I love you and I'm sorry."

Clay screamed as someone grabbed his shoulder from behind. He whirled around with balled fists and suddenly felt relief as he saw Randy standing there looking surprised at his reaction.

"Oh, God, Randy, I'm so sorry. Please forgive me. I was wrong and I promise not to be jealous like that again. Please don't hate me!"

Randy smiled and the two boys rushed together, clutching at one another like long lost brothers.

"I forgive you, Clay. I had no idea how much I meant to you and it was probably wrong of me to spend so much time with Claude."

"No, you were right to spend time with him. If Albert had been here, I would have done the same thing. I did some hard thinking running around this damned trail and I'm so glad I found you. Can I kiss you?"

"Sure. I love you, Clay, but I love Claude too. I'll probably love Albert if I ever get to meet him. I'm not mad that you spend time with Henry either. He's in love with you too, you know. He told me so."

"He did? This is getting so complicated. Jerry was right when he said love sometimes makes people get crazy and mean. It sure did it to me."

"It's okay. I understand."

"If I ever do that again, Randy --- Hit me. Hit me hard and knock some sense into me. I have some of the best friends a guy like me can have and I almost lost one of them this afternoon. Remember; hit me."

"Okay, I will. Just don't hit me back. I don't know how to fight." He looked up at the sky. "We better start back. It'll be almost dark by the time we get there."

"Where was it you wanted to take me to, out here? This trail is a nightmare of forked paths and crazy names. What the heck is Skeeter Bog? Sounds like a place to get mosquito bit."

"It is. It's a real wet area and frog pond. That wasn't where I wanted us to go. The place I wanted to take you is near the Hollow Oak Bridge. It's a place off the main trail. No one could have seen us there. I wanted to make us feel good, like we like to do."

"I know and I ruined it for us both. Tomorrow we'll go. We'll go and you can do anything in the world you want to do to me. I can't wait."

Randy looked around and then gave Clay one of the longest and most intimate kisses he'd given him up to that point.

After the kiss, Randy said, "I have two of the most wonderful boyfriends in the world. I love them both equally and I want them to understand that I don't pick favorites. I told Claude about you and he was a little jealous at first too, but I told him to get over it and that I had enough love in my heart for the both of you. I want you two to get together someday; you can love and touch each other any way you want. That excites me, because I have you both in my heart and that's where you guys are going to stay. Understand?"

"Yes. Again, I'm sorry I was a snake."

"I'm sorry I called you that. If it's any help, I have a pet snake at home and I love him too." Randy giggled and got that cute impish grin on his face. Clay kissed him again and gave him a squeeze below saying he felt something shaped like a snake in Randy's pants before they took off at a trot for the camp.

As they ran, Clay managed to tell Randy, between breaths, how he'd seen Henry crying his eyes out, just before going to look for Randy.

"Think he's just homesick with his folks leaving and all?"

"I don't know, but I plan to ask him. Maybe I did something to hurt him too. Damn! Love's just too complicated sometimes."

After returning to the Camp --- just as the sun was setting --- Clay and Randy ran to their bunks, grabbed their towels and fresh underwear. Both were sweaty and stinky from all the running in the woods. They stripped and showered side by side, as usual. One boy, another fourteen-year-old that neither cared much for, made a snide remark about them and referred to them as faggots. Neither had ever heard the word before and would have to ask around as to what was meant by it. Clay and Randy had a good idea it had to do with the way they were, however. Clay whispered, "Who cares what others think? After next Sunday, we won't ever have to see them again."

"Yeah, but after next Sunday, we won't be able to see each other again for a while. I'm gonna hate that."

Clay nodded in agreement, "Yeah, me too."

It was about nine before Clay was able to ask Henry to join him for a talk. They stepped out on the cabin's porch and found an empty wooden chair near one end of the veranda. Henry was looking bad. It was obvious he'd been crying, as his eyes were bloodshot and puffy around the rims.

"You've been crying, Rascal; are you mad at me or Randy?"

"No. I was going to talk to both of you about this anyway."

"Should I go and get Randy?"

"I guess so. I'd appreciate his advice too."

198

"Sit tight, I'll get him." A few minutes later, he returned with Randy in tow.

Randy patted Henry's shoulder before sitting down on a nearby single chair. "What's wrong, Rascal? Your eyes are all red. You look like ten miles of bad road."

"I feel like it too, guys. My heart's broken."

"Huh?" asked Randy, wrinkling his nose and glancing at Clay.

"Something awful has happened. It's about Sajid. He can never be my boyfriend now."

Clay looked at Randy and both shrugged their shoulders. "Did he tell you that? Did you come right out and ask him if he liked boys?" whispered Clay in case any other campers were close enough to hear them through a window. All of them dragged their chairs away from the building at Randy's suggestion.

"No. He showed me a picture of his wife. He's married."

This time the "Huh?" from Clay and Randy was more like **"HUH???!!!"**

"Married?" hissed Clay. "He's only thirteen! He can't get married."

"He showed me her picture and told me her name. I can't remember it, or pronounce it. She's ugly and has a big, black, ugly mole right in the center of her forehead. All of Sajid's sisters had a mole like that too. Indian girls must all grow them in the same place. They're gross."

"Wait a minute, Henry. Those are religious marks they wear because they're Hoodoos," said Randy.

"That's Hindus, Randy," giggled Clay.

"Whatever. They put 'em on like makeup. They come off."

"Oh," said Henry. "Well, his wife's still ugly. She has a mustache just like Sajid's. I like Sajid's mustache, but on a girl, it's just plain nasty looking. His wife is only twelve, too."

"She can't be his wife. Sajid's pulling your leg," said Randy.

"No. I asked him how she could be his wife and he said that in India, parents arrange ahead of time for who will be a boy's wife and while his father was in India a few days ago, he set everything up and they're married. It's already done, but they won't be allowed to see one another in person until both are sixteen. In India though, they really are married and he said the only way the whole mess could be stopped is with a divorce."

"A divorce?" asked Randy incredulously, "For two kids?"

"Yeah, he said that would be *very, very dishonorable.*" Henry mimicked Sajid's reedy voice and accent. "He sounded so happy about the whole thing. Arrrr, I wanted to hit him."

Henry started bawling and buried his face against Clay's chest. With all Clay had gone through today, he was about at his wits end to figure out what to do. He certainly didn't want some other boys to see him holding Henry against his chest and he didn't want to hurt Henry's feelings by pushing him away. He looked at Randy and whispered, "What am I supposed to do?"

Randy got the giggles and had to hold his sleeve against his mouth to keep from bursting.

Clay frowned at Randy and hissed, "You're no help at all. Henry, lets take a walk around the back of the cabin or something. Come on, Rascal. We don't want the other boys seeing us like this. They'll tease us both to death."

Henry was beginning to suffer a bad bout of hiccups. "Please... hic... Clay... hic. Promise me... hic... you'll never say... hic... you're getting married. I... hic... couldn't stand it."

Randy was holding his hand over his mouth and shaking like he was having a fit. He had to step away and Clay heard a sound like a loud fart off to the side as Randy managed to bleed off some of his laughter through pursed lips. Clay was leading Henry into the darkness beside the cabin and trying his best to calm the poor kid.

"I promise, Henry, I'm never gonna get married. If Dad came home and told me he'd fixed me up with a wife, as much as I love him, by God, I'd run away from home all over again."

"You... hic... ran away from... hic... home?"

"Long story for another night, Rascal. Now calm down and let go of me for a minute. You've got my shirt all twisted up in a ball and it's pinching the heck out of one of my nipples. Thanks, that's better. Now look at me and get yourself under control. Gees, you're a wreck. I think you need some of my spicy deodorant too. Your armpits smell like an old onion."

"I wish I was fourteen and could sleep with you guys tonight. My bunky is always making fun of me. He heard me crying and thought it was because my family left. He called me a momma's boy and a sissy. I couldn't tell him why I was really crying." Henry's voice dropped an octave and came out as a growl, "I hate Sajid and his ugly wife with her nasty, Hoodoo, mole thing and her black, hairy mustache. If I ever see her, I'll spit on her."

200

"Whoa! It's a good thing she's on the other side of the world tonight. I thought you were such a nice quiet boy and now I'm learning you're pretty darned vicious when you're angry. Maybe Badger would have been a better nickname for you." He heard Henry giggle a bit in spite of himself. "That's better. It's dark here. Give me one of your nice kisses and a hug and we'll go back inside."

"I love you Clay. I love Randy too. I wish boys could get married to boys, because I'd marry you any day."

"I appreciate the thought, Henry, but my life's complicated enough."

Chapter 19

The next day, Henry was doing much better. He was avoiding Sajid, however, who glared at him every time they passed; something else must have happened between them. Sajid was spending all his time hanging around with two other boys. Henry was now a permanent attachment to Clay and Randy. He asked Clay to tell him about running away from home and after breakfast as they worked on making willow baskets in a craft class, Clay filled him in on his history.

"You mean your father is not really your dad, yet?"

"He will be, after a year goes by; it's just the way the law works. He's my guardian until then, but I think of him as my dad. It was awful losing my original family, but after that, having to live with my aunt and uncle and their two boys was terrible. They hated me and I guess I sort of hated them. My uncle would get drunk, beat me up and I finally had to run away."

"Wow. He sounds like a real nasty man. He beat you up?"

"Yeah; he punched me in the face, knocked me down and kicked me a couple of times. I was all bruised up when I ran away to Les's house. Les and I went to see a judge and after he saw the bruises, he agreed to make Les my guardian."

"Gee wiz!"

"Les took me in and now I finally have a parent again who loves me like my real mom, dad and little brother did."

"So, Henry," asked Randy, who had just joined them after stepping away for a few minutes to use the bathroom. "Are you and Sajid no longer friends? He was looking at you with a mean expression when he passed us a while ago."

"I guess so. I told him I'd make sure and send his new wife a razor as a wedding gift."

Clay whispered, "Oh, Henry, that's low. Don't be that way. You're just mad because he seems to like girls all of the sudden. None of us knew if he liked boys the way we all do or not. He liked to romp naked in the water, but that doesn't mean anything. He's pretty young and maybe doesn't know what he likes or doesn't like yet." Clay leaned even closer and whispered even more carefully, "There's a lot *you* still don't understand, Rascal. Remember I was going to tell you more, but Parent's Day came along and we all had a bunch of problems. You and I still have a long talk ahead of us."

Randy said, "Clay told me how he let you explore a bit in the canoe the other day."

"Clay! That was supposed to be a secret."

"You never said that, Rascal. Besides, Randy is like us anyway. Relax. Maybe we'll both have that talk with you before you go back home to Cresaptown."

"When?" Henry said with a grin, his mood suddenly brighter.

"Soon," said Clay as he gave Henry's head a knuckle-rub. "Concentrate on your basket. It's crooked."

On Monday afternoon, Randy and Clay managed to slip away from Henry for a little while and went for a walk along the nature trail where Randy led him to the special place near the Hollow Log Bridge. The location got its name from a partly hollow  log that was used to cross a brook to reach a small picnic ground. Just before the bridge, Randy led him off along a nearly invisible trail; it was easy to see it hadn't been used anytime this summer. It twisted around until reaching a ravine choked with wild may apples, small umbrella-shaped plants that had oblong, yellow fruit hanging beneath them. Both boys knew the fruit wasn't worth eating, as it tasted somewhat like soap.

Randy knew of a place near the bottom of the ravine, where it was impossible for anyone to see them because of a stone ledge overhanging the area. Beneath the ledge was a flat, dry rock surface about ten feet wide that extending back under the bank six or seven feet. The two boys crawled underneath and soon had their clothing off and started doing what they both enjoyed. An hour later, they left the tiny cave-like niche, sweaty, but satisfied from their efforts.

When they returned to camp, it was nearly time for supper and Henry had a thousand questions about where they had been and why they hadn't asked him to go along.

"Henry, now don't get mad or jealous, but sometimes, Clay and I like to have some time alone when we can cuddle and hug each other and talk about things. Both of us are soon going to show you some things you need to know before you go home. You just think you know how nice it feels to kiss and hug another boy. There are things you can do with your boy parts that are out of this world. Just you wait. You're going to love what we'll teach you to do."

"When? You keep teasing me with that, but I want you to do it soon."

Clay said, "How about tomorrow morning, right after breakfast? We have optional activities. Randy and I were going to try to water ski, but I'm not sure I'm ready for that this summer. Does a morning spent with Henry sound like a good idea to you, Randy?"

"Oh, yeah, you know how much I like doing what we're going to teach Rascal here to do. We'll take you to our secret hideout and show you just how amazing your body can make you feel."

Clay had been a little sorry that morning when mail call brought no letter yet from Albert. *Maybe tomorrow,* he thought, as he left the counselor who was passing out letters.

Just before bed that night, Clay and Randy were talking while they waited for lights out. They discussed what they planned to do with Henry the next day.

Clay said, "I'm kind of having second thoughts. Do you think we should be doing this with Henry? I know he's thirteen and we know he's queer like us. I don't know what it is that bothers me about it, but something does."

"I think it's because he looks eleven instead of thirteen until you see him with his clothes off. He's got plenty of hair down there and his penis is almost as large as ours. His body just hasn't caught up with his privates and his interest in guys. He's not entirely innocent, you know. He's grabbed at both of us in the water while we were swimming at the island; he did it to me yesterday in the lake when he was sure no one else was around."

Clay said, "Yeah, I know. He didn't need a second invitation in the canoe either. He started playing around and if we had been a little farther from camp, I would have let him keep rubbing; that way he'd know what happens when you play with another boy's dick too long. I really wanted to."

"I bet. I would have dropped back enough with the canoe and let him do it. I bet he'd panic if he'd seen you squirting all over the place and let go before you finished."

Clay said, "Well, anyway --- tomorrow's Rascal's big day."

Randy said, "He'll love it and I have to be honest, so will we. I've often had daydreams about doing it with several boys at the same time. How do you want to do it?"

Clay said, "I don't know. What do you think?"

"I think we should do it by hand, the first time. Some other time, maybe we can show him how to do it by mouth."

"That sounds good. I know I sure liked my first time last week in the tent when you did it to me. Wow! I wanted it to last forever."

"It was great for me too, and I've done it that way for a long time. For your first time doing it to another boy, you did good too. I sure can't complain."

Clay furrowed his brow as he said, "You know, that's something that surprised me. It was as if I knew exactly what to do. I'd never even dreamed guys would do that, but the minute I felt you in my mouth, I knew what to do. That's one of the reasons I know I was born this way. Randy, I've never had a single thought about doing *anything* with a girl. Once when I was about five or six a little girl my same age let me look at her down there. She asked me to look, not the other way around."

"Is that all you did?"

"No. She asked me to touch her too. After I did, I smelled my finger and thought she smelled bad, like something fishy."

"I bet regular boys probably like that smell just like I like your smell. When you think about it, that's a little stinky too; but it affects me a lot. I'm sitting here just waiting for lights out so I can smell it tonight and make myself come. I wonder sometimes how many times a day a guy can come without getting tired of doing it?"

Clay answered, "I think we'd both do it all day if we didn't have other things to do, or have it get sore. Last month I did it about five times one night at home, but I got sore and couldn't do it for half a week. It wasn't worth it."

"That's the advantage of sucking on it instead of using your hand. Claude stayed over one night and he and I did it to each other about five times each. If we hadn't fallen asleep, we could have kept it up 'till dawn. Claude does it so many different ways too."

"How do you mean?"

"Well, sometimes he does it as I kneel over his chest, like you and I did today. Sometimes we do it to each other at the same time lying in different directions on our sides. Claude has some French word for that, but I forget it."

205

"How come French kids know so much about stuff like that?"

"He had a cousin in France who did it with him from the time he was six until he moved to America. His cousin was three years older and knew all the tricks I guess. Anyway, Claude taught me everything he could remember and I've started teaching you. You're pretty good on your own though. Like I said, you knew exactly how to make me feel good that first time."

The lights finally went off, so each of them kissed quickly, Randy reached in and felt around enough to have something exciting to sniff before the two of them jumped into their respective bunks and did what they most enjoyed doing.

Morning came with the usual bang of the cannon. Right after breakfast, mail was passed out and Clay was thrilled to get the letter from Albert. He, Randy and Henry dashed off to a bench so he could read it. He read it to himself first and then read it aloud to his friends.

Dear Clay,

Boy I sure do miss you. Debusy misses you to. After checking on him yesterday and giving him water and food I laid down on your bed and petted him for a wile. I acidently fell asleep and it was almost seven when I woke up. Mom and Dad were worried and had been calling but I had shut the door and didn't hear the phone. What woke me up was Dad pounding on the door downstairs. He was mad.

Like I say I miss you terrable and cant wait to see you. I have lots to tell you to. I'm a little worried about high school and ninth grade. I was going to go swimming at the mill, but I'll wait for you to come home. It's not as fun alone and I don't like to go with Toby that much. I almost hit him a few days ago because he made fun of you and your dad. I probably wont play with him ever again after that. He's almost as stupid as your two cousins.

Have you missed me? I have had dreams about you since you went to camp. Is it fun there? Have you made any friends? Please don't forget me because I wont forget you. I miss you to much to do that. Debusy pooped in your fathers new plant thing with the palm trees. I cleaned up all the sand he spilled though. He's a nice cat and I hold him and kiss him whenever I'm there. I wish I could be there with you. Please don't make to many friends and forgit about me. Maybe we can go camping when you get back. Your dad said he would take us when he called us last night to check on the house. I told him about the mess Debusy made. He misses you to.

Please write to me to and tell me if you miss me. I cant wait to see you on Sunday. I might even give you a hug. I know boys aint supposed to do that, but I think best friends should be able to. I will anyway, cause I miss you so much.

Well, I will see you on Sunday. Call me on the phone as soon as you get back. If it's not to late I will ride over to see you. Maybe I can spend the night to. Ask your dad. I miss you.

Love,
Albert

"That's a nice letter," said Henry with a giggle. "I'm not sure, but I think he misses you."

"I think you don't have to wonder about Albert being like us," said Randy. "It sure sounds like he wants to hug you as soon as you get back. Most boys would never write that in a letter."

Clay was smiling and nodding his head in agreement. "I sure miss him too. Darn, I wish he had been able to come to camp with us. I just hope you can meet him sometime, Randy. I know Rascal here will get a chance to meet him since he'll be coming over to my house. Maybe you can go camping with us too, Henry. The tent holds four."

"Great. I'd like that."

"Randy, I'll talk to Dad about ways you and Claude can visit by train. If he's the conductor on a train passing through Harper's Ferry, your folks could put you on his train and he'll watch out for you."

Henry asked, "When are you guys going to show me stuff about --- well, you know?"

Randy said, "How about right now? The whole morning is free-choice time and we've already said we're not taking water skiing. Does everyone feel like a walk to our secret place?" All nodded and grinned.

Before they left, Randy ran back into the cabin and brought along two large towels. He said, "These will make it easier to do stuff instead of being naked on the sandy rocks." The three boys started walking toward the nature trail that Clay had searched along the day before.

"Will we take our clothes all the way off?" asked Henry, looking excited.

"Uh huh," confirmed Clay. "Does that bother you? It seems to me that lately, you've gotten over being so shy."

"I'm not shy with you guys. Exactly what are we going to do?"

Randy said, "Some of it will be a surprise. Did you like touching Clay in the canoe the other day?"

"Yeah, he was really stiff and slippery; so was I."

Randy asked, "Do you get wet every time your penis gets stiff?"

"Not every time. Mostly when I'm talking with you guys about it, or thinking about certain things, it'll happen. It did the other day in the canoe. Clay saw it dribble out and he felt how slippery it made me. Is it always supposed to do that?"

"Yep. Has white stuff ever come out of your opening when you rub yourself?"

"Clay asked about that too, but nope, just clear stuff. Do some boys make white stuff instead?"

As they walked along the trail, passed the first fork, and took the Stone Fort trail, which Randy said was the shortest way to go, Clay picked up the conversation. "Have you ever heard of sperm, Rascal?"

"Uh, yeah, in health class; it takes sperm to fertilize an egg."

"Right. Well, boys start making sperm when they are about eleven or twelve right after they grow hair down below. When it comes out of your body, it's white and slippery just like the clear stuff. It doesn't come out except at special times when you're feeling real good deep inside."

"Am I old enough to make sperm?"

"You've probably been old enough for a year or two. When did you first get hair over your penis?"

"When I was ten a little bit started growing, but I got a whole lot when I was eleven. Now, it's getting thick and curly."

"Well, you probably could have made sperm when you were ten then."

"I've never seen it."

"You will soon," said Randy. "You have to do something special to make it come out. When it does, you feel real good inside and sperm squirts all over the place as you feel a pumping feeling up inside of you."

Clay said, "We're going to show you how to make your body pump it out and once you feel that, you're going to want to start doing it to yourself just about every day."

"Every day?"

"Yeah, it's just about the best feeling a boy can have," said Clay. "For boys like us, who like other boys, we can do it with one another and not have to worry about getting pregnant. You see men put their thing inside a woman's body and squirt their sperm up inside her where the egg is and that's how a baby gets started. Even teenagers can make a baby, so most boys and girls have to be real careful and not have sex until they're older and get married. Boys like us can do most anything we want and not worry about babies."

It wasn't long after that when the lads reached the cutoff to Hollow Oak Bridge; they left the trail just before the bridge and soon arrived at their trysting place.

"This is really something," said Henry as he crawled around and looked at the space under the overhanging rocks. Randy spread out the two big towels and said, "Everything's all set. Are you ready, Rascal?"

"I think so. What should I do?"

Clay said, First, let's all take off our outer clothing. If you want, you can leave on your underwear for a little while until we're ready to start making you feel good. We'll all touch each other a little bit and that will help to make us hard and probably wet. Then we can take off everything and it will be your turn first. Randy and I will do things to make sure your very first time is special."

Clay took Henry by the shoulders and looked right into his eyes and said, "Henry, I want you to remember something. Randy and I love you a lot and are doing this to make you feel how much we love being together. You'll understand that better after your first time. Right now, it probably doesn't make much sense, but it soon will." Clay and then Randy gave the boy a full kiss on his lips while hugging him close.

During the next hour or so, Randy and Clay taught Henry what pleasure and love was all about for boys like them. A bond was formed between the three that would last for many years to follow as Henry took his first steps along the road to maturity. He had gentle and wonderful teachers who showed him that sex and love together was one of the most wonderful experiences possible in this world. Even young men of their different nature could feel rich and fulfilling love through the wondrous secrets of their bodies.

Afterward as they lay in each other's arms looking up at the trees above, contemplating what they had just felt, Henry was the first to speak. "I love you guys so much. That was the most amazing thing I've ever felt or done. Thank you. You're both so special and made me feel so good. I don't ever want to leave you guys. I have two boyfriends now and want to love you guys forever."

"We love you too, Rascal," said Randy as he leaned over and nuzzled in Henry's soft hair.

Clay did the same from the other side, as he ran his fingers through Henry's soft pubic hair and said teasingly, "What about Sajid?"

"Sajid who?" said Henry with a sly grin. "I love my best buddies Clay and Randy and know for sure they love me back. Besides, I never mess with married guys."

Chapter 20

The last few days of camp were extremely interesting to say the least as Randy, Clay and now Henry further explored many aspects of their natures. Sajid was forgotten as the three formed a solid friendship. If nothing else, a group of three drew less attention, or mean-spirited catcalls about being queers or sissies. Henry apologized to Sajid for what he'd said about his wife to be, but that was as far as it went. He continued to stick with Clay and Randy.

They managed to visit their secret trysting place at least once a day and on one day twice. All three knew that on Sunday they would be forced to part. For Henry and Clay it was less of a concern as they were more confident they would be able to visit one another. Randy, though, as the days passed, seemed to become more and more melancholy. Usually the lively one of the group, always quick to tease or laugh, he was becoming the quiet one, sometimes quick to shed a tear. Shy, quiet Henry, who a week before could barely speak to other kids, was fast becoming a joy-filled, exuberant youth, finally comfortable with himself and being around others.

As the last day of camp approached, Randy, Clay and Henry started preparing to leave. All of them had changed over the fortnight and all for the better. Clay had written a long letter to Albert and sent it off on Wednesday. In it, he invited Albert to stay over the first night he was back and was sure Les would be okay with it. Albert should receive it before he arrived back home.

Clay was called out on Saturday evening for a phone call just before nine o'clock and was pleased to hear his dad on the line.

"How are you doing, buddy? All ready for pick-up tomorrow?"

"Uh huh, I'm real anxious to come home and be with you and Debussy and see Albert again. Oh, while I think of it, can Albert stay the night when I get back? He asked me to ask you in his letter."

"Sure, that's fine. We should be back before suppertime. I'll give his folks a call from here and make sure everything's okay. We'll pick him up on the way."

"Thanks Dad. You're the best."

"Thanks, so are you. Well, I just wanted to make sure you were okay. That and I miss you. Adults are just kids in bigger bodies sometimes. I get homesick too now that we're a family. How are

211

your friends?"

"They're fine. I'm really going to miss them, though. Henry can visit pretty easily, but Randy's so much farther away."

"If his parents are there on Sunday, I'll talk with them and we'll see if they'll allow him to ride the train. I can get him a free pass occasionally. It looks like my assignment will be the Baltimore or Washington to Cumberland run and sometimes Cumberland to Pittsburgh. That will be perfect as I'll be home three days a week and the other four days I'll be able to get home from work around six. You're old enough now to take care of yourself until I get there. I'm not sure yet what days will be my three days off. They might vary from week to week. Whatever it is, we'll manage. I know one thing; this nearly doubles my pay and I won't have to breathe smoke and cinders anymore."

"That's great, Dad. When will you start as a conductor?"

"It looks like I'll have a whole week off --- that's next week --- before I start my new job. You and I can go on that camping trip we've been talking about --- Albert too, if you want."

"Could Henry maybe come along too?"

"If his folks say it's okay, sure. I'm glad you've made some good friends, son. Summer camp is often good for that. Well, listen, I have to go now. I'll see you tomorrow at about eleven. Have all your stuff packed and don't forget anything. We'll be heading straight home from the camp as there will be no need for me to stop anywhere in Hagerstown. I'm all through with the classes. I love you son, and always will."

"Thanks Dad. I love you too. Bye."

Clay felt warm inside finally having a loving parent again. He ran off to tell Randy and Henry both the good news that Les was going to talk to Randy's folks about train trips to see him and talk to Henry's folks about a camping trip. Both were pleased. Their parting on Sunday would be much less bitter.

On Sunday, Les arrived a little before eleven as planned. He used the opportunity to talk with both Henry's and Randy's people and arrangements were made to allow the boys to get together once in a while during holidays or weekends once school got underway.

At the closing ceremony, Clay and Randy both were awarded special certificates for their efforts working with younger campers. Both had received a surplus of merits for their work and no demerits. The Dragons came in first in the cabin competition. After the ceremony, Colonel Lincoln himself pulled them to the side and told them they were both qualified to work at the camp next summer if they were interested. Todd Lincoln, the colonel's son gave them a wink and so did Jerry.

While Les chatted with the other parents, Clay and Randy made sure to talk to Jerry and Todd alone for a few moments thanking them for being good friends and wishing them well in their relationship.

Todd said, "Guys like us have to stick together and help each other out sometimes, because the world can be pretty mean to homosexuals. You guys be good and be careful. Pick your friends well and keep a low profile. You guys look great together, but Jerry and I have one question we wanted to ask just you two alone."

Randy said, "What is it?"

"It's about the younger kid, Henry. Is he involved with you two, or is it just hero worship?"

Clay grinned at Randy and said, "He's one of us too and the three of us have had a lot of fun together. He looks eleven, but, whew! That guy nearly wore us both out a couple of times."

Jerry and Todd roared with laughter and Jerry said, "That's five bucks you owe me Todd. I told you these two were corrupting the little squirt. Maybe it was the other way around though. You have to watch the quiet ones; sometimes they're tigers in disguise. We really like you guys and hope you can be on staff next year. Have a good year fellows and write us once in a while --- here's our addresses. We already have yours from the camp records." He handed Clay and Randy both slips of paper with their addresses printed on them. Todd said so long, winked and excused himself, as his dad was calling him.

Jerry offered to shake hands, but Clay stepped forward and gave him a big hug. Randy followed and did the same thing. After Jerry stepped away and left, Clay and Randy both ran to a nearby water fountain and washed the red, stamp pad ink off their palms. They looked at Jerry walking away from them with two sets of red handprints on his white camp jersey showing that he'd been hugged. It wasn't as good a trick as he'd pulled on them, but he'd have something to remember them by. Clay dropped the red ink stamp pad Todd had given them in a nearby trashcan as they went off to join their parents.

A few tears were finally shed as the boys parted, even though all of them knew it was only for a short time. Bonds had been forged that would stand unbroken for many years to come. Les had brought along a camera, took photos of the boys and their families, and promised prints for everyone.

Sajid came over to say goodbye and shook hands with Henry at the last minute. They seemed to be over their snit, but as soon as Henry returned to his pals he whispered, "I hope his wife's a nag. I still think she's ugly."

Clay ruffled the boy's hair and gave him a hug and a hidden kiss on the neck. "Love ya, Rascal. See you soon."

Clay's goodbye to Randy was a bit more emotional. Try as they might, both boys lost their battle to say goodbye without a tear. As they embraced, both broke down and cried. Their parents stood nearby and smiled as they saw the love and friendship between their sons. Little did they know how very deep it went, but all were proud that their sons, at fourteen, could show their feelings so freely.

Clay was unusually quiet as Les and he drove west, in their new Roadmaster, along State Road 77 toward Hagerstown, where they would then follow Route 40 into Cumberland. As they crossed South Mountain, just east of Hagerstown, Clay switched on the radio; it had a much better tone than the one in the 1939 Buick. He was scanning stations when all the sudden he heard a man singing to a familiar melody. Tony Bennett was singing *Stranger in Paradise.*

"Dad, that sounds like the song you played for me by that Russian man. His name started with a B, I think. I didn't know there were words to it."

"You're pretty sharp, Clay. The song he's singing, *Stranger in Paradise,* is based on *The Maiden's Dance* from Borodin's music. There's a new musical coming to Broadway in New York this December called *Kismet,* featuring Borodin's music. It's currently playing to record audiences in San Francisco. You have a good ear to recognize it that quickly. I'm going to have to give you some tryouts to see how well you can pick up the piano."

Clay saw an opportunity and jumped on it. "Dad, it's awfully heavy. I don't think I can pick it up."

Les looked at Clay who was only able to keep a straight face for a few moments before beginning to laugh. "You're quick witted and have a wicked sense of humor too. I'm going to have to keep my eye on you, mister. You'll be smarter than me before I know it."

"That's to get you back, Dad, for that awful mothball joke." Clay slid across the seat and leaned up against Les, who leaned over enough to give the boy a quick kiss on his temple.

"I am so lucky to have you, Clay. Something tells me we were fated to be a family. It's *kismet*."

"Huh?"

The name of the musical, *Kismet,* means fate --- something that was supposed to happen for a special reason. Now, I'm not saying your parents' and little brother's death was all part of that, but I do believe that you weren't meant to live with your uncle and aunt. There's something special about you, son. I don't know what it is yet, but it's special."

"I don't feel special."

"Maybe all parents think their kids are special, even adoptive parents, but, for some reason, Clay, you're different from most boys your age. For one thing, you have the wonderful ability to show affection. Most fourteen-year-olds would never want to snuggle beside their dad or, god forbid, put up with having their dad give them a hug or a kiss. Don't ever change, son, because what you are and what you feel is magnificent."

"I won't change, at least in wanting to be loved by you. I used to be so lonely, Dad. I used to make up stories in my head after the fire about an imaginary family who loved me, bought me Christmas gifts, and remembered my birthday, because Uncle Warren and Aunt Martha sure didn't. Loneliness hurt more in some ways than the pain from the fire."

"Why do you say that, Clay?"

"Well, with the burns, you know what caused it and other people know you're feeling it, but with loneliness, most times nobody knows how much you're hurting but you, and most times, nobody cares. If someone was around who did care, you wouldn't be lonely anymore. Does that make sense?"

"More than you can know. Some of us, Clay are lonely for different reasons. I had a great childhood with a loving mom and dad, but still there were times I was unbearably lonely. I could hardly stand it." Les thought this was a good time to lay a little groundwork for deeper discussions in the future. "I didn't fit in well with other kids and didn't have many friends."

"Why, Dad? You get along with people now. You get along

great with Albert, his folks and my friends from camp."

"Well, growing up helped with that. As a kid, I wasn't like most boys my age. I loved classical music and art and the kids around southern Pennsylvania just didn't understand a boy like me. I liked to dress neatly and read a lot and was always getting high grades in school. The other boys talked about sports, farming, mining and girls and I was awkward with all those subjects."

"Even girls?" Clay giggled.

Les nodded with a smile. "Especially girls. That's probably why I'm a confirmed bachelor. How about you, Clay? I know you're beginning to mature and grow up. Have you started thinking about young ladies?"

"No, not yet, I think I'm going to be a confirmed bachelor too. It sounds like a great idea."

Les laughed and said, "Oh, you never know, son. One of these days --- probably very soon --- you're going to look at those girls in school a whole new way. Do you ever have daydreams or even night dreams about girls?"

Clay was silent for a few seconds too long. Les asked, "Clay? If you're having daydreams about girls and feeling your body react in strange ways, it's okay. It's normal for boys your age to do that. There are certain parts of a girl's body that might make you experience what's called an erection. Do you know what I'm talking about?"

"Maybe."

"I thought you might. There's all number of slang terms for it like boner, hard on, or even stiffy, which I always thought was a silly word for it." Both of them shared a chuckle.

"You're at the age when I might need to have a talk with you about the birds and the bees. You know, sex."

"Uh huh." Clay was feeling strange as he considered his true nature. He wanted Les to love him but if Les ever found out he liked boys and got erections from thinking about and especially touching and sucking on boys, Les would hate him.

"I'll soon have to stop somewhere for gas; I should have filled up in Hagerstown, but forgot. The Roadmaster uses a little more gas than the old '39 model. It has a big four-barrel carburetor and with gas at eleven cents a gallon, I'm glad I'm soon getting a major raise."

"Yeah that'll be good." Clay was unusually silent.

"I'm not embarrassing you, am I, with talk about the birds and bees? If so, we can talk about this some other time. I just thought this might be a good time to chat since we still have about fifty miles to go."

"No, I'm not embarrassed, Dad. Some of the stuff about sex I know already. I learned a lot from friends." Clay thought how true that was, considering all Randy had taught him that first day by the dock and during their campout.

"Okay. That's good I suppose, as long as what they told you was accurate. Sometimes other boys have some warped ideas about sex. Uh, part of my job as a dad is to make sure you get the facts. Can I ask you a few questions to see how much you know? That is, unless it bothers you."

"No, it won't bother me. Go ahead."

"If I ask you anything that disturbs you, please let me know, okay?"

"Sure."

"Let's see, where should we start? You're fourteen and a half and I've noticed when you're undressed that you've already grown pubic hair. You have some hair growing under your right arm, too. So, with that in mind, let me ask this. Do you know what a wet dream is?"

"Uh huh."

"Have you ever had that happen?"

"Uh huh."

"How old were you when that happened? I'm not embarrassing you, am I?"

"Nope. Uh, it was about a month ago I think, just after you became my dad and I moved in. I woke up and my underwear was wet and smelly from sperm."

"Yep, that's a wet dream. So, have you also learned how to do it yourself? Do you know what I mean by that?"

"Yeah, Dad, I know. I, uh, do it sometimes. You aren't angry with me for doing that, are you?" He looked closely at Les's face to see how he was reacting.

Les was smiling. "Not at all, all guys do it until they get married usually. I'll even tell you a secret since I'm asking you all kinds of secret things. Even adults do it sometimes too. I'm just as guilty as you. It's natural to do it and there's nothing at all wrong with it. Some people tell you you'll go blind if you do it, or it will make you go insane, or even grow hair on the palms of your hands." Both laughed about the hairy hands. "All those stories are pure crap."

"I don't think it's wrong either. It's the way we're made, I guess." Clay found himself surprised to think Les did it too, but since he wasn't married, Clay supposed Les would want to feel good sometimes like any other guy.

"So when you do it, Clay, do you think about girls then?"

"I guess, sometimes." He felt dirty lying to Les, but what else could he say. An answer of no would just prompt Les to ask what he did think about.

"Okay. Now we come to the important warning part of our talk. Do you know how a man or even a teenaged boy can make a woman, or a teenage girl pregnant?"

"Uh huh."

"And..."

"Uh, a boy or a man gets hard and puts his penis inside a girl's or a woman's opening down below and moves in and out until he has sperm squirt out. The sperm goes inside the woman and reaches the egg cell and sometimes makes it change into a baby which is born about nine months later."

"Wow! You got it exactly right. Where did you learn that?"

"Some I learned in health class and some from my friends. Some I kind of figured out as soon as I learned how to make the sperm come out of me."

"Uh, that's good. You got everything exactly right. Now that you know that, what do you think could happen if you and a girlfriend got very carried away kissing, hugging and touching and all of the sudden you get the urge to put your penis in there and..."

"Well, a boy doesn't dare do that till he's married, Dad, or he and especially the girl would be in a lot of trouble. She might get pregnant and her daddy would get a gun and start looking for the boy." Clay had to laugh as he said that. Les did too and ruffled Clay's hair.

"Yeah, that's been known to happen. Do you think you have the will power to resist that kind of urge if it ever happens? And believe me, sometimes things get out of hand real fast when you feel those urges."

"Dad, I swear, I will never do that with a girl. I know what could happen and that's why I'm a confirmed bachelor like you."

Les, while keeping one eye on the road, glanced at Clay from time to time and said, "Well, right now you say that, but things change, buddy and you always have to be ready for anything. You might think you're too young to try sex, but you'd be surprised how things just happen. Once the horse is out of the barn, it's damned hard to put him back in sometimes."

"Dad, may I ask you a question?"

"Sure, Clay, anytime. Go ahead."

"Dad, you've said you're a confirmed bachelor. Once I asked you if you fell in love and a lady hurt you in some way and you said that wasn't what happened. Is there some other reason?"

Les had been dreading this question for some time and wasn't sure exactly how to deal with it. He drove along in silence for a few seconds. "Clay, I simply never fell in love with a woman. When I was younger, I wasn't interested in the girls at my high school or church like most other boys were. I had other interests that occupied my time and my thoughts. There was my music and art and some other issues that I will explain better to you one day soon. I'd like to wait until you're a little older and we get to know each other better. Is it okay if I put that part of the answer off for a little while? It's a real personal thing and I have to tell you about it in just the right way, so I need a little time."

"That's okay, Dad. Whenever you feel it's right you can tell me. I have some private stuff like that too and maybe once we're together longer I'll tell you about some of the things that bother me and make me feel scarred."

Les thought about the fire and some of the memories Clay had to deal with. "Sure, son, we'll both wait a little while, but whenever you're ready to talk, I'm ready to listen."

"Me too, Dad. Me too."

Chapter 21

Les pulled into a Texaco station a few miles past Hancock, Maryland, where three teen-aged attendants rushed around filling the gas tank, washing the windows and checking the oil and tires. Les

tipped them each a quarter. A few miles ahead was the rather steep climb up Sidling Hill --- really a mountain --- that had always challenged their older Buick. Les was anxious to try out the Roadmaster on the twisting road he described as difficult and downright dangerous in winter. Les bought them each a Coca Cola and an Oh Henry candy bar which made Clay think of his buddy who was somewhere ahead of them traveling home with his parents.

He looked forward to seeing Henry again, but wondered how Albert might perceive him in light of what had happened at camp. Would Albert react the way he himself had? His own jealousy was still an embarrassment he had to recognize and guard against daily. If Albert turned out to be homosexual, would he be understanding and accepting of Clay's other friends? These were questions with which Clay would soon have to wrestle.

Once back on the highway, Les was pleased at how well the Roadmaster climbed Sidling Hill. Its powerful engine never skipped a beat as it powered the heavy automobile along the twisting road. It

was a little past three, while crossing Green Ridge Mountain, that Clay started getting sleepy. Les turned on the radio and tuned in a station featuring the kind of music he played on the piano. When Clay asked about it, Les said it was a classical music station out of Cumberland and that the particular piece playing was *Waltz of the Flowers,* by another Russian named Tchaikovsky.

"How do you remember names like that and that other Russian guy you said we might someday name a cat after?"

"Hey, I used to be a music teacher; remember? I had to know those things. If you truly love something the way I love music, the names and stories about the composers come easily." Les started humming along with the music and Clay listened carefully and found he enjoyed it himself. As the road passed beneath them, his thoughts turned to other things.

Again, he considered Albert. He'd learned a lot about himself and his homosexual nature during the two-week camp experience. He'd been spending much thought on the question of whether Albert was homosexual or not and how he was going to find out. He couldn't just blurt it out and tell Albert how he felt about him. Or could he? Clay remembered how he'd decided to tell the boys at camp about his burns and how he'd showed them what the burns looked like. After that, no one had any problems seeing his scars and never once had another boy made fun.

The situation with Albert was different, of course, but maybe it would be better to just talk to him about his feelings and see what happened. If Albert was shocked by it and didn't want to be his friend any longer, it might be better to find out right away rather than slog along watching for hints of how he felt. If Albert was the same way, they would both feel better and be able to grow closer. He remembered how good he had felt when Albert had snuggled close in bed and hugged him.

He also remembered how Albert and he had both had a wet dream that night. Albert had never said anything about the switched underwear. Maybe that was a bad sign, and maybe it was a good sign. *How can I bring up the underwear? Albert's spending the night tonight. Maybe I'll stay awake and see if Albert snuggles close again.* He continued to pose questions in his mind. *I wonder what Albert would do if I snuggle close to him first? Should do it before or after Albert falls asleep? I wonder if...*

As they continued along Route 40, these and other thoughts bounced around his mind until he finally drifted off to sleep. It was nearly an hour later when he felt a series of bumps and woke up. Les looked over at him as he sat up, rubbed the sleep out of his eyes and looked around. They had just crossed over a section of bad road under repair near his school in Sand Patch. He'd slept all the way through Cumberland and beyond into Pennsylvania.

"Whew! I was sound. Sorry I wasn't much company, Dad. Guess

I was tired from all the stuff we did at camp. We're almost to Albert's house."

"Here; comb your hair, buddy. It's all pushed up on one side." Les chuckled and handed Clay a pocket comb he pulled from his pants pocket and pointed out a small mirror on the back of the passenger side's sun visor. "You'll need a trip to the barber with school starting soon."

"Ooooo, don't remind me, high school."

"Are you looking forward to it?"

"Yes and no, I suppose. I have to go whether I'm willing or not."

"That's true. You'll do fine and like it too. There's Albert's place."

Les turned in along the driveway to the Stiles property. Les tooted the horn as the Roadmaster came to a stop in front of the house. Les left the engine running. A few moments later, Albert came running around the side of the house and his parents stepped out on the porch.

Les and Clay both got out of the car and stretched. Before Clay could get his balance, however, Albert threw himself on him and hugged him tightly. Clay was surprised, but pleased. He returned the hug and said, "Boy, I've missed you. I sure wish you could have gone with me. I had a lot of fun and thought of you every day."

"Me too, I never missed anyone as much as I did you these last two weeks. You have a nice tan. Been swimming a lot?"

"Yeah, the lake there was great," he said aloud, but added in a whisper, "I would have rather been skinny-dipping with you at the mill, though."

Albert grinned and agreed with a, "Me too."

Les was talking with Mr. and Mrs. Stiles, as they looked over the new car. He opened the trunk so Albert could put his bike inside. Albert wanted to make sure and have it if he and Clay decided to go somewhere the next day.

Les called out, "Okay fellows, we need to get moving. I'm bushed and I'm sure there's an anxious cat waiting for us at home. Albert, grab your things, kiddo, and jump in the Buick; you guys have all evening to chat."

He said to Albert's folks, "Clay slept the last thirty miles, I didn't. It was a long two weeks and a long ride. Thanks for watching out for the place. I've picked up a small gift for Albert, to go along with his cat-sitting pay; I bought a watch like the one I got Clay. I heard he fell asleep on the job the other night and gave you all a scare."

"He sure did. I had to drive over and pound on your door to wake him up," said Albert's dad with feigned anger as he gave his son a side hug.

"He's a great kid and Clay and I both think the world of him. You both have a good night."

Mr. Stiles said, "You too, Les. We're happy for you and the boy. His people should have been jailed for the way they treated him."

Les drove the remaining third of a mile to their house listening to the two boys catching up. Clay had jumped in the back seat along with Albert and the two chatted about some of the things Clay had done at camp. After pulling into their driveway, everyone pitched in to carry all their belongings inside. Les then drove the car into the garage, but left the big door open so the car could better cool. The boys were already inside having their shins polished by Debussy. Clay picked him up and gave his soft belly a kiss. Albert came close and did the same while Clay held the cat in his arms. Clay did something without thinking about it. He had gotten so used to being affectionate with Randy and Henry, that he leaned forward and gave Albert a quick kiss on his cheek.

Albert looked at him with wide, surprised eyes.

Clay, realizing what he'd just done, first checked to see if Les was around. He wasn't. Clay said, "Sorry, I didn't mean to surprise you with that, but I've missed you so much and it just happened before I thought about it. Sorry."

"It's okay. I don't mind. It was nice, but you know..."

"Yeah, sorry, I won't do it again."

There was a pause as Albert just stared at Clay intently. He finally said, "I don't mind if you do it again, I just wasn't expecting it. Uh, we're best friends and all, so it really can't hurt; just don't do it when other kids or our folks are around."

"Sure, I understand. Some people might take it the wrong way," Clay added.

"Yeah." Albert smiled and Clay knew everything was okay. For a few moments, he'd slipped, but had also learned something. Albert had said he didn't mind if it happened again. *I wonder what might happen in bed tonight? I hope he hugs me again like last time. If he doesn't, I might hug him and see if he likes it.*

223

Clay led the way into the parlor and shut the French doors behind them. He sat down on a nearby sofa that faced the grand piano and invited Albert to join him. Debussy jumped up and found Clay's lap and made himself comfortable. As usual, as Clay stroked his neck and back, Debussy started pushing at his knees with his paws. Both boys laughed at the cat's familiar actions.

Albert asked, "Uh, did you make any new friends at camp? Your letter mentioned one boy who lives near Cumberland."

"That's Henry Winters. He lives in a place called Cresaptown, a little southwest of Cumberland. His dad and mom said he could come visit me once in a while. I'm looking forward to having you meet him."

"What's he like? Is he shorter or taller than I am?"

"He's thirteen, but looks about eleven; he has blond hair and light brown eyes. He's kind of shy until he gets to know you and then he's more playful and fun." *Boy is he ever playful and fun once he gets to know you.*

"When's he coming over?"

Maybe I should wait a bit before I tell Albert I've invited him to go camping with us. "Uh, I'm not sure, yet. Sometime before school starts probably. I met another boy at camp named Randy Meadows from Harper's Ferry. Once dad starts working as a conductor, Randy might come up by train to see us too. He has a best friend who was born in France, named Claude."

"Was he at camp too?"

"No. He couldn't come because he had a broken leg; I met him when he visited Randy on Parent's Day though. He might come along with Randy when he visits."

"Wow, you met a whole lot of new friends. Hope you don't forget about me." Albert was looking at the carpet as he said that. Clay thought he saw some moisture in Albert's eyes.

"Hey, you're my number one friend. I like them, but not the way I like you. You're special. That's why I gave you a kiss a minute ago. I love you as a friend, Albert, and always will. Are you okay?"

"Yeah, I just missed you so much, Clay. I wanted to go to camp too, but had to visit my cousins in Philadelphia; Mom would have been hurt if I didn't. My aunt is her sister. I'd much rather been with you."

"Well, I'm home now and you're staying over. We can spend all kinds of time together doing things until school starts. Tomorrow I want us to go swimming at the mill. Would you like that?"

"Yeah, I almost went on my own, but it wouldn't have been as much fun and I didn't want to go with Toby. He's always saying mean stuff about you and your dad."

"Yeah, you said that in your letter. What did he say?"

"Oh, he was just trying to get me angry. He said that your dad was queer and that he was a perfect match for you because you're probably queer too."

Clay felt himself getting both angry and fearful. Part of him wanted to confront Toby, but another part was saying, *Stay clear of him because he's right about me and could cause a lot of trouble.*

Instead, he asked, "Albert? Do you know what Toby means when he calls me a queer?"

"I think so. He means you're odd or weird and not like other kids. I think that's what it means. Does it?" Albert was looking intently at Clay, waiting for his response.

"No. The way he's saying it means that he thinks I like boys instead of girls. It means I want to fall in love with a boy and not a girl." Clay watched for Albert's reaction.

"Oh. I've heard it meant that too, but I wasn't sure. That's kinda mean for him to say that about you and your dad both. Les is a good man and I'm glad he got to be your father. Toby's just jealous."

"If he says anything like that at school this year, I'm gonna punch him in the nose. I won't have anyone saying my dad is queer, or anything else. I don't care what he says about me, but saying stuff about Dad is gonna get him hurt."

Albert looked intently at Clay before saying, "Wow. You've changed. I never heard you say you'd hit someone before. Let me ask you something, now that I know what queer means. Are there really boys who want to fall in love with other boys?"

"Yeah, the real name is homosexual. Some boys are born that way, I think. They really like other boys and that should be okay if the other boy likes them too." Albert's eyes were open wide as he listened to Clay.

"You don't think it's wrong and unnatural?"

"Not really. Everybody's different in some way. People should be able to be themselves and not be judged by others."

"If you had a friend who was queer, would you still like him and do fun things with him?"

"I sure would. What about you?"

Albert flinched and looked odd as he said, "You mean, am I queer?"

Clay giggled, "No, I mean if you had a queer friend, would you still be his friend?"

"Oh. Yeah, I'd still be his friend. It wouldn't bother me at all." Clay thought there might be a wealth of meaning behind what Albert had just said and what he'd slipped and said before.

About that time, Les joined the boys in the parlor. "You guys catching up on news and gossip?" They grinned and Clay nodded. "Tell you what, I'm too tired to cook supper this evening and since I'm on vacation for a week before I start my new job, I want us to celebrate. Let's go out to eat. How about I drive us up to Somerset? We'll visit that restaurant on Main Street. They have good food, they fix it fast and it's not too expensive; all the right reasons to eat there."

Clay said, "Sounds good, Dad." Albert agreed as well, so Les told them to put Debussy on the other side of the French doors, so he couldn't dig in the planter, and then the three of them left through the other parlor door that led to the garage. The big door was still open, so Les started the Buick and backed it out. Clay and Albert jumped in after Clay closed and locked the garage door. They headed off to Somerset.

Just after they got under way, Clay asked, "Albert, have you ever smelled mothballs?"

The rest of the evening went well. Les gave Albert the wristwatch he'd bought for him and paid him ten dollars for his two weeks of cat-sitting duties. They all watched the television for a half hour before Les got up and said he was going to bed. "You fellows make sure and close the parlor doors when you're done so Debussy can't water and fertilize the palms and don't stay up too late. What have you fellows got planned for tomorrow?"

"Albert and I want to go swimming at the millpond tomorrow morning, if that's okay."

"Fine with me, fellows, just be careful. Check for rocks and glass before you ride the flume. One crack on your backsides is enough." Both boys laughed. "Goodnight, boys." They wished him goodnight as well. Clay gave him a hug and a kiss. Surprisingly, Albert gave him a hug also.

It wasn't long before Clay suggested they head off to bed.

Actually, Clay wasn't sleepy; but was looking forward to what might happen after the lights went out.

Each boy took a quick bath in the big, claw-footed tub before dressing in their pajamas. The heat of the summer day had eased off somewhat, but Clay left his bedroom windows open. His room was located on one corner of the house, so there were two windows on each of two walls and the air circulated well, keeping the room cool and comfortable. Clay's big double bed was positioned cat-a-corner with its head in the outside corner of the room between the two windowed walls.

Clay put fresh sheets on the bed since they'd been gone two weeks and he had a guest. Albert gave him a hand making the bed and soon everything was ready for them to crawl in. Clay asked, "Ready for the lights?" Albert smiled and said he was all set as he jumped in bed along its left side. Clay switched off the main lights but left on a glowing, railroad lantern. Les had it modified by one of the B&O shop workers into a night-light for Clay's room. It was brass with four Fresnel lenses; two were red and two were blue. It hung on a chain above Clay's bed and filled the room with soft-colored light.

Debussy chose to sleep in one of Clay's dresser drawers he'd purposely left open for the cat to use. Debussy had seen the bed would be crowded and decided the drawer would provide a better night's sleep.

Outside they could occasionally hear the call of a whip-poor-will and the chattering of flying squirrels that lived and played at night in the two, tall, sugar maple trees that overshadowed that corner of the house. A bright gibbous moon was shining through the western windows casting twin shafts of moonlight across the floor and eastern wall.

Albert looked up and said, "I love that lantern. It wasn't here when I stayed over last time, but I noticed it when I was taking care of Debussy this week. When did you get it?"

"Just a few days before I went to camp. Dad got it from the B&O. It's one of the rear lights from a caboose. One of the men he knows, who works in the shops there, fixed it up with a cord and an electric light inside. It makes a super night-light."

"It sure does."

"It's not too bright and I like the colors. Les gave me a set of different colored lenses that I can change to make it light up in any way I want. I can leave the lenses off, but that makes it pretty bright in here. I usually use blue and red, but I have yellow and green lenses too. The colors signal different things on the railroad."

"It's really nice. I like the red and blue, too."

"If you want, I can turn it off when we're ready to sleep. I'm tired from the long day, but not sleepy yet."

"Me neither. We can talk for a while if you want. Tell me more about camp."

"Well, we stayed pretty busy. Our cabin's theme color was red and we were called Dragon Squad. Tomorrow I'll show you the shirts, shorts and bathing suit they gave us with our color and dragon label on them. The bathing suit is one of those tight-fitting ones and I was a little embarrassed to wear it at first."

"Why is that?"

"Well it fits so tight that it sort of shows everything. Anyone can see the shape of your dick and balls."

"Criminy! Did everyone have to wear that kind of suit?"

"Yeah, every cabin and team had a different color."

"Tomorrow, Clay, will you put it on, so I can see what you look like in it?"

"Yeah, if you want me to." *I'd like to see you in it too. Maybe I'll let you try it on,* thought Clay. In fact, he went ahead and said it. "I'll wear it for you, but then you have to put it on for me."

"Why?" Albert grinned and looked sideways at Clay.

"Well, if you get to see me practically naked in that suit, I get to see you."

"We've seen each other all the way naked lots of times. You were just brushing your teeth while I took a bath in your bathtub. I was naked then. Why would I look any different in the suit?"

"Why did you ask me to put it on then? You just want to see my privates in a tight bathing suit --- Come on, admit it."

Albert was frowning a bit and said, "That wasn't the reason. I just wanted to see what you looked like at camp."

Clay sensed he might be pushing Albert a little too much. He could tell the boy was very guarded about the subject, so he backed off a bit. "I was just teasing, Albert. I'll put it on for you."

"Maybe. We'll see."

228

Chapter 22

They rested in silence for a few minutes until Albert turned on his side, looked at Clay and said, "Clay, do you ever have weird dreams that bother you?"

"You mean about the fire and stuff?"

"Oh, yeah, I guess you would have dreams about that. That wasn't what I was thinking of though."

"I sometimes do. I dream about you sometimes, so maybe that qualifies as a weird dream."

"Aw, it does not. Come on, I'm being serious. Sometimes I have dreams that bother me. They bother me a lot."

"Sorry. I was just joking, but I do dream about you. I like having those dreams because I like you." Clay reached over and ruffled Albert's soft hair. "Like I said before, you're my very best friend and I love you like I would a brother."

"Thanks. That means a lot to me 'cause I love you the same way. I dream of you too; nice dreams."

"So, you have dreams that bother you; do you want to tell me about them?

"Maybe, do you ever have dreams about girls, Clay?"

Oh no! Please don't say you've started dreaming about girls! "No, for the most part now, I dream about Les and you and even Debussy sometimes. At camp I dreamed about the new guys I met there, but you were always with me in those dreams too."

"I'm the same way; you're in a *lot* of my dreams. Clay, what bothers me is that I *don't* dream about girls. Toby and the other guys are always talking about their dreams about girls and their boobs and parts down below and I don't. That bothers me."

"I'm the same way, Albert. I've never had a single dream about a girl."

"Really? That makes me feel a little better. Something happened to me a couple of weeks ago and I've been thinking about telling you about it, but I was a little ashamed. Now, I don't feel so bad, so I'm gonna tell you, but please promise that it will be a secret between us, okay?"

"Always, Albert, you know I've never broken my word. Go ahead and tell me." Clay was certain Albert was about to talk about the wet dream he'd experienced the last time they slept together before he went to camp, but that turned out not to be the case.

"I was playing with Toby, Curt and Curt's older brother, Mike about three weeks ago. I'd gone over to Curt and Mike's house and we were up in that tree house they built back in the woods. Mike had brought along a magazine he wanted to show us. It was one he wasn't supposed to have."

"What kind of magazine?"

"It was written in a foreign language, German I think, and had a whole lot of pictures of naked women in it. There weren't any naked men."

"Wow! I just bet he wasn't supposed to have it. Where did he get it from?"

"Mike said their older brother, who's in college up at Harrisburg, had it and he swiped it when his brother was visiting."

"What were the women doing?"

"Weird stuff. Some were lying around on carpets, couches and on fancy beds and a few were sort of touching themselves down below. It was kind of strange the way they were using their fingers to spread themselves open so the person taking the picture could see right inside."

"Wow! I've never even seen what a grown woman looks like down there. I remember seeing Mom dressing when I was little. I remember seeing her breasts and private hair, but nothing more."

"Toby, Curt and Mike were going crazy as they looked through the magazine. I had to say a few things once in a while like I was excited too, but I really didn't like looking at the women. Toby had a boner and kept bragging about it. So did Curt and Mike."

"How about you, did you get one?" *Please say no. Please say no.*

"That's what really bothered me. I didn't. I told the others I did, but I didn't."

Clay said, "I wouldn't have either. I think it's awful that grown women would let someone take their picture naked while they touched themselves. That's wrong."

"Boy, I'm glad to hear you say that, because I was afraid I was the only one who thought that way." Albert truly looked relieved.

"I sure hope none of those ladies were moms, because that would be awful for their kids to find out their mom did that. I guess they get paid for doing it; it's sorta like prostitution."

Albert then said, "Toby asked to borrow the magazine."

"What would he want to do that for?"

"He said he wanted to use it to play with himself that night."

"Oh. Did Mike let him take it?"

"Nope. He said if he wanted to use it that way, he'd have to do it right there in the tree house. He wasn't going to chance letting Toby's mom or dad find it."

"Did he?" asked Clay with a grin.

"Did he what?"

"Did Toby use the magazine right there?"

"No. He was too chicken and shy I guess. If he would have, I would have left before he did it anyway."

"Yeah, I guess I would have too."

There was a period of silence before Albert spoke again, "Clay, can I ask you something?"

"Sure. Go ahead."

"Now don't think I'm getting weird or something, but since we're best friends, I want to ask you this."

"Go ahead."

"Do you ever play with yourself?"

"Sometimes, I guess all guys our age probably do. Dad and I just had a talk about that today."

Albert blinked and looked surprised. "Les talked to you about playing with yourself?"

"Yeah, it was while we were traveling home in the car and the first time he talked to me about sex. He said since he's my dad now, it's his job to answer questions about sex and tell me things I need to know. He asked me if I ever did it, just like you just did and I told him the truth."

"That's cool. My dad and mom get all flustered when they have to talk about sex. Dad can hardly say some of the words and gets real embarrassed. Mom can't say penis. She always calls it my 'little thing'." Albert laughed and said, "She hasn't seen it lately." Both boys giggled at that. "Dad calls it my member. That really sounds stupid."

"Member? That is kinda goofy. I've never heard anyone call it a member."

"Now every time Dad talks about being a *member* of the Elks Club I get this mental picture of a moose with a big dick." Both boys laughed hysterically for nearly a half a minute at that.

"That's awful, Albert. Is your mom a *member* of the sewing

circle?" That started another laughing jag.

After a few more interesting uses of the word, the boys finally calmed down.

Clay wanted to bring the conversation back to where it had been before so he said, "So, Albert; I told you that I do it. How about you? You're talking about it so I guess you do. How often do you exercise your member?"

A few more laughs ensued before Albert said, "Pretty often, about once or sometimes twice a day."

"Wow! That's a lot. I skip a night once in a while, but not often."

Clay started giggling until Albert finally said, "Okay what's so funny? Spit it out." For some reason that last statement made Clay laugh even more.

Finally, he was able to say, "When I told you I did it just about every day I almost said, I want to make sure it's a *member* in good standing." He once again lost control and both erupted in more laughter.

Albert panted, "No more member jokes; I can't breathe."

After settling down Clay asked, "Have you ever had a wet dream?"

For some reason Albert looked odd and sobered up right away. He finally said, "It happened once, how about you?"

"Yeah, just once; when did it happen to you?"

"Uh, I'll tell you tomorrow. I'm getting kinda sleepy now. I think I wore myself out laughing just now. Let's go to sleep. Okay?"

Clay knew now that Albert had found the soiled underwear and knew not to push the issue just yet. *He said he'd tell me tomorrow. I can wait.* Instead, Clay replied, "Okay. I'm kinda tired too. It's been a long and busy day. I'm probably gonna sleep till about nine or ten tomorrow morning."

"Don't forget, we plan to go to the mill."

"We can do that anytime we want tomorrow. We'll make it up as we go. You want the lantern on or off?"

"Probably best if it's off. It's super nifty, but still kinda bright. The moonlight will give us enough light, I think. I'm gonna go to the toilet before you switch it off though. All that laughing made me fill up with pee."

"Yeah, me too, let's go."

They padded off to the john and a few minutes later returned. Clay switched off the lantern and they settled down under just a sheet.

"Good night, Albert. It's great being back home with you."

"Yeah, I feel the same way. Would it be all right if I give you a hug goodnight?"

"Sure, I was gonna do it anyway," said Clay.

"You were? That's cool."

The boys embraced side by side and the hug lasted an unusually long time. Clay felt his body reacting after a few seconds and secretly didn't want to let go. He was far enough away from Albert that his buddy couldn't feel what was happening below. Clay was wondering if Albert was behaving the same way.

Clay whispered in Albert's ear, which was right beside his lips, "I love you Albert and missed you."

"I love you too. This feels nice. I almost wish we didn't have to let go."

Clay whispered, "If you want, we can hug each other and still go to sleep. I won't mind if you want us to."

Albert thought in silence for a while and then said, "Maybe for a little while. That would be nice. I feel so safe and happy when you hug me. I hope you don't think I'm weird or something, but I wish we lived together and we could do this all the time."

"Maybe when we're older and finish school we could share a house or something. I'd like to live with you all the time."

"Maybe, I hope we can."

The boys continued their embrace and before long drifted off to sleep. Their dreams that night, as they lay in each others arms were dreams of contentment and love.

Les looked in on them the next morning and found them both still sleeping soundly. Albert was lying on his back; Clay was on his belly with his right arm across Albert's chest and his hand on his friend's neck. Clay's head was cradled in Albert's right armpit while Albert's right arm was around Clay with his palm resting on Clay's back. Les smiled and thought to himself, *I'm beginning to wonder about those two. Maybe I need to ask Clay a few questions that are more pointed. They are, after all, fourteen.* To find two younger kids cuddled like that was one thing, but to find two teenagers about to enter high school so close could mean something entirely different.

Les sat for a while in an armchair just watching the boys sleep and enjoying their innocence. He thought to himself, *if they are homosexual, Clay certainly has found the right home. He'll never be judged and always be loved for who he is. God, I love that boy.*

Debussy wandered in about that time and looked like he was about to jump on the bed, but Les whispered, "Come here, fuzz face. Leave 'em be and let 'em sleep. Come on." He patted his lap and the cat jumped up, settled himself and, as usual, began to purr and push with his paws against Les's lap. The two of them spent another half hour contentedly watching the two boys at rest.

Sometime around nine, Clay's eyes fluttered open. He was on his side facing the edge of the bed. He could easily see that the morning was well underway. He rolled to the left and saw Albert looking at him and smiling.

"Hi. I thought you were gonna sleep till noon."

Clay smiled back and yawned. "Whew. You should have waked me up long ago. What time is it?"

Albert looked at his new wristwatch and said, "Five 'till nine. I've only been awake a little while myself. Your dad looked in on us a few minutes ago and said to let you sleep as long as you want. He's going to be out in the yard mowing with the tractor and said we can fix our own breakfast."

"Yeah, and I'm hungry too. Be back in a minute. I have to go." Clay sat up and stretched again before padding off to the bathroom. As he pulled down his pajamas to go, he noticed that he hadn't had a wet dream this time. *I wonder if Albert did.*

Just as he returned to his bedroom, Albert was changing clothes. For a moment, he caught sight of his briefs as Albert pulled on a pair of jeans. He hadn't needed to change into fresh underwear, so he must not have had an emission. Albert glanced around and grinned. He tossed his pajamas on the bed and headed off for the bathroom.

Clay walked over, picked up the pajamas, and brought them to his nose. They were still warm from Albert's body and Clay could smell the pleasant natural scent of his friend. He felt such a surge of love for Albert at that moment that he nearly sobbed from happiness. Hugging him as they went to sleep was nearly as satisfying as anything sexual they might have done. He was firmly convinced at this point that Albert loved him, but was still not sure if it included sexual attraction. It probably did, but he had to be sure.

Clay heard the toilet flush and dropped the pajamas back where he found them. He still wondered how Albert had reacted several weeks before when he found Clay's underclothes instead of his own in his duffle bag. Albert re-entered the room, came right to Clay, and gave him a hug as if it was a natural thing to do. Maybe now it was. Clay hugged him tightly and gave him a kiss on the cheek as well. Albert pulled away, looked deeply in Clay's eyes and kissed him back on the cheek.

"If Toby saw us," Albert said as his hands still rested on Clay's shoulders, "we'd be in for so much trouble. I don't care though. You're my best friend and even though we're fourteen, I just feel different with you. Now that I know you don't mind a hug, or even what we just did, as long as it's just us, it's okay."

"I feel that way too," Clay said as he placed his hands along Albert's sides. "It felt so nice hugging you last night as we went to sleep. I woke up about three and had to pee and we were still hugging."

"We were?"

"Yep. And when I laid back down I hugged you some more and went back to sleep. I used to be so lonely at my uncle's place, but now living with Dad and having you over and being able to hug you, I don't feel lonely at all. I feel good for the first time since my family died."

"Good. That's what I'm here for. I really meant what I said last night too about us getting a house together someday. I like being with you better than being with any other person I know."

"Me too, maybe that's what will happen. We better get something to eat." They finished dressing and went downstairs. Debussy was waiting for them outside Clay's bedroom door, so he snatched up the cat as they passed and cuddled him on the way down the stairs. Clay fixed them some fried eggs and toast with apple juice. Outside, they heard Les passing the house occasionally with the tractor as he mowed the high grass.

By ten, they had cleaned up the kitchen and were all set to leave for the millpond. Clay went outdoors and waved at Les as he made a pass by the back door. Les shut off the tractor and made his way toward the porch. Clay ran and met him halfway with a warm hug.

"Les laughed and said, "Sorry I'm so sweaty, kiddo. Boy, I enjoy your hugs. Where's Albert?"

"He's inside feeding Debussy. We're going to ride our bikes to the old mill and go swimming. You want to join us?" Clay grinned as he and his dad walked toward the house.

"Not this time, but sometime soon I will. Don't forget, we'll soon be going camping. I'd like to do that while I have a few days off, so we need to pick a date. Henry can join us if you want."

"I'm really looking forward to that, Dad."

"Good. I'm going to get something cold to drink and then, while you boys are off having a grand old time skinny-dipping, I'll be slaving away on the tractor mowing the rest of our seven acres."

Once indoors, Les sat down with a tall glass of iced tea at the kitchen table while he chatted with Clay and Albert, who had joined them, about a date to go camping.

"I figure we'll spend two nights wherever we decide to camp. Any ideas where we might want to go?"

Albert suggested Dan's Rock, a nearly three thousand foot high crest atop Dan's Mountain a little southwest of Cumberland where he and his parents had once gone for a picnic. There was a public park and overlook there. Plans were underway to make the site a Maryland state park.

Les commented, "That's not far from Henry's home, you know. In fact, Cresaptown, where he lives, is just east of Dan's Mountain and from up there, you could probably look right down on his home. I was also thinking of Deep Creek Lake out in Western Maryland. Also, there's Shawnee Park, near Bedford. It has a big lake for swimming, but its campground isn't as nice. Another great spot is Muddy Creek Falls. It's not far from Deep Creek, so even if we camp at the falls, we can still enjoy the lake. There are a lot of great places to visit in that part of Maryland."

"Dad, in your room there's a picture of you and a friend standing in front of a waterfall. Is that Muddy Creek Falls?" Clay already knew that it was, but wanted to see what Les would say.

Les looked a little surprised, but said, "Yeah, that's Muddy Creek Falls. Todd and I used to go there a lot."

"Who was Todd, Mr. Mills?" asked Albert. "Is he still your friend?"

Les smiled and said, "No, he died a couple of years ago, after the war. He was hurt pretty badly during the war and kind of lost his will to live. He was my best friend; kind of like you fellows are best friends. His name was Todd Garrett. His people actually came from over in that part of Maryland. Deep Creek Lake is located in Garrett County."

"Do you miss him, Mr. Mills?"

Les hesitated, cleared his throat and said, "Yeah. I still miss him a lot. He was my closest friend and I loved him like a brother. Well, we'll talk some more about where we'll go camping later. Think about these suggestions and before supper we'll decide. That way you can call Henry and see if he wants to join you fellows."

Albert said, "Is Henry going to be coming along?"

Clay had to do some fast thinking. He hadn't yet told Albert about his plans to include Henry. He said, "He might. I told him that he could come over sometime before school started and asked him if he might like to go camping. Dad and I asked his folks at camp and they said it would be okay. It doesn't bother you does it?"

"No. I was just surprised to hear he might be along. It'll be fun. If he's your friend, he'll probably be my friend too."

"You'll like him. He's a lot of fun.

Chapter 23

Clay had been the one to remind Albert to bring along his bike when they'd picked him up the night before, so they'd have a way to get around. A half hour later found Clay and Albert arriving at the old mill. They were glad to see that no one else was there. Today, Clay and Albert wanted it all to themselves.

They'd packed along some sandwiches and drinks for later, but now the cool-looking water looked too inviting, so both started shedding clothes on the flagstone footpath that ran along the pond beside the mill. Just before they took off their underwear, Clay pulled something red out of his bike's saddlebag. The bright color caught Albert's eye and he asked, "What's that?"

"That's my dragon squad bathing suit from camp."

"Oh, yeah, wow, it's so small. Put it on. I want to see you in it."

"Why?" ask Clay with a sneaky look on his face.

Albert opened his mouth to say something, but suddenly was temporarily at a loss for words. Clay giggled and at last, Albert was able to say. "Well, you were the one last night who said you'd put it on so I could see you in it. Why?"

"I don't know," stammered Clay as he realized he'd painted himself into a corner. I just wanted you to see how a person hardly needs it since it shows everything anyway. I'll put it on and you'll see." He pulled off his underwear and pulled on the suit. He noticed that Albert didn't turn away through the entire process and Clay glanced occasionally at Albert's front for any reaction he might have. After pulling on the red suit he stood in front of Albert, spread his arms apart, and said, "Well, you tell me. Might as well wear nothing, right?"

"I don't know. If I was a girl, I'd sure like to see you wearing that. You're right. It shows the shape of everything."

Clay couldn't be sure, but thought he saw something stirring behind Albert's briefs. He felt a minor change himself. Before much else happened, he pulled off the suit and tossed it to Albert. "It's your turn."

"Huh?"

"Come on. I showed you mine now show me yours. Let's see if you have what it takes to make the girls sigh."

"Oh, okay. Just don't laugh. Albert pulled down his briefs and quickly pulled on the suit, but realized too late he'd put it on backward. Clay chuckled as Albert said, "Shit!" and pulled it back off. While reversing it, Clay noticed Albert was on the rise and got the giggles.

"I said, don't laugh, you nut. Shut up!" Albert couldn't help laughing too as he finally got it on right.

"You'd really please the girls with that boner you got going, Albert." Albert turned away and Clay could see the back of his neck getting red.

"I can't help it. Just happens sometimes."

"Well, turn around and let me see anyway. You ain't alone." Clay was wearing nothing and his private parts were at full attention; he grinned as Albert glanced back over his shoulder. His eyes opened wide and went right to the center of attraction.

Albert had to laugh and said, "Darn it, Clay. What made you get hard?" He finally turned around and sure enough, his --- or rather --- Clay's suit was poking out and upward at the limit of the stretchy fabric. He pointed at Clay's front and teased, "You could hang your hat on that thing."

"Yeah, just don't let *that* thing," --- and he pointed --- "tear my suit. If it had teeth, I bet it would be growling and chewing its way out of there right now, ready for action."

"Shut up." Albert got the giggles and could hardly stop.

Clay asked, "What's so funny? Something's got you laughing."

In an authoritative voice Albert said, "Will all members please rise for the pledge of allegiance." That's all it took for Clay to start laughing too.

Without thinking, Clay stepped close to Albert and put his hands on his shoulders as though to hold himself up. Albert did the same, but as they regained control, both realized where they were and that their "members" were but a few inches from each other. Albert started to blink and back away, but Clay stopped laughing, looked directly into Albert's eyes instead of pulling away, leaned forward, and kissed him gently on his lips.

He felt Albert's entire body shiver and expected him to push him away, but instead, Albert looked into Clay's eyes and whispered, "You like boys too, don't you?"

"Uh huh, I like boys, but I *love* you."

Albert looked at Clay in wonder and a beautiful smile grew on his handsome face. He leaned forward and they kissed again, this time not briefly. Clay pressed his lower body against Albert's and felt his erection press against his friend's hardness behind the red suit. Clay reached and pulled down the suit allowing it to drop below Albert's knees. He pressed himself into Albert once more and kissed him again and again as both shared intimate love for the very first time.

Clay was feeling dizzy and could feel the heat of Albert's body rising as they gripped one another in this first heated embrace.

Albert whispered, "I've wanted to do this for so long, Clay. Ever since I learned about how it feels to make sperm, I've wanted to touch you and kiss you. I never thought you would want to do it though, but now, you do. Oh God, I feel so good."

"Me too, did you find my underwear in your duffle bag last time you stayed over?"

"Yeah! I couldn't figure out what happened, or what I should do. When I realized they were yours I... Well I kissed them and smelled them as I played with myself and I wanted to be with you then so much. Did you have mine?"

"I did the same thing. I could smell your sperm on them and I did the same thing. I still have them, except they smell a little bad now."

"Yours do too." Albert giggled. "Maybe we can wash them now. I won't need them anymore. I have the real thing. Can I touch you down below?"

"Oh yeah, go ahead. Pull the skin back too and be careful. It won't take much to make me come."

"Come where?"

Clay explained the word much as Randy had explained it to him. Again a little thread of guilt tickled the corners of his mind as he thought about his Harper's Ferry friend. *What would Albert think if he knew what Randy, Henry and I did at camp?* His thoughts were broken, however, as Albert gently pulled back his foreskin and played his fingers over his moist tip.

Albert squeezed and Clay's body jerked from the sudden intensity of sensation. Albert raised his fingers to his nose to smell the mucus, but was surprised at the unexpected new odor there and looked up at Clay with a questioning expression.

Clay watched him and said, "Do you like the way I smell down there?"

"What *is* that? It smells kinda odd. It smells good though." He kept sniffing.

Clay explained about the scent and how he purposely didn't wash it too thoroughly as he liked the smell too. He told Albert to bend down and smell it directly.

Albert blinked and seemed surprised, but bent anyway and did as Clay suggested.

"That's really something. Oh gosh, seeing you this close has me... Clay can we do it to each other today? I want to do it to you, if you'll let me. I've wanted to do it for a long time." Albert was still staring at Clay's erection and sliding his foreskin up and down.

Clay was already climbing and warned Albert, "Better go easy, or you're gonna get a face full."

Albert giggled and stood back up. Clay took him in hand and started playing with his tip. Albert closed his eyes and made soft sounds deep in his throat.

"That feels so good, Clay. God, I love this."

Clay looked around and said, "We have to be careful, Albert. If some other kids come out this way and catch us doing this, we'd be in for so much trouble. I can hardly wait to do it with you, but right out here in the open is too risky. Maybe we should walk up along the stone path near where the flume starts. The way the path curves, you can't see the beginning from here."

Albert said, "That, or we could get in the water and do it. We could see anyone coming ahead of time from there and keep our clothes close by."

"I'd kind of like us to do it the first time lying down. I want to do it with you a special way and it would be better if we were dry."

"How do you want to do it?"

"Let's take our towels and things up to the head of the millrace and I'll show you. We'll hear anyone coming from there because the sticks and dead leaves crunch when anyone walks on them. Let's take our bikes along too."

The boys pulled on their briefs long enough to gather their belongings and walk their bikes along the path to the funnel-shaped beginning of the millrace. Clay broke a limb from a nearby bush and used it like a broom to brush away as many fallen leaves and sticks from the flagstones before laying out their towels. He pulled off his briefs once more and turned to Albert smiling.

He opened his arms in invitation and Albert, after removing his underwear, joined him once more in an intimate hug. Both kissed

241

long and intently, exploring new emotions and sensations they'd both only dreamed about. Clay reached downward and guided their erections between each other's warm thighs where soon their natural moisture made them slippery and sensitive. As they kissed, they slowly moved in and out, carefully allowing their tension to build without going too far.

Albert whispered, "I see why you wanted us to stay dry. Oh gosh, Clay, I feel so good. Now I know we *have* to promise to live together someday. After this, I couldn't stand to be with anyone but you. I love you so much."

"I've loved you since we were in about sixth grade and I started liking boys. I didn't even understand it then, but I was always looking at you and wishing you were my brother, or that I could live with you at your house. Life with my uncle and aunt was terrible and I looked at you and wished I had a mom and dad again. Now that I have Les, and we both know how we are, I'm the happiest guy in the world." He shivered and a moment later felt Albert do the same.

Clay whispered, "Careful. I'm getting too close. We need to stop for a minute. I don't want us to come like this."

"Why not? It feels so nice. I'm almost ready." Albert kissed Clay's nose, and shivered as they slid apart. Clay sucked air between his teeth, as the sensation was almost more than he could control. Both stood panting for a moment or two.

"Lay down on the towel, Albert. I want to help you come first, and then you can do it to me any way you want."

Albert complied and Clay thought he'd never seen someone as handsome and exciting as the golden-haired youth lying before him with his knees slightly raised and his head resting on his folded jeans. His sex was moist and throbbing with every heartbeat. The most beautiful smile was on Albert's face as he waited to be loved.

Clay bent and spread Albert's legs apart gently kissing his raised knees, nuzzling along the inside of his left thigh and gradually moving between his legs as Albert shivered occasionally and looked at him with wonder. Clay nestled down between Albert's legs and kissed his inner thighs, his sack and his lower penis. Albert was quivering and gasping from the unexpected way Clay was showing his love.

"That feels wonderful, Clay. I never dreamed of anything like this." Clay simply smiled and petted Albert's soft, golden pubic hair, his smooth, tight belly and his warm chest with his left hand as his right hand encircled and squeezed his sex. Albert's mouth opened in surprise as Clay bent his hardness downward and kissed its wet tip, sucking away the salty fluid gathered there. Nothing, however, prepared him for what happened next as Clay slid his soft, warm lips down and over Albert's hardness, sliding deeper and deeper along its length until Clay's nose was buried in Albert's beautiful hair. He nearly came from that alone and managed to gasp for Clay to stop.

But Clay couldn't stop. He slid upward, tightened his lips, and wiggled his tongue against Albert's hardness, sucking and sliding, sucking and sliding, as Albert's body grew tense, his inner muscles gathering for a climax he'd never forget. Albert had taken hold of Clay's face with both hands and was playing over his cheeks, eyes and ears as he lost his battle for control.

With a growled moan and a violent shiver that coursed throughout his entire body, Albert erupted within the boy he loved. Never had he felt sex like this. Pounding waves of pure joy and ecstasy swept through him as he grunted and pushed upward into Clay's mouth. Clay felt and tasted the warm, sweet semen he'd craved for so long, bursting again and again within his mouth. The orgasm seemed endless, as over and over Albert's loins pounded. Clay touched Albert's opening below, felt the heat and moisture there, and had to press deeper inside where Albert felt like warm velvet.

As if from a distance, Clay heard sobbing. It was Albert's cry of joy as he reached the end of his climax. With a shudder, Albert said, "It's over. Oh, god, it's over. I love you Clay. I love you so much! Please lie against me and hold me now. I want to hold you close!" Albert was almost frantic as Clay slipped his lips from the boy's shaft and crawled up and over his lover. Their lips found one another and Albert cooed with pleasure as Clay allowed Albert's own semen to flow into his mouth as they exchanged it back and forth in a silent, loving communion.

Clay felt his own need suddenly growing and swallowed his half as he rose from Albert's lips. "Please, Albert. Please love me now. I can't wait another second. Please." Clay was sobbing as he rolled to the side and opened his legs for Albert who quickly found him and took him tightly in his mouth, sucking and moving frantically. Albert's hands were everywhere, on him and in him, pulling at him and pushing at him until finally Clay's body could stand no more

243

and he released his love into Albert's hungry mouth. Six, seven, eight and eventually ten times he drove his living, liquid, life-fluid into Albert as he felt his lover petting and caressing him everywhere.

After the final rush of semen, Albert crawled over him and they kissed once more, sharing Clay's sweet semen back and forth until it was slowly swallowed and spent. Between their thighs, where Clay had maneuvered their erections, they pushed and wiggled until both had a simultaneous second orgasm and more of the warm fluid flowed against their tight, slippery thighs. Both thought, *would it never end* as nature made sure the love and life-bond between these two young men was a strong and vital one.

Finally both could do no more and they lay together, gripping each other in quiet love, kissing gently now and kissing often. Clay was the first to say something. "I had no idea how much I really loved you, Albert, until just now. I never want us to be apart."

"I know," said Albert. "I'll love you forever, Clay. Promise me you'll always love me."

"I promise. I'm so lucky to have you."

"Me too."

They lay a few minutes more, side by side, simply looking into one another's eyes and smiling with the wonder and joy of young love.

Finally, Clay said, "We'd better get up and clean off now. I'd like to lay here and hug you the rest of the day, but I'm afraid someone will come along and we'll be caught. Are you all right?"

Albert was getting up but was shaking as though in the grip of a fever. "Yeah, I think so. I'm kinda weak all of the sudden. That took a lot out of me. I didn't want it to end, Clay. How did you ever learn how to do it with your mouth? I never dreamed of anything like that. I thought we'd do it with our hands, but... criminy wiz!"

"Let's take a ride down the race. I want to swim with you now and as long as no one comes around I want to just hold you close to me in the water."

"Yeah, that would be great. What about glass and rocks? We better check first. Remember what your dad said, neither one of us needs another crack back there."

"Yeah, I liked what I found back there and wouldn't want it all cut up and ruined."

"That surprised me when you put your finger in me. That's

244

something else I never thought about doing, but I liked it. Where did you learn to do all of this?"

"I'll tell you sometime soon, but not right now. I just want us to enjoy ourselves and remember today forever. I don't ever want to stop loving you, Albert. We're different from most boys and we're always going to be this way. I don't ever want to be alone."

"Me neither."

After an hour of flume-riding, swimming, touching and quiet cuddling beneath the water's surface, they climbed out and got dressed. Still no one had disturbed their perfect day. They ate their picnic lunch and spent some time simply basking in the sun while talking quietly about what they'd experienced. It was nearly three o'clock when they gathered their things and cycled back to Clay's house.

They heard piano music as they entered the house, quietly put down their things in the dining room and tiptoed into the parlor where Les was deep into the music. The boys sat down on the love seat, snuggled carefully and waited until Les reached the end of a very complicated piece. As he touched the last few keys and the sound faded to silence, he was startled as two boys hugged him from two directions. Clay planted a kiss on his cheek.

"That was beautiful, Mr. Mills," said Albert. "That's the first time I've heard you play more than just a few simple tunes. I could listen all day to music like that."

"Yeah, Dad, it was great."

"Well thanks, fellows. You kind of snuck up on me. How long have you been listening?"

Clay said, "About five minutes. Was that another Russian guy's music?"

"No, that was by an Englishman named Fredrick Delius. He wrote a suite --- that's a set of music with one theme --- and called it the *Florida Suite*. He came to America when he was younger and tried to grow oranges in Florida, but he failed at that. He was too filled with music and spent more time composing than tending to his orange grove. A frost wiped out his crop, but the world got a lot of great compositions. I was playing one part of the suite called *On the River*. He lived in a little place called Solano Grove, along the Saint Johns River a little south of Jacksonville. He based that part of the suite on a floating trip he once made there."

"Is he still alive?" asked Albert.

"No, he died a few decades ago back home in Central England. It was tragic, but right after going back home he caught a disease called syphilis and lost his sight. He still wrote music though for some time. A very close friend, Eric Fenby, helped him put it to paper. I especially love his work because it's so gentle and meaningful."

"Did you play that from memory, Dad? I don't see any sheet music like you sometimes play from."

"Yeah, some of my favorites I know so well, they're like old friends. You never forget them. I can hear the music in my head --- every single note. The *Florida Suite* was written for an entire orchestra to play though. One of these days, I'll take you boys to Washington or Baltimore and we'll hear a symphony orchestra; that's about eighty or so men and women all playing together. I used to dream of conducting an orchestra like that someday." Les laughed and added, "Now I'm finally going to be a conductor, but not exactly the kind I wanted to be as a kid."

He and the boys shared a laugh.

"So boys, how was your day *on the river* --- or what passes for one in Sand Patch? Did you have a good time swimming?"

Albert said, after a meaningful glance at Clay, "Oh, yeah, Mr. Mills. It was the best day of the whole summer, so far."

"Albert, you can call me Les, if you want. We're all buddies around here. You're like one of the family now too. That was a nice hug you gave me just now. It's good to see fellows your age who aren't afraid to show their feelings. It's kind of rare. Don't ever change boys. It'll help you stay young."

Les noticed that the two boys were standing side by side and leaning against each other. There was an aura about them of joy and contentment. *I wonder,* he thought as he smiled at the boys.

"So," Les said as he closed the keyboard cover and got up from the bench. "Have you guys decided where you want to go for our camping trip?"

Albert said, "I'm happy with whatever Clay decides. I'm the guest. I'll love wherever you and he decide to go."

246

Les said, "It's up to you then, Clay. What's your choice?" He lowered the top of the Steinway and listened while the boys make their choice.

Clay said, "I think Muddy Creek Falls and Deep Creek Lake would be best. Like you said, there's a lot to do around there. I'd like to see the waterfall in the picture and go swimming in the lake and whatever else there is to do there."

"Then Deep Creek it is. I know of some nice hiking trails in that area too. Why don't you give your buddy Henry a call before it gets late and tell him your plans. I'd like us to go the day after tomorrow --- that's Wednesday --- and come back on Friday evening, or at the latest Saturday afternoon. I have to drive into Cumberland tomorrow and pick up my new uniforms."

"Uniforms?" asked both boys in unison.

"Yeah, I'm a conductor now --- blue suit, boxy hat, brass buttons and everything. I'll look kinda silly, I suppose, but it sure beats eating cinders and baking in front of a firebox. I'll get a new, official, B&O pocket watch too."

Clay said, "Oh yeah, I forgot you'll have a uniform. I bet you'll look great in it. Can Albert and I go with you tomorrow?"

"Sure. I was planning on you going anyway and Albert, you're always welcome. Just clear it with your folks."

Clay wrinkled his brow in thought before saying, "Dad, I just thought of something else. If Henry's folks say it's okay for him to go camping, maybe we could pick him up tomorrow afternoon while we're down that way and it will save his folks a trip up here early on Wednesday morning."

"That's good thinking, son. We'll suggest that and see if it works out for them. Boy I have a bright child, don't I, Albert?"

"You sure do, Mist... er, Les. I'll get used to it, sorry. Clay's very smart. He's taught me all *kinds* of things I never knew before." Albert looked at Clay and grinned. Clay blushed and grinned back.

Les noticed the exchange between the boys and almost asked, but refrained. *There's something going on between these two, but what it is, who can tell. Ah, to be fourteen again.*

Albert whispered something to Clay as Les looked on. He waited as he sensed he'd soon found out what they were discussing.

Clay nodded to Albert and said, "Dad, since Albert's going with us to Cumberland tomorrow, could he stay over again tonight?"

Les grinned and said, "As I've said, you're always welcome,

247

Albert. Call your folks though and let them know all of the plans for the next few days. Cumberland trip, camping trip, sleepovers and what not. They may want to use this opportunity to move all of your belongings over here and be rid of you for the rest of the summer." Les smiled and gave Albert a hair ruffle.

"That wouldn't bother me one bit, Les. I love every minute I spend with you and Clay."

Chapter 24

Les left them in the parlor saying he had to take care of a few things to get ready for dinner and to let him know if Albert was staying over, so he could put on an extra plate.

Clay asked Albert something privately before they left the parlor, however. "Albert, I want to know if it's okay if Henry comes along with us on this trip. After what happened today, I want to make sure you won't be bothered by having him along."

"No. It'll be fine. I'd like to meet him anyway. Now that I know we love each other and all, I won't mind. Is he friendly?"

"Oh yeah, he and I got along great. *Should I tell him now or not? Maybe later, I'll have to think about this later.*

"Good. Then call him up and see if he can go. First, let me use the phone and call Mom and Dad about everything."

The phone was in the parlor, so Albert made his call. His folks approved everything, but said he'd have to come home, join them for supper and gather all his things. His dad said he'd drop him off after supper.

"I can't stay for supper, Mom fixed something special, but I'll be back right after I eat and pack my stuff. I'm gonna wait until you call Henry though before I leave. That way I'll know if he's going too and be able to tell my folks. What's his last name again?"

"Winters, Henry Winters, like the season. Let me get his number and I'll call him. I'll have to go through the operator since it's long distance. Wait here, I'll be right back." Clay ran out and as he passed the kitchen, he told Les that Albert was eating at home, but would be back later. "I'm going to call Henry, Dad. Is it okay to call long distance?" Les told him to go ahead.

Clay ran up the stairs, with Debussy running along behind as he must have thought Clay was playing. Sometimes Debussy behaved more like a dog than a cat. Clay dug through his desk drawer where he'd put the slip of paper with Henry's number written on it and then ran back downstairs once again followed by the exuberant cat. Clay noticed Debussy had followed him into the parlor and said, "I'll play with you in a minute, Debussy; I have to make a long distance call."

Albert picked up the cat, sat with him on the love seat and rubbed his belly while Clay dialed 0. A moment later he said, "Hello ma'am. This is Sand Patch 2-4536, I need to call Pinto 4-3434 in

249

Maryland." A few moments later he said, "Yes ma'am, I'm fourteen and have permission." After another pause he said, "Thank you." He grinned at Albert and felt important as he made his very first long distance call.

"Hello, Mrs. Winters? This is Clay Parker from camp." There was a pause. "I'm fine; how are you, ma'am? May I please speak to Henry?" A few moments passed before he heard his friend's voice.

"Hi, Clay. Wow! I was afraid you'd forget about me and not call. You know how some kids say one thing and mean another? Whats-ya doing?"

"I wanted to call and see if you'd like to join my dad, Albert and me for that camping trip we talked about?"

"Oh, wow! You meant it then. You really are my friend."

"Good grief, Henry. Why'd you think I wasn't?"

"I don't know. Sometimes people forget about me. You didn't." Henry whispered, "I love you, Clay."

"I know; me too. Right now though, we have to talk fast. It's long distance. Here's what we plan to do." Clay went on to fill Henry in, but after a minute Henry interrupted saying Clay had best tell his mom all the details. He called her to the phone; after an explanation of the itinerary for the next few days, she gave her permission. Clay could hear Henry squeal in the background.

Henry got back on the line and asked, "What time will your dad pick me up and can he find our house?"

Clay said, "Just a minute, Henry." Off the line he said, "Albert, go get Dad. He'll need directions to Henry's house."

After Les talked to both Henry and his mother, all the plans were made and it was agreed that they would pick him up in the morning before their trip into Cumberland as that worked out best for Henry's family.

Before they hung up, Clay handed the receiver to Albert and said, "Say hello to Henry. He wants to say hello to you too."

Albert blinked, took the receiver and said, "Uh, hello, Henry. I'm Albert. I uh, look forward to meeting you tomorrow."

"Oh hi, Albert. Clay talked about you all the time at camp, so I'm looking forward to making friends with you too. You and I have something special in common."

"What's that, Henry?"

"We both have the best friend in the world."

"That's for sure, Henry. I better go now since this is long

distance. Be good and I'll see you tomorrow. Bye."

Clay said a quick goodbye and heard Henry hang up. He waited for the operator who told him the cost of the call was a dollar forty-five for nine minutes. Clay winced at the price and hoped Les wouldn't be angry.

Les wasn't around; they could hear him whistling in the kitchen, so Albert snuggled close to Clay and the two exchanged a kiss.

"Dad or Mom will bring me back with all my camping gear after supper. Clay, I can't wait for tonight."

"Me either. I love you." Clay kissed Albert and ran one hand down inside the front of his pants for a gentle squeeze and caress. Albert grinned and did the same as they kissed again. After removing his hand, Albert sniffed his fingers and grinned.

"Wow! Even after all that swimming, you smell so good. I love that and I love you too. See you later."

Albert startled Les when he said goodbye, as he passed through the kitchen, got on his bike, which was parked beside the back porch, and took off for home.

A few minutes later, Clay wandered into the kitchen and gave Les a hug from behind. Les jumped again and said, "Whew! You and Albert keep sneaking up on me. All these years by myself have made me jumpy, I suppose. So, it's just the two of us for supper, right?" Clay nodded and snuggled close. Les gave him a squeeze and said, "So everything's all set with the Winters family? I figure we'll take the road down through Finzil, Mount Savage and LaVale and turn off there for Cresaptown. Henry lives in a little place called Triple Lakes, about two miles southwest of Cresaptown. From there we can take Route 220 back north into Cumberland."

"That sounds good, Dad."

"Is Henry pretty well behaved? He seemed so at the camp." Clay assured him the boy was no trouble.

"I'm going to be taking you boys into the main rail yards, so I want you to tell the others to stay close and not wander off or touch anything. There are a lot of safety rules around that area. The railroad discourages young visitors, but now, as a conductor, I have the authority to take you there as long as there are no problems. The supply office is in South Cumberland and that's where I have to go to get my five uniforms. They do the cleaning there too, so I'll be visiting the place often."

"Five uniforms?"

"Uh huh, for the most part, I'll be working four days in a row, so on the fourth day I'll turn in four uniforms for cleaning and have one left for the next work cycle. Then I'll pick up the clean ones when I go back. The B&O takes care of the cleaning and that's fine with me. I had to wash my own coveralls here at home before, so it'll be nice not to have to bother with that anymore. The coal, oil and grease were pure hell to get out of my clothes. The new uniforms are wool and have to be dry-cleaned."

"Will we get to see some engines, Dad?"

"If possible, I'm going to try and take you guys to the roundhouse. Maybe you'll get lucky and a Mallet will be in for service. They often are, as most of them are wearing out. I know how much you want to see one of those monsters up close. Just tell the other boys to be perfect gentlemen; and we'll be able to do it again sometime."

"I was going to ask you, Dad. At conductor school, what kind of grades did you get?"

"Well, they don't give A's or B's, but they do rank us according to our scores and our practical tests. I scored very high in my class and became certified for passenger service."

"What are practical tests?"

Les chuckled and said, "They have four passenger coaches parked at the training center and we have to act out what conductors do and say. At the same time we're training, there are also other men training to be porters, cooks and waiters. The dining car is where everyone at the school eats lunch when classes are in session. That gives the cooks and waiters practice. Most seats in the coaches have manikins in them like store dummies, but some seats have the instructors too. Once in a while they give you a difficult time just to see if you maintain your temper. Some cuss at you and they even had one short guy pretending to be a kid who'd snuck on board. I was supposed to politely put him off at the next imaginary station and let the station master there deal with him."

"How'd you do?"

"I saved time and just chucked the little bastard out the window."

"Dad! You didn't."

Les laughed and said, "No, but I wanted to. The guy playing the kid called me an asshole and tried to kick my shin. He did it gently, but in reality, we sometimes have to deal with that sort of thing. I had to promise to buy him a candy bar in the club car before he quit giving me a rough time. That was the test." Clay laughed.

They ate supper and talked of the coming trip to Cumberland and the camping trip on Wednesday. After supper, Clay washed, dried and put away things while Les took a bath before Albert came back.

Clay wandered upstairs and saw the bathroom door was standing open so he walked in thinking Les had finished and he could use the toilet. Les was toweling off and was completely undressed.

Clay gasped and said as he left, "Oops, sorry, Dad. I thought you were finished."

"It's okay, Kiddo. I'm not bothered. I'm so used to leaving doors open around here and it doesn't matter if you see me bare or not. I've seen you and my eyes haven't melted yet."

Clay *had* noticed his new dad, however, and thought he was very handsome with his clothes off. He was also pleased that his body didn't react to seeing Les nude. He was just Dad and nothing more. He noticed that Les hadn't been circumcised, either, and somehow that made him feel proud that he was just like his new father.

Clay waited in the hall until Les left, wearing only a pair of briefs. Clay went inside and peed, leaving the door open as Les was talking to him from his bedroom.

"Clay, when we get back from our vacation trip to Deep Creek, I want to talk more with you about some things like we did in the Buick coming back from camp. Over the next few days, if you have any questions about bird and bee topics, keep them in mind, because I want to hear your thoughts and ideas. Remember I told you I would share some personal things with you once we get to know each other better?"

"Uh huh," said Clay as he entered Les's bedroom where Les had put on clean, comfortable clothing. "I remember."

"You said you had some things that bothered you and caused you to be afraid sometimes. We can share our ideas and problems then. But, in the meantime, if something bothers you, there's no need to wait. I'm here for you anytime." Les was sitting on the edge of his bed and patted it for Clay to join him. "You going to get your bath now or after Albert gets back?"

"I'll wait a while. It's still light out and we might want to mess around outside and I'd only get sweaty all over again. I'm not too dirty since we spent about three hours swimming at the mill."

"Was anyone else there today?"

"Nope, we had it all to ourselves."

"Did you guys skinny-dip?" Les said, with a nudge and a grin.

"Yeah, we almost always do as long as no one else comes around. We keep our clothes where we can get them fast, so if we hear someone coming, especially a bunch of girls, we can grab them and get dressed."

"Does Albert have a girlfriend, yet?"

"Nope, he and I talked about that and he likes the idea of becoming a confirmed bachelor too."

Les smiled and said, "You know you don't have to do that just because I said I'm one, Clay. You guys are young and have a lot to discover about life. I'm willing to bet you'll change your mind about bachelorhood soon."

"I doubt it, Dad. I'm happy with the way things are working out right now."

I wonder what he means by that, thought Les as he gave Clay a push backward and started tickling him. *He's fourteen, but still there's a lot of little boy left,* Les thought with pride as he quit and gave the boy a kiss on his forehead. Downstairs they heard the door shut and Albert's voice.

"I'm back, Clay and Les. Where are you guys?"

Clay ran off toward the stairs to greet his buddy.

That evening a storm swept across the mountains and from nine o'clock on, thunder and lightning dominated the evening until nearly midnight. After they ran around the house closing windows, Les asked the boys to unplug the television, radio and several other appliances for safety's sake. Les couldn't help himself and asked Albert to unplug the piano and Albert, not thinking walked once around the Steinway looking for a wire until he heard Les and Clay both laugh.

"That's mean; I'll get you guys for that. I wasn't thinking straight."

"Sorry, buddy. I couldn't pass up the chance."

There was an especially bright flash and crash as another bolt of lightning struck close to the house. All three of them jumped.

Les said, "I really need to have a couple of lightning rods installed on the house. There used to be some, but when the roofers replaced the shingles just before Mom died, they never put them back up. When we get back from our trip, Clay, help remind me and I'll get some new ones and do the work myself."

"Okay, Dad."

"Another thing I plan to do before winter sets in, is replace our coal furnace with a modern fuel oil system. I never want to shovel another lump of coal or smell the damned stuff burning that close again." Les laughed.

"Tomorrow afternoon, when we get back from Cumberland, we'll gather all our camping supplies and pack the Buick. As you think of things we might need, fellows, make a list, so we won't forget anything. I looked at a map of Western Maryland and I think we'll go to the town of McHenry. It's next to Deep Creek Lake and I bet someone there will be able to tell us about a good place to camp. There's no private campgrounds marked on the map, but I'm sure there's some around there."

"What if there's not, Les?" asked Albert.

"Well, it would be nice to have a campsite on the lake, but not absolutely necessary. We can always use the campground at Muddy Creek Falls. It's close to the lake. That's where Todd and I used to camp. We had some good times there." Les stared off for a few minutes and Clay saw his eyes glisten a bit.

"You miss him a lot don't you Dad?" Clay said as he stepped close to his dad and hugged his shoulder.

"Yeah, he was the closest friend I ever had. We knew each other all through grammar and high school. We went to college together for a while too."

Albert asked, "Could I see his picture, Les?"

"Sure. Clay, run upstairs and get that photo so Albert can see that I was young and good-looking once too."

"Aw, Dad, you're still young and handsome. Thirty-three is young," said Clay as he ran off upstairs.

Albert took this opportunity to say something, "Thanks, Les. Thanks for being Clay's dad. He sure deserves a good dad for a change. He's had a pretty tough life so far. I love him, Les. I really do. He's like a brother to me and no other person I know cares about me like he does. We've decided that someday we want to get a house and live together."

Les smiled and said, "Well, how about if you guys find some nice girls in high school and fall in love someday? I don't think your wives would care much for the idea of everyone living in one house."

"Neither one of us are going to get married, Les. We've talked about it and I want to be a confirmed bachelor just like you and Clay."

"You guys are only fourteen. You're just at the age where you're about to discover romance and I bet within a year at high school, you'll both have girlfriends and the idea of bachelorhood will be a long gone memory."

"No, sir, I doubt it. I'm not interested in girls and neither is Clay. We get along well and like the same things and we've made up our minds. I looked up the word confirmed in that big dictionary you have and it says that confirmed means definitely determined, established and firm. That's Clay and me, Les. We're definitely determined to share a house and be friends for life."

Les smiled and said, "Well, if that's what you guys end up doing, I'll back you all the way. That's the same way I felt about Todd when I was your age, so I can understand and respect your determination and loyalty to one another."

They heard Clay coming back down the stairs so Albert whispered conspiratorially, "I'm glad we had this talk, Les. Thanks again for being a good dad for Clay."

"You're very welcome, Albert," said Les with a straight face and a solemn voice. Albert was so serious and cute while he said what he had to say. *I really need to have a talk with Clay. This sounds serious. Do they really know what's going on between them?* Les smiled at the very determined-looking young man and ruffled his soft, golden hair.

That night, after the two boys went to bed, they cuddled for a while before getting down to more serious activities. Clay made sure to lock his bedroom door before they were intimate and unlocked it afterward.

As they lay side by side after loving one another, they talked briefly.

Albert asked, "Where did you learn how to do all those things we did today at the pond and here in the bed? I never dreamed of two boys doing it with their mouths before. I thought about kissing you down there, but that was about it. I thought about kissing your butt cheeks too, so next time we do this maybe I'll do that." Albert giggled. "See how weird I am."

256

"I love every weird bit of you. You can kiss my butt anytime you want. Before we go to sleep, you can give me a smooch or two if you want. I'll save a big fart and make it something you'll never forget. I'm weird too."

"You better not fart or I'll bite your butt instead of kissing it. Either way, it sounds like fun." They laughed and Clay snuggled close and gave Albert a love nibble on his nose.

"I sure love you. I've wanted to do things with you now ever since I learned about how neat stuff like this feels."

"Yeah, me too, but, you still haven't told me where you learned to do stuff with your mouth."

Clay paused for a short interval before asking, "Have you ever done anything with another boy, Albert?"

Albert was silent just long enough to get Clay's attention.

"If you have, it's all right. I won't be mad. You can tell me."

"Uh, you know the cousins I went to see in Philadelphia?"

"Yeah, If you did anything with them, I won't be mad or jealous."

"You sure?"

"Cross my heart."

"Well, last December and again just last week, my cousin, Carl and I did some things. He's the one who taught me how to play with myself the first time. That was on Christmas Eve last year. Are you sure you won't be mad?"

"No. Boys often try out stuff." W*hew! This will give me a way to explain Randy and Henry,* thought Clay. "So, what did you and Carl do? How old is he?"

"Well, he's a little older than me. He was fifteen at Christmas and now he's sixteen. I sleep in his room when we visit, because my other boy cousin is only seven and sometimes wets the bed. My other cousins are all girls. They're nine, eleven and twelve and I sure didn't sleep with them."

"Better not. I'll be jealous and damned worried if you ever do. That's a big family."

"Yeah, there's another boy who's nineteen, but he's married and lives in Camden, New Jersey, across the river. Carl's like us, I think, because he always wants to do stuff when I'm visiting. Up until last Christmas, he just wanted to see me and feel me get hard. I wouldn't let him do anything else, because I was too young and didn't really know what he was trying to do."

"What changed your mind?"

"At Christmas, I hadn't seen him for almost two years. Before that, I didn't have hair yet and my *member* wasn't much bigger than my thumb. It was still my 'little thing'." Both had to giggle at the reference to Albert's member. "On Christmas Eve, he asked me a bunch of questions about if I'd ever made sperm and I had no idea what he was talking about. He told me he could show me and since he was my cousin, I let him. I was pretty surprised and had a very merry Christmas." Clay laughed and Albert continued, "The next two days we did it to each other at night and in the morning."

"So he never did it with his mouth?"

"Nope, just his hand; he wanted to put his dick in my crack one morning, and I let him, but only between my legs. I told him I didn't want him to do it to my opening. His uh, member, is a pretty *big* thing."

"Did he come, doing it that way?"

"Uh, huh, it made me real sticky down there and I had to take a bath after getting up. I liked the smell of sperm too. Carl's like me and doesn't have the extra skin like you do, so he didn't have that special smell like you do. I really like that."

"Did you ever feel like you loved him, when you did stuff with him?"

"A little, but he's my cousin. I had a few dreams about him for a while after I got back home, but then I started wondering about you and when I did it by hand each night, it was you I wanted to do stuff with. Now I can." Albert paused a moment or two before adding, "Uh, Clay, a couple of times while I was here at your house taking care of Debussy, I did a few things too."

"With someone else?" Clay asked with slight alarm.

"Oh no, it was just me. I, uh, played with myself here on your bed a couple of times and thought about you as I did it. Hope you don't mind."

"No. I wish I could have joined you, but now I can, of course. How did you do it?"

Albert giggled and whispered, "You left a pair of dirty underwear in your laundry basket and I sort of snuggled with them and... well, you know. I was wishing you were in them, I guess."

"Cool. I'm not mad. I'm kinda glad about it. I know you did it 'cause you love me."

"I sure do. The one time, after I did it, I fell asleep. That was the day my dad had to come looking for me and I caught hell for scaring him and Mom. They'd called, but I had your door closed and when the phone rang, I guess I didn't hear it. Dad had driven over and was pounding on the front door and that's what finally woke me up. He told me afterward he was about to break in. He thought I might have fallen and knocked myself out or something."

"Gees!"

"I'm glad I woke up and heard him before he had to break in. If I hadn't and he'd found me here in your bed I would have been in super deep trouble."

"Why's that?"

"Well, I was laying on your bed naked and had your underwear on my chest. Dad would have had a heart attack."

"Oh god, I can just imagine." Clay kissed Albert's nose and asked, "Any other midnight confessions?"

"Nope, just that and what I did with my cousin. I hope you're not mad at me."

"Thanks for telling me, Albert. I'm not mad or jealous."

"Good. I've been a little worried about that."

"Would you be mad or jealous if I told you I learned some of the stuff I did with someone else?"

"No. I don't think so. Have you?"

"Yeah, it was at camp."

"This summer? At Camp Cunningham?"

"Yeah. One junior counselor told us that a lot of boys at camp try things out like that. He was right. I did some stuff with Randy and Henry. Both of them are like us. Are you gonna be mad at me?"

Albert looked a little odd and his eyes were blinking rapidly. "You did stuff with Henry? The boy we're picking up tomorrow?"

"Uh huh, I don't love him like I love you though. We just tried stuff out. Randy showed me how to do it by mouth and he and I both showed Henry."

"All three of you at the same time?"

"Uh, huh, I hope you're not mad. Please don't be mad. It's you I really love."

Albert was fighting to hold back the tears. Clay reached out and tried to pet his hair, but he pulled away just enough to signal he wasn't ready for anything like that.

"Please, Albert. Don't be mad. It was never like it was for you and me. Oh, damn. I was hoping you wouldn't be jealous or hurt. I never should have gone to that damned camp in the first place. I should have asked to stay with you while Les went to school. Shit!"

Albert was crying softly, but said, "I'll be okay. It was just a shock to know that it happened just a few days ago before you and I loved each other for the first time. I'll be all right."

"Do you still love me?"

"Yeah, I love you. But it's going to be hard camping with Henry now that I know he and you did stuff. Do you love him?"

"In a way I do 'cause he's a good friend and queer like us. But I don't love him the way I love you."

"You said you did stuff with Randy too?"

"Yeah, there're a lot of things I want to tell you about, so you'll know exactly what happened. I still wasn't sure yet if you were like me and when I found out Randy was and he asked me to do stuff, I just went along with it. One of the camp counselors, Jerry, who's like us, said that sex and love can make people get crazy and sometimes do stupid things and I found out he was right."

Albert sniffed and asked, "Is he another boy you did things with?"

"No. Jerry's seventeen and his boyfriend, Todd, was at camp too. Todd's dad, the colonel, runs the camp. Jerry was just trying to give us advice. He was smart enough to spot Randy and me and knew we were queer. He tried to help. Let me tell you the whole story and maybe then, you'll understand why I did what I did. Just know that I love you in a different way than any of these other friends."

"Okay."

"Albert, I decided to tell you all this stuff tonight because I wanted you to know. If I weren't in love with you in a special way, I wouldn't even let you know about Henry and Randy. All three of us were just trying things out and learning from each other. I want you to know too, that once you meet Henry, you can ask him if everything I tell you is true or not. If you want to do things too with him or later Randy, I won't mind. One of the things I learned the hard way was how terrible it is to be jealous. That's part of what I need to tell you right now, because I made a fool out of myself too."

"You did?"

"Boy did I ever."

For the next hour, Clay poured out his heart and told Albert the whole story from beginning to end. As he finished, he said, "Albert, no matter what, I love you and I want to be your closest friend. I want us to be together forever and please, I want you to forgive me. If you want, I'll even call Henry and cancel his invitation to go camping and never see him or Randy ever again. You're too special to me to ruin what we both want us to have."

Albert smiled and said, "No, I understand better now. I probably would have done the same things you did if it had been me at the camp. I enjoyed doing things with my cousin and I still love him, but not the same way I love you. Henry can come along this week."

"You're sure?"

"Yeah, I do want to talk to him and make sure we all know about each other's feelings. I want you there when we talk. Albert and Claude will be okay too if we get to see them later on. I hope we can all get along and not be jealous. I still love you."

Clay rolled close and hugged Albert harder than he had ever done before and sobbed against his chest. "I'm so glad you can forgive me and that you understand how everything happened."

"I tell you one thing, Clay. If you go to that camp and work next summer, I'm going with you. Maybe I can get a job too. If not, I'll volunteer. That way we can keep our eyes on one another and at the same time keep each other happy. If Randy's there or Henry and we decide to play around, I'll at least be a part of it. I forgive you. Just hold me close for a while until I go to sleep, okay?"

Clay did just that.

Chapter 25

Albert was feeling much better the next morning as the two awakened to Les rapping on Clay's bedroom door and announcing breakfast in fifteen minutes. Clay looked at his clock --- now an electric model with a built-in radio --- and found it was seven-fifteen. He recalled their plans to drive south into Maryland to pick up Henry before paying a visit to the B&O shops and yards in Cumberland.

The storm had long since passed, leaving behind a fall-like crispness to the air, even though it was still the month of August. That happened occasionally in the higher elevations of the Allegheny Mountains where brief hints of the coming autumn were common.

Clay gave Albert a warm hug and kiss before they both tossed aside the covers and headed for the bathroom, both in need of morning relief. Clay said, "I love you, Albert. Hope you're feeling better this morning."

"I am. I just had a lot to think about last night and I'm looking forward now to meeting Henry. I'm not going to be mean to him or anything. From the way you described him and how he sounded on the phone, he seems like a nice kid. We both can share his friendship."

"Good. You'll like him. He can be a tease once he gets over his shyness with you, so be ready for anything." Clay and Albert had entered the bathroom by now and Clay left the door stand open. He washed his face while Albert emptied himself and then they traded places. Just as Albert was finished washing his face and Clay flushed the commode, they were greeted by Debussy, who came tearing into the room meowing, ready for his morning petting. Clay snatched him up and both boys gave him what he desired.

As they left the room, Les spotted them as he ascended the stairs and said, "Ah, good. I wanted to make sure you were both up before I start pouring waffle batter." Les turned, preceded them to the ground floor and led the way to the kitchen. Debussy started in on a small bowl of evaporated milk, one of his favorites, while Les prepared golden brown cheese and bacon waffles. Clay set the table for three and soon all was ready.

After two savory waffles apiece, they cleaned up the table and readied for their trip south. All three wore sweaters, as the air was cool outdoors, somewhere in the mid-fifties; it was rather unusual for mid-August, but not unheard of. Les mentioned that they might want to pack a few extra blankets with their camping supplies just in case the cool weather held for the next few days or dropped even lower.

The drive south was uneventful and before long they reached Cresaptown and turned south along U.S. 220. Triple Lakes was a scattered collection of houses, a mile south of Cresaptown and by following the directions Les had been given the night before, they had no trouble finding the Winter home across from a public baseball field where games were no doubt a regular event in summertime. A few teenagers were there playing a pick-up game.

Les and the boys had no difficulty deciding which house was Henry's as the boy in question came running toward their car waving his hat and yelling. A mile-wide smile split his face. A heavy woman, Henry's mother, stepped out on the porch wiping her hands on a dishtowel. Les pulled up in front of the yard and switched off the engine; Clay and Albert got out, as did Les.

Henry flew toward Clay and gave him a quick hug before turning to Albert and offering his hand. Albert shook it with a smile as Henry said, "Wow! I'm glad to meet you finally, Albert. You're all Clay talked about the whole time we were at camp. He drove us crazy saying how much he missed you. You're just the way he described you too."

"Thanks, Henry. He's told me all about you and I'm glad you could come along camping this week."

Henry greeted Les as well saying, "Hi, Mr. Mills. It's good to see you again too. Thanks for making sure I have a friend come and visit. Clay's one of my two best friends and I bet Albert's gonna be number three."

As Henry shook Les's hand, Albert leaned close to Clay and whispered, "I thought you said he was shy. He's a nice kid. You're right though, he looks about eleven."

"All I can say is, he's changed. I think camp got him out of his shell. Let me say hello to his mom. I only met her briefly at camp and want to mind my manners."

"Me too, I'll join you."

After all the introductions were made, Mrs. Winters said, "Okay, Henry. Gather all your stuff, I'm sure Mr. Mills and the boys are rearing to get started."

While Henry and the boys went inside to help him with his gear, Mrs. Winters and Les talked and shared parental conversation about their boys. She was complimentary and said that it was like she'd picked up a different boy after camp. Les asked her to use his first name. She asked him to do the same and call her Betty.

"Les, he was always so quiet and shy. It was getting worrisome; he'd sit for hours and watch the other boys playing ball across the road, but we couldn't get him to go and join in. He always seemed so lonely and sad. All he talks about now is Clay and Randy and since last evening, Albert."

"That's good. Camp is often good for children."

"We're so glad Henry's changed. Leo and I were seriously thinking of taking him to a doctor to see if he was well. A thirteen-year-old shouldn't be as moppy and dismal as he was. Whatever your boy and Randy did, they did us a favor. He's like a new person and it's all for the better."

"That's good to hear, Betty. Camp did a lot for Clay as well."

"Thanks for including him on this trip. Can we give you some money to help with things? I gave Henry five dollars spending money, but his daddy and I want to help out."

"Not to worry. Everything's fine. I'm sure there will be times when Clay comes to visit and I'm just happy he has some friends like Henry now as well. He's had a rough time in life since he lost his parents." Les went on to tell Henry's mother about the fire and his difficulties with his uncle and aunt.

"That poor child. I heard Henry say something about the burns, but had no idea he'd lost his whole family. He's a sweet boy and I'm glad he has a parent now who loves him. He's welcome here anytime --- Albert too. He seems very well-mannered as well."

About then the boys returned toting Henry's camping gear. Les opened the trunk of the Buick and helped the boys arrange his things. After Henry gave his mom a warm hug and kiss, they all boarded the car and headed back northeast toward Cumberland. Within fifteen minutes, they were driving through downtown headed for the southern part of the old city.

Cumberland, in one form or another, was over two hundred years old having once been the site of a British wilderness outpost and fort in the mid-1700's. In 1755, George Washington, then only twenty-two years old, had served as a guide and scout for General Edward

Braddock at Fort Cumberland. Since then, the city had grown into the second most populous city in Maryland, mostly due to the railroads that met and crossed there. Three, the B&O, the Pennsylvania and the Western Maryland Railroad all shared right-of-way and exchanged passengers and goods in the extensive train yards of South Cumberland.

Before long, they reached the yards where Les stopped at a gatehouse and presented an identification card to a B&O yard officer who waved them in. Les spent a few minutes telling the boys the rules of behavior and said if all went well, he'd take them on a tour of the shops and roundhouse. He pointed out the large round structure not far away, as they passed the various shops and freight car repair and construction facilities located there. He drove them first to a three-story, brick structure not far from the gatehouse. Les described it as the yard office and supply depot. It was here he would be picking up his uniforms and daily orders once he started work as a conductor.

After parking the car, he led the boys inside and down a long hallway on the first floor. At a door labeled, in gold leaf, **Uniforms**, Les ushered them inside and asked the boys to have a seat on several leather-covered benches along one wall of the room. He stepped to a wicket and rang a hand bell. A thin, frazzled-looking lady appeared and asked how she could be of service. Les showed her his identification card and asked about uniforms. She wrote down his measurements and asked him to wait for a few minutes until she could contact another employee to take care of his needs.

Before leaving, however, she smiled at the boys and asked, "Conductor Mills, are these all your sons?" The boys giggled as Les explained that only one was his boy and the others were his friends. She smiled and said, "I have something special for young visitors. I'll just be a second." She left the window and two minutes later returned with three small cardboard boxes.

"You'll have to have Conductor Mills carry these out of here, boys, because technically, they're B&O property. We found a couple of cases of these that had a small flaw in the inside bands, so we don't issue them to employees, but I like to give them out to boys like yourselves when they come by. Open them up and take a peek, but don't wear them until you leave the yards."

The boys looked inside one of the boxes and found that she had given them each an official B&O conductor's hat just like the one

Les would soon be wearing. Each had a bronze B&O, capital dome herald set above the bill. The boys were awestruck and thanked the lady several times. Les was soon called away to try on his new uniforms and a few minutes later came back out so the boys could see him.

"Oh, Dad, you look super!" said Clay as Les smiled, pulled out and consulted his new gold, railroad watch and said, "All aboard!" All three boys stepped close and pawed over the fine navy-blue, wool outfit.

Les told them he had to change back and would rejoin them soon. Ten minutes later, he emerged with two sets of clothing in boxes, saying the other three outfits he would leave here, as they needed slight adjustments while the two sets he carried were perfect. He let the boys help carry his outfits as well as the boxes containing their new hats.

Their next stop after stowing the suits in the Buick was the giant roundhouse. Again, Les presented his identification card along with his new conductor's badge and asked the roundhouse foreman if he could show the boys around. It was a courtesy to ask, even though his ranking as a conductor gave him the authority to take most anyone, anywhere on his own responsibility. The foreman, who knew Les well, grinned and said he would show them around himself as it beat doing paperwork. His name was Pete Hickey and as they entered the grand central bay and turntable area of the roundhouse, Clay's mouth flew open. There was a Mallet on the turntable as they entered; it was being revolved to allow it to back into one of the service stalls.

Les said, "Boy did we ever time this right, Clay. There's your Mallet: Number 74. I've worked that old girl a couple of times and she's a balky bitch if I must say so. Excuse the official railroad lingo, boys, but that engine has never been my friend. Her oil feed pumps never stay at one setting for more than ten minutes and it takes constant fiddling to get her to behave."

Pete said, "Your daddy's right, Clay, that's what she's here for now, oil feed problems. This is her last chance too, Les. If we can't solve the problem this time, she's going to the scrap yard."

"You're going to throw it away?" said Albert and Henry, both at once.

"Can I have it?" asked Clay.

Les and Pete roared at the boy's naive request. Les said, "Where are you gonna put it, Clay, in the train room? It might be a tight fit. That damned thing, even without the tender, is about seventy feet long and weighs what, Pete?"

"I never wrestled it onto a scale, but I'd guess about three or four hundred tons. Back your car up, Les, and we'll couple 'er up."

Les ruffled his son's hair and said, "It's a little big for the yard, kiddo and the last I checked our house is not beside any tracks."

"Aw Dad, I spoke before I thought; quit teasing. It sure seems a shame though to see it go to a junkyard."

Pete said, as the Mallet began to chuff and its engineer backed it into its repair bay, "I know how you feel, young fellow. I've been working on these beasts for almost forty years and I hate to see 'em go too. The diesels are all right, but they're just not the same. Steam engines like these have pulled America's trains for over a hundred years and it'll be a shame to see their time end. I just wish they would put a steam whistle on the diesels if for no other reason then to honor the big iron locomotives that pulled their weight all those years. Enjoy that sound while you can, boys, you won't hear it much longer."

Pete walked the boys around the outer edge of the great turntable showing them the machinery that moved it and the giant electric motor that drove its gear work.

"The turntable used to be run by a steam engine too, but electric motors were easier to maintain, so in 1940 we switched over to electric. Come on, I'll let you guys climb aboard 74. Just watch what you touch, some things are very hot. Most are marked, but a few signs have fallen off and I don't want trouble from the safety bulls."

Clay whispered, "What's a safety bull, Dad?"

"Railroad police, if one of them says jump, you ask, 'How high, sir?' Their word is law and it's for a good reason. See that sign over there with the number 257 on it. That means two hundred fifty-seven days without an accident in the roundhouse. We want to help Mr. Pete keep it that way."

They'd reached the Mallet, Number 74, just as its engineer stepped down from its cab. He turned and saw Les and smiled. "Les, I heard an awful rumor that you went and got yourself made into a damned, stinking conductor. Cab's not good enough for you anymore?" He offered his hand for a shake and got it.

"It's true, Mick." Les held up his new badge and grinned. "No more cinders and singed eyebrows for me. Mick, this is my son,

Clay, and his two buddies, Albert and Henry. I brought them along with me today so they could see some of the horses in Pete Hickey's barn. Clay's been a Mallet fan for some time, so I was glad to see 74 on the table. Think she'll make it through surgery one more time?"

"I hope so. Same problem: oil feed. If we can get that fixed, I think she'll make another hundred runs before they scrap her. It's a damned shame, but the Mallets are wearing out. Come on up here boys and I'll show you the cab."

He spent the next ten minutes showing the boys the controls of the enormous locomotive. He let each of them give a short toot on the engine's whistle before the steam pressure died away. The fire had been dumped into an ash pit below to burn out once the engine was backed into its bay. Another man, the current fireman, was there for a few minutes, and shook Les's hand wishing him well with his new job.

When Clay stepped down from the Mallet, he came face to face with his uncle. Both stopped short and simply stared at one another. Les stepped behind Clay, rested his hands on the boy's shoulders, and said, "Hello, Warren."

Warren said nothing, but turned to the side and spit a stream of tobacco juice into the glowing cinder pit beneath the engine, where it sizzled and hissed. He turned and walked away.

Clay was shaking and almost said something as he saw his uncle turn, but Les must have sensed it coming and squeezed his shoulder. He whispered, "It's not worth it, son. *He's* not worth it. He's from your past and can't hurt you again. Let's get going."

Albert was whispering to Henry, probably filling him in on who they'd just met. Clay had told Henry at camp about his abusive uncle. Henry looked up and frowned at Warren's back now a hundred feet away as he walked off toward another bay of the roundhouse.

Henry yelled, "Asshole!" but not loud enough for Warren to hear above all the noise of the roundhouse. Les, Albert and Clay all burst into laughter at the *shy boy's* exuberant courage. Henry turned and glared. "He hurt Clay and someone needs to tell him what he is."

"I like him, Clay," said Albert with a laugh. "*Shy?* I don't think so." Clay was blinking at Henry, more surprised than anyone. Les was biting his lip trying to hold back a belly laugh.

After a tour of the nearby B&O shops, where freight cars were built and repaired, they ate lunch at the Queen City Station and

Hotel before heading home.

They arrived at the house around two o'clock and all three boys pitched in to get their camping gear packed in the Buick for an early start in the morning. After that, Clay showed Henry the train room where they spent a fun-filed afternoon playing with the model railroad while wearing their new conductor caps.

After supper, Les asked Henry, "Clay told me you play the piano. Would you play for me, Henry?"

"Yes, sir, I've been taking lessons for five years and I'm getting much better. I don't have any of my music with me, but I can play a few pieces from memory. Clay told me you used to teach piano and music. I'd like to hear you play too."

Les led the way to the parlor where he gestured toward the Steinway. Henry's eyes bulged as he walked around the classic grand piano and ran his hands over its mirror-like, ebony wood finish. He carefully lifted the keyboard cover and sat down. Les raised the top of the instrument and propped it open.

Clay and Albert joined Les on the sofa as Henry looked back, grinned and said, "I'm going to play one of my favorites. It's a piece by Arthur Rubenstein and it's called *Melody in F;* most people know it as, *Welcome, Sweet Springtime*." He began to play and even Les leaned forward in surprise as the boy played the well-known song without a single error. His expression and technique were excellent. When he finished, he turned and smiled. Everyone applauded.

"My god, Henry; that was wonderful!" said Les. "Son, you've a great deal of talent. What else can you play for us?"

"Uh, I'll try a piece I've been working on since May. It's a little more difficult and I might make a few mistakes, so forgive me if I do." He turned once more, composed himself and started playing Frederick Chopin's *Nocturne*. Les closed his eyes as he listened to the boy who was playing so very well. Five minutes later, Les had only noted two minor errors and felt much the same way he did when he first heard his protégé, Charlie, years before.

Clay and Albert clapped as did Les who then said, "Henry, you are destined for greatness, son. You have the talent to become a world-class pianist. I hope you plan to continue to take instruction. Who's your teacher?"

"It was a lady, Miss Hindrick from LaVale, but she had a heart attack last month and won't be back as a teacher. She's in her seventies. Mom and Dad are looking for someone to take over for her."

"I know Miss Hindrick. She's a fine teacher and I'm sorry she's had health problems. Whew! If it weren't for my new job and crazy schedule, I'd do it myself. I'll be happy to coach you along until your folks find someone who can truly help you grow your talent. Son, I had another student once who was every bit as good as you at thirteen and he's now an honor student at Julliard and will be playing in London for the Queen of England later this month."

"Wow, the queen?"

"That's right. Don't ever give up on music, for you have what it takes to be great. You feel the notes and express the emotion written into the composition."

"How come you work for the railroad instead of teaching music, Mr. Les?" asked Henry.

"It's a long and complicated story, but I can't do that any more. It doesn't pay very well in this part of the country either. I don't usually take on students, but I'll gladly fill in until you can find a new teacher, even if it's only one evening a week. I'll speak to your parents when we get back. No charge. It will be my pleasure to work with you."

"Thank you. Will you play for me now, Les?" said the bright-eyed boy.

"I sure will. Do you have a request?"

Henry frowned in thought but suddenly grinned and said, "How about some cat music?"

"Cat music? I don't know what you mean," said Les with an expression of bewilderment.

"Well, you have a cat named after one of my favorite composers, so I'm sure you know something by him, the composer, not the cat. You know Randy from camp? He has a boyfriend named Claude, just like Claude Debussy."

Clay felt himself growing warm as Henry said the word 'boyfriend'. *Oh, crap! What's Les gonna think now.* Clay waited, expecting the unspoken question, but was pleased when it never came. Albert too was nudging him and looking panicked.

Les smiled and glanced at Clay before saying, "I'd be more than happy to play some cat music for you fellows tonight. What about *Golliwogg's Cakewalk?*

"Oh, yeah, that's a fun piece. Have you ever played it for Clay and Albert?"

"Not yet, but I will now. This piece, guys, is from a suite Debussy called *The Children's Corner* and is a lot of fun. I'm not sure what a golliwogg is, but the tempo and rhythm is a cakewalk. Give a listen."

All three boys enjoyed the short, but fun composition whose tempo varied from slow to fast and whose volume changed from very soft to extremely loud. As it ended, all applauded.

He played one more piece after saying, "Enough for classical music, fellows. This is a piece by Scott Joplin called *The Maple Leaf Rag.*" Once again, Clay and the boys were surprised by Les's versatility in talent and expertise. All applauded once more for Les, who felt complete once more, being able to share his music with young people.

Les had to call an end to the evening's fun by saying, "Well, boys, it's almost eight-thirty. By the time you fellows get bathed and dressed for bed, it'll be nine-thirty and we have an early start tomorrow as we set off for the lake. Let's go now and get ready for bed. I'll use the bathroom down here so you fellows can use the one upstairs. Henry, do you want to sleep on a cot in Clay's room or use our guest room?"

"I want to sleep on the cot with Clay and Albert, if that's all right. They're my best friends now and I want to spend as much time as possible with them."

"That'll be fine, Henry. I'll set up a rollaway bed in the room before bedtime. One's stored in the guest room closet. Go now fellows --- scoot. Get your baths and get ready for bed."

Chapter 26

Clay pulled Henry aside when Albert went off to use the bathroom. "Henry, be careful using words like boyfriend around my dad. He doesn't know about what we did at camp."

"Well Claude's a boy and he's Randy's friend, so he's a boyfriend. Your dad didn't seem bothered by it. I'll be careful though. Hey, does Albert know about what we did?"

"Uh huh, he knows. We talked about it just last night and he was a little bothered by it at first, but after I explained how things just happened, he understands. Maybe we can talk about it later, but not tonight, unless Albert brings it up. I'd rather wait until were on our trip and can sit down privately and talk about that sort of thing."

"Did you and he finally do stuff? At camp, you said you weren't sure he was like us or not. I take it he is, by the way you've been talking."

"Yeah, he is and we've done a lot of stuff. The first time was the day after I got home from camp. I'll tell you more about it later, okay?"

"Okay. Maybe all three of us can do some stuff together while we're camping," said Henry with a grin. "Albert's really nice-looking and he's friendly like you and Randy both."

"We'll see, Henry. I don't want to push Albert too much to do things until I know for sure he's not jealous. He was a little bit upset and sad at first and I was afraid I'd really messed things up and hurt him. Henry, I want you to know that Albert is still my number one friend when it comes to loving him and I don't ever want to do anything to hurt him. I love you too, but Albert will always be special. Does that bother you?"

"Nope, I can love you both and I promise I won't do anything to hurt him either. If you see me doing something wrong, let me know and I'll be careful."

"Thanks, Henry." Clay gave the boy a quick kiss and a hug.

"Are you guys going to do stuff in bed tonight?"

"Maybe just hug each other close. We like to do that when we sleep. We have to get up early, so we won't do anything else."

"I wish I could hug you guys while we sleep, too."

"Maybe soon we'll be able to. For now, just be patient."

"Okay."

Albert came back and asked, "Who takes the first bath?"

Clay said, "It doesn't matter. Henry, since you're the guest, why don't you go first?"

"Okay, but you guys have to keep me company." Henry smiled and winked at them.

"Thought you said he was shy, Clay," teased Albert. "The way you told off Clay's uncle today was nifty, Henry. I wonder if he heard you."

"I don't know, but I hope he did. It was awful noisy in there, though. I used to be real shy, Albert, but since I met Clay and Randy, I feel like a different person. I was bothered by the way I was thinking about boys and stuff and now that I know I have friends who think the same way, I feel better, especially when I'm around you guys. Can I give you each a hug?"

"I don't mind," said Albert and held out his arms. Henry grinned and wrapped his arms around his new friend. He managed to plant one of his kisses on Albert's cheek and was happy when it was returned. Clay hugged and kissed him too.

Henry said, "See, we're all going to be super good friends. I love you both."

After their baths, all three climbed into bed. Les had set up a rolling bed right beside Clay's big four-poster. Les had swiveled the big bed slightly out from the corner of the room, so the smaller bed would fit beside it. He figured all three boys would want to sleep that way so they could talk and enjoy being boys.

Les stopped by Clay's bedroom a little later. The door was slightly ajar, and he heard them talking and laughing from time to time. The second time he stopped by, about twenty minutes later, he heard soft snoring, so he peeked in. All three were sprawled in odd positions and sleeping soundly. Les again felt that wonderful surge of love, not only for his new son; but warm affection also for his two friends. These three were good for one another and he looked forward to three days of relaxation and fun as it gave him the opportunity to feel young and boy-like himself, something he thought he'd never enjoy again.

At six o'clock, Les's alarm went off, so he arose and started dressing. Before he could get completely dressed, he heard Clay knock at his door. "Come on in, I'm decent." Clay ran to him and gave him his usual warm hug and a kiss. Right behind him was Albert and Henry waiting their turn. Les had to laugh as he realized how in-tune these three were as he got two more hugs.

"Everybody sleep well?"

Clay said, "Oh yeah, Dad. We talked a little bit, but since we knew we had a busy day ahead, we decided to try and sleep and we did. What should we fix for breakfast?"

"Let's keep it simple this morning. How about cold cereal and a sweet roll? I bought a pack of sticky buns at the store. There're two for everyone. I packed some for the camp meals too. You guys set the table and I'll be right down after I visit the john."

Once breakfast was over, Debussy's bowls and sandbox were prepared for three days and their last few belongings were packed in the Roadmaster. Les locked up the house and they got underway. He headed south through Sand Patch, Callimont and soon took the right turn off toward Finzil, just over the Mason Dixon line in Maryland. Les pointed out the home of his former student and prodigy and told Henry about Charlie and his recent debut at Carnegie Hall, in New York.

"If you keep going the way you are, Henry; that could be you someday. You really do have the talent to go far."

"Thanks, Mr. Les. I'll keep practicing."

"I'll be taking Clay with me to Chicago sometime this fall to see Charlie in concert. If it's possible, I'll see if you and Albert can go along."

"Oh, that would be wonderful, but won't that cost a lot for the train and everything?" asked Henry, wide-eyed."

"Since I'm a conductor for the B&O, the train will be free. I'm arranging a pass for Charlie's mom and dad too. The B&O is good to its employees. We can stay at the Chicago Terminal Hotel cheap too. I think seeing the concert would be great for you all, especially you Henry."

"Thanks, Mr. Les. Thanks so much. It's one of my dreams to go to a concert like that."

Just below Finzil, they met U.S. Route 40 and took it westward to Grantsville, Maryland. From there they left 40 and headed south along State Road 495. It was a twisty mountain road through some of the most beautiful, old growth forestland in Maryland as it wound toward Deep Creek Lake. By nine-thirty, they neared the lake and Les pulled off the road at a scenic overlook where they were able to view a historic marker and see part of the large reservoir created in 1925 when a dam was built where the original Deep Creek flowed into the Youghiogheny River.

Deep Creek Lake was the largest fresh water lake in Maryland and in 1953 was fast becoming a major recreational resource for the western end of the state. Garrett County had always been a depressed area with little industry or work other than timber and a few coalmines. The lake was beginning to change the economy to that of a vacation spot which would draw new visitors and much-needed money to the area. Winters there could be fierce, however, and very few visitors came to Garrett County during those months. There were plans underway for a future ski resort that would attract a whole new crowd to the Western Maryland highlands someday soon.

Les pointed out several features from the overlook and told the boys he thought the campground at Muddy Creek Falls was their best choice for a campsite. The falls was one of two, well-known falls along the Youghiogheny. The other was Swallow Falls, less than two miles from Muddy Creek Falls. "My friend Todd and I camped at Muddy Creek once in a while and it was pretty nice. I think you fellows will like it too. It'll be less crowded than campsites nearer the lake."

From the overlook, Les took a secondary perimeter road that skirted the lakeshore for a number of miles. They saw an arched, ironwork span coming up ahead that enabled one to cross to the south shore of the lake at a narrow spot.

Les said, "That's the Glendale Bridge. We'll cross it later to get to Muddy Creek Falls, but for now, we'll head for a swimming area  along the lake's north shore." He took a right, just before the bridge and followed a perimeter road along the lake. A mile farther found them parking at a public swimming area featuring a log-style changing room, a white sand beach, two life guard stands and several floating docks and diving platforms. After gathering their swim suits and several inner-tubes Les had packed along, they headed for the changing room and soon emerged, ready for the water. All of them ran for the lake, Les included.

Like the lake at Camp Cunningham, Deep Creek's water was chilly at first, but soon the swimmers got used to it as they romped and played in the crystal-clear water. The three boys never gave Les a moment's peace and he loved every minute of it. Before long, the cool water was taking its toll, however; everyone's lips started turning blue and several of the boys were shivering. Les called them together and told them it was time for lunch. That's all it took to get them out of the water as everyone was famished.

Les led them to the car where they retrieved a large wicker hamper in which he'd packed a picnic lunch. They carried the basket to a covered wooden table and soon everyone was enjoying ham and cheese, or egg salad sandwiches along with potato salad, canned peaches and bottled soda pop from an ice cooler.

"So, guys?" asked Les, "What say we head for Muddy Creek Falls next and find a nice spot for our tent? We can get it set up so it's ready for this evening and still have time to hike to the falls." Everyone agreed that sounded good.

Albert asked, "How far is the campground from the falls?"

"If I remember right, the trail's only about a quarter of a mile and a pleasant walk. I brought along a camera, so we can take some photos of everybody at the falls. I'll get some pictures of you all swimming tomorrow if we come back to the lake again."

Les drove back to and crossed the Glendale Bridge. The falls were to the west after crossing a narrow part of the lake which stretched off to the south and east. Passing through the little town of Thayerville, while heading west, they soon arrived at the state park and campground. After driving past various campsites, they selected a pleasant level spot near a restroom building and laid claim to it. Les had the boys wait there to hold the site as he drove back to the entrance and paid a fee for two days with an option on a third. The total cost was only seven dollars. That included a little extra for a key that switched on a power receptacle near the tent site and would give them power for a small electric light in the tent. Les had brought along a portable gas stove for cooking as well as a gas lantern for light.

After erecting the tent and preparing their campsite for the evening, Les locked anything valuable in the Buick and he and the boys set off along the trail to the falls. As he walked the familiar path, Les thought back to the several times he had come there with Todd. He couldn't help shedding a tear or two as he remembered his once happy and later troubled friend. The war had not only taken Todd's arm, it had stolen a part of his soul.

Les looked ahead at his new son and his best friend, Albert. Both were walking side by side with their arms around each other's shoulders. Henry too was flanking Clay's other side and from time to time Clay wrapped his other arm around Henry. *If he is like me, I'm going to make sure he'll be happy and never have to feel unloved because of the way he is. I think I'll soon need to talk with him about it, though, before someone else figures it out and scars him with hatred.*

They soon arrived at the end of the trail. It brought them to the top of the falls where they could easily walk out along the edge of a rock ledge that during the spring rainy season or storms became part of the falls. In summer --- the dry time of year --- the falls was only a twenty foot wide stream of clear water, plunging past the edge of the rocks and cascading over step-like rocks below, dropping roughly thirty feet and ending in a wide, clear, plunge pool.

Albert said, "I expected the water to be muddy since it's called Muddy Creek Falls."

Les said, "I think in the spring when the water's flowing very fast from rain and snow melt, it might be pretty muddy."

Clay asked, "Dad? Would it be okay for us to take off our shoes and walk in the stream?"

"Sure, guys. Just don't get too close to the edge of the falls. The rocks might be slippery with algae and it's a long, bumpy way down." Les pointed to a path nearby and said, "There's a trail along the falls that starts there and leads to the pool below. There's great wading and swimming down there too. After you explore up here a bit, we'll walk down. Todd and I used to swim there when we visited."

Henry looked at Les and asked, "Did you and Todd ever go skinny dipping here?" Clay put one hand over his left eye and gave Albert a look. Albert was grinning and mouthing the question, *Shy?*

"No, Henry," laughed Les. "It's a public park, so don't get any ideas. If you want to skinny dip, have Clay and Albert take you to the old mill near our house. Those two will never wear out a bathing suit there. I think they swim naked most times they go there just like Todd and I did when we were kids."

Clay said, "You never told me you and Todd used to swim naked, Dad."

"Well, a guy has to have some secrets; besides, I've only been your dad a few months. Give me time to share all my dark deeds. I have a feeling you probably have a few of your own you're holding back." Les grinned as he dropped the hint.

Clay gave Albert and Henry a quick look and raised his eyebrows. Les noticed it too and chuckled before continuing: "I know it's hard sometimes for kids to realize that their folks were kids once upon a time. When we grow up, we get to relive our youth through our kids. Up until recently, I never thought I'd have a son or daughter, but now things have changed and I can enjoy you, Clay and your two great buddies while sharing in your fun."

Henry simply had to say it. "Good, Mr. Les. When we get back and go skinny dipping, you can go along with us too."

"Oh no, my skinny dipping days are over; I could be arrested. You guys can still get away with it for a year or two, I can't. Take your shoes and socks off now --- just your shoes and socks, Henry --- and enjoy the water. I'll join you for that. Maybe we can catch some salamanders or hellgrammites."

"Huh?" three voices queried.

Clay said, "What are heg...uh, hegramites?"

Les grinned and said, "Hel-gram-mites. They're the larvae of large insects with big pincers called dobsonfies that fly around out here at night. The larvae live under rocks in streams like this. Just turn over a few flat stones in the stream and I bet you'll eventually find some."

"Cool," said Henry.

"Be careful though as they pinch pretty hard. They're the absolute best bait for trout fishing, but it's illegal to use them. It's a twenty-dollar fine or a night in jail if a game warden catches you fishing with one. The trout can't resist them."

"That's something else we'll have to do, Dad; I love to fish and so does Albert."

"Me too," added Henry.

After entering the shallow water that seldom was deeper than a foot, Les showed them how to turn over flat rocks carefully to find the larvae without scaring them off. Within a few minutes, they'd found a few of the extremely nasty-looking creatures. Henry just had to try and pick one up and got his fingers pinched as warned. He yelped and flung off the tenacious bug. It had punched two tiny holes in the boy's fingertip that bled for a few minutes. Henry took it in stride, however, and started looking for another.

A short time later, Les and the three boys headed down the trail to the base of the falls. A few other people were there; two adult couples relaxing on nearby rocks, watching as their children splashed and played in the plunge pool beyond the stair-like waterfall. Les and the boys pulled off their jeans, since they all were wearing bathing suits beneath and everyone went into the water. It was a bit cold --- even though it was summer --- and Les shivered as he gradually eased into a deeper part of the pool.

Clay spotting Les's reluctance started splashing him; he was soon joined by Albert and Henry. The boys were squealing with delight as Les tried to avoid the cold spray. Finally giving up, he made a growling sound, ducked completely under and swam toward the boys who fled, knowing Les was out for revenge. Albert was his first capture and was pulled under from below and tickled. Both he and Les broke the surface laughing while Clay and Henry moved closer.

Les tossed Albert to the side and made a grab for Henry who yelled and tried to flee, but Les was too good a swimmer and caught the smaller boy, dunked and tickled him. This time when Les and Henry surfaced, Clay was nowhere to be seen. Les looked around in the water as best he could, but still couldn't spot Clay. Albert was grinning and motioning to Les that Clay was underwater just behind him trying to hide. Les said thanks and slowly approached.

"He's got to come up for air soon and then I'll have him." Sure enough, Clay carefully stuck his head up to snatch a breath of air and that quick, Les was on him tickling and dunking him too.

After their frolicking, all four kids --- even the thirty-three year-old one --- settled down and swam about in the clear, clean water as Muddy Creek Falls cascaded endlessly over the rocks.

By four o'clock, all were chilly, tired and ready to return to the campground for supper and a quiet evening around the campfire.

Chapter 27

At each of the campsites, there was a carefully constructed stone-lined pit for campfires to lessen the chance of forest fires. Les set the boys to work gathering firewood as soon as they returned to camp and changed back into regular clothing for the evening. The temperature had been pleasant all day, but as the sun sank toward the west, a slight chill could be felt. It looked as though the night might be cool and a campfire would be welcome, not only for cooking their supper, but as a warm place to sit as they enjoyed the evening.

Henry located a pile of ready-cut logs not far from the campsite where the local forestry people had cut a firebreak and piled up a number of split logs for campers to use. Once Henry returned and told the others, they had no lack of wood for the evening's fire. Les wanted to build a quick-burning fire first of small branches to make enough coals for roasting corn and potatoes. He also had planned to grill some hamburgers on an iron grill that could be swung into place over the coals. While Albert and Clay arranged smaller branches and twigs into a cone-shaped arrangement, Henry surrounded it with dry leaves, twigs and some scraps of newspaper Les had packed along to help start the fire.

Les was curious to see if Clay was still experiencing anxiety around a fire. Clay had talked with him before going off to camp about bad dreams he often suffered due to seeing his little brother die in the fire and the terrible pain and slow recovery he'd endured after surviving the horror. Les hoped that Clay's time at camp had helped somewhat to lessen those fears. He intended to ask Clay to be the one to start and tend the fire this evening under his supervision. If he saw that Clay wasn't ready, he wouldn't push the boy, but eventually he hoped to help him overcome those fears.

Once the fire cone was ready for lighting, Les called Clay off to one side and asked him, "Son, I want to know how you feel about being the one to light and tend the campfire this evening?"

Clay blinked and looked at Les with some degree of surprise. "I don't know, Dad. I guess I can try. I suppose I have to get over it eventually, but just using matches makes me nervous sometimes. But, I'm fourteen now and having a home with you has made me feel a lot better about a lot of things."

"That's good. Have you had any dreams about the fire lately?" Les asked as he put one hand on his boy's shoulder to let him know he was supportive.

"Since I came to live with you I've only had one dream and it wasn't one of the really bad ones. It was about being in the hospital afterward and not the fire."

"Okay. That's probably a good sign. To be honest, son, I was expecting you to have more nightmares, but I'm so glad you're doing so well. I think you're ready to face your fears, or I wouldn't ask you to do this."

"Okay, Dad, I'll light the fire. I was hoping Albert and Henry would do it, but now that I know you want to help me, I'll give it a try."

"Good for you. I'll be right there and if you get uncomfortable, you can pass the duty off to one of your buddies. With your permission, I'm going to tell them why you're the one to light the fire tonight; okay?"

"Okay. That doesn't bother me, Dad."

Les and Clay walked back over to the fire-pit and Les spoke to the two boys who were waiting and wondering why Les had pulled Clay to the side.

"As you both know, Clay has had a terrible experience with fire and often it's caused him to fear being around one. He and I just talked and he feels he's ready to start recovering from those fears. I've asked him to be the one this evening to light and tend our fire." Henry and Albert both smiled at Clay and nodded their support.

"It might seem like a simple thing to do, but it's important for each and every one of us to face our fears and not let them control us. Now I know that both of you boys love Clay enough that if he has difficulties tonight with this, you won't make fun of him or tease him in any way, right?"

Both boys pledged they would never do such a thing to Clay, who smiled and thanked them. Les reached into his sweater pocket, pulled out a box of matches and handed them to Clay after giving him a hair ruffle and a pat on the back.

Clay looked at the small wooden box and approached the fire pit. He bent to one knee, opened the box and extracted one match. His hand trembled, just a little, as he grasped the match as far from its tip as possible. He closed the matchbox and turned it to the side where the striker strip was located. He looked up at Les and his buddies who all gave him a smile and a nod. He held the box close to a tuft of newspaper, said a quick prayer and struck the match along the strip. With a sputter, it burst into flame. As Clay felt the heat and saw the flames leap up from the tip, he nearly let go, but managed to grit his teeth and hold on. He lowered the match to the paper and hoped it would start quickly before the match could burn too close to his fingertips.

The paper caught and the flames spread up and over the newsprint. Clay tossed the match into the flames and withdrew his hand. Part of him wanted to get up and back as far away from the fire as possible, but he fought the urge and remained kneeling nearby as the flames spread through the arrangement of twigs and tinder. Only after he saw the fire was well underway did he stand up, take a deep breath --- he realized he'd been holding it --- and turn to Les and his friends who were smiling and nodding, proud of what he'd accomplished. First Henry and then Les and Albert started clapping. Albert ran forward, hugged him, and without a thought, gave him a kiss on his left cheek. Henry hugged him from the other side and soon Les joined in and he was surrounded by the three people he loved the most.

"I did it," he said with pride as he sniffed and his eyes filled with tears. "I did it, Dad."

"You sure did and we're all proud of you. I had no doubts you could do it." Les had seen Albert's kiss and smiled inwardly as he saw more evidence of the close relationship that was growing between Clay and his friends. Henry especially, who was nuzzling against Clay's shoulder, seemed very affectionate and able to express his feelings. *Maybe Clay's found a number of boys of his nature. Randy seemed to be the same way when the two had to part at camp.* He remembered both boys crying a bit as they hugged and said goodbye that day. *More and more, I think I need to have a talk with Clay. He needs to know that I'll love him and support him if my suspicions are true.*

Before long the small logs had burned down enough to create a bed of hot coals and Les tucked four large potatoes and four ears of sweet corn, all buttered, salted and wrapped in aluminum foil, under the embers. Henry and Albert had scrubbed the grill and now Les placed four thick hamburger patties laced with chopped onion, green peppers and steak sauce on the grill. The meat began to sizzle and four bellies began to growl as the aroma of the cooking meat reached them. It was nearly eight o'clock and, by now, all were extremely hungry. The sun had recently set behind the trees and the surrounding hills to the west. A few stars were beginning to appear overhead.

So far, Clay had proudly tended the fire throughout the evening and Les complimented him on his bravery and determination to battle his greatest fear. It wasn't long before their meal was done and ready for eating. Henry and Albert had set the picnic table and soon all were seated, busy building their hamburgers on toasted buns. The baked vegetables were still singing and popping as Les brought them to the table on a platter; he warned them not to try and open the potatoes and corn right away until they could cool a bit. After finishing their burgers, it was time to enjoy the corn and baked potatoes; they were cooked to perfection. Les uncovered a bowl of fresh white butter and soon all four of them were digging into their potatoes and chomping at their corn on the cob.

"Oh, god, Mr. Les, this is the best corn I've ever had!" Henry managed to mumble as he came up for air after munching along two whole rows of the corn. His face was greasy and speckled with bits of corn. "I love this! Thanks so much, Les, Clay, and Albert for having me along. I love you all so much. It's so good to *finally* have some friends."

Les smiled as he considered the small boy's openness and enthusiasm. Clay had described him as shy, but so far, Les would have to say he was the least reticent of the three. Henry was sitting beside Les so he gave the boy a hair ruffle and said, "I'm glad you're having a good time, Henry. What grade will you be starting in the fall?"

"I'll be in eighth-grade, Mr. Les, at Cresaptown School. Next year I'll be going to high school; probably Allegany High in Cumberland. Where will you and Albert be going, Clay?"

"There's a small high school in Wellersburg, Pennsylvania. It's about twelve miles south from our houses, but we can ride a school bus. The next nearest high school would be in Somerset, but it's about twenty miles north."

Albert said, "Do we have to talk about school? I hate to see the summer end."

"Yeah, me too," agreed Clay. "This has been the best summer of my life, so far. I've made new friends, grown a lot and best of all I have a dad who loves me. Oh, and I've finally learned how to strike a match without having a heart attack." Everyone laughed.

Once they cleared off the picnic table after enjoying their dessert of pound cake and canned peaches, Les and the boys gathered around the fire. Clay proudly added several large logs and branches that would burn higher for some time providing heat and light. The air temperature had indeed dropped about twenty degrees, so their sweaters felt good as they all sat around the fire on the folding, wood and canvas, camp chairs Les had packed along. The boys roasted marshmallows on coat hanger wires as they talked of various things.

Clay at one point said, "I wish Randy was here too. It would be nice if he lived a little closer."

"Yeah, I miss him too," said Henry.

"Well, as soon as I get back to work," said Les, "I'll make arrangements for him to come see you fellows. I'll be passing through Harper's Ferry often and his dad and mom already said he'd be able to travel with me to Cumberland. We'll try and get him up to visit before school starts. He's starting high school too, right?" Clay told him he was. "I'll make sure you can join us then too, Henry. We might have to get a bigger tent if you fellows keep collecting buddies." Clay giggled and said he was happy with the great ones he had now.

Les tested the waters a bit and asked, "Henry, do you have a girlfriend back in Cresaptown?"

"Heck no, I hate girls!" He giggled a bit before adding, "Well, I don't exactly hate them, but I don't want to have any as close friends. They're too hard to figure out and I never seem to know what to say to them. Whenever I say anything, they just make fun of me and laugh, so I say, to hell with 'em. Oops, sorry about saying hell, Mr. Les. I forget you're an adult and Clay's daddy. You're like one of the guys when we're out here. Hope you're not mad."

Les chuckled and said, "No, Henry. When we're out here, I *am* just one of the guys. I can forgive a few slips when we're just having guy talks. You know though, you might soon change your mind about those girls. A lot of boys do when they start growing up. Things change a lot at your age."

"Yeah, I know. I'm finally growing faster. I grew an inch since June already and I have a bunch of hair over my penis already." Clay and Albert went wide-eyed at Henry's frankness. Les was smiling as he listened to the *shy* youngster.

Clay thought he'd better change the subject quickly before Henry started in on recent discoveries, so he said, "What classes are you gonna take in eighth-grade, Henry?"

"I haven't decided yet. Mom and Dad said they'd help me figure out what electives I should take. I get to choose two this year. I'm thinking about taking an art class and I'm already taking band. I've been playing in the band since sixth grade. They usually don't let sixth graders join up, but no one else plays as well as I do and they made an exception."

"You're an exceptional player, Henry," said Les. "I assume you're

285

not in the marching band at your school. It's a little hard to march with a piano."

Henry giggled. "Well, that's true, Mr. Les. I'm in the orchestra and play for the chorus class too. I have to stay after school for that sometimes, but I enjoy it. We had a concert last May and I won a prize for best solo performance."

"What did you play?" asked Albert.

"The song I played for you guys yesterday, *Welcome Sweet Springtime --- Melody in F,* by Arthur Rubenstein. That's how I know it by heart. Then I played one of my own songs. I have several I've written on my own."

Les said, "I want to hear those when we get back, for sure." With an air of authority, Les added, "Boys we have a *prodigy* in our campsite this evening."

Albert looked around and said, "Where? What's a prodigy?"

Before Les could explain, Clay said, "Oh, Albert, they're small, vicious rodents that sneak up on you and nibble at your feet. They're very common in these woods."

Les was laughing and Albert realized he had been fooled. "Okay, I almost fell for it. Now really, what's a prodigy?"

Les said, "It's an exceptionally brilliant young person who has a skill that comes very naturally to him or her without effort. After hearing young Henry play our Steinway, I hereby declare him to be a prodigy."

Henry was beaming with pride. "Thanks, Mr. Les. I'm going to keep practicing too and become an even better player."

As the fire died down and they continued to talk, Les remembered some of his visits to this same park with Todd. The first time he and Todd had camped here, they'd been with Les's father who took them on a combination fishing and camping trip. He and Todd were fourteen or thereabouts and at that time had not acted upon their natures. Les remembered how he felt about Todd, however, and remembered how his mind and body reacted to his handsome friend. Todd was tall and dark-haired with a beautiful smile and a quiet, gentle voice. He could sing in perfect pitch and would often sing along as Les played popular tunes on the family spinet --- the one residing now in the little guest house. *Good memories, good times*, he thought. Les only wished life had been kinder to Todd. *God, I still miss him so much. Wherever you are, Todd, I'm thinking about you this evening and still love you, buddy. I wish you could have met my son; you would have loved him too.*

He looked at Clay and his friends as they smiled and laughed and again wondered if they might all be homosexual. Many clues led him to believe that could be the case. Had they figured it out yet? Had they experimented? Were they starting to hate their nature the way he had until he finally accepted his difference around age twenty? None of the boys seemed unhappy or ashamed, especially young Henry, the so-called shy one. Les smiled as he remembered the boy's frankness discussing his recent growth. *I'm going to talk with Clay as soon as we get home. I may have to tell him more of my own story. I don't want him to begin hating himself if he is different. He'll be loved no matter what.*

Around ten, as the fire was nearly spent, Les suggested they all go to bed. He'd seen the telltale yawns from the boys who, like most youths their age, never wanted to give in to sleep especially when having fun and enjoying their fellowship. None of them complained when he said it was time for sleep, however. Everyone made a quick trip to a nearby restroom; a new addition to the campground Les was very pleased to see. When he and Todd had camped there years before, there were no such amenities as a flush toilet. The only option then was an especially smelly and spider-infested outhouse.

Once in the tent, Les helped them arrange their sleeping gear. He'd brought along two heavily padded quilts that he first spread on the tent's canvas floor. They would at least insulate the boys and him from the rough and chilly ground. The outside temperature had dropped into the low fifties as best Les could estimate, so their sleeping bags would help keep them warm. There were also several heavy blankets each boy could spread over his sleeping bag to provide even more protection from the cold.

He noticed that Henry and Albert both wanted to sleep on either side of Clay, but the tent was simply too small to fit three boys in a row along one side comfortably. Clay, however, placed his bedding beside his dad's gear. As soon as everyone was tucked in, Les turned off the gas valve on their camping lantern and the bright glow slowly faded away to utter darkness. It wasn't long before Les heard Henry snoring lightly. Clay, resting beside Les, giggled as either Albert or Henry farted loudly on the other side of the tent.

Clay whispered, "Glad I'm over here with you, Dad." Les laughed and agreed. "Thanks again for taking us camping."

287

"You're welcome. We'll do it as often as we can, but I have a feeling we're in for an early fall and a hard winter this year. It's slightly cold for August, but that's Garrett County for you. They have much harder winters here than we do in Sand Patch, although I've seen it get very cold there too. Part of it's due to the elevation and the way the mountain ridges run from north to south. Cold, moist air flows off the Great Lakes eastward across Ohio, which is mostly flat country and suddenly it has to rise up over the Alleghenies. The pressure change forms ice and snow and one of the first places it falls is in Garrett County, Maryland."

"I had fun at the falls today, Dad. Albert and Henry did too and wanted me to tell you thanks."

Les whispered back, "Good, I'm glad. They're good boys and I'm sure happy to see they care a lot about you. Henry's a handful. I thought you said he was shy. I almost busted out laughing when he told us about his pubic hair."

"Yeah, I was kind of embarrassed when he did that."

"I noticed you changed the subject real fast. Henry's a very affectionate boy for thirteen. I noticed he doesn't mind giving you a kiss once in a while. When you lit the match and started the fire, Albert pecked you on the cheek, too. Does that embarrass you?"

"Maybe a little, Albert was real happy for me. Henry just does that. He'll get over it as he grows up some more."

Les was silent for a few moments before saying, "It's okay if he doesn't. It's not wrong to show emotions. Some boys think it's unmanly, but I want you to know that I'm proud to have a son who can accept and share love with his close friends. Some boys are different in that way, Clay, and if that's the way you are, I won't be mad at you, or think there's something wrong with you. Even if you had given Henry a kiss in return, it would have been all right. Do you understand what I'm saying, son?"

"Uh huh."

Clay's mind was going a mile a minute as he realized what his new father was saying. "That's nice to know, Dad. Sometimes I worry that I'm not like most other boys. Some of my other friends say mean things that bother me a lot."

"Really, what do they say?"

"You know Toby Anderson?"

"Yeah."

"Well he sometimes says mean things about you and me both now that you're my dad."

"Oh? What kind of mean things?"

"I hope you don't mind me telling you this, but he says that you and I are both queer. He says that's why you're not married and that's why I don't have a girlfriend."

"Do you know what he means when he says that, Clay?"

"Uh huh. It means that queer guys like to fall in love with guys instead of girls."

"Okay. How do you feel about men or boys who might be like that?"

"I think it's just the way they are and the way God made them. It's none of Toby's business. The preacher at the church Aunt Martha and Uncle Warren made me go to was all the time preaching about men like that. He did a long sermon not too long ago about two cities in the Holy Land that God destroyed because there were men like that living there. He called them Sodomites after the one city, Sodom. When I was little I didn't completely understand that story, but now I do."

"You think God was right to do what the Bible says He did to those cities?"

"No. It makes Him seem like a hateful, mean God. Maybe those men were just being themselves because God made them that way. I don't think that story is all that true. I don't think Jesus would've done anything like that to a whole city. I sure hope he wouldn't kill men like that just because they loved their friends and maybe had sex with them. I sure hope God wouldn't send boys like that to hell after he made them that way in the first place."

Clay suddenly burst into tears and was doing his best to try to stay quiet as he sobbed into his blanket. Les pulled back his covers, pulled Clay close, and rocked him, kissed his head as he whispered in his ear, "Don't you worry, son. God isn't like that. The Bible was written by many different people and some of them put their own hatred into those words. Don't you pay any attention to Toby, or other boys like him. I want you to know that no matter what you are like, or who you choose to love, I will still love you as your dad and soon, you and I are going to talk about this subject more. I think I know what's bothering you and I want to help you better understand yourself. I love you no matter what."

Clay managed to say softly, "Thanks, Daddy. I want to talk about it too. I love you so much right now and just want you to hold me for a while if you can."

"Oh, son, I'm happy to. Just relax now and try to get some sleep. You and I have a lot to talk about in the next few days and after we do, I think both of us will feel a lot better." Les held his son close until he finally drifted off to sleep.

Now that Les knew for sure, he could help the boy deal with his nature better. Les himself slept soundly that night relieved that he had jumped the first hurdle in opening up communication with his son on such a delicate topic.

Chapter 28

Clay awoke just after dawn with a desperate need to relieve himself. Les was sound asleep and snoring lightly. Across the tent, his two friends were still buried in their sleeping bags, dead to the world. As Clay carefully got up so as not to disturb his dad, he started thinking about what Les had said just before holding him while he cried. *He knows and somehow it doesn't matter. He still loves me.* That thought alone gave him so much courage and comfort. He looked down at Les who was turned on one side smiling at some dream he was deeply immersed in. Clay felt such a surge of love that he nearly cried out loud with happiness.

Clay turned away though, and pulled on a sweater before stepping outside. It was *cold*. His breath was visible as he stepped toward a nearby bush and peed. The air was crisp and clean, with the scent of a healthy forest; the sky above was clear and deep blue. He hoped the day would warm up so they could go swimming again sometime during the day. If it stayed this way, however, swimming would be out of the question. Just as he finished, Albert exited the tent and took Clay's place at the bush with a giggle and a grin.

"Whew! I had to go bad. I heard you zipping the tent closed and got up. Your dad and Henry are both still asleep, I think. I love you, Clay. I haven't had much of a chance to tell you with Henry and your dad around, but I want you to know that I do love you."

"Me too, Albert, you're my number one guy. I wish I could give you a hug and a kiss right now, but can't --- especially since you're holding your member." Both had to laugh at the familiar running joke. First chance I get, when your hands are free, I will."

Albert said, as he finished up with a shiver, "Henry's downright scary sometimes, Clay. I thought I was gonna gag holding back a laugh when he talked about his pubic hair with your dad, gees!"

"I know. When we get some privacy today, I'll tell you something about Dad that makes me feel better about being the way we are. I think he knows and it looks like it doesn't matter to him. He'll love me no matter what."

"Really? Did he say that?"

"Yep. He said that no matter what I was like, or who I loved, he'd still love me."

"How did he figure out you might be queer? Did he say anything about me? I sure don't want my folks to know."

"He did mention you and Henry too, since he saw you give me a kiss when I lit the fire last night. He'd seen Henry giving me little kisses earlier. That's what started Dad talking about things. He said it was okay and that if I ever wanted to kiss you or Henry back, it wouldn't bother him. He said he understands."

"Wow! You got to be kidding! I realized I'd done that after you started the fire and hoped he hadn't seen me. It's just coming naturally now."

"Albert, I think maybe Dad is just like us too."

"Really?"

"I think Todd was his boyfriend and it hurt him real bad when Todd died. That's why he isn't interested in getting married and said he's a confirmed bachelor. I think that's his way of saying what he really is thinking. He said he and I have to have a talk about it sometime soon."

"Wow."

"I feel so much better now that I know Dad understands how I feel. I had a good cry last night about things and he hugged me until I went to sleep. God, Albert, I love him so much. He really understands me and now I know he'll love me no matter what."

"That's good. I wonder how my mom and dad would feel if they knew how I am? I'd be scarred to tell 'em." Albert rolled his eyes and laughed. "Remember, Mom and Dad can't even say penis." Both boys got the giggles and Clay risked giving Albert a hug anyway. "I wouldn't even know *how* to tell them."

"It's easy, Albert. Just invite Henry to stay a few days at your house. He'll just up and tell 'em everything." They laughed as they re-entered the tent where they found that Les was awake. Henry was naked and pulling on a clean pair of underwear. He looked up and grinned at the boys as they said good morning. Les was already dressed in blue jeans and a flannel shirt. He dug out a roll of bathroom tissue and headed out the tent flap before Clay could zip it shut saying he had to visit the restroom and would be back in a few minutes. Just before he left, he asked them to put on heavy clothes and boots, as he would be leading them on a hike after breakfast.

"Morning guys," said Henry as he came over and gave each of them a hug and a kiss. Albert grinned and kissed him back as did Clay. "Where are we going on the hike today?"

"I'm not sure yet, Rascal. Dad didn't say. I have to talk to him and see where he's planning on taking us. I think swimming might be out unless it warms up soon." He and Albert started getting dressed in warm clothing as Henry finished doing the same.

Just as they finished, Les returned and offered the roll of toilet paper to anyone who needed to visit the john before breakfast. Albert took the roll and headed off toward the restroom. Clay and Henry said they'd wait until after they ate. They told Les they'd give him a hand getting breakfast.

After leaving the tent, Les set up the small two-burner gas stove on the wooden picnic table and said he'd cook some oatmeal since it was such a cold morning. By the time Albert came back, the water was boiling and Les added the oatmeal and started stirring it. He asked Clay to fill a coffee pot with water and measure out enough grounds to brew four cups of coffee. As soon as the oatmeal was done, he set aside the hot cereal and replaced it with the coffee pot to bring it to boil. By the time they sat down to eat the oatmeal and two sticky buns for each, he'd packed along, the pot was making burping sounds and soon they each had a cup of the good-smelling brew. Les took his black, but the three boys preferred milk and lots of sugar. Henry said he'd never had coffee at home and after tasting, said it was good.

Les refused to tell them where he was going to take them for their hike even though they pestered him for a hint. After securing the campsite, Les drove south along Maryland State Road 219 until they crossed into West Virginia at a little border town called Gnegy Church. Four miles into West Virginia, just past the small town of Silver Lake, Les turned left on a gravel secondary road that wound uphill through several miles of dense woods. It ended at a gravel-covered parking area by a small, fenced-in, cement block building labeled with the United States Forest Service emblem. A sign gave a warning that the building was government property and what fines and penalties would be levied for anyone who molested the structure. Les was being mysterious and still refused to tell them exactly where they were going. He pointed however to a sign just past the building saying:

Backbone Mountain Trail
Summit - 2 Miles

They began walking and after a rather steep and strenuous hike along a jeep road, they arrived at a cleared area at the top of a high ridge where they could see for a number of miles in all directions. A U.S. Forestry jeep was parked by a cement block building. By the

293

building, a tall, steel-constructed, fire tower had been erected. A new-looking historical marker, erected in 1952, designated the spot

as Hoye Crest, the highest point in Maryland atop Backbone Mountain.

Les announced, "Boys, you are standing on the top of Maryland."

Albert said, "I thought we were in West Virginia! When did we cross back into Maryland? I must have missed the road sign."

"We crossed back there, somewhere along the road to the U.S. Forestry building. Because of the way the mountain and the roads are situated, you have to start along the way in West Virginia to get to Backbone Mountain and the tip top of Maryland." Les pulled a folded map of Maryland from his jacket pocket and showed them Maryland's highest point near the very southwestern tip of the state's panhandle.

From above they heard a call. "Hey, mister, if you want to bring the boys up for a look-see, you're welcome to come on up. There's a key under that flat rock beside the gate.

Les yelled back his thanks and went in search of the key. It fit a padlock on a gate to the high fence that surrounded the tower and after opening it; Les locked it back and pocketed the key until their return. After climbing twelve flights of metal stairs in a dizzying square spiral, they arrived at an open trapdoor. A jovial-looking man in a bright red flannel jacket over his army green, Forest Service uniform greeted them and welcomed them to the top of the state.

"Hi, I'm Ned Shoemaker." Les introduced himself and the boys.

Ned continued: "It's good to have some company this morning. Not too many people hike up here. The view's worth it though."

Albert spoke saying, "Thanks, Mr. Shoemaker. This is great. How high is this tower?"

"It's a hundred fifty feet, but seems higher after the climb. Look around. You can see about fifty miles in all directions from up here. If you brought a camera, it's a good place to get a few snapshots. You picked a nice clear day too."

Everyone thanked him for his friendship and welcome. The boys walked around the interior of the tower looking out at the forests and mountaintops below in all directions. Ned showed them his fire-spotting transit and described how it worked as they looked through it. He also let them use a massive pair of sixty power binoculars whose weight was almost more than Henry could handle.

"I bet this is a heck of a place to work in the winter," said Les.

"It's okay once you get up here as we have a good heater --- either electric or gas in case we lose power --- but sometimes the snows are so heavy that we can barely get up here with a jeep. Sometimes we get snowed in for days at a time and have to stay overnight in the bunkhouse."

"Is that the building beside the tower?" asked Henry.

"Yep, it has bunks for four, a bathroom and a well-stocked kitchen. In the spring and summer, four of us work single man shifts, but in winter, we trade out two men, working three days at a time. It pays well and I like the solitude. We have a phone and a two-way radio for calling in and out. The few visitors to the mountaintop provide just enough company from time to time to keep me from becoming a complete hermit."

Henry asked, "Don't your wife and family miss you in the winter?"

"My kids are all grown up and gone and as for my wife, well, like I said, I enjoy the solitude." He laughed, as did Les and the boys.

Les said, "Well, we sure appreciate your kindness. How often do you have a fire start around here?"

"We've been lucky the last few years. The only big one that caused a lot of damage was back in 1949, over near Swanton, Maryland. I was a firefighter then and that fire damn near got me. It killed two close friends. Wind shifted and swept it through so fast we just couldn't outrun it. I got burned some, but my buddies didn't make it. After that, I asked to work the towers. Being that close to fire and getting burned does something to you."

Les glanced at Clay who was gazing downward at the floor in thought. Les was waiting to see what Clay might have to say about the subject. He felt it might be good for Clay to share his experience with the man and wasn't surprised when Clay looked up and said, "I was burned too, Mr. Shoemaker. My mom, dad, and little brother were killed in a house fire. See." Clay raised his shirt and showed Ned his belly and chest.

"Oh, son, I'm so sorry that had to happen. It's bad enough that you got burned, but to lose your family... I'm really sorry."

"I was ten when it happened, but now I've been adopted by my new dad, Les Mills, and he's the greatest dad a guy could ever want. I'm sorry you got burnt too."

"It was mostly my legs and backside and if it's all the same to you, I won't show you my scars. I don't think anyone wants to see an old man's burnt behind." He laughed, as did the others.

"You know, I've got something for you, son." He went over to a cabinet and pulled out a brown Forest Service hat and said, "You'll look like Smoky the Bear in this. I wish I had two more for you other fellows, but I'm gonna give this one to young Clay here, as he's felt the fire firsthand and survived it. I can get another from the service anyway and seldom ever wear it. I've got some Junior Forest Ranger, Smoky Bear badges here for all three of you young gentlemen, though." He took three stainless steel badges from a drawer and gave one to each boy. They thanked him and pinned them on. He turned to Clay and said, "You can hang that hat on your bedroom wall, Clay, and remember your visit to the top of Maryland."

Everyone thanked the man and shook his hand before descending

the tower, re-locking the gate and hiking back to the car. Along the way, Les told Clay he was proud of how he shared his experience with the man and bravely showed him the scars. Clay had to adjust the band on his new hat, but wore it as they walked the trail.

That afternoon it warmed up enough for them to go swimming again in the plunge pool of Muddy Creek Falls.

Les asked Henry and Albert to give

Clay and him a few minutes to talk privately during their time at the falls and led Clay to a high flat rock that looked down upon the pool where the other boys played. Les was still close enough in case one of them had a problem.

"Dad, I'm having so much fun. Thanks again. It's been super."

"I'm so very proud of you, son. You're everything a man could want in a son. You've made my life a lot fuller and I'm happier than I've been in a long, long time. We both know how bad loneliness can be."

"You miss Todd a lot, don't you Dad?"

Les nodded and finally said, "Yeah. I loved him very much. He and I were a lot like you and Albert and maybe Henry too. I see the love you have for your friends and it's the deeper kind that sometimes happens to guys like us. You know how I've talked about being a confirmed bachelor. Well, maybe you've figured out what I meant by that. You're no dummy, Clay and I think you know what I'm referring to." Clay nodded but remained silent looking at his dad and smiling.

"You aren't interested in girls are you?"

Clay shook his head and said, "No Daddy. I like boys. You like guys too, don't you?"

"Yeah, does that bother you?"

"Oh no, Dad, it makes me feel great. I know now that you'll keep on loving me. You know what it's like and now I can talk about things without feeling embarrassed and scarred. I sure got lucky and found the right dad. I was scarred to death that Uncle Warren would somehow find out about me."

"I'm sure you were. I think God made things work out just right for us. I've been lost since Todd died and never wanted to team up with anyone else. I still have no desire to do that, but it sure is nice to know that I have a son now to love and share my home with."

"It makes me feel good too."

"Todd and I used to sit right here and watch the falls when we visited this spot, so it has good memories for me. Now, having you here adds to those special moments."

"I'm glad we don't have to be so lonely any more."

"Yeah, me too; I have a few questions for you, if you don't mind."

"Sure, Dad. Go ahead."

"What about Albert? Does he have any idea how you feel about him. I can tell you love him."

"He's queer too, Dad, and loves me as much as I love him. Henry and Randy are the same way. I found out about them at summer camp."

"My gosh, you've been busy." Les chuckled before going on, "It took me two years to finally get up the courage to ask Todd about it and we were about sixteen before we knew what it was all about. Uh, have you and Albert experimented a bit? If it's none of my business, you can say so and I'll let well enough alone."

"Oh no, Dad, as long as you're my dad, it's your business too. I want you to know about how much I love him. He and I have done stuff together and Dad, it's the most wonderful thing I've ever had happen. Henry and Randy at camp and I did stuff too, but Albert is the one I want to spend the rest of my life with."

"Wow! So, you've fallen in love and at fourteen, no less. I'm glad for you. You deserve a nice partner like Albert. He's a good boy, so very honest and loving. Henry is too, but be careful getting involved with other boys as it might cause Albert to feel hurt. Does he know you and Henry; and I suppose Randy have experienced sex with one another?"

"Yes. I told him right after we had our first time together. It happened at the old mill the day after I came back from camp. We just looked at each other and hugged and somehow we knew what we wanted to do and we did it. It was the second best day of my life."

"What was the first, Henry and Randy?"

"Noooo! The best day was when you asked me if I wanted to be your son and we went to see the judge. That will always be the best day. I love you so much, Dad, I feel like I'm gonna bust sometimes. I love you and Albert and Henry and Randy and I'll probably love Randy's boyfriend, the French kid, Claude."

"Well, don't over-do it, you just *might* bust. Love and sex are very powerful things. They can make people get mean and crazy sometimes with jealousy. Be careful about..."

"Oh I know! Sorry to interrupt you, Dad, but I know how awful jealousy can be. I made an absolute ass out of myself at camp when Claude came to visit Randy. Sorry about saying ass."

"It's okay, you were referring to the animal, I do believe. How did you make an ass of yourself?"

Clay went on to tell Les that story as well as several others --- without exact details --- as they spent another fifteen minutes on the rock. Albert and Henry were watching them from time to time below and Clay could see that Albert had a good idea what was being discussed, as he nodded at Clay and gave him occasional smiles and a thumbs up sign, occasionally. Clay smiled back and nodded.

Once Clay finished talking to Les, who told him to go enjoy his time with his friends, he shared with them that Les now knew about his nature. Clay, at his dad's request, did not discuss Les's own inclinations with the boys. Clay did make it clear that Les understood and respected what they were and would not pass on their secrets to their parents.

"Dad said that if you guys need to discuss things with an adult, he would be glad to answer your questions."

Henry asked, "Did you tell him that you've done things with Randy and me, Clay?"

"Yeah, and he warned me about jealousy and that's when I told him what happened to me when Claude visited Randy. I've told Albert about that already. As I've told you, and I'll remind Randy when I see him, Albert is my number one guy. I still love you, Rascal, and we might all do things together once in a while just for fun, but Albert is the one I want to live with someday. Does that bother you?"

"Nope, I understand. I won't get mad if you want to be alone with Albert either. I think it will be fun for us all to do things together at the same time, 'cause we like one another so much, but you two guys love each other in a different way and I'm glad about it. I hope I find a boy who I can love that way and maybe live with, as I get older. 'Till then, I can have fun once in a while with you two."

Albert gave Henry a quick hug and said, "You're a good friend, Henry, and what you said means a lot to me. I love you too, just like Clay, but with him and me, well; it's different somehow."

As they finished talking, they saw Les motioning them to come out of the water. They were becoming cold anyway because they'd been so still. As long as they were romping and horse playing, their bodies could fight off the chilly water, but now it felt good to come out and bask in the warm sunlight. They joined Les on the flat rock above and laid back on its warm surface.

It was late afternoon and Les asked them what they wanted to eat for supper. "We have more hamburger meat packed in the ice chest, lots of baked beans, a canned ham I can slice and fry and canned fruit for dessert. What'll it be, fellows?"

Clay suggested, "Well, the hamburger meat will spoil if we don't use it up, so how about we each have a hamburger again. They were good last night. In the morning, we can have fried ham with scrambled eggs. All of us boys will fix breakfast for you, Dad and give you a day off from cooking before we have to go back home." His buddies second the suggestion, so that topic was settled.

Henry broke the ice about the topic he and Albert were most anxious to hear about. "Mr. Les, Clay told us that you know about how all of us are different from most boys and I want to thank you for loving Clay enough to keep on loving him no matter what. I think when I'm fourteen, or maybe fifteen, I'll tell my mom and dad too, but I might need you and Clay to help me out with that when the time comes. They're kind of used to me being weird anyway, so it won't surprise them very much. I just have to get over my shyness."

Les laughed and said, "Henry, you're doing just fine with that already. I'll be glad to help when the time comes and I'm sure Clay and probably Albert too will lend some moral support."

"Thanks. I feel better knowing that."

Albert expressed his concerns about his folks by saying, "It's not me that's shy in my family. It's my mom and dad." He went on to tell everyone how his parents had trouble talking about sex and soon everyone, Les included, was laughing at his dad's uncomfortable use of the word 'member'.

Chapter 29

The remainder of their camping trip went well, but all were sad to leave Garrett County, and head back toward home. Henry asked if he could stay a few days more at Les and Clay's house, and after a call to his family, arrangements were made for them to pick him up in three days. Les offered to drive him home, but the Winters family wanted to see where Clay lived and talk with Les concerning their son's piano education. He gave directions and invited them for dinner.

Needless to say, after returning to Sand Patch, Albert and Clay took Henry to the old mill for a stimulating day of swimming and other enjoyable activities. Both he and Albert were introduced to the V-seat --- as Clay called it --- and other novel things possible at the remote location. There was no evidence of jealousy among the three as they shared intimacies.

On the morning of Henry's last day visiting, Clay received a long distance call from Harper's Ferry. It was Randy and he was very upset. He started talking, but soon broke down and started softly sobbing as he told Clay that Claude and his family were returning to France in September. It was something to do with an inherited family business that Claude's father now had to manage and maintain.

"I feel awful, Clay. I'm probably never going to see him ever again unless when I'm older I can go to France. By then he'll have another boyfriend and he'll forget all about me. I sure wish I was there with you guys right now. I miss you and Henry too and now after Claude leaves next week, I'm going to have nobody." Randy started wailing and said he had to hang up before his mom heard him and wanted to know what was wrong.

Clay said, "Randy, hang on just a minute. Don't hang up yet. My dad knows all about me now and what you and Henry and I did at camp and he'll do whatever he can to help you come see us on weekends."

"He knows we're all queer and he's not angry?" Randy was incredulous.

"Uh huh, he knows and he's not bothered by it. And don't worry, he won't tell your folks. He'll be starting to work as a conductor on the Baltimore trains this coming week, so maybe you can travel back and forth with him. He said he'd talk to your parents soon and set everything up. We all love you and we'll help you feel better. Don't hang up yet. Hang on a minute."

Clay shared what was going on with Henry and Albert who were nearby. After talking with them, he turned back to the phone and said, "Are you there, Randy? --- Good. Listen, Henry wants you to know that he wants to be your boyfriend now that Claude is going to France. He says... Wait a minute... Here, he wants to talk with you."

Henry took the phone. "Randy, I'm so sorry to hear about Claude. I know you're sad. We all wanted to get to know him better too, but I guess we won't be able to. I love you very much too and I'm gonna be right here and not move to France, or anywhere else for that matter. I would love to be your boyfriend since we already love each other. I know Harper's Ferry is still far away, but with Clay's dad and the B&O Railroad, we can see each other a lot. Maybe I'll be able to come and see you there with Mr. Les's help. Please say you'll be my boyfriend, 'cause I love you so much already."

There was silence on the other end for a few moments before Randy finally got himself under control. "That sounds nice, Henry. I love you too and with Mr. Les's help, maybe we can see each other often. I'm gonna miss Claude and might feel lousy once in a while, but I love you and think you're one of the nicest boys I've ever known. You're very good looking and I love the way you always hug and kiss. You've made me feel better already. I'll be your boyfriend."

Randy was nearly deafened by the loud squeal coming across the line as Henry whooped and keened his happiness. "I'll be the best friend you've ever had and we'll have so much fun. I can hardly wait to see you again. Maybe Mr. Les can get you on a train real soon. I love you, Randy. You're the best. Here's Clay now. Nope, wait a minute; Albert wants to say something too. Here."

"Hi, Randy, I'm Albert, Clay's boyfriend. I'm anxious to meet you too. I think it's great that Henry and you will be together. It's going to be so nice for the four of us now. We'll each have someone to love in that special way. Clay and I want to get a house someday and live together for the rest of our life. Maybe we can all get a real big house and all four of us can be a family. That would be so cool. I hope to see you soon."

Randy responded, "Me too. I'll miss Claude, but now I know I'll never be lonely since I have good friends like you guys. I have to go now, Mom's back from the clothesline and I have to wash my face from crying so much. Tell Clay I'll call again soon. See what his dad can do about the train and we'll soon get to meet. Tell everyone I love them. Bye." The phone clicked off just after Albert heard Randy's mom in the background asking who was on the phone.

Albert giggled and told his buddies that maybe Randy didn't have permission to make the long distance call. Clay grimaced and said it would probably be all right.

Before supper that night and the visit from Henry's parents, Clay talked with Les about Randy and Claude. Because Les understood what Clay and his friends were feeling, he could commiserate with Randy and pledged to help with transportation so he could visit soon. He'd have to spend a few days at work and learn his schedule before anything definite could be worked out, but he told Clay he'd make sure it happened, perhaps before the upcoming Labor Day weekend.

Clay hadn't said anything about Henry's offer to be Randy's new beau as he felt that was their business. The rest of the afternoon, the three boys helped Les prepare for the Winters family visit. Les chose to slow-bake a rump roast of beef and serve it with mashed potatoes, gravy, fresh creamed garden peas, a green salad from their garden, French bread he'd bought at a bakery in Wellersburg and ice cream for dessert.

The Winters arrived at two as planned and dinner was served shortly thereafter. During the meal, conversation focused on Les's discussion about Henry's musical talent. Henry blushed as Les compared his ability with that of Les's former student, Charlie, who had performed at Carnegie Hall.

"Your son could easily be a world class pianist, as he has a phenomenal command of music. Henry *feels* the notes and doesn't just play them mechanically. He's one of those rare young people who are able to get inside the minds of the composers and know what they were trying to say as they wrote the music. Not only that, but he's already writing his own compositions at thirteen! That's so rare. He played two of his personal compositions for me and they're fantastic."

Leo Winters said, "That's mighty kind of you, Les. I know we love hearing him play at home. My sister gave us an old upright, player piano when Henry was about six and before we knew it, he was playing songs using both hands that he'd heard on our radio or Victrola. Betty and I knew he had something going, so when he was eight, we signed him up with a neighbor lady who taught him to read music. Pretty soon, she said it was beyond her ability to teach him much more and suggested we get him a better teacher. That's when we contacted Miss Hindrick, up in La Valle, but now she's unable to teach him."

Betty Winters said, "Les, I know you're just starting a new job and are very busy, but anything you can do to help Henry would be most appreciated. We'll be glad to pay you double what you normally charge to teach students."

"It'll be my pleasure to fill in until we can find a worthy teacher for him. There's absolutely no charge. I can work out a series of lessons and exercises that will enhance his style and challenge his technique, but he's ready for a full time master teacher. I have the training for that, but now with the new job and my new family duties, I just couldn't do him justice. Tell you what; I know of a man in Keyser, West Virginia. He's retired now, but he has the experience and the knowledge to further Henry's talents. He's a tough old bird though. Henry, I'll warn you right now, he'll work your fingers off. Keyser is only about fifteen miles from Triple Lakes, I think."

Leo Winters nodded and said the distance wasn't a problem. Betty said she was home all day long and would make sure he got to his lessons as they had a second car.

Henry piped up and said, "I'll do it, Mr. Les. I don't mind working hard."

"He's a good man and kind, but very demanding. That's what it takes to make a good piano teacher. I'll give him a call tomorrow and see if he'll take on a special student. He taught me during my middle to late teens and for a while, I hated the stress as he nearly worked me to death, but by heavens, I learned and learned well. His name is Doctor Aloysius Dent. He's not a medical doctor, but has a doctoral degree in music and composition from Boston University. I have a feeling he'll balk at the idea of coming out of retirement, but once he hears you, he'll come around. No true piano teacher would refuse someone of your potential."

"Thanks, Mr. Les. I won't let you down. I'll work real hard."

"I know you will Henry, because you love the music. After supper, we'll both play for your folks. I've been practicing something really hard so you won't show me up."

"What are you going to play, Dad," asked Clay.

"The last movement from *Rachmaninoff's Second Piano Concerto.*"

"Oooooo," said Henry, wide-eyed. "That *is* a hard piece; it's one of my favorites."

"I'm glad these two know what the heck they're talking about, Betty, because I'm lost. I just like to listen," said Leo, as he gave his son a hair ruffle and a kiss. Les was pleased to see the easy and open love between the father and son. That was extremely important in the life of any creative person as they were often shunned and misunderstood by others, even family. He had little doubt that when they learned of Henry's sexual nature, they would be supportive and still love him unconditionally.

Later that evening, Henry played a portion of *The Emperor's Waltz*, by Johann Strauss and several short pieces by Modest Mussorgsky from *Pictures at an Exhibition.* By far though, Les came across as the master maestro that night with his flawless rendition of the final movement from *Rachmaninoff's Second Piano Concerto.* Clay and Albert both sat wide-eyed. They'd both heard Les play before, but never with that level of power and passion. Playing Rachmaninoff was always a strenuous workout and Les was perspiring and breathing hard as he finished the piece.

After the concert, it was time for the Winters family to return home. Poor Henry was nearly in tears as he hugged his friends and Les while saying goodbye. His folks assured him they would soon bring him back for visits and piano lessons until arrangements could be made with Dr. Dent.

Albert had to return home that evening too, and Les drove him since it was dark. Clay and Albert rode in the back seat and just before they arrived at Albert's house, Clay and he embraced and kissed. Les smiled as he saw them in the rear view mirror. He said, "You two look great together. Remember, you have my blessing. When the time comes to talk to your folks, Albert, I'll help if you want. We both love you as family now; goodnight, son."

"Thanks, Les, I love you too. Goodnight." Albert jumped out as soon as the car stopped. Les opened the trunk so he could unload his camping gear. The Stiles family thanked Les for taking the boys camping and asked Clay and him to join them for dinner some evening soon. Les said they'd be honored to accept before saying goodnight and driving off with Clay, headed for their home.

Once back home, with no other distractions, they sat side by side on the parlor sofa chatting while listening to a stack of records playing on their Motorola record player.

Les asked, "In talking with the boys, did you mention anything about my relationship with Todd?"

"No, Dad. I think Albert has it figured out on his own, but if so, he knows to keep it to himself."

"I'm not concerned about him; in fact I may soon have a talk with both of you and make things clearer to Albert at that time. I was more concerned with young Henry, who seems to say whatever pops into his busy little mind. He is one unusual kid, but lovable. He's such a free spirit and my god, Clay; he has enough musical talent to go far."

"I know. Those songs he played were really something. I still want to take a few lessons myself."

"We'll do it soon. Let me get started with the new job and settle in a bit and I'll start you out on some beginning exercises. You did pretty well picking out a few tunes the other day for me. It shows that you have a good ear and a sense of timing already."

"Thanks. I don't think I'll ever be as good as Henry, or you for that matter, but I'd still like to learn what I can."

"Any ideas about what career you might want to pursue someday? I'll do whatever I can to pave the way for you. What school subjects do you most enjoy?"

"Well, in eighth-grade we had science and health class; I guess I liked that better than anything. I like English and especially literature. I've read a lot of good books that I really love. I do okay in math and social studies, but they're not my favorites."

"What about sports. Are there any that especially interest you?"

"I don't like team sports much, but I'd like to try out for track and field. As I've told you, I'm good at running, thanks to Uncle Warren." Both shared a chuckle.

"What about art; have you ever done any drawing or painting?"

"I like to draw. I had a lot of drawings I'd done over the last few years, but Aunt Martha decided to clean out my room one day while I was at school and she burned all of my drawings in the trash barrel. I got angry and complained and Uncle Warren swatted me and made me go without a couple of meals. He threw my colored pencils in the fireplace."

Les growled and said, "Damn those two! How can two people be so hellishly mean? I want to see what you can do. I draw and paint too, but lately I haven't had the urge to do anything."

He stroked Clay's dark curls and added, "Up until you came into my life, I was even slipping with my music. I was sad most of the time and had no one to share my life with. That's changed and I want to get back into things like never before."

"That's good, Dad."

"I'll dig out my art supplies and set up my studio again in the guesthouse so you and I both can do some work there. I want you to draw something for me as soon as you feel like it, okay?"

"Sure. I like to use colored pencils. The set I had was only sixteen colors, but I learned how to blend them together and did pretty well."

"I have a fine set of forty-eight colors from England."

"Oh wow! That sounds super."

"I'll dig them out for you tomorrow and give you a sketch pad to work in. Tomorrow's my last day off before I start work, so we'll have to start making plans for that as well. Let's see, Labor Day will fall on September the seventh this year and school will start for you the next day, Tuesday. That means you'll have a number of days on your own here, while I go to work. Will you be okay with that?"

"Sure, I'll be fine. Can Albert come over while you're at work?"

"Absolutely, he's always welcome. You can go over to his house too, just make sure the house is locked up while you're gone and leave me a note on the fridge."

"Okay."

"I should be getting home before six each day. I'll call the dispatcher tomorrow and see what days I'm scheduled and for what runs. All I know now is I'm on the *Shenandoah #7,* come Monday, for a run to Baltimore and then a turnaround on the eastbound *Shenandoah* that afternoon. It leaves Cumberland at six-twenty and arrives in Baltimore at eleven-ten. The *Shenandoah #6* leaves Baltimore at noon and arrives in Cumberland at four-fifteen."

"Wow Dad, you have those times memorized."

"It's my job, kiddo. I'll be in charge of those trains so I have to make sure my trains leave and arrive on time. On Monday, I should be home about five-thirty."

"I'll have supper ready; that's another thing I learned at my uncle's place. I had to help cook the meals and Aunt Martha was a pretty good cook, if nothing else."

"I sure wish I could have adopted you right after the fire and the hospital stay and spared you all those years with them. At least at fourteen, you're responsible enough to be at home while I'm working. You know, it just occurred to me. I've never asked you when your birthday is. When is it, Clay?"

"January third. Yours is on October first, right?"

"Yep; I'll be thirty-four."

"That gives me a month and two weeks to come up with your birthday present and fix a special dinner for you, Dad."

"You don't have to do anything special. Just becoming a dad has been the best gift I've gotten this year." He gave his boy a hug.

"I'm really looking forward to Christmas. I'm gonna spoil you just a bit, no matter what I've said before. Christmas was always special for me and my parents while I was growing up. I haven't had a tree since Mom died, but we'll sure have one this year though --- a nice, big one."

Clay snuggled close and asked, "Dad, did your parents know you liked guys?"

"Mother did after a while. She figured it out and finally asked about Todd and I. Dad never did find out. He died of a heart attack when I was eighteen, just out of high school. That was 1938. He and I were close and I missed him a lot. He was a good father. Todd and I had been loving one another since we were sixteen, but we did it secretly. Mom didn't figure it out until just before the war in 1941. When Todd came home after his ship was torpedoed in 1944, and he'd lost his arm, I had him move in with me in Baltimore where I was teaching at the Maryland Academy of Fine Arts. Mom was living here, in Sand Patch alone and we often came up on weekends for visits. Todd's parents were both dead by then, so Mom and I were the only family he had. Mom, by then, accepted things and loved him like a second son."

"Why was Todd so sad, Dad? I believe you said he tried to kill himself." Clay thought about it before Les could answer and added, "Daddy, if this makes you feel bad, we don't have to talk about it right now."

"Thanks, but I'm okay. Todd had a lot of pride. He felt like he was dead weight and that he had to depend on me for everything. He was left-handed and had lost his left arm; he had to learn how to do everything with his right."

Yeah, I can understand that; I had to learn how to walk again after my legs were burned and I'd been in a hospital bed so long. It's hard."

"It was hard for him too and he'd get so frustrated at times. Then I lost my job and things were hard for us. We had to move back here. Mom was ill with cancer and soon died. Todd loved her like a parent by then and that made him feel even more depressed."

"I wish I could have been here then and helped him feel better too."

"That's so nice for you to say that, Clay; you're such a treasure. He would have loved you too. When a man sees the kind of things Todd saw in that war, it changes him. It's just like you seeing your little brother in the fire. You'll never forget that and it will always hurt. Todd saw his shipmates crushed by a fallen bulkhead and trapped in flaming oil. He was pinned too and the flames had nearly reached him, but other sailors managed to get him free and away from the fire."

"Wow. I can see how it must have made him feel."

"Todd couldn't get that horror out of his mind and move on, Clay. You know what it's like; you've seen horrible things that have caused nightmares, too."

"Yeah, for a while they were pretty bad."

"I bet. Son, I want you to promise me something. If ever your memories begin to eat at you; come to me and let me help. Don't wait."

"I won't Dad. I promise."

"Good. Todd kept it all bottled up and it ate away at him until he couldn't stand it any longer. I'd try to cheer him up and keep his mind occupied, but he'd get angry with me for doing it and that was putting a strain on our love. He finally tried to shoot himself and instead only ruined his eye and damaged his brain. It took him nearly six months to slowly die in the hospital and all during that time he..." Les had to stop and suppress a sob before going on.

"Daddy, you can tell me later; don't make yourself feel bad, please."

"No, Clay, I have to finish. I want you to know, because I've never been able to tell anyone else this. All the time he laid and wasted away in that hospital, he didn't know who I was."

"Oh, God, Dad I'm sorry."

"His mind was damaged and his memory of me was completely gone; but unfortunately, his memory of the ship and the fire was there *all the time*. He'd wail for hours about the fire and his burning friends. That's all his mind would let him see for hours on end. I remember asking God to let him die and after he did, I felt guilty about praying for that to happen."

"You just wanted him to be at peace, that's all."

"I know that now, but for a long time it ate at me. Remember how you broke down that first day and told me you felt it was your fault that you couldn't save your little brother?"

"Yeah."

"That's the same thing. We often blame ourselves instead of accepting that we really had no other course to follow. I hated most that I couldn't say goodbye to Todd and tell him how much I still loved him as he died. He had no idea who I was. He'd push me away and call me the devil, or other terrible names. It wasn't Todd in there anymore, Clay. I was in love with a stranger and was losing him; it hurt so much, Clay, it hurt so much." Les buried his face in his hands and slumped forward on the sofa where they were seated.

Clay hugged Les tightly from the side and together they cried silently for some time arm in arm. It was good for them both to let go and share the grief in both of their pasts. It was time now to move on to a happier life together.

Chapter 30

Clay decided to get up very early on the morning of the thirtieth to fix his father's breakfast and see him off on his first day of work as a conductor. Les would have waited and donned his new uniform at the station before boarding and assuming control of the train, but Clay insisted on seeing him decked out in his new navy blue outfit. Les did say, however, that he would eat breakfast first before getting completely dressed so as not to mar the uniform with spilled food. Once the meal was over, Les went to his room and soon came down the stairs completely dressed.

Clay smiled and said, "Oh, Dad, you look super. I'm so glad you have a better job now away from all the coal dust and stink. I almost wish I were going along with you today, but I know you'll be busy your first day and need to keep your mind on your work. Will you be the only conductor on board today?"

"No, most long run passenger trains have two and sometimes even three conductors. I'll be the assistant conductor on the long run trains for a little while; it's sort of a probation period and a chance for me to get used to the routine. The assistant conductor has charge of the dining, club and observation coaches. Today's train will have a Vistadome coach too and that will fall under my watch." Vistadome coaches were slightly higher than a conventional passenger coach and had a second floor with wide picture windows for sightseeing.

"I'd like to ride up there, Dad. I bet the view is super."

"It's pretty impressive, especially along the Potomac Valley, between Cumberland and Baltimore."

"If you were the head conductor, what would you have to do?"

"The senior conductor has charge over arrival and departure times, the porters, baggage and Pullman coaches. He also has all of the paperwork to handle, and for the first few days, I'm glad of that. I'll look over his shoulder and learn the ropes that way. Sometime before you start school, I'm going to take you along to Baltimore and back, so you can see what my jobs like while enjoying the train ride too. Maybe it'll be a train with a Vistadome coach. I won't be able to spend much time with you though, as my duties come first."

"That'll be super, Dad. I've never been to Baltimore and I'm looking forward to it."

"Maybe Albert and Henry can join you for company and when we make a stop in Harper's Ferry, well..."

"Oh, Daddy, you're the best. Can you do that? Let us all on the train?"

"Yep, a conductor has the power to do that; plus I'm allowed to use my employee pass for family and children under sixteen. I already asked and got the okay for whatever I wish to do for you and your buddies. Just don't say anything to them until I find the right date and time to have them join us."

"Okay, I won't."

"Well, son, I have to hit the road and the rails. The sun's soon to rise. You get back in bed and get some more sleep. You're looking sleepy."

"A little bit, I guess," said Clay as he yawned and smiled.

"I'm glad you got up to see me off and I love you more than life itself. You be careful and if anything happens, call Albert's mom. She said she could be here in a few minutes. If Albert comes over, have fun but be careful. If you fellows go swimming, or anywhere else, let Albert's mom know where you'll be and call her when you get back. And..."

"Dad, I'll be fine. We went over all this last night and I'm just fine. You go and do a good job on the train. Let me give you a hug before you leave though. Mmmm, yeah --- Bye, Dad."

"Goodbye, Clay. See you around six."

Les and Clay headed for the garage, where Les opened the door and soon backed the Roadmaster out. Clay waved before closing the garage door and returning through the parlor. He headed for his bedroom after closing the parlor door behind him. Debussy, waiting in the hall, mewed for attention and soon they were curled up in Clay's big, four-poster bed where they drifted off to sleep.

That evening, as promised, Clay and Albert --- who'd spent much of the day with Clay --- had supper ready when Les arrived home at five forty-five. They spent a pleasant evening together as Les told them of his first day on the job.

"What a difference, boys. No coal, oil or soot. I'm tired mainly because of all the time on my feet walking from one end of my coaches to the other and back again. I'll have to get used to that. There's little time to sit down, as passengers always seem to have so many little problems, concerns and complaints. It goes with the job though. The pay makes it worthwhile and it sure beats eatin' cinders."

"What train will you be on tomorrow, Dad?" Clay asked.

"I have a short run tomorrow, Cumberland to Pittsburgh and back on the *Daylight Speedliner #21,* going west and the Daylight Speedliner #22, going east. I'll be home about three tomorrow. For both of those runs, I'll be the only conductor; there are no Pullman or sleeper coaches since it's a short run, so I won't have to worry about roomettes and cranky, overnight passengers."

"What kind of engine was pulling the *Shenandoah* on the way back today, Les?" asked Albert.

"It was an F-7 Diesel and one assist unit. It was the same this morning on the *Shenandoah* eastbound. That's becoming pretty much routine. The *Capital Limited* to Chicago will still be using the

Streamliners for a while, but they're doomed for extinction too. The B&O only has four of them in service. All they are is a stinky, dirty, steam locomotive in a pretty dress. They look exciting, but all that streamlining metal just makes them harder to service. I give the streamliners about another three years and they'll be gone for scrap too. And no, Clay, you can't have one for the backyard."

The boys laughed.

"So what did you fellows do all day long?"

"Well, after our chores were done, Albert came over and we went swimming at the mill. I packed along a lunch and we swam until about three."

"Was there anyone else around out there today?"

Clay answered, "There were some younger boys and girls who came to swim for a little while, just after we arrived. They had an older teenaged girl along watching them. She was about sixteen, I'd guess."

Albert chuckled and added, "We were lucky we weren't skinning dipping yet when they arrived. She kept giving Clay the eye. He was wearing that tight red bathing suit he got at camp, Les, and boy he sure looks slick in it."

"Shut up, Albert." Clay admonished.

"Albert, you speak from personal tastes, I assume." Les said with a laugh.

"Quit it, Dad."

"Oh yeah, I was the one who insisted he wear it. I was just about to ask him to take it off when we heard the other kids coming."

"Shut up, Albert."

Les said, "Albert do you hear something occasionally?"

"Yeah, but I'm not paying much attention."

"I've found that's best. Oh look, Clay's turning red," said Les, while grinning at his son.

"It matches his bathing suit."

"Ah, come on; both of you quit."

"There he goes again. He's rather noisy, but I guess we both have to put up with him. Love conquers all." Clay who was sitting between Les and Albert got a hug and a tickling from both sides.

After a few minutes of fun, Les said, "Albert and Clay, you guys are so good for one another. I've wanted to talk with you fellows together for the last few days, but things have been busy, Henry was here and maybe now's the best time to do it before we hit the sack."

Clay had been expecting this and had told Albert the topic might come up.

"As you know, Albert, I'm well aware of how you boys are different from most other boys and I have no problem with that. Being homosexual just happens. It's still frowned upon by most people, however; so I want to make sure you both know how very careful you have to be as you grow older and move into adulthood. Maybe someday things might be different for boys and men and I suppose women too who like people of their own sex."

"I know how careful we'll have to be," said Albert, now serious as they dealt with a serious topic.

"Clay has told me that you might also have figured out why I'm so tolerant of what you and he are. Is that the case?"

Albert looked funny and glanced at Clay as though to ask for his help in answering. Clay said only, "It's okay, Albert, you can say whatever you need to say."

"Uh, okay. Les, I kind of get the feeling that you might be like us too and that Todd was your boyfriend when you guys were younger. Hope I'm not saying anything wrong."

"No, son --- and I do look at you now as a son too. What you're saying is true. I'm homosexual too, so it gives me a lot of experience in helping Clay, and now you, with your lifestyles. Henry as well, but right now I don't need to discuss this with Henry and I'd like to ask you fellows to keep my nature a secret as far as he goes."

"I understand. Henry's tongue wags and his brain lags."

Les laughed and said, "Cleverly put. I trust your good judgment, Albert, and want to let you know that I'll be happy to answer any questions you and Clay have about being the way we are. I may have a few questions for you fellows too, so I can better appreciate just how experienced you might be in your relationship."

"That's okay with me, Les. Whatever you want to ask, go ahead."

Les went on to ask them just how active they were and was not entirely surprised to find they had moved past mutual masturbation and had even experienced oral relations. He assured them it was the usual progression of things with homosexual boys and men. He also warned them of the health dangers of anal sex, which they told him they had not tried yet, and went on to explain the dangers also of venereal diseases, which neither had heard about before. That prompted a number of questions that needed answers. Les supplied them with all the facts and stressed the importance of fidelity in any good relationship. He pointed out how jealousy could break up a good pairing quicker than anything. He told them to be very careful as they experimented with Henry and Randy, who Clay now told him was Henry's new beau.

"You're going to try these things, I have little doubt. Just take it slow and talk about things with each other as you do. Don't sneak around and keep secrets from one another. That will destroy what you have quicker than anything."

Les then told Albert and Clay how he had lost his job in Baltimore, simply due to rumor and innuendo. Clay hadn't heard of that before, so it was new to him.

"That's another reason, fellows, why I don't teach in a school any longer. It's just too risky. For some reason, some people associate homosexuality with child molestation and that's simply not the case. Sometimes it is and everyone gets the blame. Both of you, as you consider future vocations, keep that in mind. There are a few careers that I would discourage Clay from considering for the same reason. Even the work at the summer camp you have planned for next year must be done very carefully. Once your reputation is marred, it's damned near impossible to change peoples' minds about you."

They discussed much that evening before it was time for bed. Les retired shortly after nine and told the boys they could stay up until ten if they wanted, but warned them to begin to adjust their sleep habits because school would soon be starting and they would be getting up early too.

Albert, who was staying over that night, asked Les if he had any problems with Clay and him sharing a bath or shower sometimes. Les grinned and said it was fine with him. He assured them that Todd and he had done that every chance they got when they were still teenagers.

"All of those things help to forge close ties and love between partners, boys. I know how you think and feel, and I understand. I wouldn't recommend sharing a bath at your house, Albert, until after you have a long talk with your parents."

"Oh, no sir, I don't intend to. I'm thinking that once I turn fifteen in December; maybe that will be a good time to have a talk with my folks. I know they love me, but I know it's gonna come as a shock. I just don't want them to feel hurt in any way, thinking it's their fault that I turned out this way."

"Clay and I will help when the time comes, but you'll have to be the one to tell them, Albert. That's important for both you and them. As scary as it seems, you'll feel better once you don't have to live a secret life. Most of the guilt of being homosexual comes from having to hide it from the people you love the most. Right now, I bet you feel better being able to talk with me and Clay openly about your feelings and concerns."

"And how! I think of you now like another parent and knowing that you're homosexual and once had a boyfriend and all, makes me feel very good. I really do love you, Les and appreciate how good you are to Clay and me."

"I love you too, Albert." Les gave both boys a warm hug before he went off for bed.

On Wednesday, September 3, Les arranged for Clay, Albert, and Henry to travel with him to Baltimore on the eastbound *Shenandoah*. He would be working the train only one way this day and had booked himself and the boys for two nights in the Baltimore & Ohio's Grand Hotel in Baltimore's Union Station. That would give them several days to enjoy the big city before Les and they returned to Cumberland on the afternoon of the fifth, aboard the westbound *Shenandoah*.

Arriving in Harper's Ferry at 8:40, a grinning and very happy Randy Meadows boarded the train where the conductor, somewhat to his surprise, greeted him with a warm hug. Randy's mother and little sister waved goodbye as the boy boarded the train. Waiting just beyond the vestibule in the next coach was a frantic Henry who made no excuses as he hugged and kissed Randy fervently, somewhat to the boy's initial embarrassment.

Henry covered it however as he squealed, "Cousin Randy! I'm so glad to see you again. It's been so long! Mom and Dad and Grandma each send a kiss too." That gave him the excuse to plant three more kisses on Randy's cheeks. Randy was blushing and had barely recovered when two more *cousins* gave him matching hugs and kisses. Other passengers were smiling at the *family reunion* and one lady even said how very sweet it was to see young relatives reunited and gave them each a pat on the head and a peppermint candy as they passed her on the way to their scats. The conductor grinned and rolled his eyes.

A few minutes later, Les called from the platform, "All aboard," and signaled the engineer. The train pulled out of Harper's Ferry station and crossed the Potomac on the wide stonework bridge. It immediately passed into a quarter mile-long tunnel where Henry took advantage of the semi-darkness to nuzzle a bit more with his *kissin' cousin* as he now termed Randy. Henry and Randy managed a few quick feels in the dark, as well, that had nothing to do with cousinhood.

317

Les had made sure they got seats at one end of the coach where two sets of seats faced one another. A porter had helped Randy stow his luggage in the overhead rack and Les came by just after they exited Harper's Ferry Tunnel and played his part asking for Randy's ticket, whereupon he showed Les his three-day rail pass. Les winked, used his capital dome-shaped punch to validate the card and went on to visit other passengers.

Les came by shortly thereafter and told them to watch for the next stop at Point of Rocks, Maryland where the rail line split, one line heading southeast for Washington, while the other went to Baltimore. The *Shenandoah #7* would continue on to Baltimore. Another passenger train, *The Washington Express #10* (which Les would occasionally work) ran toward Washington on a different schedule. It would take the southeast branch of the rails at Point of Rocks.

At noon, they arrived in Baltimore's Union Station and waited for Les before exiting the train. After all other passengers had left the coaches; Les stepped off with the boys. The other conductor had agreed to ride on to the yards for the normal turn-around process. He'd be joined there by another secondary conductor for the trip back in the afternoon as the *Shenandoah* headed west.

Les led them to the hotel desk and picked up their room keys for the overnight stay. He paid an employee-discounted fee for the night's lodging and asked for an extra single bed for himself, knowing the boys would no doubt sleep in the two double beds the room normally provided. Their room was on the fifth floor and looked out over the city to the north. Les pointed out several well-known buildings including Baltimore's old Shot Tower, where lead shot had been made for nearly a hundred years during the nation's early history. From an observation garden on the hotel's roof, Les pointed out Chesapeake Bay, Baltimore Harbor and Fort McHenry, where a crucial battle in 1812 had inspired Francis Scott Key to write the lyrics to the *Star Spangled Banner*. Les told them they would visit the fort the next day.

After an early dinner in one of the three restaurants within Union Station, Les and the boys returned to their room to change clothes. Les had told them each to pack their best clothes and a suit if they had one. He'd bought Clay a handsome, black and gray, pin-stripe suit a few days before. Henry, from having performed in several school concerts, had a nice suit, but it was obvious by looking at his

318

ankles and sleeves, that he'd grown recently and would soon need another fitting. Randy and Albert both brought along their church suits and by six-thirty all four boys as well as Les looked their best.

Les had not told them exactly where they were headed as they exited the hotel and he flagged down a cab. He even handed the cabby a note rather than say where they were bound. Clay looked at him curiously and Les simply grinned and repeated his usual frustrating phrase, "It's a surprise."

After a ten-minute ride through the beautiful old city, they arrived at a magnificent building a few blocks from Johns Hopkins University and Hospital. It was obviously a grand theatre and Les finally had to tell the boys they were there to see the Baltimore Philharmonic Orchestra perform Antony Dvorak's *Symphony from the New World*.

Henry was beside himself. Clay remembered one record he was fond of that he often played on their Motorola record player. It was entitled *Largo* from that symphony and was famous by another name, *Going Home*, as it had been set to words and recorded as a separate vocal piece by a number of performers.

Once inside the grand concert hall, they made their way to center section seats just eight rows back from the massive stage whose burgundy, velvet curtains were still drawn. As they waited, Les explained how a guest conductor would be leading the orchestra this evening.

"Boys, I bet you've heard his music before as he writes and conducts for a number of Hollywood studios. He wrote the music for that science fiction movie, *Day the Earth Stood Still,* with Michael Rennie and Patricia Neal. His name is Bernard Herrmann and he's one of today's foremost conductors. Let's see --- the program lists several pieces he'll be offering this evening. First is *March to the Scaffold,* by Hector Berlioz. You guys will like that one, as it's a powerful and exciting piece. Next is the Scherzo from Dvorak's *Serenade for Strings.* Third will be the feature performance of Dvorak's, *Symphony from the New World.*"

Les went on to explain the other features of the evening's concert and just as he finished, the house lights began to dim and the curtain was raised to reveal the entire ninety piece orchestra in their seats. As a hush fell over the audience, Bernard Herrmann walked across stage to enthusiastic applause and bowed before the audience. He turned to the orchestra and acknowledged the first violinist with a nod. As tradition demanded, the man stood and took a bow for himself and his eighty-nine fellow musicians. There was more applause. Next, Maestro Herrmann nodded to the first chair oboist who blew a single A note. All the other members of the symphony orchestra used that note to make sure their instruments were in perfect tune. Once that was completed, the conductor tapped his baton on the podium and raised both hands at the ready. With a flourish from the maestro, the orchestra began Berlioz's, *March to the Scaffold.*

All four boys sat captivated throughout the entire two-hour performance. As the encore, Tchaikovsky's *March Slav* ended, the entire audience rose to a standing ovation. The boys cheered loudly as the orchestra took its bows. Les was pleased to see the four enjoyed the experience that all too few young people were able to witness firsthand.

During and after the cab ride back to the hotel, all the boys could talk about was the music, bombarding Les with a hundred questions about the composers, the instruments and the history of the pieces they had heard. It was nearly eleven o'clock by the time everyone was settled for bed. Les found that he was expected to tuck in not only his own son and Albert that evening, but also Randy and Henry who thanked him repeatedly for taking them to see the orchestra. Henry especially was nearly in tears as he told Les how very inspiring it was for him to hear a live concert as he'd always dreamed of doing.

The next morning saw them visiting the nearby B&O Railroad museum, Fort McHenry and one of Baltimore's beautiful parks. They had lunch in a restaurant along North Avenue before heading to a grand theatre where Clay was finally able to see Walt Disney's, *Twenty Thousand Leagues Under the Sea.*

The next day it was time for Les to go back to work on the twelve o'clock westbound *Shenandoah* that would carry them home to Cumberland. Randy and Henry were able to spend several days at Les and Clay's home before school began.

Chapter 31

On the Saturday before Labor Day, all four families arranged to meet for a grand picnic at the C&O Barge Canal Park on the Maryland side of the Potomac River near Paw Paw, West Virginia. Les and Clay along with Albert and his folks rode in the Buick, while Henry's parents and Randy followed along in the Winter's family car on Maryland Route 51. Randy's family would drive west from Harper's Ferry, West Virginia and meet them there.

Soon everyone had gathered at the designated rendezvous. The weather was perfect and all four boys and Randy's younger sister, Sara, enjoyed hiking along the towpath within the old tunnel that had been bored through a mountain in the early eighteen hundreds so the Chesapeake and Ohio Barge Canal could carry freight along the canal from Cumberland to Washington.

The canal, first envisioned by President George Washington, was an engineering marvel for its time, but was doomed to obsolescence by the invention of the steam locomotive and the advent of America's railroads. The B&O had been the first chartered railroad in America and within only a few years, the old canal had fallen into hard times due to lack of use. Now it served only as a source of recreation in the few areas where it was still maintained.

While the youngsters played and enjoyed the last few days of the summer of 1953, the parents became better acquainted and grew closer because of the friendship shared by their sons. Plans were made between the adults for a second holiday outing and reunion during Thanksgiving weekend.

Just after their picnic meal, Randy's father, Randal Meadows

Senior, asked to speak to Les privately, so they walked a short distance from the other parents to chat. "You know, Les, something happened between those boys at summer camp; Randy's like a different boy at times."

"I think camp was good for them all. Clay made some good friends," Les observed.

"I uh, want to ask you something, Les, and I hope I'm not going to alarm you, or cause you any concern, but I simply want to talk to another father about this. You seem so well-adjusted with your boy even though I understand you just recently adopted him."

"Thanks, Randal, we're doing great together." Les was feeling some degree of alarm, fearful a certain subject was about to be brought up. It turned out he was right, but not in the way he expected.

"This is kind of a delicate topic and was one I was about to discuss with the parents of another of Randy's buddies, a French boy he was always spending time with. The French boy, Claude, however, moved back to France a few weeks ago and I let it go. Les, I'm kind of worried about Randy, as he seems a little odd at times. I have a brother who reminds me a lot of my son. He, uh, well, Les... How can I put this? My brother's not the marrying kind. He uh, sort of prefers the company of other fellows, if you know what I mean."

Les nodded and Randal continued: "I love my brother, however, and understand him. My sister does too, but one other brother won't have anything to do with him. Do you know what I'm talking about? This is difficult for me to discuss."

"I understand, Randal. You think maybe Randy leans in the same direction?"

"Yeah, he and the French boy were very close and he cried for three days straight when he heard the kid was leaving. Then he called your place and talked to Henry and your boy and since then, he's been fine and all he talks about now is Henry this and Henry that. Les, do you think my son might be uh, homosexual?"

"Randal, I, uh, don't know how to answer you exactly. If he were, how would you feel about that?"

"Oh, I'd still love him. Nancy and I have discussed it and we'd still love him just the same. Our main concern is for what he might be going through. He might not be able to figure it all out. My brother went through pure hell during his teen years. He damn near committed suicide at one point too. I'm worried that my boy might hate himself inside and has no one to talk to about this."

"Have you ever tried to broach the subject with him?"

"No. I really don't know where to begin. I'm afraid if my wife and I are wrong, we'll make him feel bad by thinking he's queer. I even hate that word, queer. Even though homosexual is the proper term, it has so many negative meanings. Uh Les, I'm sorry to bother you with this, but I simply wanted another parent's opinion. You get along so well with your boy and he seems so well adjusted and normal and well... I just want to help my boy, if he needs help." Randal sniffed a few times and looked away to hide any tears that might be appearing in his eyes.

Les placed one hand on the man's back and said, "Listen, Randal, I know what you're going through and maybe I can help. Would you like me to talk to Randy and hint around at the subject and see if I can learn anything?"

"Oh, Les, would you? This is beyond me. He and the other boys seem to look up to you and you have such a good way of communicating with them. Whatever you can do would help me and Nancy so much. I just want my boy to be happy and know that we love him no matter what. We were thinking about having my brother come down and talk with him if all else fails."

Shortly after their conversation, Les asked to talk privately with Randy. Clay and his other buddies were all looking confused and curious as Les and Randy took a short walk along the towpath beside the canal.

Les began, "Randy, I just had a very unusual conversation with your dad. He's asked me to talk with you about something that I already know about, but I'm not supposed to know about."

"Huh? What do you mean, Mr. Les?"

"I'll put it bluntly. Your dad and mother both are concerned about you and suspect that you may be homosexual." Les could literally see the blood draining from Randy's face as he stared up at Les and wavered a bit as though about to faint.

"You okay, buddy?"

"Uh huh. I think so. Oh god, Mr. Les. Do they know? Are they mad at me, or Henry, or Clay, or you?"

"No. That's the first thing you have to understand. Your dad and mom want to help you and they will still love you no matter what. They've had ideas about you ever since you were friends with Claude and now that he's gone they see how very happy you seem

323

being with Henry. It's going to be all right if they do know the truth, kiddo. They love you and want to help."

"Wow! What should I do, Mr. Les? I'm ashamed and don't know how to talk with them about this. How did Daddy know?"

"Well, for one thing, you have an uncle who's just like you, so your dad already knows about these things."

"What? Oh good golly! That must be Uncle Charlie. He's not married and lives up in Hagerstown. We hardly ever visit him, but he comes to see us. Dad, Mom, Sis and I love him a lot."

"So you see, Randy, your parents aren't going to throw you out in disgrace. You all need to have a talk about this as soon as possible. Once they know, you'll feel so much better and I bet they'll make sure you get to see Henry as often as possible. I'll help with the train transportation as best I can."

"Can you help me talk with them, Les? I'd like you to be there."

"Whew, Randy, I don't know. *When* would be the biggest difficulty. Everyone's having a good time today; just me talking alone with you has caused my boy and your other buddies are nearly breaking their necks trying to watch us. Look at 'em."

Indeed all three boys, as well as Randy's folks were watching them intently. Fortunately, the other parents were chatting among themselves at the picnic table. Les waved at the boys and they all looked guilty except for Randy's folks who smiled and nodded.

Les and the boy walked back to the table where Les could see that Nancy and Randal were nervous about the outcome of the conversation. Randy was looking rather panicked and yet anxious to talk to his folks.

Les ruffled his hair and whispered, just before they reached the table, "If you want to, Randy, we can talk right now. It looks like your folks want to find out the truth."

"Okay, Les. Let's do it now."

"I'm proud of you, kiddo. Give me a minute." Les motioned to Nancy and Randal to join him and Randy. They asked their daughter to stay with Henry and his folks for a few minutes after telling her they had to discuss something privately with Randy. She looked surprised and curious, but stayed and chatted with Henry.

Les saw them give each other a glance and take a deep breath before stepping his and Randy's way. The four of them walked over to another table and sat down. Les suggested that Randy speak to them first. The boy's eyes told Les that he'd expected Les to do the talking, but Les felt it was best for the boy to take the initiative.

Randy began, "Uh, Mom and Dad, uh, Mr. Les and I talked about something and I want to talk to you about it now too. Do you both know what this is about?"

"Yes, son," said his father. "Before we talk about it though, I want you to know that no matter what; your mother and I will never stop loving you. Did Les mention Uncle Charlie?" Randy nodded, yes.

"Good. You go ahead now and tell us about yourself. Don't worry about a thing."

"Okay. Dad and Mom, I'm kind of different than most boys. I guess you must have asked Mr. Les to talk with me first. Please don't be mad at me or disappointed, but I don't like girls. I like boys and I'm so sorry I'm that way, but I can't help it. I love Henry, who's the same way and I hope you'll not hold this against him." Randy was snuffling and tears were beginning to flow as his mom and dad took him in their arms and hugged him close, telling him they loved him and was proud of him for telling them the truth.

Les started moving away, but was stopped by Mrs. Meadows who said, "Thank you so much, Les. You're a good friend and we felt it might be easier for Randy to talk with you first about this. Do you think your boy and his friend Albert might be bothered if they learn that Randy and Henry are uh, boyfriends?"

Les smiled and sat down again before saying, "They already know, Nancy. Clay and Albert are the same way. That's why the four of them all get along so well. My boy's homosexual and I love him unconditionally. The only parents now who don't know are Henry's people and Albert's folks. I hope they'll be able to clear the air soon and then everyone will feel more comfortable with the situation."

"For a man who has never married and has only been a dad for a few months, Les, you are one great parent," said Randal senior. "We'll have a chat with our daughter so she knows about everything. Thanks again for listening to us and helping to solve our family problems."

Les thought about it for a few minutes, took a deep breath and said, "I'm going to share something else with you and I hope you continue to trust me and consider me as a friend. My ability to help in dealing with boys of their nature comes from personal experience. I'm the same way as your son. I want to assure you that I will never betray your son, my son, or their friends by acting inappropriately."

325

Randy's eyes flew wide open at that point and he looked as surprised as his parents. They then assured him that they had nothing but respect for Les and what he was doing for these four very different boys.

Mr. Meadows put it best as he observed, "Well, it looks like you were the perfect parent for Clay after all he's been through. I think it's wonderful these youngsters came together the way they did. It appears like all of us will have to keep some important family secrets especially once the other two sets of parents learn the whole story."

Les then said, "I'll do what I can to help Henry and Albert talk to their folks. They both want to already. Clay and I live just a short piece down the road from Albert's place; I know the Stiles family and I'm sure it won't affect the way they love and cherish Albert. Henry's dad and mom love that boy completely, so I don't see any problems there either. We'll all be better off once the air is cleared and all four families can share the love their boys enjoy. I thank you for accepting me as well. It's not always been easy for me and it won't be easy for the boys."

Randal senior said, "People can be so damned cruel to anyone who's different, whether they're colored folks, Jewish, handicapped, or whatever."

Les agreed, "Unfortunately that's so very true. Look how easy people made it for Hitler to do what he did in Europe. People like our sons and me were targeted for the death camps just as often as the Jews and Gypsies once that madman got started."

Mrs. Meadows said, "Let's hope and pray that things change someday in the future and Americans can learn to accept peoples' differences."

"I'm afraid it will take a long time, Nancy," said Randal. "Look at the way colored folks are treated in the south and even here in the north. They have to go to separate schools, separate churches and even have to use separate restrooms and water fountains. America has a lot of dirty laundry to wash before everyone can be considered equal. Hopefully it will happen someday and boys and girls like our children can be whatever the Good Lord made them to be."

The Meadows and Les joined the others and the rest of the day was one to remember for all four families. As four o'clock arrived, the families gathered their belongings and prepared to return to their homes. Everyone looked forward to gathering in the future for holidays or weekend outings. The parting between Randy and Henry was especially difficult due to the distance between their homes, but Les assured them he would make sure they could get together on weekends occasionally if his schedule worked out to their advantage.

Les had pulled Clay and the boys together and explained how Randy's parents now knew the facts and how it did nothing to change the love they had for their boy. Henry pledged that he would soon talk to his parents, but asked if Clay and Les might be there when he did so. Albert said he would make a decision soon about talking to his folks and he too asked for Clay and Les's help.

At four-thirty, everyone left the C&O Canal Park heading east and west to their homes. Les and the Winters agreed to stop in Cresaptown where their ways would part. Everyone was surprised when --- after parking in the lot at Cresaptown School, where Henry would attend eighth-grade --- he told Les and Clay privately that he'd told his parents about liking boys on the way and that they might soon want to talk to Les about the whole thing.

"Mom asked me why I was crying after we left and I just decided to tell her and Daddy the truth about how much I love Randy. They were surprised, but they both still love me. Did I do the right thing?"

Les gave the boy a hug and said, "You are one brave young man, Rascal." Les and everyone had started using the nickname Clay had given Henry at camp. It just seemed to fit.

"Now all we have to do is help Albert with his family and everyone will be more settled and comfortable. I'll drop by soon and talk with your folks. I have a few things to share with them as well that will help them understand you better. We love you; son and I'll see you for lessons until Doctor Dent can take you on as a regular student. Be good, Henry, and once again, Clay and I are proud of how brave you were."

Clay gave the boy a hug and said, "I love you, Rascal and just like Dad said, we're proud of you. See you soon."

After driving on to Sand Patch and dropping off Albert's mom and dad at their house, Albert asked to ride along home with Les and Clay. Once they arrived, Les and Clay told Albert that Henry had come clean with his folks. Albert thought a while in silence before saying, "I guess I'm the only one left. Let me sleep on it tonight, but tomorrow, I'll talk with my mom and dad. I want us all to stop having to keep so many secrets. Les, could you and Clay be there with me when I tell them?"

"We sure can," Les assured the boy. "You'll have to do the talking, because it's important for you to be the one to tell them. After that, we'll be there to answer questions. I'm also going to tell your folks about my past and assure them that I mean you and the other boys no harm. I have a feeling your folks, like a few other people around Sand Patch, have their suspicions about me anyway. I don't mind telling your parents, but from the rest of the town, I have to maintain my secret. Some folks might use that to take Clay away from me and right now, he and I need each other."

"I know," said Albert. "Those folks don't know you like we know you and what a good man and dad you are for Clay. You're like a second father to me and I love you just as much as I do Mom and Dad."

"Thanks, Albert. That means a lot to Clay and me both. We're all family and once your folks know, they'll be a part of the family too.

At Les's request and suggestion, Albert spent the night at his own home and the next day called Les and Clay and asked if they could come over for supper. He'd asked his parents to invite them for dinner and they agreed, not knowing what Albert's real motive was for the invitation. After a delicious supper of fried chicken, home-made dinner rolls and potato salad with chocolate cake for dessert, the families settled down in the Stiles parlor for conversation.

Albert's parents were surprised when Albert asked to talk to everyone about an important topic. "Mom and Dad, I have something that I have to say to everyone here. I'm a little scarred to talk about this, but I have to do it."

"Is everything all right, son?" asked Mr. Stiles. "You're not in any kind of trouble are you?"

"No Dad, I'm not in trouble. Dad and Mom, you know how I never talk about having a girlfriend and how I spend all my time with Clay. Well, it's because I'm different from most boys. I really don't want to date girls. And I don't want to get married someday. I...uh...I like boys instead. I like Clay and want to be with him the rest of my life." Albert hung his head, sobbed and said, "I'm homosexual. Please don't hate me."

He sat down beside Clay and started crying. Clay put his arms around his boyfriend and hugged him tightly. Albert's dad and mom came over, knelt in front of their son, and hugged him as well.

His mother spoke first. "Honey, we'd never hate you. Your daddy and I sometimes wondered if you might be that way, and we love you nevertheless. Some boys are just born that way. We love you and we love Clay." She gave Clay a kiss too before directing her next question at Les. "I suppose you know about this, Les, or you wouldn't be here?"

"Yes, ma'am, I do. Albert has talked it over with me during the last few days and I urged him to talk with you. Clay and he truly love each other and I hope you can accept that as I don't know of any way Albert or Clay can change the way they feel."

Mr. Stiles was petting his son's hair and said, "We're not disappointed at all with you, Albert. Clay is a fine young man and if you love him, as it's your nature to love him, then we love him too. I kind of thought you might be this way, so it's not a complete surprise. Don't you ever think we love you any less because of the way you are."

"Thanks, Dad and Mom; I love you both so much too."

Mr. Stiles said, "My only concern is how mean other people can be when it comes to this subject. I'm sure you know all about that. This has to be kept a secret from everyone else, or you'll never be able to live a happy life. People are mean spirited and won't let you."

"I know, Daddy," Albert managed to say quietly as he was still crying a bit. "I know. Mr. Les has talked with me about that too. My two other friends, Henry and Randy are the same way and I love all of them as friends too. They've all told their parents now, so we all have to be very careful and keep our secrets. We were all tired of keeping it from our families and the people we love the most. Now everyone knows and I feel so much better."

Les then took the floor and explained his own history to the Stiles family, assuring them that he had no intention of every doing harm to the boys. They both said they had no qualms about his nature or past and that they trusted him completely.

Mrs. Stiles said, "I believe it was God's hand that brought all of us together.

Epilogue

High school began for three of the young men the day after Labor Day. Henry, started eighth-grade in Cresaptown School, but wasn't there very long. Les had suggested to the Winters family that Henry be tested and all were pleasantly surprised when it turned out that indeed he was more advanced and ready for a greater challenge. In mid-September, Henry was advanced a grade; he started attending ninth grade at Allegany High in Cumberland. He'd be turning fourteen in late October.

Doctor Dent, after witnessing Henry's expertise at the keyboard, agreed to come out of retirement and take on the boy as his student. He told Henry's family that not since he'd taught Les, had he seen such promise in a pupil and predicted great things for the boy.

Mr. and Mrs. Winters sold off several heirlooms and antiques and bought Henry a better piano for Christmas that year after consulting with Les about a choice of instruments. It made their parlor a bit crowded, but Henry was beside himself Christmas morning when he returned from Les and Clay's house after a two-day visit and found a baby grand Steinway squeezed in beside the Christmas tree. He sat down on the bench and cried for nearly five minutes before he could play a single note. Clay was along and sat beside him as he played *Oh Holy Night* and several other beautiful Christmas songs for Les and his family.

Clay then surprised everyone by playing *White Christmas.* He'd been taking lessons from Les and was doing surprisingly well. Henry sat wide-eyed as Clay performed. Henry hugged him warmly as he completed the song beautifully, without a single mistake.

Henry had a triple surprise that day as Randy and his family arrived for Christmas dinner with the Winters. Henry's mom and dad hadn't told Henry they were invited, so he was utterly thrilled as his boyfriend hugged and kissed him openly and without any shyness in front of both families.

Randy's younger sister, Sara, wrinkled her nose as they embraced and said, "What a shame. Last summer, after meeting him at camp, I was sort of thinking about asking Henry to be my boyfriend, but I guess I can forget about that." She giggled and gave them both a hug and kiss anyway.

"I've always wanted a little sister and now I have one, Sara. I love you too," said Henry and he gave her a warm hug and another kiss.

The Stiles family spent the latter part of Christmas day with the Mills family. Les had encouraged Clay in both his musical and artistic efforts throughout the fall. He was pleased to find his son had real potential; his ability to draw and paint was miles above average. For Christmas, Clay received a professional-quality drawing table complete with a variety of art media and supplies. Les bought him several other items for their model railroad, as well.

During the fall months, Clay had labored in secret on a beautiful colored pencil drawing of a B&O Mallet for Les's Christmas gift. The drawing was over three feet in width and was so realistic that Albert's parents said it looked like a photograph when viewed from more than five feet away. Clay had used his model Mallet as a guide for the drawing and if one looked closely, Les, Clay and Albert were visible standing side by side in the cab waving. The background was the rolling hills of the Alleghenies. Les wept like a child when he unwrapped and revealed the picture on Christmas day. He said it would be given the place of honor above the mantle of their fireplace in the parlor once he had it framed and glazed.

Clay's gift for Albert was a set of drafting tools Les helped him pick out as Albert was showing an interest in becoming an architect and was nearly as skilled as Clay when it came to drawing and sketching buildings and structures. Albert gave Clay several model kits for buildings to add to the family railroad. One was a model grist mill and Albert told Clay he expected him to add the mill and a millpond somewhere on the railroad in the near future complete with a millrace and path. Clay secretly asked him if he wanted it to include two boys in the buff. Albert said, he'd rather wait for summer and act out the scene in person.

A few days after New Year's and by chance on Clay's fifteenth birthday on the third, Judge Brand surprised both Les and Clay by dropping by one evening with adoption papers for Les to sign. He asked Clay if he wanted to adopt Les's last name, or keep his own name of Parker. Clay decided on Clayton Parker Mills to honor both his birth parents and his new father. The good judge told him he would have a birth certificate issued in a few days reflecting Clay's choice.

Les was happier than he'd ever been in his life, finally feeling complete and at peace with himself. After the judge left that evening, he and Clay sat together on the sofa in the parlor listening to music on the record player and watching the snow falling outside in their front yard. Clay turned to Les and said, "Dad, thanks for everything you've done for me this year. I never thought I'd ever be happy again after everyone died in the fire, but now I am. Thanks for understanding me and allowing me to love Albert."

"Clay, I want to thank you too. After Todd died, I felt like my life was over and that I was only going through the motions of living. There was a empty hole in my world and son, you've filled it. I am the happiest I've ever been. Seeing you and Albert sharing love fills me with love too. Like Albert's mom said, I think God helped us all find our place in the scheme of things. Randy, Henry and their families are happy and I'm glad you and I could play a part in that as well."

"Yeah, me too."

"We're different, son, but we have the same right to pursue happiness as everyone else. Don't ever let the meanness and negativity of the world drag you down. It'll try sometimes to do just that, but as long as we cherish the love we have for each other and our friends, we'll continue to enjoy the blessings we've all shared this year. I foresee a bright future for you and your three friends, especially now that they have their family's love and support behind them."

"Yeah, I do too."

"Son, you played a big part in all of that. You were the keystone that held it all together. It was your love for your friends that brought Albert, Henry and Randy into not only your life, but mine as well and the lives of all the parents. Think how wonderful the parents feel now that they can talk comfortably about their sons and their nature without embarrassment and shame. We all owe you a lot. Love just naturally radiates from you, Clay, whether you realize it or not. What a shame that your uncle and aunt never could see what a treasure they had under their roof."

Les pulled Clay close and kissed his head as he breathed in the wonderful man/boy scent of his son. "I'm going to be very selfish now and say that I'm glad those two didn't realize what a treasure they had, because now, Son, you're *my* treasure and I will never cease to love and cherish you. We're going to have so much fun together as you grow up and I grow old. And best of all, neither of us have to worry about loneliness, ever again. God, I love you."

"I love you too, Dad, and always will."

The End

Author's Closing Words

Having been born in Cumberland, Maryland in 1951, I lived and spent my first eight years in a small house much like Henry's in the little village of Triple Lakes. My maternal grandfather, Howard, (Shown at left sharing a nap with me in 1956) worked in the Cumberland shops of the B&O Railroad and I remember to this day the final days of steam-powered locomotives like those described in this novel. I've taken a few liberties with times and dates for the demise of the great Mallet locomotives. I remember seeing only one in the mid-fifties when my grandfather took me to visit the shops in Cumberland where he built and repaired freight cars. The monster Mallet he showed me and allowed me to crawl over at age six or so, was only a rusting hulk on a weed-choked siding; by then, most of the Mallets had been reduced to scrap-iron. I can only imagine what they may have been like during their heyday in the twenties, thirties and early forties. I've seen a few films that preserved their sights and sounds. I recently learned that a Chesapeake & Ohio mallet has been found and is being restored. It will soon be a new addition to the locomotive inventory of the Western Maryland Scenic Railroad. They operate steam trains for daily excursions out of the restored Western Maryland Station in Cumberland, Maryland. You can learn more at www.wmsr.com.

I remember other steam locomotives that regularly pounded across the Alleghenies during those early years of my life. Most were 4-8-2 Mikados, 4-6-2 Pacifics and 4-6-4 Hutsons. In 1958, when my family left Western Maryland and moved to South Florida, only a few were still in service, but I still recall them with fond wonder. They made an indelible impression that continues even today.

I was, since the age of eight, and still am, an avid model

railroader. Believe me, steam locomotives are still my favorite although I have a number of diesel electric locos on my HO scale model railroad. My layout is set in the 1950's, in the rolling hills and low mountains of the Alleghenies.

All of the characters from my story are completely fictitious, of course, but being gay myself, I'm very familiar with the inner emotional struggles young teens of that era experienced as well as the lie they often had to live, to keep their secrets from friends and family. Being born in 1951, my teen struggles took place during the sixties and believe me, it still wasn't easy to accept and adapt to the things I felt and the fears I experienced as I was forced to keep so many secrets about the real me. Thank God, it's a little easier on gay teens in our world today.

Clay's story has a happy ending mainly because that's the kind of stories I most enjoy writing. However, life isn't always so rosy and perfect. I have been accused of being a Pollyanna when it comes to my novels, seeing only the bright side of things, but I am who I am and will continue to be, I suppose. The world is a dark enough place with entirely too many sad and tragic stories, so I figure maybe I can bring a smile, a laugh or a few tears of joy to my readers. I experience all of the above when writing, as I'm a sentimental softie and write with a handkerchief, or box of tissues handy. I write primarily for nostalgic, gay, male readers, but I sincerely hope others who read my work --- straight men and women --- can better appreciate the experiences of those of us who were born with a different set of sexual interests.

I enjoy hearing from my readers and encourage you to send me your comments, compliments and gripes via my Author's Page at Amazon Kindle Books. You input helps me be a better writer who can satisfy the needs of my loyal readers. I cannot answer all your comments, but I will try and answer the more pertinent and thought provoking ones. Hey, if I spend all my time writing answers, who's going to write the stories?

By the way, De Cessna is a pseudonym. Authors use pseudonyms mainly to separate their works of imagination from their real lives and the lives of their family. Please respect my privacy.

Thank you for purchasing and reading my novel. I hope I have entertained you and made your world a little brighter. That, more than anything, is my ultimate goal. You keep reading and I'll keep writing.

Maps

Southwestern Pennsylvania

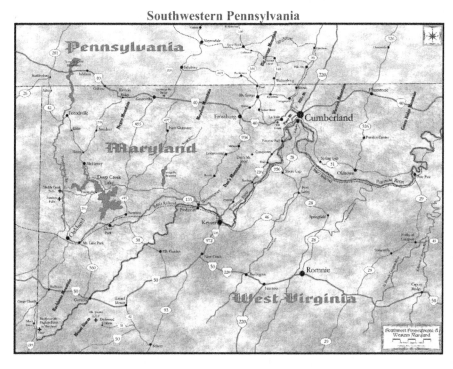

Sand Patch & Cumberland Area

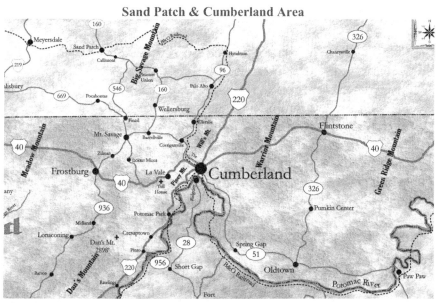

Printed in Great Britain
by Amazon

87246287R00195